W9-BYG-466

THE COLOR OF PASSION

Standing under the shelter of the gazebo, Nathan drew Lydia into his arms. His silver-gray eyes held her motionless and when he spoke his voice was a low, deep whisper. "Are you as curious as I am?" he asked.

Lydia's natural honesty kept her from pretending ignorance. She knew exactly what he was talking about and denying it served no purpose. He fascinated and frightened her. In that moment she really didn't care what his intentions were; she wanted him to kiss her.

His lips were softer than she expected. Lydia's hands rose between them, not to push Nathan away as he first suspected she might, but to grasp the front of his jacket and hold on.

At the first faint stirrings of passion he pressed for a more intimate response. Tilting his head, his mouth slanted across hers. They shared a breath, an indrawn gasp, and he tasted the sweetness of her mouth as she gave him what he sought.

Nathan's kiss excited her senses. Lydia knew the hard, angular planes of his body in contrast to hers, the beat of his heart through her fingertips, and heard the sounds of her own passion rising. Behind her eyelids was a sunburst of color and in the center of her was another one of heat . . .

Jo Goodman

Sweet Fire

ZEBRA BOOKS
KENSINGTON PUBLISHING CORP.

For Wendy:
Her interest, support, and encouragement
have been invaluable to me.
Thank you.

ZEBRA BOOKS

are published by

Kensington Publishing Corp.
475 Park Avenue South
New York, NY 10016

First printing: July, 1991

Printed in the United States of America

Also by Jo Goodman:

Prologue

London, 1852

She was dead. There was no question about that.
Looking at her, Nathan's wiry young body became still as
stone, and his eyes, lightly gray and ringed in blue, darkened with fear. He paused, half in and out of the
bedroom, and wondered what he should do. He had seen
dead people before, but they had mostly been drunks who
slept in gutters or crept into a shop stoop huddling for
warmth and never woke again. He'd once seen a man's
throat cut in a tavern brawl and two gentlemen mortally
wounded in a duel. But he had never seen anything like
this.

"What's wrong?" The urgent, furtive whisper came
from the dark alley below Nathan. "Get on with it!"

Nathan swallowed hard and tried to clear his throat. It
was no good. His mouth was bone dry. He couldn't say
what was wrong so he did what he had to do. He raised the
window he'd been holding a few more inches and
shimmied through the opening. Snakelike, he crawled on
his belly over the sill and onto the floor.

The candles on the nightstand and the burning coals in
the grate were a mixed blessing. Nathan could see what
he was doing, but he could also see the blood. It was on
the bedding, on the brass headrails, in her honey-colored

hair, and, just below where the woman's left wrist dangled over the thick feather tick, it was pooled on the floor.

The first thing Nathan did was check the door. It was locked from the inside. Satisfied he wasn't going to be surprised, he returned to the foot of the bed, careful to stay clear of the blood. The last thing he needed was a trail for the peelers to follow. The peelers derived their name from the man who had established the law force, and they were the object of ridicule and scorn, or gratitude and respect, depending on one's contact with them. Nathan and the company he kept held the former opinion. The peelers had played a game of tag with Nathan for over three years, ever since he'd turned eleven and earned his place as one of the best sneaksmen in all of London. Sometimes they caught him, mostly they didn't. Nathan didn't like to think of the celebration on Bow Street if they pinned a murder on him.

Nathan Hunter started out as a lowly puzzler, throwing muck from the street in the eyes of some unfortunate gentleman, then running away while his more experienced partner picked the poor fellow's pocket. Nathan wasn't satisfied with his role, for there existed among the impoverished a class system just as stultifying and rigid as the one accepted by more respected society. So Nathan worked his way up in the kingdom of thieves. From starglazer, where he learned how to cut the panes out of shop windows and take off with whatever was behind the glass, to chiving the froe, where he cut off a woman's pocket with a razor, Nathan showed an uncanny aptitude for his chosen career.

He was possessed of a pair of the finest rum daddles in London—deft, coordinated hands that could lift a watch, take a purse, or draw out a snowy silk handkerchief without jostling the victim. Still, it wasn't enough. He practiced the fam lay, a technique for shoplifting where the palm was dabbed with a little hot ale so that it became sticky. Something light, a diamond earbob, a ring, an

8

unset stone, could be palmed easily in such a fashion. Nathan had done it all. At fourteen he'd already been in jail on three separate occasions, not a bad record for a young man eager to prove his mettle and apt to make mistakes marked of inexperience. There were other sneaksmen his age who had already been to jail a dozen times, but Nathan didn't believe they should be lauded for it. Surely, he thought, it was better not to get caught than to risk transport to Botany Bay. Each time a sneaksman appeared at the assize house to face his charges, his chances of being banished from his homeland grew greater.

That thought raised goose bumps on Nathan's thin arms. In spite of the fact that his brow was beaded with sweat, he shivered.

"God! Would ye look at that!" Brigham Moore squeezed his body through the opening Nathan had left. At seventeen years and one hundred fifty pounds, Brigham was broader in the shoulders and thicker in the waist than his protégé. He was still light on his feet, but he'd never possessed the catlike quickness and agility that Nathan had. What Brigham lacked in manual dexterity was mostly compensated for by his quick wit and his brash daring. Tonight's scheme had been his idea.

Nathan spun on his heel and faced the window. "What are ye doin' 'ere? Ye're supposed to be me lookout. In or out. C'mon wi' ye. Quick. Someone's bound to see ye." He turned his back on Brigham as the older boy hefted his body through the opening and closed the drapes.

"Did she do 'erself in?" Brigham asked as he came to stand beside Nathan. He couldn't take his eyes off the dead woman. Her open, sightless eyes held his and he imagined he saw an accusation in them. It was unnerving. "Well?" he prompted, pulling his cap lower over his sandy hair.

Nathan shrugged. He wished he could find it in himself to cover the woman's naked body. The tangled, bloody sheet left most of her exposed. There was no dignity in it, he thought. She was dead, and the first thing he had noticed after the blood was her breasts. He didn't especially like himself for that.

"Did ye do it?" Brigham asked. "Ye 'ave a way with a razor."

"Don't be daft. O' course I didn't do it. I found 'er like this."

"So ye weren't losing yer nerve. I wondered when I saw ye 'esitate in the window."

Nathan didn't make a reply. The shock of finding the room occupied, and occupied by a body, was finally wearing off. Nathan realized he'd already spent too much time doing nothing. "I could use yer 'elp," he said, dragging his eyes away from the same vision that held Brigham captive. With an effort he hardened his heart. "Quit starin' at 'er and 'elp me get 'er trinkets." Taking a cotton drawstring bag from beneath his jacket sleeve, Nathan went to the vanity and quickly surveyed the available booty. He passed over the perfumes and creams, knowing he couldn't get much for them, and settled instead on helping himself to a pair of pearl drop earrings, a cameo brooch, three gold sovereigns, and a few farthings. He held up a locket to the candlelight, examined it, and made out the fine engraving on the golden face: BAO. A feeling of sadness washed over him, though he couldn't have said whether it was pity for the woman whose life had been so brutally ended, or if he pitied himself for not being able to take the locket.

"Don't ye want it?" Brigham asked.

"It's engraved. Wouldn't take the peelers long to trace it back ta 'er and then ta us."

"Take the chain then. It's worth somethin'."

Nathan found himself strangely reluctant to do that. He glanced over his shoulder at the woman. She wasn't looking at him any longer. Her eyes were closed now. He picked up the locket, tore the chain free, and dropped it in his bag. "Did ye touch 'er?" he demanded.

10

"I shut 'er lids," said Brigham. "I didn't like the way she was lookin' at me."

"Don't touch 'er again." He looked down at Brigham's feet. "Look! There's blood on yer stockings." There was a trace of disgust in his sigh as he turned his attention back to the vanity and rifled the dead woman's jewelry box. "See what's in 'er wardrobe. 'Ave a care not to take anything too personal." Nathan wondered what was wrong with his mentor. Usually Brigham confronted danger with clear-headed calm. Nathan had noticed that Brigham was peculiarly excited about what he'd seen, his green eyes feverishly bright. Nathan's stomach was churning with equal parts disgust and horror. Brigham seemed more fascinated than frightened.

"What do ye suppose 'appened?" asked Brigham. He picked through the gowns in the wardrobe, looking for something that might be valued in the thieves' market.

Nathan didn't want to speculate, at least not out loud. He was certain of several things, and none of them were particularly comforting. The woman hadn't killed herself, although he was fairly certain it had been meant to appear that way. After all, her wrists were slashed. But there wasn't a razor blade, a knife, or broken glass in sight. It was hardly likely that she had cut her own wrists then taken the time to put away the object she'd used. Nathan had already seen that the blood was largely confined to the area of the bed. She'd never made it farther than the edge of the feather tick.

Above the deep slashes on her wrists were faint markings that looked as if they had been made by a rope or shackles. Nathan recognized them because he'd known the feel of rope and irons each time he visited prison. She'd been bound, probably gagged, then brutally cut. He wondered if her murderer had watched her bleed to death. It was a certainty the murderer had used the window to exit since the door was locked from the inside, and just as certain that he hadn't left long before Nathan

11

arrived. The candles hadn't been gutted, the coals glowed, the blood was still dark crimson, not black, and when Nathan had been close to the bed he could feel the dead woman's body heat.

Nathan thought back to what he'd been doing a half hour ago. While he'd been waiting for Brigham to meet him in the alley behind King Street, this woman was being murdered. If Brigham hadn't been late Nathan might have very well surprised the murderer. He didn't have any illusions that he could have saved the woman. He wasn't particularly strong or menacing. It was far more likely that he would have been easy prey himself.

Brigham closed the wardrobe and handed Nathan some lace trimming and handkerchiefs that he'd pilfered. "She's kind o' pretty, don't ye think?" he said lowly.

"She's dead."

"Sure. But before that." When Nathan didn't answer, Brigham went on to examine other parts of the room. He found a Bible in the nightstand drawer. "Here," he said, tossing the book to Nathan. "Take this."

Nathan fumbled the Bible, scooping it up a moment before it thudded to the floor. He glared at Brigham. "Ye lookin' to get caught? Someone might o' 'eard this if it fell."

"Who's to 'ear? I told ye she lives alone."

"The 'ousekeeper."

"Gone tonight. Gone every Friday. I wouldn't 'ave suggested it otherwise."

Nathan breathed a little easier. He opened the Bible. The woman's name was written on the frontispiece. Beth Ann Ondine. Another shiver of sadness and sympathy traveled down Nathan's spine. He set the Bible aside.

"What's wrong with it?" Brigham asked.

"I don't want ta take it. It should be buried with 'er."

"Oh, for God's sake. Do ye think she cares about that?"

"I do," Nathan said quietly.

Brigham's tawny brows knitted. He fixed Nathan with

12

a sharp glance and detected a trembling in Nathan's taut body. His jaw was set stiffly, as if to hold himself in check, and his bony chin poked out defiantly. Brigham set out to bring him down a few notches. "That Bible will bring a few shillings."

"We're doin' all right without it."

"What about those pistols we 'ad our sights on? Wouldn't 'ave to steal 'em. We'd each 'ave our own pops and a galloper. A cinnamon stallion for me and a wild black rogue of a 'orse for ye. Highwaymen we'd be, and none'd be lookin' down their noses at us. Flash as Dick Turpin in our finery, kissin' the ladies and cullin' the gents of their trinkets."

Nathan shook his head stubbornly. The Bible wasn't worth so much as all that and it wouldn't have mattered if it had been. "I'm not takin' it."

"She's a whore, Nath. That Bible's fer show, naught else."

A whore? Brigham had never said anything about their mark being a whore. Besides, a whore didn't have pearl earrings, exquisite brooches, or expensive gold lockets. "These baubles don't belong to an ordinary whore," Nathan said, then added, "And it doesn't matter what she was. She's entitled to a Christian burial just the same." He hoped it was so. He knew it was something he wanted when his time came. If God could accept a whore, then surely He would accept a sneaksman with rum daddles.

"I didn't say she was ordinary, but she's a whore just like any o' them waterfront doxies. She's a rich gent's mistress and that makes 'er a whore."

Nathan's heart hammered in his rib cage. A rich man's mistress! The peelers would be everywhere looking to catch the murderer. Almost against his will he heard himself asking for a name.

"Lord Cheyne."

Nathan closed his eyes briefly, shaking his head. He repeated the name under his breath then swore softly. "Whut was goin' through yer mind when ye thought o'

13

this mad scheme? Lord Cheyne's mistress! It's Botany Bay for sure if we're caught. It won't matter if anyone believes we done 'er in or not!"

"Don't worry. I tell ye, we're safe enough. 'E won't be 'ere for another hour or so. Never comes before ten bells on a Friday night."

As far as Nathan was concerned they had already stayed too long. He was known for the speed of his heists as well as the cleanness of their execution. Tonight's caper was one unwitting blunder after another. "Let's go. I 'ave all we need." He headed for the window but stopped when he saw Brigham drop to his hands and knees near the bed. "What are ye doin'?" he demanded nervously. "C'mon, Brigham. Don't play—"

Brigham made one sweep beneath the bed with his outstretched hand. "I thought I saw . . ." He paused, his fingers touching something cold and wet. A moment later he was smiling triumphantly, holding up a dagger. The hilt was encrusted with seed pearls. The blade was crusted with blood.

"Put that back!" Nathan said, nearly stamping his foot in frustration. He raked a free hand through his dark hair, his expression frankly disbelieving.

Brigham paid no attention. "Would you look at this! It's beautiful!" He examined it in the pool of flickering candlelight. He felt Nathan come up behind him. "Give me yer bag," Brigham said.

Used to taking orders from Brigham, Nathan responded to his tone without thinking. He watched as Brigham took out one of the handkerchiefs he'd stolen and used it to wipe blood off the dagger. "What are ye goin' to do wi—"

"I want it," Brigham said firmly. "I've never seen the like before."

Nathan's gray eyes widened and he offered a protest. "It's what was used to kill 'er. Ye can't be thinkin'—"

"I want it," Brigham said again.

And that, Nathan supposed, was that. He shifted

14

uneasily on his feet as Brigham stuffed the lace-edged handkerchief into the bag and followed it with the dagger. The bag was unceremoniously jammed into Nathan's hands, just as Nathan had known it would be. He might be an accomplished sneaksman, but Brigham was still older, still more experienced, and still the leader. It was up to Nathan to take the lion's share of the risks. He said somewhat sulkily, "Don't know what good it is. Ye don't know 'ow to use it. Not a dagger like that."

Brigham raised one brow. "I could slit yer throat easy enough." Then he laughed lightly, putting his arm around his young accomplice's shoulders. "But where's the profit in that? Ye're still be best, Nath. None of the other boys can 'old a candle to ye." He felt the stiffness ease out of Nathan's thin frame. "That's better. If it'll make ye feel more the thing, it's not a dagger at all. It's for opening letters." He pointed to the escritoire in the far corner. It was littered with correspondence.

Nathan thought about that. He wondered if Miss Ondine had been surprised while she was sitting at her desk, answering an invitation or writing a letter to her lover. He wondered if she had tried to fend off her attacker with the opener and found it turned against her. He banished the thoughts with difficulty. "Let's go," he urged again.

"All right." Brigham's arm dropped away from Nathan and he started for the window. "Blow out the candles. Darkness will help cover us. I'll go first." Brigham raised the window and put one leg over the sill. He turned to see what was holding up Nathan and caught the sheen of tears in the boy's clear gray eyes. "Ye wanted to go," he said harshly. "Let's go. Don't turn soft-hearted and cotton-headed on me now."

"She could 'ave been me mum," Nathan said softly, rooted to the spot.

"Or mine. She was a whore after all."

Nathan was moved by Brigham's bitterly cold tones. Sucking in his lower lip and bracing his shoulders, he

15

stayed by the bed long enough to cover Beth Ann's lifeless body with a sheet, then he followed Brigham out of the room. At street level the boys disappeared into the shadowed, dangerous alleys that were their home.

Twenty-three days later Nathan was nabbed by the peelers while he was working the crowd at Vauxhall Gardens. It would have ended with a light jail sentence if it hadn't been for the cameo brooch they found concealed in the heel of his shoe. They recognized the quality of the ivory cutting, the fineness of the gold filigree, and knew it fit the description of a particular piece of jewelry missing from the home of Miss Beth Ann Ondine.

He was tried at an assize in London for the murder of Miss Ondine. Some days he saw Lord Cheyne sitting at the back of the crowded courtroom, trying to express disinterest in the case when it was obvious, at least to Nathan, that his lordship was a broken man. Beth Ann was loved, he thought, and he wanted to scream from the stand that he hadn't killed her, that he was wrongly accused. Yet he said nothing of his innocence, protesting it not to his solicitor or to the jury. There was no question of ever raising Brigham's name as his accomplice and Nathan did not expect Brigham to step forward and clear him.

Yet that was precisely what Brigham attempted to do and for his pains was clapped in irons and tried for his part in the robbery. His sentence was four years. Nathan got twenty. They were both sentenced to hard labor in Australia and thus exiled from England forever.

"Looks like we napped a winder this time," Brigham said, using the slang expression for transportation. He raised himself to the iron bar window of the cell he shared with Nathan and looked at the scaffolding in the courtyard. "Goin' across the world, we are. Under it, too. Van Dieman's land I 'ear it called."

Nathan knew what his friend was seeing beyond the

16

confines of their cell. He had watched men work on the gallows while he was waiting for his trial. Without Brigham's help he might have been taking the walk to the noose himself. Transportation was not as popular as it once was and the crime of which he was accused was particularly heinous. The jury had had no doubt he was guilty, but perhaps the judge had. All things considered, the sentence was a reprieve of sorts.

"Why did ye do it?" he asked, moving out of the shadow Brigham cast across the damp stone floor.

"Ye're me friend, ain't ye?" Brigham answered simply. "Couldn't let ye go to the bay alone, could I? Who'd look after ye if I wasn't around?" He lowered himself to the floor again. A smile touched his mouth as he tilted his head at a rakish, cocky angle. "Besides, there's gold ta be 'ad in Botany Bay, or ain't ye 'eard?"

"I 'adn't 'eard."

"Well, I 'ad. Jimmy Faughnan got 'imself sent off as soon as the news came in. No shame in that. He'll do his time then 'ave the last laugh when he strikes it rich. Just the way we will."

Nathan said nothing. He had wondered how the cameo found its way to his shoe and why the peelers singled him out at Vauxhall Gardens. Now he knew.

Part One

San Francisco

Chapter One

She was dead tired. There was no question about that. It showed in her bowed head and in the intermittent slowing of her steps. Puddle water splashed the hem of Lydia's gown and soaked her right shoe. She sighed wearily and took the time to skirt the next one. Lamplight from the dance halls and gambling palaces was reflected on the rain-glazed street. It shimmered and flickered beneath Lydia's feet, an effect that went unappreciated until she turned into the alley behind the Silver Lady.

Lydia hesitated, standing at the edge of the dark alley, wondering if she dared take it. Common sense dictated no. Anything, *anyone,* could be in the black shadows and recesses behind the gambling hall and hotel. On the other hand, she thought, she was going to be late for her own party. She hadn't taken a carriage because she hadn't expected to be gone more than a couple of hours, and by leaving home on foot she had been able to avoid the inevitable questions. She didn't have fare for a cab, and though her parents would have paid for it, again, there would have been questions.

Those questions were the reason Lydia Chadwick took

the alley. A few short cuts, shaving minutes here and there, could get her home before she was missed by anyone but her maid. Pei Ling wouldn't raise the alarm unless it appeared that Lydia was going to miss her first guests, and Lydia wasn't going to let that happen.

Darkness and Lydia's active imagination played an equal role in prompting her to hurry. She kept to the center of the alley, prepared to dart for safety in any direction. She knew her senses were heightened by her circumstances. It was as if she could hear each individual raindrop as it splattered on the cobblestone, or see shadows separate from the vacant doorways. Her breathing was a roaring in her own ears and fear was a dryness in her throat.

Yet when she first heard the footsteps behind her, she denied they existed. An echo, she thought, an echo of her own steps. But when she stopped, the sounds went on a beat too long. Worse, there was more than one pair of feet. Anyone had the right to come this way, she reasoned. Anyone. She told herself she was being unnecessarily cautious to suppose she was being followed.

No one behind her could know she was Lydia Chadwick. No one could suspect by her dress or her manner, by the fact that she was on foot, that her parents were Madeline and Samuel Chadwick, that her home was a granite-and-glass mansion on Nob Hill, and that someday she would inherit one of the greatest fortunes in San Francisco. Her presence behind the Silver Lady, a location she would have avoided in daylight without an escort, encouraged Lydia to believe that whoever was behind her now wasn't there because of who she was. There was a modicum of comfort in that.

Raising the hem of her gown a few inches in one hand and securing her shawl in the other, Lydia picked up the pace again, daring to glance behind her one time. She saw two dark figures, large enough that they could only

22

be men. They were walking closely together and they didn't pause when she turned her head to see them. She felt them match her steps, then, when she faced forward again, she heard them break rhythm, lengthening their stride and closing the distance between them quickly.

Lydia started to run. Her shoes were heavy with water and the wet cobblestones made the going slippery. The restrained coil of her sable hair loosened from its anchoring pins and fell down her back. Rain-slick strands were matted to the crown of her head and dark tendrils fell across her eyes, blinding her momentarily. When she reached to brush them away she lost her grip on her shawl. The fringe caught on the brooch she wore at her throat while the rest of the plaid garment fluttered behind her. She tried to recover it, but the hands that finally gripped it were not her own.

Lydia screamed. The large hand clamped over her mouth smothered the sound and her breath. Lightheaded, she struck out at her assailants with her feet and managed to catch one of them on the shin. She heard a grunt, but it was small satisfaction as pain shot from her toes to her leg. Lydia clawed at the hand covering her mouth as she was backed into a doorway. It was only after she was cornered, blocked by the door behind her and by the pair of men in front of her, that she felt the pressure on her mouth ease.

Sucking in air, tasting blood on her inner lip, Lydia leaned weakly against the door and stared widely at her tormentors, trying to make out their features in the darkness. She smelled spirits on their breath and sensed a certain wildness in their eyes as they unashamedly returned her scrutiny. She reached blindly behind her for a doorknob and was immediately pushed to the other side of the door.

"None of that, missy," one of the men said in a low tone. "We only want a look at your wares."

Wares? "I'm not selling anything," said Lydia. The men exchanged glances and burst out laughing. Lydia recoiled from the raucous noise and the nauseating odors.

The man sporting a mustache, the one who had held his hand over her mouth, stopped laughing first. He placed a hand on the curve of her neck and shoulder and forced her chin up with his thumb. "Give me a light here," he said. In short order a match was struck and the meager light was thrust in Lydia's face. Her features were illuminated, revealing a heart-shaped face, grave, rebellious eyes, the sulky lower lip of her widely cut mouth, and a glowing rain-washed complexion.

Lydia blew out the match. After a stunned silence, both men laughed again. "She's not so bad as I first thought," the mustached man said to his friend. "A little plain, perhaps, but in the dark one's not so different from another." He leaned closer to Lydia. "I'd say by the way you pucker those lips, you have something worth selling."

She blanched, realizing now what they had meant by her wares. "You're mistaken," she said quietly, forcing a calm she didn't feel. "I'm not what you think."

The clean-shaven man, the brawnier of the two, chuckled deeply and managed a touch of sarcasm as he spoke. "And I suppose we just didn't follow you out of Miss Bailey's?"

"Well, yes, perhaps you did, but I—"

"But you don't know what Miss Bailey's place is," he suggested, patently skeptical. "Is that it?"

"No . . . of course I know, but you don't—"

"Enough chatter," Mustache interrupted. "I still want a taste of those lips."

Lydia ducked, averting her face, and pushed out between the men at the level of their waists. Surprise was on her side, for neither of the men anticipated her escape. Sprinting toward the lights from the cross street that

24

intersected the alley, Lydia yanked up her skirt and petticoats and ran with her head bowed against the wind . . . and came to a breathless halt when she ran full tilt into a wall.

At least she thought it was a wall until it reached out to steady her. She struggled against the arms that held her upright, supporting and imprisoning her in the same embrace, but they were like ribbons of steel across the small of her back. Lydia twisted, butting the hard chest with her head. She heard a soft groan as her captor rocked on his feet and was forced to take a few stumbling steps backward to regain his balance. Just at the moment she thought she was free—Lydia felt herself spun around, her arms crossed in front of her and held in a basket carry that locked her elbows and secured her wrists in a viselike grip.

"I'm not going to hurt you." The grating whisper just behind her left ear was punctuated by a rough little shake that demanded her full attention. The voice raised itself a notch and addressed the other men in the alley in clear, even tones. "You're not going to hurt her, either, are you, gentlemen?"

Lydia looked up and faced the men who had cornered her moments earlier. They were slowly backing away. *Good,* she thought, *they're afraid of this stranger.* Then she wondered if she had more to fear from him as well.

"Never were going to hurt her," the broad-shouldered one said. "Just having a little fun with her. No harm in taking a kiss."

"There is when it's not given freely," the stranger replied. "Now get out of here before I decide to let her go and settle the score with the two of you."

The pair seemed to measure the threat and decide it was a real one. They turned quickly and ran back the way they'd come, kicking up raindrops in their wake.

The hold on Lydia didn't loosen right away. Panic welled inside her and took the form of a hard knot in her

25

throat. She made a tentative move against the hands that held her wrists.

"Easy now." The words were said softly and meant to gentle. The grip was eased. "Are you all right?"

Lydia freed herself completely and stepped away, rubbing her wrists. She didn't bother answering the question. The man was distracted, looking past her and into the depths of the dark alley. For a moment Lydia thought the others had returned. She moved closer to the stranger for safety.

"It's nothing," he said.

"But you thought you saw something."

He didn't deny it. He'd seen something, and he hadn't lied. It *was* nothing. A soft hiccup drew his attention. "You're soaked through," he said. Thanks to holding her against him, so was he. "Let's get out of this rain."

The suggestion startled Lydia. "Oh, no. I couldn't go anywhere with you." She bit her lip, belatedly realizing how ungrateful she sounded. "I'm sorry, I didn't mean . . . I'm in a hurry, you see. I have to get home. My parents will be worried."

"They'll be more worried when they see you like this. Your dress is ripped." He lifted his hand and pointed to the base of her throat.

Lydia's fingers flew to her collar. Her brooch had been torn away and the lace trimming along the high, modest neckline was hanging raggedly. "My shawl," she said, looking around for some sign of it. "It caught on my brooch and—"

"I think I see it over there." He took her hand and pulled her back into the pitch-black center of the alley.

He must have eyes like a hawk, she thought as he scooped up the shawl. She was certain she couldn't have found it. Lydia waited for it to be thrust into her hands.

"It's filthy," he said.

The trace of disgust in his tone, as if he didn't like having his hands soiled, brought a smirk to Lydia's lips. "I'll take it," she said. "I don't mind a little dirt."

The stranger's grunt was noncommittal, leaving Lydia to wonder if she had correctly divined his thoughts. "You can't wear this home," he said. "Come with me and I'll wash it out for you. I have a room above the Silver Lady. We can be there in a few minutes."

Lydia held back, digging in her heels when the stranger made to pull her along. She shook her head vigorously, appalled by his suggestion. "I'm not going anywhere with you," she said firmly. "I don't even know your name."

His rare, beautiful smile was wasted in the darkness. Amusement, however, was rife in his tone. "Circumstances have rather played hell with propriety, haven't they?"

She was silent, unable to find the situation as funny as he obviously did.

"Nathan Hunter." He dropped her hand and made a small bow. "Now may we get out of the rain?"

"Mr. Hunter . . . I really don't think—"

"You're not the only one with somewhere to go this evening," he said. "I myself was on my way to an engagement when I came across you and those two thugs. Now, I could have gone on and left you to fend for yourself, but I didn't. I'm going back to my room, change my evening clothes, and attempt to start this night over. You can come or go as you wish, but if you have a care for your health or what you're going to tell your parents, you'll come."

He turned to go, seemingly uncaring of her decision. That decided Lydia. She followed.

In the lobby of the hotel and gambling hall, Nathan slipped out of his evening jacket and put it across Lydia's shoulders when she sneezed. It was damp but warmer than nothing. "This way," he said, pointing to the wide

27

center staircase. "I'm on the third floor."

Lydia kept her head lowered, hoping no one coming or going from the gambling hall would see her. She'd never been inside the Silver Lady before, but she could think of at least a dozen men of her acquaintance who frequented the place.

They mounted the carpeted stairs quickly, their tread soft. Water squished between Lydia's toes and through the leather seams of her ankle boots, leaving a trail of wet footprints. Nathan extracted a key from his vest pocket and unlocked the door to his suite, pushing it open and ushering Lydia inside.

Lydia was having third and fourth thoughts as she entered. She immediately put what she hoped was a safe distance between herself and Nathan. Crossing her arms in front of her, warming her hands close to her body, she nervously studied the man who had helped her.

She measured most men against the man who raised her, who called himself her father even though he had no claim to her blood. He was the man she loved best in all the world, the man she knew better than all others, and the only man she knew who didn't care anything about her money, since it was his in the first place.

There was nothing about Nathan Hunter that brought her father to mind. He was taller, leaner, darker, and harder. Lydia's sweeping assessment gave her pause. She wouldn't have come with him if she could have seen him clearly in the alley. She would have turned away in the lobby if she hadn't been so concerned with hiding her face and avoiding his scrutiny. Now it was too late.

One corner of Nathan's mouth turned up in a sardonic smile. "I'm not a white slaver, you know."

It wasn't very comforting that her thoughts were so transparent. He looked, if not like a white slaver precisely, then a pirate at the very least, or the way she imagined a pirate might look. He had the eyes of a predator, wolf's eyes, icy gray edged by a ring of dark blue.

They were clear and penetrating, implacable in their expression, cold and hard in a way that a smile could not touch. The lines fanning out from the corner of his eyes had not been put there by laughter or age. He did not have the look of a man who laughed easily, and she guessed he was perhaps only a few years above thirty. He had a narrow, sculpted face, a Roman nose, and a mouth that was barely softened by the faint suggestion of a dimple on either side of it. His hair was several shades darker than her own, his brows nearly black, and his skin was tanned, giving him a saturnine appearance that embraced both danger and attraction.

His clothes marked him as a man of some means. His shirt was white silk, tailored to his broad shoulders. His vest was pale gray, shot through with silver embroidery threads. He checked his watch, a pocket affair on a platinum fob, and turned toward the bedroom.

"I'll get you a blanket, some towels, and wash out this shawl," Nathan said, unbuttoning his vest as he went. "Feel free to stoke the fire and add some coals. The sooner you get warmed up, the sooner we can get you out of here."

He disappeared into the bedroom and returned a few minutes later, his arms ladened with the warmth he promised. He was greeted by a blazing fire and an empty room. Nathan wasn't completely surprised that he'd frightened her off. He shrugged, dropped the blanket and towels on a nearby chair, and headed back to the bedroom. Standing in front of the large cheval glass he tore at his bowtie and smiled faintly at his reflection. Had Lydia been there then she would have had good reason to be afraid, for his smile was a cold one and never came close to reaching the frosty depths of his eyes.

"Oh, Lydia," he said softly, "I think you've only postponed the inevitable."

*　　　*　　　*

"It's not as if you're pretty." The words were not said sharply, nor were they born of envy. They were cruel by virture of being stated so simply, as a self-evident fact that could not be argued. "I mean," the speaker continued in the same vein, "I could understand it if you were attractive to men. For a young woman in your position, money is sometimes a curse. I don't think I would worry nearly so much if I thought they were only interested in you."

"Mother," Lydia said quietly, lowering her eyes away from the mirror. She bore her mother's concern stoically, not dwelling on the hurtful side of her message. "I need to get ready. Couldn't this—"

"No, I don't think it *can* wait. That's what you were going to say, isn't it?" Madeline Chadwick smoothed the satin bodice of her ball gown and cast a quick, surreptitious glance in the same mirror her daughter was avoiding. Satisfied that her gown was not wrinkled, Madeline focused on the strand of pearls at her neck, straightening them so the clasp was hidden beneath the thick auburn coil of hair at her nape. She caught Pei Ling watching her, the dark almond-shaped eyes giving nothing of her thoughts away. Even when Madeline returned her steady regard, the maid's gaze did not waver. "You can go," said Madeline, waving Pei Ling off. "I'll help my daughter get ready. See if Mrs. Church needs you in the kitchen."

Madeline pretended she didn't see that Pei Ling looked to Lydia for direction before she agreed to leave the room. Lydia's faint nod was the permission Pei Ling sought. Making a slight bow, Pei Ling slipped out of the room.

"I'll never get used to her," Madeline said as soon as the door closed. "She moves in and out of a room like a dark spirit. I don't know why you insist on keeping her. I could find you a perfectly acceptable Irish maid who knows something about—"

"Mother," Lydia said quietly.

Madeline sighed. "Oh, very well. We won't talk about Pei Ling. Here, let me do something with your hair." Madeline approached Lydia from behind, reaching over her shoulder to pick up the brush on the vanity. She gave her daughter's hair a few hard strokes, alternating the brush with her threading fingers. "It's still damp."

"I just left the tub a few minutes before you came in." Lydia was amazed the lie did not stick in her throat. Usually her explanations were not so facile. She supposed that desperation lent her courage. She couldn't imagine telling Madeline anything that had happened to her today. Taking the brush from her mother's hand, Lydia began dressing her own hair.

"Why do you have to wait until the last minute?" Madeline asked.

Lydia did not respond to the rhetorical, sniping question. Her fingers worked expertly as they swept her hair into a smooth chignon and anchored it with a half dozen strategically placed pins. A few tendrils curled damply at her temples and ears. Lydia pushed them back. They rebounded stubbornly. She looked at the clock on the mantel and saw she didn't have time to spare. She abandoned the attempt to make her hair obey and stood, giving Madeline her back. "Fasten me, please."

"I don't think you should have napped so long this afternoon. Look at you," she said, focusing Lydia's attention on her reflection again. "There are shadows beneath your eyes. I came by your room several times, but that sloe-eyed witch you keep wouldn't let me in to wake you. She said you didn't want to be disturbed."

"I'll speak to Pei Ling. I really was exhausted this afternoon, but I never meant that you shouldn't come in." Of course that was exactly what she had meant and her maid had followed her instructions to the letter. Somewhat belatedly Lydia realized Pei Ling must have had her hands full keeping Madeline at bay. She promised herself that she would find some suitable reward for Pei Ling's undiminished loyalty.

"Pinch your cheeks," Madeline admonished. "Perhaps that will distract from those violet bruises under your eyes. Honestly, Lydia, would you look at yourself?" Exasperation crept into her voice. "Could you have found a more unflattering gown for this evening?"

"You had this dress commissioned for me," Lydia reminded her softly.

"So I did." Madeline's dark green eyes made a swift assessment of Lydia's ball gown. Daffodil yellow did not flatter Lydia's complexion, making it appear unappealingly pale while emphasizing the shadowed look of her eyes. The rounded bodice should have drawn attention to the high curve of Lydia's breasts, but the stiff taffeta material flattened her chest and the ruffle that edged the bodice looked as if it had been sewn there to compensate for an inadequate bosom. The line from Lydia's waist to her ankles was broken by two tiers of ruffles which adorned the hem. Extra material draped heavily from her waist until it was swept into a bustle at her back.

"I don't understand it," Madeline said. "It was beautiful on the young girl who modeled it at the salon. I thought it would be perfect for you. How could it make you look so thick and awkward?"

"Perhaps because I *am* thick and awkward." Although Lydia's smile was brittle, she used the same matter-of-fact tone that Madeline had used ealier. She only had to look at her mother to know the truth of her statement.

Madeline was everything Lydia accepted she wasn't. She was several inches taller, gracefully slender, and at the same time generously curved. Her face was a classic oval with fine-boned features and wide green eyes the exact shade of emeralds. In the depth of the color was a blue flame which darkened with her mood, lending Madeline a smoldering, and somehow distancing, glance.

Her lustrous auburn hair held its coif no matter how it was styled. The deep, understated fire of her hair offset a flawless, alabaster complexion. She was long of limb, with a narrow waist, slender neck, and beautifully sculpted hands and tapered fingers.

Madeline finished fastening the gown. She placed her hands on her daughter's shoulders, adjusting the gold locket at Lydia's throat. "Nonsense," she said, but her voice was not encouraging. "It's only the gown that makes you appear that way."

"Perhaps I should change."

A faint frown pulled down the corners of Madeline's full-lipped smile. It disappeared so quickly that it was easy for Lydia to believe she had imagined it. "I don't think so, dear," Madeline said, pushing at Lydia's shoulders to adjust her posture. "There's really no time. If you hadn't waited, you might have been able to—"

"I know, Mother," Lydia interrupted wearily. She 'tood straight, her spine like a ramrod until Madeline's hands stopped their prodding and poking and fell away. "I'm sorry I'm such a disappointment to you." Lydia moved from the vanity and out of the line of the mirror's harsh reflection. Caught in an old memory, Lydia's smile held a hint of sadness. How many times before going to sleep she had prayed to wake up looking like her mother!

"Lydia! How could you think you're a disappointment? Have I really given you reason to believe I'm disappointed in you?"

Lydia answered as expected. "No."

"Well then, I fail to understand what you meant by that remark."

Feeling two instead of twenty, Lydia bit her lip. The inside of her mouth was still bruised and tender from her encounter in the alley and she tasted blood almost immediately.

"Don't do that. It's unattractive."

Lydia released her lip. She felt like crying. "I only

meant that I must remind you of him and that must be disappointing."

Madeline did not have to ask who "him" was. "How can you bring up Marcus?" she asked, her eyes expressing both astonishment and hurt.

"He's my father."

"*Your* father is waiting for us downstairs, preparing to greet *your* guests, opening his home to *your* friends for *your* charity affair, and you choose this moment to bring up Marcus."

"I didn't mean—"

"I don't think I'll ever understand you, Lydia."

"But—"

Color heightened the contours of Madeline's cheekbones. Her eyes darkened. "We are not going to discuss it." She drew a deep, calming breath and let it out slowly. "Now, let me look at you. You could use a pair of earrings." She went to Lydia's jewelry box and sifted through the jet beads, pearls, and sapphires. She found a pair of dainty gold drop earrings with yellow diamond centers. "These will do fine," she said, handing them to Lydia. "Much better. They brighten your face. I'm really very sorry about the gown, darling. I thought it would be perfect for you. The next time perhaps you'll go to the salon with me instead of letting your charity commitments overwhelm your time."

"It's fine, Mother," Lydia said. "I don't mind. Really, I don't. No one will notice me with you in the room."

Madeline did not appear mollified. "I'm not the one in need of a husband. You are."

Rather than argue the point, Lydia said, "That isn't what this evening is about, and I'm sure you realize it. You and Papa agreed to help me raise money for St. Andrew's. Please don't make the ball into something it's not."

"I don't see that there's anything wrong with mixing two agendas."

"I'm interested in the orphanage, Mother."

"And I'm interested in you. Why can't we find anyone who cares more about you than your money?"

But Lydia knew why. She couldn't hold a candle to her mother. Madeline's flame was intoxicating beauty and artful conversation. Beside it, Lydia's light was all but invisible. Too often a man who professed interest in Lydia was soon captivated by her mother. Lydia observed it, accepted it, and used it as a test, a trial by fire as it were, to determine if the man's interest lay with her or with her money. Mustering a smile, she approached her mother, stood on tiptoe, and kissed Madeline's smooth and unlined cheek. "You distract them while I pick their pockets. That's the best way to mix our two agendas."

Samuel Chadwick was pacing the area in front of the library fireplace when the double doors slid open. He looked up, saw his wife and daughter framed in the doorway, and put down his pipe. "Here are my beautiful girls," he said, opening his arms wide to welcome them.

Lydia walked quickly to her father's arms and returned his warm hug, kissing him on either side of his graying handlebar mustache. "Papa, you look wonderful! So dapper. Is that a new tie?" She straightened the black silk around the stiff points of his starched collar. "All gussied up for me? You're a darling, do you know that?"

"I've already made a contribution to the orphanage," he said dryly.

Lydia feigned a wounded expression. "I'm not an idle flatterer."

"All right. Five hundred dollars. Not a penny more, thief. I'll have to hit the mother lode to support you and St. Andrew's at this rate."

Madeline took the hand her husband offered and raised her cheek for his kiss. "Since you'd rather be digging inside some dark mountain anyway, perhaps you should donate a thousand."

There was an edge to Madeline's tone that did not go unnoticed by Samuel or Lydia. Both, however, had their own reasons for ignoring it. Samuel released his wife and picked up his pipe. "Won't you each have a glass of sherry before our guests arrive? I confess, I thought I was going to have to drink alone. Always need a bracer before one of these shindigs."

"Oh, Papa. You always exaggerate your misery." Lydia went to the walnut sideboard and began pouring the sherry. "I'm not going to feel sorry for you. After the first few dances, you'll slip away with three or four of my guests and spend the rest of the evening in here playing poker."

Samuel puffed harder on his pipe, an endearingly sheepish light in his pale-blue eyes. "Winnings go to charity," he muttered around the pipestem.

"Of course they do." Lydia gave her father his glass and offered another to her mother. "I wouldn't countenance it if they didn't," she said saucily. She raised her glass a moment later and toasted her parents, thanking them for their help with her dearest worthy cause.

They were an odd pair, she thought, not for the first time. It seemed that she had always known her parents were suited to each other the way oil was to vinegar: individually distinctive in their own right, mixing briefly for some shared purpose, then separating.

Samuel was his wife's senior by a score of years, fifty-eight to her youthful thirty-eight. While Madeline's mein was often cool and her anger icy, Samuel was warm and even-tempered. He rarely raised his voice or showed his displeasure in any way save for a frown that knit his eyebrows. He was not one to suffer fools, but he believed in second chances, and played fair with every partner he'd ever had.

Samuel was in California when gold was discovered in '48. He'd struck a rich vein and mined his first hundred thousand by the time the initial horde of greenhorn easterners arrived in San Francisco Bay. He parlayed that money into millions through shipping and railroads, and never minded admitting that he'd been lucky. He saw no shame in it. Striking that vein *had* been a matter of luck. Getting it out of the ground, on the other hand, had been back-breaking work.

That work showed in his hands, hard, gnarled hands, tough with calluses that years of leisure had never quite erased, and in his shoulders, broad and thickly muscled from the burden of pickax and shovel. He shifted now in his black-tailed dress coat, and reminded his daughter that unlike his wife, he'd never grown comfortable with the trappings of wealth. He was supremely happy to wear a pair of overalls and putter in the garden, or take a lantern and pickax a half mile deep into the Sierra Nevadas. It was Madeline who gloried in affairs like the one they were about to host. Samuel merely suffered them.

Madeline set down her glass. "I think there's just enough time for me to check the seating arrangements for dinner." She was out of the room before Lydia could protest.

Lydia shrugged helplessly, shaking her head. "She's going to select a dinner partner for me, I know it. A gold piece says it's Henry Bell on my left and James Early on my right."

Sam winked. "You're on." He drew on his pipe and looked at Lydia thoughtfully. She seemed to be trying very hard to keep the sparkle in her eye and the smile on her face. "Did you and your mother have words?" he asked.

"How did you—" Realizing she had given herself away, Lydia sighed and her agitation surfaced. "I'm sorry, Papa, I can't seem to avoid having words with her

37

these days. It was my fault really. Once Mother saw this gown on me she decided she didn't like it, or rather she didn't like *me* in it, which I understand perfectly. I should have gone with her to choose it, but I was caught up in planning this evening with Father Patrick, and what do I care about a gown anyway?"

"Don't you?"

"No." But she didn't look him in the eye. "All right," she said after a short pause. "I do care. Just a little. I'm sure Mother thought it would be fine, but you can see that it isn't. I was standing beside her, in front of the mirror, and I realized how different we are, how I'll never have even a tenth of her beauty, and somehow I just thought of Marcus. Before I knew it I was blurting out his name."

"I see," he said without inflection. He would always regret that Madeline had chosen to tell Lydia that she was another man's child and that the other man was a rapist. He could only guess of what Madeline's motives were for sharing that with her daughter. He had never been consulted before the fact, and afterward Madeline had been characteristically tight-lipped. It had been left to him to console the stunned, confused, and heartbroken child he had raised from birth as his own. In the six years since that day, the only good to come of Madeline's revelation as far as Sam was concerned was the unbreakable bond he forged with Lydia in the aftermath. "Shall I still call you Papa?" she had asked, her eyes grave and wounded. "I think I should die otherwise," he had answered. His response was so sincere, so heartfelt, that Lydia could not doubt it.

"I shouldn't have mentioned Marcus. It can't be anything but painful for Mother to remember him, but sometimes I wonder if she doesn't see him when she looks at me."

"I don't think that's the case at all," Samuel said, rolling the stem of his glass between his large palms. "I have an idea what your mother sees when she looks at you, and it certainly isn't Marcus O'Malley.''

Lydia looked at her father expectantly, waiting for him to expound on his thoughts. He seemed about to when Mr. Hardy appeared in the doorway and announced the first carriage had just arrived. Hiding her disappointment, Lydia looped her arm through Samuel's and escorted him to the entrance of the ballroom where they prepared to greet their guests.

"I wondered if you were going to come this evening," Nathan said as he alighted from a hired carriage and saw Brigham Moore waiting for him.

Brig's sandy hair caught the light from the carriage's lanterns. A boyish, mischievous smile touched his mouth. At thirty-four he was not so far removed in appearance or temperament from the boy he had been half a lifetime ago. "I was invited, wasn't I? The same as you."

"Hardly the same. Mr. Chadwick asked me. *Mrs.* Chadwick asked you."

"So? End's the same. I'm here, you're here. The game's afoot."

Nathan put his hand on Brig's forearm as the other man would have approached the Chadwicks' palatial home. "That was a stupid stunt you tried to pull this evening."

Brig stopped and looked at Nathan with new interest. One tawny brow was raised in a rakish salute to his old friend's cunning. "So you did see me. I wondered."

"I heard you first," Nathan corrected. "You were never particularly light on your feet."

Brig shook his head, not accepting Nathan's explanation. "I think you were expecting me, that's why you heard me. Somehow you found out about my plan for Lydia and intervened in my place. That wasn't very sporting, you know. But don't worry, I don't hold it against you. All's fair. That's what we agreed to at the outset, didn't we?"

"I think we've interpreted that phrase a little differently," Nathan said softly. "I discovered what you had in mind quite by accident. I tell you that because you should be cautious about confiding in strangers. One of the men you hired to follow and frighten Lydia had a loose tongue before he set out on your mission. God only knows what he's telling people now. Perhaps you want to get sent back to the bay in chains, but I don't. Once was enough."

"Good. You protect my back and I'll see to Miss Chadwick."

"As you saw to her this evening?" Nathan's icy gray eyes narrowed. "I don't think so. She was terrified by those men and with good reason. You were late getting there."

"An accident," he explained. "I followed them following her. I still don't know how I lost sight of them. You obviously didn't."

"I wasn't approached by the whores on the corner of Montgomery."

"Lucky me, eh?"

"Brig," Nathan said, trying to reason. "It was a foolish attempt at winning her confidence. Your hirelings might have done anything to her before you arrived."

"Raped her, you mean? I don't think so. I wasn't paying them to toss up her skirts. I've seen her, remember. I'd have had to pay them."

Nathan's hand dropped away from Brig's arm. He clenched it at his side. "Don't hurt her, Brig. She's an innocent in this bit of madness."

"Hurt her?" The open, boyish smile split his handsome face again. "That's no part of what I have planned. I'm going to marry her, Nath." He turned and went up the walk. Light scattered across the portico as the door to the mansion opened and Brig was ushered inside. Nathan watched the house swallow him up and still he did not move. He stood alone on the sidewalk, hands thrust in the pockets of his evening coat, wind ruffling his dark hair, and wondered why he could not approach this evening's outing with the same nonchalance or confidence Brig displayed.

"Mr. Moore," Madeline said, a thread of excitement in her voice. "How good of you to come this evening. I wasn't certain you would, given the fact we're going to twist your arm for a donation."

Brig made a slight bow, then gallantly offered his arm. "Twist away. I promise you, I consider the pain a small price to pay for the pleasure of your company."

Madeline responded to Brig's engaging smile with light, trilling laughter. For the first time since the guests had begun to arrive, her gaiety was not forced. "I'd like you to meet my husband. Samuel, this is Mr. Brigham Moore. I told you about him," she prompted. "The gentleman who rescued me outside of Sheridan's department store last week."

"Oh, yes," Samuel said, extending his hand. "The little tremor. It's a pleasure to meet you, Mr. Moore. It was good of you to see to my wife's safety at your own expense."

"I believe you've been misinformed," Brig said genially. "I recall your wife pushing *me* out of harm's way. That *little* tremor lasted only a few minutes short of eternity as far as I was concerned. I thought it was the end of the world."

Smiling, Samuel withdrew his hand. "Then it's all the more commendable that you kept your head. From what Madeline has told me, you reacted with incredible calm despite your own injuries."

Brig touched the back of his head. "Nothing that a few stitches couldn't take care of."

41

Samuel turned Brig's attention to Lydia. "Let me introduce our daughter Lydia. Lydia, Mr. Moore."

"It's a pleasure to meet you, Mr. Moore," Lydia said. "Mother's sung your praises. She's told us you've recently come from England. It's rare for someone not of this area to react with such presence of mind." Lydia watched with some astonishment as color flushed Brigham Moore's cheeks. Why, he's embarrassed, she thought. Then he turned the full force of his smile on her and all coherent thought left Lydia. Had he gushed over her, made some asinine remark about her resemblance to her mother, or her beauty, or her gracefulness, Lydia would have recovered her senses, but Brig did none of these obvious things and managed to hold Lydia in his thrall because of it.

"It's an honor to be here," he said sincerely, making another small bow. His green eyes held Lydia's all the while, displaying his interest openly. "I'd be happy to hear about your plans for the new orphanage. No arm-twisting is necessary, I promise you."

"Oh?"

"I was raised in a London workhouse," he said. "I've no parents myself."

Though he said it simply, without apology, Lydia thought she detected pain in the depths of his eyes. She was moved.

"Go ahead, darling," Samuel said. "I know you want Mr. Moore to meet Father Patrick. Your mother and I will greet the remainder of our guests."

Madeline's encouragement was noticeably cooler than her husband's. "Perhaps you'll start the dancing as well. I think there are several couples who would like to begin."

Lydia, who had already accepted Brig's proffered arm, stood rooted to the floor at her mother's suggestion. She could feel the tide of heat rushing to her face. Her mind worked furiously, searching for something to say that

42

would extricate Brigham Moore from an obligatory offer. It came too quickly.

"I'd be honored, Miss Chadwick, if you'd allow me to partner you for the first dance."

Wishing she were anywhere but where she was, Lydia forced a smile to her lips. "Of course." She felt herself being led away and was grateful for her guest's calm, because she had none of her own. When they were out of earshot of her parents Lydia whispered, "I apologize for Mother. You needn't feel that you have no choice but to dance with me."

Brig halted in his tracks and bent his head slightly in Lydia's direction. "I'm afraid I should be the one to apologize for taking shameless advantage of your mother's suggestion." He looked quickly around the ballroom. "There are a number of gentlemen here this evening without obvious partners. Perhaps there is one to whom you'd rather give the honor?"

At first she was taken aback, then Lydia's tremulous smile brightened. She stopped biting her lower lip. "No . . . there's no one," she admitted, and added, "I've danced with all of them before."

Brig's tawny brows raised slightly, his handsome face full of good humor. "And none of them met your standards?" he asked. "That doesn't bode well for me. I'm not very accomplished on the dance floor."

"Oh, no . . . I didn't mean . . . that is . . ." Her voice trailed off when she realized he was teasing her.

"I'm sorry," he said. "You rise so beautifully to the bait that I can't help but dangle my hook. Shall we?" He placed one hand on her waist and lifted his chin in the direction of the musicians warming up at the opposite end of the room. "I believe they'll take their cue from you."

Lydia raised her face to look up at her partner and take measure of his sincerity. He was tall and slim, square-jawed, and even-featured. There was something young in his smile, a youthful excitement that made his green eyes bright. There was eagerness and expectation in his stance. His head was tilted to one side and a lock of sandy hair had fallen across his forehead. By slow degrees, as if full realization was against her will, she acknowledged that she liked what she saw. Her solemn dark-blue eyes widened a shade. "All right," she said softly. She caught the attention of the leader of the small orchestra and nodded once. Almost immediately the room was filled with the heady, lilting strains of a Strauss waltz.

"What power," Brig said as he turned Lydia gracefully about the ballroom.

"Pardon?" Was that her voice? she wondered. That breathless, slightly husky tone, did it really belong to her? He had lied about his skill in the dance, she thought distantly. He led her through the steps almost effortlessly.

"I was referring to the way you cued the orchestra. A regal nod from you and suddenly there's music and laughter and dancing."

"Regal?" She shook her head. "I don't think so, Mr. Moore. My mother, perhaps, but not me."

"At the risk of arguing, I'd like to point out that I've seen the queen. *You*, Miss Chadwick, were regal."

Feeling more comfortable than she could ever have imagined, Lydia laughed. "Tell me about London, Mr. Moore, and how you came to see the queen . . ."

At the entrance to the ballroom Nathan's hand was taken in a warm embrace. "Glad you could make it, Hunter," Samuel said. "You're the last guest to arrive. I was afraid you were going to stand me up. This is my wife, Madeline Chadwick. Madeline, Nathan Hunter. I invited him for the—"

"Poker game," Madeline finished. "Don't apologize, Mr. Hunter. I assure you, I'm quite used to this. I had hoped my husband would partner me in one dance . . ."

44

Her voice fell away and she looked at Samuel with a sideways glance that was more suffering than amused.

"Oh, but . . ." Samuel began, looking quickly for his poker partners.

Nathan interjected. "Perhaps your husband would permit me the pleasure. I admit I enjoy holding a good hand at poker, but I enjoy holding a beautiful woman more." Samuel looked as if he were about to object and Nathan shook his head, sweeping Madeline Chadwick into his arms and onto the floor. "Too late," he told Sam over Madeline's white shoulder.

Samuel shrugged good-naturedly. "I'm going to go mark the cards." He disappeared into the hallway, making a brief stop in the dining room on his way to the library.

"So, what do you think of the plans, Mr. Moore?" Lydia asked. They were standing in a relatively quiet corner of the ballroom where Lydia had arranged the three-dimensional model of the proposed orphanage as well as the architect's drawings on a table. "This will take the place of the mission Father Patrick's using now. It's been the site of the orphanage since fire destroyed the old one about a year ago. The mission was never really intended to house so many people, certainly not children, and is wholly inadequate to their needs."

Brig casually rested one hip against the table and studied the model. "It's quite an undertaking. I'm impressed that you want to offer so much to these children. There was nothing like this when I was growing up."

"You make it sound like a lifetime ago."

"I'm thirty-four, Miss Chadwick. It *was* a lifetime ago—your lifetime."

Lydia extended her chin a notch, not flattered that he thought her so young. "I'm twenty, Mr. Moore."

"I beg your pardon," he said, setting his mouth so as not to betray his amusement. He was not entirely successful.

"Laugh if you will," Lydia said. "I'm used to people not taking me seriously."

Brig straightened. "You're wrong there. I'm taking you and your project very seriously." He pointed to the model. "It's plainly evident that you've given a lot of thought to the planning of this home."

"Father Patrick and I worked closely with the architect."

"You seem to know the sort of place children need to grow comfortably."

She warmed to the compliment but admitted, "The Father's influence more than mine, although I spend as much time as I can at St. Andrew's, doing what I'm able. They're wonderful children and they deserve much better than they're receiving from the community now. In a city where quakes and fire are part of life, where children can be orphaned in the blink of an eye, it only makes sense to provide for—" She stopped and concentrated on smoothing the curled edges of the blueprints. "I'm sorry. I tend to go on about my causes, this one in particular. Mother says it's my worst fault."

"If it's your worst fault, then you're a paragon among women. There are worse things than feeling passionate."

Brig's softly spoken words washed over Lydia and she blushed at his phrasing. Had he meant to be provocative? She stole a glance at him, decided his comment had been innocent, and felt a small pang of regret. His head was bent over the model. He was studying the area at the rear of the orphanage set aside for play. How different it must have been for him, she thought. He'd shared little about the London workhouse during their dance, and Lydia did not press, but she knew enough about such things to fill in the pauses in his story.

Lydia pointed to the expanse of land adjoining the

46

orphanage property. "We'd like to be able to buy this as well. The goal is to make the orphanage as self-sufficient as possible by raising our own beef and poultry. The garden would not only support the needs of the children but allow us to sell some of the crop in the city. I think most children will find a measure of satisfaction in farming; a few may even enjoy it. The outdoors will be so much better for them than tedious piecework, and they tend to love being around animals. We'll be able to have pets and—" Smiling guiltily, she shook her head. "I'm doing it again, aren't I?"

"I'm not complaining," Brig said, his expression frank.

"You're too kind," Lydia said, an impish grin touching her lips as she added, "But I'll wager you'll think twice before saving another woman in a Frisco shaker. Look where it's got you."

Brig laughed, and Lydia knew she liked the sound of it.

"Darling..." Madeline said as she and Nathan entered the circle of light laughter. "You can't monopolize Mr. Moore. You have other guests."

The light that had been building at the back of Lydia's cobalt-blue eyes was shuttered now. "Yes, of course," she said quietly. For the first time she noticed the man on her mother's arm. Surprise paralyzed her voice and her feet.

Madeline made the introductions all the way around, and Lydia realized she must have responded in some appropriate fashion. At least no one was looking at her as if she'd grown a third eye. "Let me allow Mr. Moore the opportunity to meet some of our friends," Madeline was saying, "while you show Mr. Hunter your plans." She smoothly disengaged herself from Nathan and gave Brig no choice but to accompany her on a tour of the room.

When she and Nathan were alone, Lydia turned her

47

back on her guests and betrayed her nervousness by speaking quickly. "How did you find me and what do you want?"

Nathan's predator eyes narrowed slightly and he studied Lydia a moment before answering. She was clearly agitated by his presence, a factor he hadn't counted on. While he hadn't expected gratitude, as Brig had when he'd devised the scheme, neither had Nathan anticipated his earlier rescue would result in such an annoyed greeting. "This may come as something of a surprise, Miss Chadwick, but I didn't *find* you and I don't want anything."

Lydia pursed her mouth to one side in plain disbelief. With an air of impatience, she crossed her arms in front of her.

"Your posture speaks for itself," he said tightly. "Excuse me, I'll find your father." Nathan turned on his heel and had taken three steps when he heard Lydia call his name. He kept on walking.

Frustrated by his actions and embarrassed by her own poor manners, Lydia hurried after her guest. Trying not to be obvious, she slipped her arm through his and pulled him up a little.

Nathan halted and turned cold eyes on her. "I'm not a horse to be reined in, Miss Chadwick."

Lydia had the grace to look away and stammer an apology. "But you can't blame me for being startled," she added, defending herself.

"I don't blame you for being startled. Only for being rude."

At the far end of the ballroom Madeline and Brig were passing in front of the orchestra. Madeline's head was thrown back, a bright smile on her face as she laughed with evident enjoyment at something her partner said. With a coy tilt of her head and a sideways look, Lydia said, "A dance might improve my disposition."

Nathan had seen the direction of her gaze before it

48

came to rest on him and understood her intent. "Don't flirt. It's not becoming."

Lydia blinked widely, not certain she had heard him correctly. And he called *her* rude! She considered telling him so, but then he was pulling her into his arms and spinning her across the floor.

Chapter Two

He was not an accomplished dancer. He lacked the fluid grace and practiced rhythm that had made Lydia so comfortable in Brig's arms. She followed his fits and starts as best she could, but more than once she found herself trouncing his toes. Each time she apologized for her clumsiness. He said nothing. Lydia thought she heard him counting out the three-quarter time under his breath.

Against her better judgment she ventured a question. "How do you know my father?"

There was a pause several beats long before Nathan answered, confirming Lydia's suspicions. "What?"

"You said you were going to find my father. How do you know him?"

"I met him a few weeks ago at the Silver Lady."

"You're a gambler?"

"On occasion."

Lydia gasped softly.

Nathan frowned. "What's wrong? Do you have something against gamblers?"

"No," she said quickly. "No, not at all. I . . . you . . . that is . . ." She did not want to call attention to the fact that his fingers were pressing painfully hard into her waist, or that the hand holding hers was grinding her knuckles together. His concentration was fierce, and unexpectedly Lydia found herself harboring a measure of admiration for his grit. "It's nothing," she said. "Please, go on."

"There's nothing much to add," he said somewhat stiltedly. "I told you earlier this evening that I was on my way to an engagement. This is it. Your father invited me for the—"

"Poker game." Lydia finished his sentence as her mother had before her. "Papa isn't much for dancing."

"I knew I liked him," Nathan muttered under his breath.

"Pardon?" she asked politely.

"Your father seems to be a fine man. I've enjoyed his company on each occasion we've met."

"I had no idea Papa frequented the Silver Lady."

"You're jumping to conclusions, Miss Chadwick. I only met Sam there once. We've seen each other at the Wells Fargo office, the Exchange, and at least one time riding in Golden Gate Park."

"So you're going to play cards with my father this evening."

Nathan nodded, lost his timing, and caused Lydia to stumble as he changed his lead. He grimaced. "Forgive me. That was my fault that time."

Which, Lydia supposed, was his way of saying all the other missteps had been her responsibility. She bit back the accusing words which came easily to mind. "I suppose Papa told you that all his winnings go to charity."

"No, he didn't mention it at all. I take it I'm expected to lose."

"Don't do it on my account, Mr. Hunter."

Turning Lydia toward the ballroom entrance, Nathan stopped on the threshold. His hand was still tight on Lydia's waist, but he dropped her hand. Without visible effort he pulled her closer so that she was forced to tilt her face toward him or bury it in his shoulder. "Don't flatter yourself, Miss Chadwick," he said coldly, hardened against the flash of pain in Lydia's wide and wounded eyes. "I doubt I could be moved to do anything on your account again. If I lose money tonight it will be for the children."

Lydia couldn't think of anything to say. By the time she did, Nathan was gone.

James Early didn't give Lydia time to think about her odd encounter with Nathan Hunter. With an eye toward the main chance, James swept Lydia back onto the dance floor and kept her thoughts occupied with light, inconsequential banter until Henry Bell stole her away. The evening progressed in such a manner, with Lydia pleading her cause for the orphanage and her suitors making their case for her hand.

Occasionally her mother would catch her eye and indicate approval or disapproval of a particular partner. Lydia ignored Madeline's directives, and to demonstrate that romance had no part in what she had planned for the evening, Lydia spent most of her time on Father Patrick's arm, mingling with the guests who were longtime family friends and could make significant contributions to St. Andrew's.

When Mr. Hardy announced dinner Madeline led the way to the dining room. Lydia extricated herself from Henry Bell's elbow with the excuse that she had to get her father and his guests away from the poker table. It was only a short reprieve, she thought, remembering her wager with her father: Henry on her left and James on her right. Given Madeline's signals in the ballroom, Lydia was certain her mother would have arranged it.

There were five men huddled around the card table. Lydia had expected her father and Nathan Hunter, and it wasn't too surprising to find Mr. Sullivan and Mr. Davis since their wives had remarked on their absence several times during the dancing, but Brigham Moore's presence caught Lydia off guard. He was the first to look up when she entered the library, and his welcoming smile struck at Lydia's young, vulnerable heart. She looked away quickly, embarrassed by the sudden wealth of feeling, certain everyone in the room would see it, understand, and know the cause.

One man did. When Lydia looked up, she caught Nathan Hunter watching her closely, studying her features with his remote, impenetrable gray eyes. She stared back a shade defiantly, and held his attention until his eyelids lowered, shuttering his glance. The insolent smirk on his mouth, however, was still very much in evidence.

Lydia went quickly to her father's side, placing a hand on his shoulder. "Papa, dinner's been announced. Mama and our guests are on their way to the dining room now."

Samuel reached over his shoulder and laid his hand over Lydia's, patting her absently. Still studying his cards, he held them up for Lydia to see. "Brigham here has proposed a rather interesting wager," he told her.

"Oh?" She was careful to keep her features composed. Her father had a full house: three sevens and two threes. She also noticed that he had very little in the way of winnings in front of him. Based on where the money lay, the lucky man at the table tonight was Brigham Moore. "And what wager is that?"

"As you can see, darling, my funds are quite low." Everyone at the table understood that Samuel had access to a great deal more money, but at the beginning of play they had agreed on a limit. "If I want to see Brigham's cards he's suggesting I offer you up as part of my stake."

"Papa!" Lydia blushed deeply, her composure shaken. "What can you be thinking? That's barbaric!" But she wasn't offended, she realized. She felt warm inside, and tingly.

Brigham laid his cards facedown on the table. "Your father hasn't explained it very well, I'm afraid. My intentions are completely honorable. If I win this hand, then you'll accompany me to the Cliff House tomorrow evening for dinner."

"Well, Daughter?" Sam asked when Lydia didn't respond.

"It's improper, Papa," she said softly, believing that she should make some sort of protest.

Samuel sighed, folding his hand. "Oh, well, perhaps it is. Hell of a time for you to come calling dinner. Another minute and the deed would have been done." He dropped his hand from Lydia's and leaned forward in his chair. "Brig was even willing to donate his winnings to your charity . . . that's supposing he won at all."

Lydia glanced shyly at Brigham. "You'd donate your winnings?" she asked.

"Of course." The eager, boyish smile lit his green eyes.

"All right, Papa," she said. "I suppose it's not so improper a wager since the children will benefit."

Nathan Hunter shifted in his chair, stretching his long legs in front of him. "By all means, Miss Chadwick, you must do it for the children."

Lydia looked quickly around the table. No one else seemed to have heard the sarcasm in Nathan Hunter's tone. They were simply taking his statement at face value, encouraging her with a nod or a smile to support her father's wager. "Certainly I'll do it," she said firmly.

"There's a girl," Samuel said, pleased with her decision. He quickly scribbled out a marker and pushed it and his money toward the middle of the table. "Now we'll all get to dinner on time."

Lydia peered a little anxiously at Sam's cards when he lifted them again. They hadn't changed. He still held a full house. She tried not to show her disappointment as she realized that Brig's cards would probably not hold up against her father's. The children would win no matter how the hand played out, she thought. Only *she* could lose.

Samuel turned over his cards. "Sevens over threes," he said, beaming at his fellow players. "You don't think I'd bluff, do you?" He started to pull the money toward him, including his marker for Lydia, when Brigham stopped him.

"Tens and eights," Brig said, fanning his cards across the table in front of him. "A better full house." He glanced up at Lydia while he started to gather his winnings. "I wouldn't bluff on a wager this important."

He meant her, she thought giddily. He was saying she was important to him! She offered what she hoped was a cool, slightly indifferent smile, afraid he might perceive her as too young and overeager.

"Apparently none of us would," Nathan Hunter said, cutting into Lydia's reverie. "You must have forgotten that I hadn't folded."

Lydia gasped softly, her smile vanishing when she realized there were three players left in the hand, not two. Knowing what she would see as Nathan turned over his cards, Lydia struggled to hide her disappointment.

"Four twos, gentlemen," he said. Nathan waited until Brig withdrew his hand, then he picked up Sam's paper marker for Lydia and put it in his vest pocket. He pushed the remainder of his winnings toward Sam. "For the children, I believe," he said, coming to his feet.

Lydia wanted to scream. Instead, she inclined her head graciously and prayed he would not offer to escort her to the dining room. She worried needlessly. Nathan hung back to speak with Brig while her father took her arm.

"He's probably consoling Mr. Moore," Samuel said in a low voice.

"More like rubbing salt in an open wound."

"What?" Sam wasn't certain he'd heard correctly.

"Nothing, Papa. It wasn't important."

They entered the dining room just as the guests were being seated. Lydia immediately looked to James Early and Henry Bell to find her place. Sam saw the direction of her glance and chuckled under his breath. "Looks like I win, m'dear. They've got Miss Adams and Miss Henderson for company this evening."

"I detect your fine hand in this," Lydia said.

"Me? But that would be cheating." He led her straight to her chair and pulled it out for her. "Then again, it wouldn't be the first time." With that parting shot, Samuel left Lydia to take his place at the head of the long table.

"This is an unexpected pleasure," Brig said as he seated himself on Lydia's left.

"It certainly is," Nathan said on Lydia's right.

Between them, Lydia smiled wanly. She couldn't imagine how she was going to get through dinner with her nerves intact.

"Are you feeling well?" Madeline asked following dinner. "I can't remember when I've seen you less animated."

Lydia drew her mother closer to the shelter of two large potted palms. Chairs were being arranged in the ballroom in preparation of the after-dinner concert, and many of the guests had chosen to take a walk on the grounds. Those who remained behind were listening to Father Patrick's colorful stories about his own wayward youth or studying the architect's drawings for the orphanage.

"I'm feeling a little tired," she admitted. "I hadn't realized it was evident."

"Evident?" Madeline took both of Lydia's hands in her own. "Darling, you practically telegraphed your feelings to me. It was obvious that you were simply overwhelmed by the attention at dinner this evening. I don't know how the mistake was made. I never intended you to be seated by Mr. Moore or Mr. Hunter. They're too old, and, I suspect, far too experienced for you. James and Henry are so much more appropriate."

"I'm sure you think so, Mother."

Madeline's eyes narrowed briefly. "What does that mean?"

"Nothing," Lydia said dully. "I'm simply tired." She gently withdrew her hands. "If you'll excuse me, I'd like to go out for a breath of air."

"I'm not sure—" She stopped as Lydia walked away from her. Madeline stood rooted for several seconds, stunned by her daughter's uncharacteristically rude behavior, then she went in search of the soprano who was going to provide the entertainment.

Lydia stepped out onto the flagstone portico. The air was still damp from the earlier spring rain and fragrant with the scent of roses from the garden. She hadn't thought to bring a shawl, and the skin on her bare forearms prickled as a cool breeze circled her. She walked over to the stone balustrade bordering the portico and watched her guests meander along the garden paths to the pond and the gazebo beyond. She would have an entertainment in the summer, she thought, with an outdoor concert and paper lanterns around the pond. She would manage the guest list completely alone the next time and make certain there were no surprises.

Dinner had been horrible for her. From the appetizer to the moment when the main course was served, Lydia was expected to converse almost exclusively with the companion on her left. She couldn't enjoy her time with Brigham Moore, however, because she was dreading the time she would have to spend with Nathan Hunter. Throughout the meal her attempts at conversation were stilted and awkward, and the horrible knot in the pit of her stomach just kept growing. At one point she thought she was going to have to excuse herself or be sick in front of everyone.

Pei Ling's soft voice interrupted her humiliating memories. "Miss Liddy," the maid said, coming to stand at Lydia's side. "Please come. Someone here to see you."

"Tonight? Who is—"

"They say hurry. I ask them wait in library." Pei Ling's dark eyes were anxious. "Hurry, please. Before Mother sees them."

Lydia was beginning to suspect who had come calling. She didn't question Pei Ling's insistence again. "You can wait here in the hallway," she told her maid when they reached the library. "Warn me if Mother or Papa comes this way. This will only take a few minutes."

Nathan had been standing on the portico, just out of reach of the ballroom's chandelier light, when he saw Lydia walking toward the balustrade. He felt trapped in the shadows, not wanting to draw attention to himself by moving, not wanting to be thought a spy if he stayed and was seen. He watched her linger by the stone rail and wondered at the drift of her thoughts. Probably considering how to get out of her father's wager, he decided. It was clear to him that she was unhappy by the turn of events at the poker table. Her civility was forced all through dinner, her comments monosyllabic or too sweet to be sincere.

In spite of the cool reception, Nathan perservered. He was used to being shown the door once women made Brig's acquaintance and he'd never cared. This time, though, there was too much at stake to quit the chase. He patted Samuel's marker in his vest pocket and thought about dinner at the Cliff House tomorrow evening. He still had another chance to set things right—this time without Brig's presence.

He was thinking about where he might take Lydia after dinner, how he might explain himself to her, when he saw her being approached by a Chinese girl he took to be a house servant. They both disappeared into the house, and the next time Nathan saw Lydia, ten minutes had passed and she was leaving the mansion by a side door, alone and on foot, cloaked in a black, hooded cape and carrying a wicker basket in one arm.

Raking back his hair with his fingers, Nathan frowned,

trying to imagine what could have taken Lydia Chadwick away from her own gala. He couldn't. There was no woman in his experience to compare to Lydia. She was shy and defiant by turns, awkward then graceful, gracious and ill-mannered in a heartbeat. She had yet to thank him for his rescue this evening. Still, Nathan thought, she had danced with him and never once let on that she found him hopelessly inadequate as a partner.

Behind him, Nathan heard the musicians warming up again. A few chords were struck on the piano. The guests were being urged to come inside for the entertainment. At the edge of the pond he saw Brig take Madeline Chadwick's arm and start toward the house. It was not an unexpected sight. Nathan remembered the first time he had seen Madeline. It had been nearly two months ago, shortly after he arrived in San Francisco, and she'd had Brigham Moore on her arm on that occasion as well.

Nathan wondered if Brig thought he could get to Lydia through her mother or if his interests lay in Madeline herself. Probably a little bit of both. Brig typically didn't leave much to chance, and tonight's poker game must have cut him on the raw. The memory of that game brought a smile to Nathan's mouth. He was smiling as Brig and Madeline crossed the portico and entered the ballroom through the French doors, and he was still smiling as he went in search of the diminutive Chinese servant he'd seen with Lydia.

Nathan felt like the sneaksman he had been as he toured the first floor of the mansion looking for Pei Ling. He viewed three parlors, the private family dining room, and an art gallery before he surprised the maid in the solarium. She was in earnest, agitated conversation with Father Patrick and Nathan suspected it had something to do with Lydia's abrupt departure.

Pei Ling and Father Patrick stopped talking and turned at the same time toward Nathan. Pei Ling made a short bow and started to back away. She was stopped by the priest, who faced Nathan squarely, assumed the younger man was lost, and gave him directions back to the ball-room.

Nathan closed the solarium doors. The room was warm, redolent with the scent of humus and hothouse flowers, and the floor-to-ceiling windows shimmered with tiny beads of moisture. "I've come to talk to the girl," Nathan said.

Father Patrick took off his gold-rimmed spectacles and wiped the lenses with a handkerchief. His thin, angular face was flushed and his wide forehead glistened with perspiration. He replaced his glasses and touched the handkerchief to his brow, then to the balding crown of his head. "You're Mr. Hunter, aren't you? Mr. Chadwick's poker guest . . . the one who made the rather sizable contribution."

Nathan nodded.

"Well, Mr. Hunter, I'd appreciate a few minutes more with Pei Ling before you speak to her. There is a matter of some importance which I—"

"This will only take a moment, Father," Nathan interrupted. He took a chance that he had correctly divined the nature of their conversation and plunged in. "I saw Miss Chadwick leave here a short time ago. She appeared to be in a hurry and was rather secretive about her departure. I came to ask Pei Ling—" He paused, looking to the maid to see if he had caught her name correctly. At her quick nod he continued. "—if Miss Chadwick might benefit from an escort."

Father Patrick raised his eyes heavenward and whispered a word of thanks. His prayers had been answered. "Yes indeed, my boy," he said, eagerly stepping forward. He put an arm around Nathan's shoulders and drew him into the room. "Pei Ling tells me Liddy's gone to Miss Bailey's."

"Miss Bailey's? But that's—" He almost said that's where she had been earlier in the evening, but he caught himself in time.

"A brothel," the priest said, finishing the sentence he

61

thought Nathan was too polite to complete. He threw up his hands and began pacing the tiled floor. "When Liddy gets something into her head, she can't let go of it. She's committed to the children, you see . . . no, you can't see. I'm not explaining this very well at all."

Pei Ling raised her head slightly. "I would explain, please. Two women come tonight for Miss Liddy. Say Charlotte is about to have baby. Miss Liddy go to help with delivery and take baby."

"Take the baby?" asked Nathan. Lydia Chadwick wanted a child?

"To the orphanage," Father Patrick broke in. "She's gone to Miss Bailey's to take Charlotte's baby to the orphanage."

"Charlotte doesn't want baby," Pei Ling went on. "Miss Liddy see it has good home."

Surely this could have waited until the morning, Nathan thought. What made taking the baby out tonight so urgent?

"Miss Liddy afraid for baby," Pei Ling said, answering Nathan's unvoiced questions. "Doctor at whorehouse not very good. Miss Liddy don't like. She say he drink too much. She think he might hurt Charlotte or baby. Miss Liddy go today to see Charlotte, but her time not come. Now it come and Miss Liddy go again."

Nathan doubted Pei Ling had ever spoken so many sentences together in her life. She seemed surprised by her effrontery and quickly bent her head and studied the floor.

Father Patrick stopped pacing. "Well, Mr. Hunter? Could we press upon you to go after Lydia? She made Pei Ling promise not to tell her parents, which is why she came to me. I'm afraid my absence from the musicale is already cause for some comment. I can't afford to be gone much longer."

"Miss Chadwick must have already been missed by others," Nathan said.

Pei Ling nodded. "I tell Father she not feel well and go to room. He want to see her but I say she not want to be disturbed. I could not find Missus."

Nathan knew why that was so. "I'll go after her. I don't know why she didn't leave with the women who came with the message. At least she'd have had an escort to Portsmouth Square."

Father Patrick's dark-red brows lifted slightly. "So you do know where Miss Bailey's is."

"Don't take me to task for it, Father. Be happy that I do."

It was drizzling by the time Lydia reached the brothel. She was happy to get out from under the rain and the thick cloud of fog and into the relative safety of Miss Bailey's. Every noise between Nob Hill and Portsmouth Square quickened her heart and her pace until she was running through Chinatown on her way to Kearny Street. She took the side entrance to Miss Bailey's and leaned against the door for several minutes to catch her breath.

"Here you are," Ginny said, coming halfway down the narrow back staircase. "Me and Mara thought you changed your mind."

Lydia unfastened the satin frog at her throat and hung her damp cloak by a hook near the door. "You could have waited for me," she said, starting up the stairs with her basket. "It only took me a few minutes to get ready."

Ginny's bright yellow curls bobbed as her head came up suddenly. "Wait for you? You wouldn't mind being seen with us?"

Remorse struck at Lydia's heart. She had been berating them for leaving her to make the trip alone and they had only been thinking of her reputation. "Of course I wouldn't mind."

"Imagine that," Ginny said. "And I was so sure you'd

want us out of the house as quick as possible. Mara didn't even want to go in. Wanted to pay a boy to give you the message and be done with it. I said we should try to look like we belong and deliver it personal."

"You did the right thing. Has Charlotte had the baby yet?"

"Soon. I think she's waiting for you. Won't let Doc Franklin hardly touch her."

At the top of the stairs they turned left and headed up another flight. Charlotte had been given a room in the attic for her delivery. In the event it was a hard labor, Ida Bailey didn't want the customers complaining about Charlotte's screaming.

"I'll help what I can," Ginny said as they entered Charlotte's room. "Mara's got someone with her, but I'm free." Her voice dropped to a whisper. "Kind of a slow night. All the swells are at your place applying for sainthood."

Lydia thought she was used to Ginny's plain speaking, but that comment made her feel heat in her cheeks. She had never given a thought to the men who frequented Miss Bailey's house. Now she wondered how many of them had danced with her this evening, played poker with her father, or made a pledge to Father Patrick. One of them might even be the father of Charlotte's child. The thought disappointed her first, then made her angry, but she didn't have time to dwell on it. Charlotte had cried out.

"I'm here now," Lydia said, ignoring Dr. Franklin's mumbled aside. She sat down on the edge of the bed and took Charlotte's hand. There was a basin filled with water on the floor beside the bed. Lydia took the cloth lying over the rim of the basin, wet it, and gently wiped the perspiration off Charlotte's pale face. "She could use a fresh gown, Ginny. This one's soaked through. See what you can find."

"She's not changing her gown now," Dr. Franklin said

64

quellingly. "She's about to give birth."

"Then she'll have it for later. Or were you going to let her lie here like this for the rest of the evening?" Lydia shivered. "And it's cold in here. Why don't you start a fire?"

Franklin sputtered and swayed a little on his feet. He attempted to level Lydia with a hard stare, but his eyes were slightly unfocused. "*I'm* the doctor."

"Yes, well, there's a mystery." Her sharp retort raised a wan smile on Charlotte's lips and captured Lydia's attention. "Good. That's all I wanted to see. You're going to be fine, do you know that? And the baby's going to be fine." She smoothed back Charlotte's ash-blond hair where it lay wetly against her forehead and placed the cloth across her brow. "Go ahead, you can squeeze my hand when it hurts. I don't mind." Lydia turned her anxious eyes in the direction of the doctor. "Isn't there anything you can do for her? Should she be in so much pain?"

"It's perfectly normal," Franklin said. "Which proves my point that you shouldn't be here at all. This is no place for you."

"This is no place for *any* woman." Lydia didn't like the look of Dr. Franklin. His thin, slight body was hunched at the foot of the bed as though straightening would have pained him. His hands, when they weren't jammed in the pockets of his jacket, trembled. His dark eyes were rheumy and he dabbed at them occasionally with a handkerchief. In the short time that Lydia had been in the room he had gone to his black satchel twice and raised something to his lips. Lydia was not so naive that she didn't realize he was drinking.

Ginny entered the room carrying fresh linens and a nightgown. Without any prompting from Lydia, she built a fire and kept herself busy tending it. The tension between the doctor and Lydia was almost a tangible thing and Ginny didn't want any part of it.

65

Lydia replaced the cloth on Charlotte's forehead several times in the next half hour. Her hand was bruised where Charlotte held it in a tight grip each time she had a contraction. Lydia's silent entreaties to the doctor went unanswered. Except to knock back a little drink, he didn't leave the bed, and save for the few times he muttered something to himself, he didn't speak.

Ida Bailey poked her head through the door once to inquire about Charlotte's progress. That said, she stated her real mission for climbing the stairs. "Someone's come for you, Lydia. He says Father Patrick sent him to make certain you arrived here safely and get home the same way." Ida's beringed fingers curled around the edge of the door and drummed lightly as she awaited Lydia's response.

Lydia sighed. Pei Ling must have gone straight to the priest. "Did he tell you his name?" James or Henry, she thought. They would have been eager to make themselves useful where her safety was concerned.

"Nathan Hunter."

"Mr. Hunter!"

Charlotte cried out again, her thin face contorting with pain. Lydia forgot about her own situation as the doctor announced the baby was indeed coming.

Impatient to be gone, Ida asked, "What do you want we should do with Mr. Hunter?"

"Entertain him," Lydia said succinctly.

Ida's rosebud mouth curved in a sly, catlike grin. "A pleasure." She slipped back into the hallway and closed the door quietly behind her.

Dr. Franklin cleared his throat and caught Lydia's eye. "It's breech. I'm not sure I can—"

"You damn well better," she whispered coldly. She turned back to Charlotte and soothed her with encouraging words and kindness. It wasn't enough. Charlotte let out a scream of terror and pain as Franklin attempted to turn the baby.

"You're going to have to hold her," Franklin said. He motioned Ginny over to the bed. "Both of you. Make sure she keeps her knees up."

"Don't tell me you're squeamish now," Lydia warned Ginny.

"I'm not," the prostitute said. "Well, not much. But you surprise me."

Lydia shrugged as if it were unimportant. She wrung out the cloth in the basin and sponged off Charlotte's neck and shoulders. The young girl's breathing was quick and shallow and her heartbeat fluttered rapidly against her chest. "What are you doing to her, Franklin?" Lydia demanded. "Can't you—"

Ginny broke in. "She's passed out."

Lydia glanced down at Charlotte. Her face was pasty white, her lips a bluish gray. There was no reason now for Lydia to mince her words. "What's happening to her, Franklin? What in God's name have you done?" She eased her hand out of Charlotte's and went to the end of the bed where the doctor stood. Lydia blanched when she saw the blood. "My God! You've torn her. She's hemorrhaging!"

"That baby's not coming out," Franklin said. He turned away and went for his satchel.

Lydia picked up the bloody forceps the doctor had been using and jammed them into the small of his back. "You take another drink and I swear I'll force these down your throat." She poked him again, harder this time, and when he turned around awkwardly, unsteady on his feet, she jabbed the forceps at his middle. "You damn drunkard. Do something for her! Make the bleeding stop!"

Franklin pushed the forceps away and took a step backward, holding his hands in front of him to ward Lydia off. "There's nothing to be done," he said without emotion.

"I don't believe you," Lydia said hoarsely. "There must be something you can do."

"She's going to die."

67

"Damn you."

He shrugged. "She's just a whore."

Enraged by his callousness, Lydia raised her arm to strike him. Ginny's hand stayed her. "Don't do it, Miss Lydia. Look at him. He can't help Charlotte."

Tears flooded Lydia's dark-blue eyes. She lowered her arm until it was pointing at the door. "Get him out of here, Ginny. Show him the door and tell Miss Bailey that I'll need towels, menstrual cloths, and boiling water to sterilize these instruments. Also, get someone up here who thinks they *can* do something. Hurry, Ginny." Lydia drew up her gown and knelt at the bottom edge of the bed. "I'm not giving up, even if he has."

Lydia began by trying to stem the flow of blood. Using the linens that Ginny had brought earlier, she made packs and pressed them against Charlotte's thighs. Charlotte went in and out of consciousness as the contractions came on more rapidly, and Lydia had no clear idea what to do with a breech birth. "Oh, please, Charlotte, you've got to help," she whispered. "You've got to."

The door opened behind Lydia. She glanced over her shoulder and saw Nathan Hunter walk into the room. He threw his jacket beside the doctor's satchel and rolled up his shirtsleeves as he approached the bed.

"You!" Lydia cried. "What are you—"

Nathan did not answer. He simply picked Lydia up and moved her off the bed. Her legs unfolded under her and he set her on the floor. "Ginny's bringing the things you asked for. Go help her."

Lydia responded to the authority in Nathan's tone and stopped questioning his presence or his right to order her around. She hurried off to lend her assistance to Ginny.

"Charlotte? That's your name, isn't it?" Nathan washed his hands at the bedside basin, then shook off the water droplets. "Well, Charlotte, I'm going to help you have your baby. You go ahead and scream if you have to, call me any name you want. It's going to hurt because the first thing we have to do is turn your baby around." He kept talking, a gentle litany of instructions and praise, as he worked between Charlotte's bloody thighs. Sweat trickled down his spine and beaded on his brow.

Lydia returned to the room and set a kettle of water in the hearth. She dropped in the instruments Dr. Franklin had used, then stood beside Nathan at the foot of the bed. She watched him work in silence, his mouth tight with the force of his concentration, his jaw clenched. There was tension in his profile and a muscle worked rhythmically in his cheek. Lydia picked up a damp cloth and wiped his forehead.

"Thank you."

It took Lydia a moment to realize he was speaking to her. She couldn't think of anything to say. She simply nodded once in acknowledgment.

"Take her hand," Nathan instructed. "Talk to her. Make her help. I've almost got the baby turned. Is Ginny here?"

"Right here, sir," Ginny said as she walked into the room. "I've got the linens."

"Find something to wrap the baby in and bring it over here." He turned his attention back to Charlotte. "It's all right to push now, Charlotte. Next contraction. That's it. Come on, darlin'. I can feel the baby's head. No, don't stop. Don't . . . Lydia, get me the forceps; Charlotte's not pushing any longer." Lydia retrieved them quickly from the kettle, almost burning her hands in the process. "Easy," Nathan cautioned. "I can only do one patient at a time."

"Are you a doctor?" Lydia asked when the instrument was cool enough to give him.

He shook his head.

"But how do you—"

"Sheep."

Lydia's lips parted in surprise. Ginny giggled nervously.

Nathan continued working. He eased the forceps around the baby's head and pulled gently on the next contraction. Though nothing of his fear showed on his face, the amount of blood loss alarmed him. If he somehow managed to bring the baby out, he wasn't at all confident he could do anything to save Charlotte.

He glanced at Lydia once. She was stroking Charlotte's hair, her lips bent near the young whore's ear. Her voice was softly encouraging, lilting and sweet. Her eyes though were infinitely sad, tear-washed, and so dark in her pale face they appeared to be black. *She knows,* thought Nathan. *She knows we're going to lose Charlotte.*

Losing the baby, however, was the first pain to be borne. Nathan held the tiny child in his palms, his own eyes closed briefly against the ache of his failure and the loss of something so precious. "I'm sorry, Charlotte," he said quietly. "He's stillborn."

Charlotte nodded weakly. A tear slipped between her closed lids and she bit down on her waxen lips. Groping blindly, she found Lydia's hand and held on tightly.

Lydia sucked in her breath and smothered a sob with the back of her hand. It didn't matter that Charlotte had vowed all along that she never wanted the child; Lydia knew it did little or nothing to lessen her anguish now.

"I'll take him," Ginny said, slipping her hands beneath Nathan's. "We'll need the scissors to cut the cord." Nathan got those for her and snipped the cord quickly. Ginny carried the baby to the basin and began washing him off while Nathan went back to working on Charlotte.

A few minutes passed before Nathan had the placenta. He wrapped it in the newspaper that Lydia was quick to provide. "Do you embroider?" he asked Lydia as he examined the damage Dr. Franklin had done to his patient.

"What?" She couldn't imagine why he wanted to know at a time like this.

Nathan didn't answer her question directly. "Look in the doctor's bag and see if he has a curved needle and surgical thread."

70

Suddenly his query made sense. Lydia hesitated. She couldn't possibly do what he was proposing. Yet when Nathan repeated his order, rapping it out impatiently this time, Lydia knew she would do whatever she had to.

She did. And in the end it still wasn't enough.

Ginny laid the baby in the basket Lydia brought and put it beside Charlotte's still body, then she closed Charlotte's eyes. "There's nothing more you can do," she said quietly. "I'll see to everything from now on."

Lydia couldn't move. Her fingers trembled with exhaustion and she pricked herself with the needle she held. Her eyes widened slightly at the pain, but that was her only reaction. She simply sat at the foot of the bed, limp with weariness, her eyes vacant, and stared at Charlotte's serene, finely wrought features.

Nathan used his forearm to push back the damp strands of dark hair that had fallen across his brow. He looked around for a clean towel and grimaced when he couldn't find one. "Is there someplace we can go to wash?" he asked, holding up his hands for Ginny to see.

"My room," Ginny said. "One floor down. First door on the left. Lydia knows where it is." She looked at Lydia, then back at Nathan. "Is she going to be all right, do you think?"

Nathan had been wondering the same thing, but he didn't say so. "She'll be fine. She got in a little over her head this time, I think."

"That's Miss Liddy." There was a certain fondness in her voice that did not go unnoticed by Nathan. "She has the heart of a lion."

And the straight-thinking sense of a Jackaroo, Nathan thought disparagingly. Hell, a tenderfoot on a sheep ranch had *more* sense than Lydia Chadwick. Nathan took the needle from Lydia's fingers and gripped her firmly around the wrist, pulling her to her feet in a single motion. She didn't resist him, a turn of events which Nathan accepted with mixed feelings. He led her into the hallway and down the stairs to Ginny's room.

71

The bedroom was warm thanks to a small coal stove tucked in one corner. Nathan watched in some amazement as Lydia meekly complied with his suggestion that she sit on the thickly padded footstool beside it. He poured water from a porcelain pitcher on Ginny's bureau into the matching bowl and washed his own hands. He carried fresh water over to Lydia. In spite of the warmth, she was chilled through.

He knelt on the floor in front of her. "Here," he said, lifting the basin to her lap. "Put your hands in here and I'll wash them off." He scrubbed her skin with a washcloth, noticing for the first time how small and soft her hands were in comparison to his. Yet he had seen for himself that they were capable hands, as deft and skilled as they were graceful. He thought of his own rum daddles, rough and calloused after more than a decade of hard labor, and realized how inadequate they had been to this evening's task.

"You have beautiful hands," she said, her voice just above a whisper.

Nathan self-consciously curled his long fingers into fists. He got to his feet quickly, picked up the basin, and emptied it. He rinsed his face at the bureau. Turning to Lydia, Nathan rolled down the sleeves of his shirt. "I left my jacket upstairs. While I'm getting it, I suggest you find something of Ginny's to wear. You're about the same size, I think." When Lydia looked at him blankly, a frown furrowing her dark brows, he pointed to her yellow party gown. "It's ruined."

Lydia's eyes dropped to her ruffled bodice. It was indeed ruined, stained with blood along the edge, at the waist, and where she had absently adjusted her short, puffed sleeves. There were handprints on the skirt of the gown, black now that the blood had had time to dry. "Yes," she said, nodding once. "You're right. It's quite ruined. I can't go home like this."

She seemed at a loss as to what to do so Nathan repeated his suggestion.

"Oh, but I don't think I could wear something of Ginny's."

Nathan frowned and asked sharply, "Why? Because it's a whore's dress?"

Lydia's head jerked up. She was not adept at hiding her hurt, and it was there for Nathan to see in the dark-blue depths of her eyes. "N-no. Of course not." *Ginny's clothes won't fit,* she wanted to say, but was too embarrassed. "Go on," she said. "I'll think of something."

Nathan wasn't certain he trusted her. He opened Ginny's wardrobe, selected a severely cut sapphire-blue evening gown, and tossed it on the four-poster. "Put that on," he said, brooking no argument. "I'll ask Ginny just to make certain there's no problem." At the door he paused. "Be here when I get back, Miss Chadwick."

In the attic he helped Ginny clean and dress Charlotte's body, then take the bloody linens to the washroom in the cellar. Ginny was effusive in her thanks, but Nathan didn't pay much attention. He hadn't done anything as far as he was concerned and his motives weren't as altruistic as Ginny made them sound. When he came to the attic Charlotte and her baby weren't nearly as important as making himself less repugnant in Lydia's eyes. He wondered if he had failed because of that. Maybe there was nothing to be gained by doing the right thing for the wrong reasons.

Thirty minutes after he left Lydia, Nathan found himself holding his breath while twisting the brass handle in Ginny's door. He let it out slowly when he saw Lydia was still in the room. She was standing at the window, her back to him, dressed in the gown he had chosen. She didn't move when he entered and he wasn't sure she had even heard him. Yet when he came to stand behind her, her slender shoulders heaved once with a sob she couldn't contain, and when she turned it was to step into his arms.

Lydia did not question that she should seek comfort and strength in the embrace of Nathan Hunter. For once she put her needs first and she needed someone to hold her now. It had never felt quite so important to have the touch of another human being. She required nothing of him save kindness. She could not know then it did not come easily to this man.

Nathan absorbed her shudders. He felt the damp stain of her tears through his shirt and the soft, silken strands of her hair against the underside of his chin. Her skin held the delicate scent of lilac and the freshness of her, the purity of her spirit touched him unexpectedly. He didn't know what to do with her; he didn't quite know what to do with himself. He held her loosely, somewhat stiffly, not pressing the sudden advantage the evening's odd events had given him. It was enough to hold her and let her imagine he was feeling her pain, when in fact he knew little about sharing any emotion.

He wasn't any better than Brig, he thought, and perhaps he was worse. Lydia was a complete innocent. What chance did she have against either himself or Brigham Moore? Did she even understand the kind of careful calculation and planning that was being used to win her trust? He set Lydia away from him and handed her a handkerchief. "Take this, wipe your eyes, and blow."

Confused by the harshness in Nathan's tone, Lydia gave him a watery, tentative smile and thanked him. Just below the surface of her skin she was cold again, and in her heart she was aching with sadness. "We should go, I suppose," she said finally when he didn't say anything. She folded the handkerchief neatly and tucked it under the sleeve of her gown. The tatted edge of the handkerchief peeked out to decorate her wrist. "What time is it?"

Nathan consulted his pocket watch on the platinum fob. "Almost midnight."

"I suppose Papa is beside himself with worry by now."

"I think Pei Ling told him you were ill and indisposed to visitors. I'm fairly confident Father Patrick will keep your secret as well."

"And you?"

"Your parents aren't going to hear about tonight from me." That would hardly win him a chance at her hand. The Chadwicks most likely frowned on their daughter delivering babies in brothels.

"Good." She raised her chin a notch, a gesture that Nathan was beginning to recognize as Lydia's challenging stance. "Then I don't want to go home just yet," she said.

Nathan didn't so much as blink. He wasn't surprised. Jackaroos did indeed have more sense than Lydia Chadwick. "What is it you want to do?"

"Get drunk."

She made it seem perfectly reasonable. "Have you ever been drunk, Miss Chadwick?" he asked politely.

"No."

"Do you even drink?"

She sniffed a shade haughtily. "Of course I do."

"Wine with your dinner or perhaps you sneak a glass of port after the meal."

"I drink sherry. In fact, I've already had some this evening."

One of Nathan's brows was lifted slightly, as was the corner of his mouth. The look of dry amusement was cool and remote on his features. "Oh?" he said blandly.

"You're laughing at me," Lydia said. "Go ahead. I don't know why men can use any excuse to drink themselves silly and a woman can't even do it when she's witnessed two deaths in the space of an hour. Charlotte was not my friend, Mr. Hunter, but I had come to know her in these past few months and I think the world's poorer for her passing. I wanted to offer her baby a good place to live, with people who care, and he never had even the tiniest chance. I couldn't get a doctor who wasn't a drunk to come here. I couldn't make a difference."

Raising her hand to her mouth, Lydia managed to hold back a harsh sob. She finished quietly. "Watching Charlotte go like that . . . the life just seeping out of her . . . just seeping out." She forgot about the handkerchief and

75

swiped at her tears with the back of her hand. Impatient with herself, angry about injustice, unfairness, and her own inadequacies, Lydia pushed past Nathan and headed for the door. "I'll take myself home, thank you."

Nathan stopped her, hooking his hand around her elbow and bringing her up short. "I promised Pei Ling and Father Patrick—" Lydia tried to shake him off, "—that I would bring you home safely. I don't . . ." She yanked harder and found herself brought flush against Nathan's hard body, "—don't think it matters if I bring you home drunk."

Lydia stopped struggling. Her eyes, when she looked up at him, seemed impossibly large for her face. They darted over Nathan's face, trying to measure his sincerity. "Really?"

"Where do you want to go?"

"I don't know," she admitted. "I don't really know any places."

Nathan eased his grip on her elbow. "Does it really matter where we go?"

She shook her head. "But I don't want to stay here."

"That wasn't what I had in mind. What would you say to the Silver Lady?"

"In the gambling hall?"

"In my suite."

Lydia didn't say anything for a moment.

"Have you changed your mind?" Nathan asked. It was difficult to read the course of her thoughts as they played on her features now. "You can, you know."

"No." The chin was thrust forward again. "No, I haven't changed my mind." She hesitated a beat, then said quickly, "I was embarrassed before . . . In the alley, when you . . . and then you insisted I go to your room . . . I didn't . . . that is, I've never done anything like that before. I couldn't imagine what you might think of me, or rather I *could*. That's why I left. And then you showed up at my party—as my father's guest. I was . . . mortified." She closed her eyes a moment, reliving the memory. "That's why I treated you so abominably. You'd seen me in that alley with those men. I thought you might believe I was—"

"Asking to be assaulted?" he finished for her.

"Something like that."

"And you're telling me now, that even though you're going to accompany me back to the Silver Lady, it's strictly because of your newfound interest in liquor."

"I was?" She flushed a little. "Yes, I suppose I was."

"What did you think you were saying?"

"Thank you," she said. "I was trying to say thank you."

Chapter Three

The suite was cold. The heavy fog that had cloaked their passage from Miss Bailey's to the Silver Lady pressed against the windows like a living thing. While Lydia stood huddled by the door, Nathan closed the drapes and started a fire.

He sat back on his haunches and raised his palms to the heat and crackle of the flames. Without looking in Lydia's direction he said, "Are you coming or going? I can't tell."

"I haven't changed my mind, if that's what you mean." Although her words held a touch of bravado, Lydia's eyes were still darting nervously about the room, taking in the things she hadn't noticed on her brief first visit.

The suite was rather expensively appointed, indicating again that Nathan Hunter had money to spend. There were two small damask sofas facing each other on either side of the fireplace. A bright Oriental rug filled the space between them. The brocade drapes were ivory and they matched the high-backed armchair situated between the two windows. The end tables, sideboard, and wainscoting were all dark walnut, lending the room a rich, warm elegance.

Lydia avoided looking to her left where the door to

Nathan's bedroom was only partially closed. Some things were better not explored.

She realized that Nathan was watching her. As if he could read her thoughts, a half-smile played at the corners of his mouth. Lydia's own mouth pursed primly in disapproval.

"Shall I take your cape?" he asked blandly, coming to his feet. "Or would you rather wear it the rest of the evening."

"I can manage, thank you." Lydia slipped out of her cape and hung it on the brass rack behind her. Because she didn't know what to do with them, she crossed her arms in front of her as if she were still cold.

"You'd be warmer over here." Nathan stood in front of the fire a little longer, waiting to see if she would approach while he was there. When she didn't, he took pity on her and went to the sideboard to pour their drinks. As soon as his back was turned he heard her move quickly to the fireplace. "The selection is somewhat limited," he said as he poured his own drink.

"I'll have whatever you're having."

He turned, raising his own tumbler for her to see. He caught her off guard, with her back to the fire and the hem of her gown raised almost to her knees. She dropped her dress quickly and looked everywhere but at him. "I'm having Scotch," he said, a small pause between each word as he tried to get his thoughts back on center. A brief glimpse of Lydia's shapely calves and slim ankles had captured his imagination and scattered his thoughts. "Scotch," he repeated. "Are you certain that's what you want?"

"I'm certain." She sat down on one of the sofas in a corner nearest to the fireplace and pretended to study the oil painting above the mantel.

Nathan brought Lydia her drink and followed the direction of her gaze. "It's not very good, is it?" He sat down opposite her. "I never cared much for landscapes. I notice your family has a considerable collection of art-work."

"Papa showed you the gallery?" she asked.

"I saw it," Nathan answered, evading the question slightly. "You're not drinking. Wouldn't you prefer something else?"

"Oh, no . . . no, this is fine." To prove her point, Lydia took a mouthful of the Scotch and swallowed. She forced a smile and blinked rapidly, fighting back the tears that appeared instantly in her eyes. In the end she couldn't quell a gasp when the Scotch hit her stomach. Fighting fire with fire, Lydia took another quick swallow.

"Just how wide would you say your stubborn streak is?" he asked, watching her struggle not to choke. "I can't think of many young ladies who have your kind of grit." It was a bit of a lie since Nathan actually couldn't think of one. He'd met plenty of women who could drink their fair portion of whatever swill was put in front of them, but they were a common sort, women of the street, thieves and beggars, hardened by life in a way Lydia Chadwick could not possibly know. They did what they had to do to survive.

Lydia, he thought, was a curiosity. She did what she did because she wanted to. As far as he knew she had never experienced a need that hadn't been met, a wish that hadn't been fulfilled. It was clear to Nathan that Samuel Chadwick doted on her. Yet she didn't appear to be spoiled, as he might have expected, but headstrong and full of purpose and determination.

Her eyes intrigued him. Sometimes they seemed impossibly large in her heart-shaped face, and so dark that the cobalt-blue color appeared to be black. They were rebellious eyes, most often defiant or stubborn in their expression, yet in their very depths Nathan had the impression of a pervasive sadness, as if rebellion were there to shutter a wounded soul.

"May I have another drink?" asked Lydia, showing

Nathan her empty tumbler. "No, you stay where you are. I can get it myself."

It was just as well that she interrupted his fanciful thoughts, Nathan decided. He wasn't certain he liked where they were headed. Sentiment had no place in his plans for Lydia Chadwick.

He handed her his tumbler and followed her with his eyes as she went to the sideboard. Her carriage was poised and graceful. The stark blue evening gown he'd chosen for her from among Ginny's things emphasized the slender line of her back and the smallness of her waist. Her shoulders were narrow and her arms were long, the wrists small and delicate. He recalled holding her against him, first in the alley, then in the ballroom, and still later in the brothel. Each time he had been struck by the way she had fit to him so easily. She was not a tall woman, yet her high and slim waist gave the impression of legs that went on forever. He wondered why he hadn't noticed that before now. It was not the sort of thing he usually missed when he was looking at a woman.

Then he remembered the yellow gown. Whoever had suggested she could wear yellow and yards of ruffles hadn't done a kindness to her.

He accepted the drink she held in front of him. "You can put your feet up," he said when she returned to her sofa. "A person doesn't generally go about getting drunk as stiffly as you. You'll find it much easier if you try to relax a little. And you can stop worrying that I'm going to attack you. I haven't yet, have I?"

Lydia blinked widely, drawing her feet up beside her more in reaction to his harsh and sarcastic last statement than because of a need to relax. "I don't think you'll attack me," she said, her voice husky from liquor and weariness. "Why would you want to?"

Nathan ignored her last query. He could give her at least three reasons why he'd like to show her the bedroom: her eyes, her legs, and her sulky, generous mouth. "Stop looking at me as if you expect the worst

82

then," he said sharply. "We're here as a favor to you, nothing else."

She nodded and quickly lifted the tumbler to her lips again. The Scotch did not taste quite so foul and fiery as it had at first. "Will it take very long to get drunk, do you think?"

"At the rate you're going, not long at all."

"Oh. That's good then."

Nathan didn't respond. A long uncomfortable silence built while Lydia worked on her drink and Nathan nursed his. When they finally spoke it was one of those awkward situations where it happened at the same time. After some disagreement about who should go first they both fell silent. Nathan filled Lydia's glass a third time and watched in some amazement as she knocked it back in three swallows. She held the tumbler out again.

"You may want to ease up some," he said, filling her glass. "Or I could add a little water."

"I'm fine." Staring up at him defiantly, she held on to the tumbler when he tried to take it back.

Nathan shrugged. "Suit yourself. It's your head." He put the decanter of Scotch on the floor by Lydia's sofa and returned to his seat. Stretching his long legs in front him, he crossed his ankles and stared at Lydia over the rim of his glass.

"I wish you wouldn't look at me like that," she said.

"Like what?"

She lowered her lids so that she could see Nathan through a narrow slit, set her mouth grimly, thrust her legs in front of her, crossed her ankles, and raised her glass to about the level of her nose. She sat like that for several long moments and simply stared back at him.

"I see," he said, tamping down a smile at her perfect mimicking. When she resumed her earlier position, he asked, "Does it bother you so much?"

"It makes me feel rather foolish," she answered honestly. "It's one thing to be foolish, quite another to be made to feel so."

"I beg your pardon," he said, sitting up a little straighter and drawing back his legs. "You're my guest after all. I'll make an effort to please."

Lydia doubted it was something he did often, and his concession warmed her. Or was that the Scotch? She giggled.

She was definitely beginning to feel the effects, Nathan realized. That girlish giggle was surely the beginning of the end. He started thinking about how he was going to get her back inside her Nob Hill mansion without alerting the entire household.

"Did you know Mr. Moore before this evening?" Lydia asked, interrupting Nathan's planning.

Except for the slight narrowing of his gray eyes, there was nothing Nathan did to reveal his surprise. "What makes you ask that?" he asked, prevaricating.

"Your accent. It's very similar to Mr. Moore's. It's natural that two Englishmen would have gravitated toward one another here in San Francisco."

"Is it? I hadn't thought about that. Did Mr. Moore tell you where he's from in England?"

She nodded. The movement made her chin nudge the rim of her glass and a little Scotch splashed the back of her hand. Embarrassed by her clumsiness, she quickly pressed her hand to her mouth and sucked in the droplets, never noticing how Nathan's cold eyes took on an edge of warmth as they followed her movement and came to rest on her wet mouth. "He's from London," she said. "Where are you from?"

"London. But don't put too much significance into that. I don't think you could understand how big London is."

"I should like to see it some day," she said dreamily.

Nathan could have said the same. It was the one place he could never return. Without a governor's full pardon, banishment from England was forever. "It's an incredible city," he said instead, remembering the place of his childhood. "Exciting. Crowded. Noisy and dirty. Narrow, winding lanes lined with tenements and palaces bordering the most beautiful parks in the world. There's mind-numbing poverty and wealth that can hardly be imagined.''

''You make it sound very much like San Francisco.''

''Do I? Yes, I suppose in some ways it is, though if you repeat that I'll swear I never said it.'' He finished his drink and set the glass aside. ''London is centuries old; poverty and riches go back so many generations they're bred in the bone, for the most part, inescapable. There's a certain acceptance of fate there that's missing in your city, Miss Chadwick. Here wealth is only decades old and people remember their roots. Men and women still believe they can aspire to be something different than their class would dictate. I admire that.''

''Do you? I confess that surprises me.''

''Oh?''

''What do you know about any of it, Mr. Hunter?'' She guestured to the room at large, indicating the richness of her surroundings. ''You seem quite content to have accepted what good fate and fortune have bestowed on you. If Mr. Moore were saying these things, it would be understandable. He came to my party this evening because he knew it was a charity event. By your own admission you came to play cards with my father. Did you know Mr. Moore was raised in an orphanage much like St. Andrew's? He escaped the London slums and made something of himself.''

''You admire him.''

''Yes . . . yes, what's not to admire? He's obviously met life's challenges head on. He's personable and interesting and—''

''Don't forget handsome.''

Lydia blushed, then asked herself why she should deny it. ''Yes, he's handsome. He has kind eyes, a wonderful smile, and he's very polite.''

''A paragon among men.''

She wrinkled her nose at Nathan, disgusted with his

dry humor. "Think what you will. You could do worse than to emulate his manner."

Since there had been a time when Nathan thought much the same way, he couldn't find it in himself to fault Lydia for her shortsightedness. "I'll take it under advisement," he said, noting that that seemed to satisfy her. She was looking around the room again, shaking her head slowly down side to side, her eyes as big as silver dollars. Nathan had no difficulty reading the expression on her face. She was still astonished that she wasn't home. Her half-smothered giggle seemed to punctuate her thought. Above the rim of her glass her smile was a trifle giddy.

"You're well on your way to being pie-faced," he observed. "How does it feel?"

Her grin widened. "Wonderful. I'm enjoying myself immensely." She spoke carefully, sounding out the individual syllables. "Are you?"

"I can't remember when I've been so entertained."

Lydia's brows drew together as she considered what he said. It wasn't worth so much effort, she decided, and her features relaxed. "Do you know I was angry with you this evening?"

"You were?" Nathan asked politely. He wondered if he should warn Lydia that the drink was loosening her tongue. Doubting that she would take heed of anything he might say, he let her go on.

"Oh, yes," she said. "I didn't want you to win that last poker hand. I think you knew it, too."

"I knew it. But what could I do? I had the winning cards. I would have won whatever wager was made. You didn't have to agree to that wager. Samuel would have let you bow out gracefully."

"I did it for the—"

"Oh, please," he said, scoffing her. "Have the decency to be an honest drunk. You agreed because it was Brigham Moore who you hoped might hold the winning hand."

"My father held a full house," she said a shade

86

haughtily. "Remember? I thought it was very likely that he would win."

"That may be so, but you *hoped* Brig would win."

"If you knew that why did you insist on showing your cards? You could have just folded. The pot would have gone to the orphanage just the same."

"Would it?"

"Of course." Lydia paused, taking another full swallow. She thought she could acquire a taste for Scotch. "Are you saying Mr. Moore would not have honored that part of the wager?"

The last thing Nathan wanted to do was say anything against Brig. That would surely send her flying into his old friend's arms. Nathan unbuttoned his evening jacket and pulled out the paper marker in his vest pocket. He leaned forward and held it out to Lydia, letting it dangle between his thumb and forefinger. "Say the word and I'll put it in the fire."

Lydia couldn't believe she'd heard him correctly. In the library, when he'd won the hand, he'd seemed so pleased with himself. She came to the only conclusion she could. "You don't want to take me out to dinner at all, do you? You only did it to spite me, because you knew I wanted to go with Mr. Moore." Belatedly she realized what she'd finally admitted to Nathan Hunter. Her chin lifted a notch. "So? What if I *did* want to have dinner with him at the Cliff House? The wager was his idea, wasn't it? At least *he* wanted to go with me."

Nathan gave her a hard, steady look. "Do you want me to pitch this in the fire or not?"

"Oh, no, I'm not going to make this easy for you by reneging on my part of the wager. You do with it what you want to do."

He leaned back, sighing. Her logic confounded him. Nathan hoped it was the alcohol that had her talking in circles. Once they were married he was going to lock the liquor cabinet and carry the key on him. He folded the marker again and put it back in his pocket. "I'm keeping

87

it," he said. "I'm taking you to the Cliff House tomorrow and I won't allow you to use your impending hangover as an excuse to get out of it. Your eagerness to go to dinner with Brig is hardly flattering."

Lydia rolled the tumbler between her palms and stared down at her empty glass. "I've been rude. I'm sorry."

Nathan shrugged.

She looked up to see why he hadn't answered. He was still watching her closely, his clear gray predator eyes holding her motionless. She refused to repeat her apology, unaware that it had already been acknowledged with practiced indifference. Leaning over the edge of the sofa, Lydia reached for the crystal decanter. "Ooooh," she said, holding her head as a wave of dizziness washed over her. "I think your rug is spinning, Mr. Hunter."

"Nathan."

"Hmm?" She glanced up at him and smiled. "What's that again?"

"You may call me Nathan . . . and judging by your grin, I think you've had quite enough."

"Oh, but—"

"Enough." He moved the decanter back to the sideboard and returned to Lydia's side in time to catch her tumbler before it dropped to the floor. "How do you like being drunk?" he asked a moment later when Lydia herself slipped off the sofa and onto the floor.

"Am I?" she asked. "Am I really?"

Judging by her voice, Nathan decided she was completely pleased with herself. "You're about as shikkered as I've ever seen a sheila. And you're going to feel crook come sarvo."

Lydia knew she was drunk. She'd heard what he'd said and hadn't understood a word. She frowned up at Nathan, wishing he'd stop towering over her and sit down.

"I said you're about as drunk as I've ever seen a girl. And you're going to feel terrible by tomorrow afternoon."

"Well, I feel fine now," she said with a sense of practicality. "Except for having to look up at you. It makes my neck ache."

The long line of Lydia's throat was completely exposed to Nathan. At his side his fingers itched to close around it and throttle her just once. "I'll sit down," he offered.

Lydia patted the floor beside her. "Here."

"I don't think—" Her eyes darted down quickly, hurt by his refusal. A moment later he was sitting beside her, his back against the sofa. "It would have been easier," he said, "if you'd have let me put you back on the sofa."

"Too high."

He found himself smiling at the grave, wise pronouncement. "I see."

"You may call me Lydia."

"All right . . . Lydia."

The silence that grew between them this time was a comfortable one. Out of the corner of his eye Nathan saw Lydia's lashes flutter as she tried to stay awake. When her head lolled toward the fireplace he gently brought it back and let her rest it against his shoulder. It was not long before she turned entirely in his direction, her legs curled to one side, and snuggled trustingly in his arms.

There were worse things, Nathan supposed, than dealing with a shikkered Lydia Chadwick.

Until the steady knocking at the door roused him, Nathan was unaware that he had fallen asleep. His dreams had been a natural continuation of his waking thoughts, one flowing into another like a stream into a river. The young woman who had figured rather largely in both was still sleeping soundly in his arms.

Nathan stumbled a bit as he got to his feet, his legs numb and unsteady beneath him. He stretched, glanced at the clock, then bent and picked up Lydia. She was lighter than he had imagined. Again he recalled the horrible yellow gown and acknowledged that her dress had indeed been deceiving. Moving quickly toward the bedroom, Nathan laid Lydia on his bed and covered her up to her neck with the quilt at the foot of the bed. She never stirred, not even when his fingers lingered in her hair at a spot just above her temple.

He shrugged out of his evening jacket, vest, and shirt, mussed his hair, slipped into a smoking jacket, and took off his socks and shoes. The knocking at the door was louder now and more insistent. Just before he opened the door Nathan worked up a huge yawn and rubbed his eyes. Anyone could be forgiven for thinking they'd wakened him from hours of deep sleep.

"What do you want, Brig?" he asked tiredly. There was no surprise in his voice, for he felt none. Indeed, he would have been surprised if it had been anyone else. "Do you have any idea what time it is?"

"Actually I do." Without waiting for an invitation, Brig pushed past Nathan. He went immediately to the sideboard and helped himself to three generous fingers of bourbon. His eyes went from Nathan, who was still leaning against the door, to the woman's cape hanging on the rack beside him. "Oh, sorry old man, I see you have company," he said, indicating the cape with a tilt of his chin. "I should have realized when you disappeared from that beano so early that you had a sheila with you." Brig meant a gala affair. He was rarely cautious about his slang when he was alone with Nathan. "Mind if I have a look?"

Before Nathan could raise an objection or move to stop him, Brig was slipping into the bedroom. All Nathan could do was pray that Lydia had not turned in her sleep or uncovered herself. Brig would find it odd that he was sleeping with a fully dressed woman.

A moment later Brig was back, his disappointment telling Nathan that all was well. "Too dark," said Brig, "but she's a bit of a thing, ain't she? Not like some girls that come to mind."

"You're referring to Miss Chadwick, I take it."

"She's the one who comes to mind. Pity she ain't more like her mother. Now there's someone who can fill out the front of my trousers."

"I noticed your interest."

"It's mutual."

"I thought it might be. I'd be careful, though. Lydia may object to your spending too much time with her mother. I have the distinct impression that that sort of thing's happened before."

"Oh?"

"No information. Just a feeling."

Brig knew he'd do well to consider that feeling. "I'm surprised you're telling me. Given that we have the same objective, I'd think you'd want me to fail."

Thinking about Lydia in his bedroom, Nathan permitted himself a small smile. "Perhaps I think I can afford to be magnanimous."

Brig snorted. He sat down in the corner of the sofa Lydia had occupied. "So, who is she?"

"That's none of your business," Nathan answered kindly.

"What made you decide to leave?"

Nathan sat down on an arm of the other sofa. "I believe Lydia retired for the evening, at least that's what Samuel told me. With her gone there was little to be served by staying. I left at about the time the entertainment began."

Brig nodded. "That's when I missed you." He took a swift swallow of bourbon. "I didn't appreciate you winning that hand. That wager was my idea."

"It was a good one."

"That's the second time you've interfered with something I planned."

"We've already discussed this, Brig. I thought you said all you cared to before we went to dinner."

"I thought I had. The more I think about it, the more bloody angry I get."

91

Brig didn't really look angry. He looked slightly drunk. Nathan knew from experience that the latter was more dangerous. "Shouldn't you be going? I do have a guest, you know."

"Might as well," he said, sighing. He gulped back his drink, set the tumbler on the floor, and headed for the door. "Maybe I'll find someone for myself tonight."

"Surprised you haven't already. That's not like you, Brig."

"I'm looking for a lady, not a whore."

"What about Madeline Chadwick?"

"As I said, I'm looking for a lady."

Nathan thought about Brig's parting remark for a long moment before he got up and locked the door and turned back the lights. He reasoned he could still get a few good hours of sleep before taking Lydia home. It would probably take at least that long for her to come out of her stupor. Padding barefoot to the bedroom, he found Lydia lying on her back, snoring softly. He turned her on her side, moved her toward the middle of the bed, and got in beside her.

He almost came out of his skin when he realized she wasn't wearing anything but a thin cotton shift.

"Lydia?" He said her name softly, on an inquiring note. When she didn't answer, he nudged her shoulder with his fingertips. She didn't respond. He touched her again, just to make certain she was sleeping. Or rather that was the excuse he put forth when a gremlin thought told him he'd never touched skin as smooth as Lydia's. "Are you awake?"

He waited for a full minute, listening to the cadence of her breathing and wondering if she'd heard any part of his conversation with Brig while she'd been undressing. The very idea made his insides curl in a hundred tiny knots. To have come so far only to lose everything because of Brig's untimely visit could have easily moved Nathan to murder. He'd killed before. He could do it again.

With that thought in mind, Nathan fell into a sleep many times more troubled than Lydia's.

His hand was on her breast. The full, smooth curve of it filled his palm and his thumb passed back and forth across the nipple. Once. Twice. Again. Beneath his calloused thumb a bud appeared. He touched it, teased it. Her breast was fuller now, harder and warmer. His fingers trailed along the underside curve to her heartbeat, rested there a moment, then moved to her other breast and stroked her skin, brushing her nipple with his knuckles.

Her hand was at the waistband of his trousers. Her fingers traced the edge, dipping just beneath the material at her whim. His skin was smooth here, his flat belly hard. His flesh would retract suddenly in anticipation of her touch.

Without a word passing between them, they inched closer, moving toward the middle of the bed. The hem of her cotton shift was twisted around her hips, pushed there by her movement and the movement of his hands. He caressed the outside of her thigh from knee to hip. His palm traveled across her skin in long, sweeping strokes, becoming slightly more urgent with its pressure and heat on each successive stroke.

Frustrated by the barrier of his trousers, her fingers slid upward, spreading out as they moved up the center of his chest. His flesh changed under her touch and the accident of rubbing his right nipple was then deliberately repeated on his left. Her hand moved along his ribs to the underside of his arm. From there it slid to his elbow and then to his shoulder. Trailing along his collarbone, her fingers slipped around his neck and toyed with the ends of his dark hair, tugging and ruffling, raising prickles at his nape and sending an excited shiver down the length of his spine.

His palm rested briefly on her hipbone, covering her,

learning the shape of her body in the curve of his hand. His fingers fell lower, between her thighs now, and nested intimately in the warm and humid contours of her body. Gradually there was movement. First him, then her. He stroked. She responded. There was a sound at the back of his throat which could be taken as encouragement. Her sigh was acceptance.

Her knee was raised, and slid between his thighs. The bare length of her leg was covered by his, and when her exploring hand reached his waist again, he took her wrist and dragged it lower until she was cupping the fullness of his sex. He pressed his body against her so there was the friction of his trousers and her palm as she held him.

Their legs tangled as they moved in unison, she on her back, he nearly on top of her. His mouth sought hers, capturing and silencing the small, agitated moan that had come to her lips. There was no nuance in the kiss. No sipping or delicacy of desiring. The kissing had been left too late for the sweetness of budding passion.

Their mouths were hungry. Their tongues entwined in earnest battle and they shared a single breath. They each pressed their advantage, greedy for pleasure. They took from each other. It was more by accident than design that they gave anything in return.

The pressure of his mouth kept hers open. His tongue swept along the sensitive line of her upper lip, touched the even ridges of her teeth. She drew him to her, unsatisfied with anything except the deepest of his kisses and the hardness of his passion.

It was the gasp they shared, the harsh sound of it when they drew back for breath, that brought them abruptly awake.

For a moment they simply stared.

"Oh, my God." Nathan fairly leaped away from Lydia. He rolled to the edge of the bed, taking some of the covers with him as he jumped up. He stumbled on the puddle of blankets at his feet, kicked them away angrily, and grabbed his snowy white evening shirt. He put it on inside out, jamming his arms into the sleeves with such force that he rent one of the seams.

The drapes were open. Lightning flashed once, illuminating Lydia's stricken features. It began to storm in earnest, and the sound of rain against the windows was as loud as marbles hitting glass. Nathan lit a bedside lamp and yanked at the drapes' tiebacks, letting them fall.

Lydia was sitting with her back against the walnut headboard, her knees drawn up to her chest and her shift covering her like a tent. She was staring at the far wall as if she were fascinated by the flicker of light and shadow from the bedside lamp.

Nathan studied Lydia's closed posture, the unyielding set of her mouth and the vacant expression in her dark eyes. Most of her hair had fallen behind her back, but a few sable strands touched her cheek and stood out in stark contrast to the whiteness of her complexion.

"I want to go home now," she said dully.

He found his vest and consulted his pocket watch. It was nearly four o'clock. "There's still time," he said. "We should talk."

"I don't think so, Mr. Hunter. I think—"

"Nathan," he said.

She ignored his interruption. "I think you should leave so I can dress."

"In a moment."

"Now."

His tone became hard and gritty. "We'll talk now. I can imagine the kind of things going on in that virgin's head of yours and I'm not going to stand by while you cry rape from the top of Nob Hill." Perhaps she was more like her mother than he first suspected. With what he knew about Madeline, he should have exercised more caution with her daughter.

Lydia finally turned to look at him. His eyes were cold and accusing, and Lydia felt herself recoiling even though she gave no outward sign. "You can imagine any sordid thing you want, but that doesn't mean it's true.

95

I'm certainly not going to cry rape. Nothing happened."
She could still feel the heat of his hand on her breast, the caress of his fingers on her thigh, between her legs. Every time she spoke she was aware of her mouth and the things she had been doing with him that did not involve speaking. It wasn't nothing, she thought, but she would never admit otherwise.

"That's right," he said tightly, raking through his hair with his left hand. "Nothing happened." He could still taste her in his mouth, feel the raspy sweetness of her tongue against his. His skin was warm where she had touched him with her fingertips, and between his thighs, where she had left him aching, he was still hot and hard. "And nothing's going to happen," he went on, "so stop looking at me as if you wish it would."

Lydia stared at him, horrified. "That's a lie! I'm not wishing any such thing!"

He was. He grabbed his vest, jacket, socks, and shoes and stalked out of his bedroom, slamming the door behind him. God help him, he thought. He was handling it wrong. All of it. He'd hoped to gain her confidence, not her contempt. He'd never touched a virgin in his life, was never even certain he knew one until Lydia Chadwick, and in less than twenty-fours of meeting her formally he'd had his hands all over her.

He stared at his hands. They were shaking. He dropped his clothes on one of the sofas, padded over the the sideboard, and splashed a clean tumbler with bourbon. He raised the glass to his lips, felt the trembling, and finally admitted that he was scared.

Lydia Chadwick held his life in her small, delicate hands and she didn't even know it. An accusation of rape from her and . . . He couldn't think about it. He wouldn't.

Nathan knocked back his drink and set the tumbler down hard. In the other room he could hear the rustle of clothes and realized Lydia was dressing. He did the same.

Lydia entered the sitting room some ten minutes later.

96

Her face was freshly scrubbed and her hair had been ruthlessly pulled back, tied at her nap with a scrap of lace from her petticoat. "I'd like a glass of water, please," she said, standing on the threshold.

"Certainly." His tone was as flat as hers, and just as calm. It was as if nothing out of the ordinary had ever taken place. Nathan poured her water at the sideboard and held it out to her. She crossed the room to take the glass. There was only the slightest pause as she accepted it, careful to place her fingers just so in order not to touch his hand.

"Thank you." She finished the glass quickly and held it out again.

"More?"

"Please. I can't remember ever being so thirsty."

"It's the alcohol. It does that." He gave her back the glass. When she was finished this time she placed it on the sideboard. "How's your head?" he asked.

"Thumping."

He nodded, expecting nothing less. "Are you ready to go?"

"Yes." She hesitated. "I don't want to start an argument. I just want you to know that you do not have to escort me home."

Nathan did not want an argument, either. He chose his words carefully. "I know I haven't given you any reason to think you're safe with me, but I made a promise to Father Patrick and Pei Ling that I would see you home. Whatever you think you know about me, I'm a man of my word." He paused a beat, waiting for her reply. She regarded him steadily and said nothing. "I'll get your cape."

Rain lashed at them during their entire journey. There were no cabs on the streets looking for fares, and not many drivers would have asked their horses to climb steep Powell Street under such slippery conditions. Nathan and Lydia were both wet and winded by the time they reached the mansion.

He escorted her to the same side door she had used to make her exit earlier. They stood on the recessed stoop under an eave and caught their breath. The rain was falling so heavily now that it surrounded them like a crystalline curtain. They were facing each other. Nathan was trying to catch Lydia's eye; she was doing what she could to avoid his stare.

"I'll come by at seven-thirty to take you to dinner," he said, speaking softly so as not to wake anyone.

That got Lydia's full attention, and her features expressed complete disbelief. "You can't be serious." But she saw that he was. "I'm not going anywhere with you tomorrow or any other day."

"You're reneging on the wager?"

"After what happened a mere hour ago I don't think your question merits an answer."

"I see. So you do blame me."

"I blame myself," she said quietly. "I blame myself for misinterpreting your character. You're not so different from any of the others."

"What others?" he demanded.

Lydia turned away, groping for the doorknob.

Nathan took her elbow and spun her roughly toward him. "What others?" Even in the darkness he could sense her fear. Swearing at himself under his breath, he let her go. This time when he repeated his question it was done with forced calm and patience.

Lydia rubbed her elbow where Nathan had grabbed her. She could still feel the press of his fingers. "The others who show any interest in me," she said. "When I tell them I'm not interested in marriage, they try to find a way to compromise me so I won't have any choice. I've fought off more advances than General Grant and I'm not about to succumb to the dubious charms of a foreigner. How much money do you need, Mr. Hunter? Perhaps I can make a draft for you tomorrow."

Placing his arms on either side of her shoulders, Nathan cornered her against the door. "You seem to be forgetting something, Miss Chadwick, and since it's pertinent to this discussion, I find it necessary to point it out. As pleasurable as that little interlude in my suite was, it wasn't initiated to compromise you. I'm not even certain *I* initiated it. You could have been any whore in my bed, snoring, stuporous, and smelling of alcohol. I seem to remember you crawling all over me, and I'll tell that to anyone you go running to. Give me some credit for getting out of that bed as soon as I realized who you were.

"As for wanting your money, put that thought away. Your money's no good to me. I'm only interested in you, and my intentions are so honorable you'd probably find them insulting."

His declaration left Lydia unable to speak. He called her a whore in one breath, threatened her in the next, and very nearly plighted his troth in the third.

"Good evening, Miss Chadwick," Nathan rapped out as he pushed away from the door. He turned and started around the house toward the street.

Lydia watched him go, then she twisted the doorknob to enter her home. It wouldn't open. She tried again. Nothing. Frantically searching the pockets in her cape lining, she came up empty-handed. She pushed at the door even though she knew it was useless. Oh, God, she thought, wanting to do nothing so much as drop where she stood and cry. Instead she swallowed every vestige of her pride and ran after Nathan Hunter.

She caught him before he had gone very far. "Please," she whispered, urging him away from the street and back toward the shadows of the mansion. "The door's locked and I haven't any key. Pei Ling either thought I had one or someone else locked the door after she went to bed. There's no light in her room; she probably went to bed hours ago."

Nathan doubted that. Lydia's maid seemed loyal to a fault and possessed of a little more common sense than her mistress. Pei Ling was far more likely to have fallen asleep in Lydia's room, waiting for her mistress to return. "What do you want me to do?" he asked.

"Help me get inside, of course."

"Of course. You're talking about breaking and entering."

"It's *my* home."

"It's *my* neck," he said coldly, "and your reputation."

"My reputation will be in shreds if I can't get back inside by morning. My father's up at first light and Pei Ling can't keep him away from my room forever."

"That's supposing she's been successful thus far."

Lydia tugged on the upper portion of Nathan's sleeve. The hood of her cape fell back and the rain quickly wet her hair, making it dark and sleek on the crown of her head. "Please," she repeated. "I have to get back inside. Won't you help me?"

Nathan was silent for a while, turning over the choices in his mind. Finally he said, "I'll be here at seven-thirty to take you to dinner. I expect that you'll be ready."

"That's blackmail."

He shrugged. "That's my condition."

Her hand dropped away from his arm. "All right," she said reluctantly. "I'll go with you." When he didn't move, she added, "You can trust me, Mr. Hunter. I know something about keeping one's word."

"Very well. Show me the other entrances."

Lydia took him around the house. Every door was secured and without so much as hairpin or penknife between them, Nathan couldn't pick a lock. All the windows on the ground floor had been closed against the rain. He tested every one and found them all to have their latches in place. Not one could be budged.

"It's hopeless, isn't it?" Lydia said forlornly.

"Not necessarily. Show me which windows lead to your bedroom."

"But my room's on the second floor."

Nathan put his hands on her shoulders, turned her

100

around, and gave her a light push in the general direction they had to go. "Show me."

Lydia's room was at the rear of the house on the northwest corner. Nathan felt their luck changing when he heard something flapping above him and realized that the drapes had been drawn outside by the wind. That meant an open window. He showed Lydia where her drapes were slapping wetly against the side of the house, but she wasn't encouraged. It was an incredible height to scale and there were no means of doing it that she could see.

A down spout hugged the face of the mansion, but Nathan knew it would never support his weight. Twenty years ago he would have shimmied up the thing and never thought twice about it. The granite blocks that made up the house's outer walls were smooth as glass and much too large to make climbing from seam to seam possible.

His eyes strayed to the portico. Its flat roof was also a balcony for some of the rooms on the second floor. If he stood on the stone balustrade, perhaps, just perhaps, he could haul himself up there. "Whose rooms are those?" he asked, pointing to the row of windows and French doors that opened on the balcony.

"The ones farthest from us are my mother's. The next one belongs to the dressing room she shares with my father. And those last two windows and door are part of my father's room." She sighed. The window that was open, the only one they couldn't reach easily from the portico's roof, was the one that belonged to her.

"What about the dressing room?" Nathan asked. "If I got up there and found the window wasn't secured, would I be able to get into the hallway?"

"Not without going through either my mother or father's room."

"But if they're—"

Knowing the direction of his thoughts, she held up her hand and cut him off. "My mother and father share a dressing room, not a bed . . . not anymore. It's not the

101

sort of thing they'd tell me, but the servants talk. I've heard things," she finished inadequately.

"All right," he said, "we won't rely on a sudden passionate reunion to make our task any easier. The dressing room's not an alternative. We're back to your room."

"Oh, but—"

"Let me worry about it." The first thing he did was go to the nearest flower bed, choose a few smooth stones, and fling them at Lydia's window.

"What are you doing?" she whispered, trying to stay his arm. "Who do you think will answer if I'm not there?"

"Your maid."

"Pei Ling's not there."

"Then what about her room? Maybe we can rouse her. It's better than taking an unnecessary risk."

Lydia shook her head.

"Why not?" When she didn't answer immediately, Nathan pressed her again.

"Because she sleeps with my father, that's why."

"I see," he said, whistling softly under his breath. What he saw was that Lydia Chadwick knew a great deal more than Madeline and Samuel probably suspected. It was too dark to see her eyes clearly, but he hadn't imagined the pain in her voice, the necessity of saying something quickly because it hurt to express it any other way. "Very well," he went on. "The balcony it is."

He led Lydia back to the portico. "Once I'm inside your room, go to the side door and wait for me."

She shook her head. "You can't do it like that. The door's not merely latched, it's locked. The keys are kept in the kitchen pantry. You can't go traipsing all over the house for them. You'll drip water and leave a trail everywhere you go. I'll never be able to clean up after you. I'm going in the house the same way you are."

Lightning seared the sky again and the low roll of thunder covered Nathan's sarcastic reply. "Wonderful," he said. "That's just bloody wonderful."

102

Nathan stripped off his jacket and tossed it over the balustrade. He stretched his arms, working them like windmills until he was limber. He was used to hard labor, digging and hauling, walking and riding, but it had been a long time since he'd been called on to do something this strenuous and inherently dangerous. He made several tentative jumps, testing the spring and stamina of his legs. When he thought he was ready, he stood on the flat stone railing.

On his first attempt he missed the balcony's overhang completely and nearly sent Lydia sprawling on the portico's flagstones as he fell off the balustrade. Glaring at her and ordering her to stay out of his way, he climbed back up and came within an inch on his next try. The third and fourth attempts were ultimately failures: Nathan caught the lip of the slippery balcony but could not hold on to pull himself up. He moved to the end of the railing where a smooth granite column supported one corner of the portico's roof. This time when he jumped, he wrapped his legs around the shaft and half shimmied, half pulled himself upward. When he was high enough he threw one leg up on the lip of the balcony and hauled himself up the rest of the way. Seconds later he was over the balcony's decorative railing.

Crouching down, Nathan hurried toward the house. Once he was safely at an angle where he couldn't be seen from the windows, he stood up, leaned back against the sheer wall of the house, and caught his breath. After a few minutes he looked over the edge of the balcony and saw Lydia standing out in the rain again, watching him. He could imagine the cobalt-blue eyes, bright with expectancy, wide with worry. At least Nathan hoped she was worried. There was a very good chance he was going to break his neck for her.

Nathan estimated the distance from where he stood to Lydia's window as a little more than four feet. The face of the house was rain-slick, as slippery and as cold as ice. He couldn't just lean toward the windowsill and hope to catch it; there was no toe-hold, no place to wedge his fingers. He would have to make an angled leap, get his hands and arms inside the window without getting tangled in the flapping and slapping drapes, and pray he didn't knock himself out when he slammed into the house. He was not hopeful. As he recalled, the flowerbed below Lydia's window was filled with rosebushes.

Wiping a combination of rain and perspiration from his forehead, Nathan paced off three feet at a right angle to the house, knowing that would make his angled leap to the window just about five feet, a distance he thought he could make, or prayed he could. When he found the proper angle and distance he climbed back over the railing, stood on the narrow lip of the balcony, and didn't give what he was going to do another thought.

Nathan jumped.

His hands caught the drapes. The rods held for a heartbeat, then tore away from the anchoring wall. Nathan felt them give. He scrambled, feeling as if he were flailing in vain, trying to crawl up something that was falling down, then he felt the solidness of the sill and thrust one arm inside the window. He hung there, swinging under Lydia's window from the momentum of his leap. With strength born of determination and a certain amount of anger, Nathan managed to get his other arm through the window. He felt another seam in his sleeve give way.

His feet slipped on the outer wall of the house as he tried to find purchase. Just pushing off the house helped Nathan raise himself a little higher. With nothing but grit and a prayer, Nathan pulled himself up until he could shoulder his way through the open window. He rested briefly when he got his upper torso in, then slid the rest of the way through, facedown on the braided area rug, his arms tangled in the fallen draperies.

He had done cleaner and slicker second-story work, but considering the amount of improvisation involved in this one, Nathan was pleased with his night's work—so far.

Water puddled on the floor as he stood up. He untangled himself, kicked the braided rug aside, and pushed open the sash as wide as it would go. Leaning out, he waved Lydia over to the window. "Take off your cape and throw it here." He was gratified to see that she didn't hesitate to obey.

The cape was heavy with water, and it took two tosses before Nathan caught it. He let it hang out of the window, twisting it so it lost water and formed a tight rope. "Grab the end and hold on. I'll pull you up."

Lydia jumped once at the makeshift rope dangling above her and hung on for all she was worth. Within seconds Nathan was hauling her into the bedroom. She stumbled when he set her on the floor and fell into his arms as he steadied her. She stiffened and he, sensing her discomfort, separated himself from her.

"Thank you," she said. "I could never have gotten here on my own."

"If I had my way," he said caustically, "you'd never get out."

"Does that mean you've changed your mind about the Cliff House tomorrow?"

"Today," he corrected. "In an hour or so this house is going to be waking. And I'm going to hold you to your promise."

Lydia could only imagine one reason that he would want to. No matter what he said, it had to be her money. He certainly made little effort to hide his dislike for her. "Very well," she said. "I'll be ready."

Nathan went to the window, hesitated, then, without warning, turned on Lydia and pulled her into his arms. He kissed her deeply, firmly, and swiftly, giving her no time to react, let alone protest. He didn't give her time to respond later, either. Easing himself out the window, he cursed softly in anticipation of the ache in his legs, and jumped.

The next few minutes he spent covering his tracks in the yard and locating his evening coat and putting it on.

He was ready to leave the yard when he heard his name. He looked up, shielding the rain from his eyes with his hand. At the last moment he dodged the missile that came flying from the window: Lydia's sodden, soiled, and borrowed dress.

"Get rid of it," she said in a loud whisper. Almost as an afterthought she added, "Please."

Nathan scooped up the gown and rolled it into a ball. What the bloody hell, he thought. After the fire Lydia had set in his loins, he'd been thinking of returning to Miss Bailey's anyway.

Chapter Four

"This has to stop, Lydia." Madeline pushed past Pei Ling and swept into her daughter's bedroom like a cold Sierra Nevada wind. "It's almost noon and you're still abed. I simply will not be put off by your Chinese dragon any longer."

Over Madeline's shoulder Lydia could see Pei Ling standing by the door, her features perfectly composed, even serene. There was nothing remotely dragonlike about her countenance. Covering her urge to smile with a yawn, Lydia dismissed Pei Ling and sat up in bed. "Is it really noon?" she asked.

"Of course it is. You'd know if you'd let a touch of sun in." Madeline went to the windows and pulled back the velvet drapes, first on the window where they were still anchored firmly, then on the window where Nathan and Lydia had made their middle-of-the-night entrance. "Why you insist on keeping this room so . . . what's this? Lydia, this drapery rod is about to fall down. What happened here?"

Lydia knew it was about to fall down. After Nathan left she'd spent close to twenty minutes securing it as best she could on either side of the window frame. A little more of Madeline's fiddling and they would . . . fall. Lydia's eyes dropped to the draperies on the floor, partly to avoid her mother's cold and disapproving stare. She felt all of five years old, clumsy and inadequate. "I left the sash up when I went to bed last night," she explained. "The heavy rain soaked the drapes. You can see what's happened as a result."

"You're so careless, Lydia." She sighed, kicking away the drapes with the toe of her shoe. She went over to the bed and sat down on the edge near Lydia's feet. "I'll ask Mrs. Leeds to fix them this afternoon. Now, tell me what possessed you to leave your own party last night. Pei Ling said you didn't feel well. You looked overwrought to me, but that was no reason for you to abandon your guests. It's not done, Lydia. Not done at all."

"I did it."

Madeline looked at her daughter sharply. "I don't find that sort of tone amusing, Lydia."

Lydia looked down at her hands. "I'm sorry." She picked up a pillow and crushed it against her chest, drawing her knees toward her as well. The barriers helped her face her mother again. "I know it was the worst sort of manners to leave the guests, but it couldn't be helped. I spent most of the afternoon before the party in my room with a sick headache; I probably should never have tried to attend."

Only slightly mollified, Madeline said, "Your guests were sympathetic, and I managed your duties."

"I knew you would, Mother. I'm sure I was barely missed. Thank you."

"Yes, well, I shouldn't want this to become a habit on your part. If you choose to host a party, then you have to see it through, sick headache or anything else that puts you under the weather. I must say, you're looking well enough now." She placed the back of her hand on Lydia's forehead, then felt her flushed cheeks. "You're not warm, but there's color in your face for a change. It even flatters you a little, Lydia. And your eyes are bright. Are you certain you feel all right now?"

"I'm fine, Mother. Really." She would have liked to run to her mirrored vanity and see what her mother was talking about. Were her night's adventures somehow evident? Lydia raised her fingertips to her mouth and touched her sensitive lower lip. It was easy to imagine Nathan Hunter's mouth on hers. Could her mother suspect? She was anxious to turn the subject away from her physical condition. "How much money was raised last evening?"

Madeline got up and went to Lydia's wardrobe. She opened it and began sifting through the contents, looking for something for Lydia to wear. "You exceeded your goal," she said. "There's no question but that St. Andrew's will be built. In fact, I understand from your father that you were responsible for one of the larger donations." She paused in examining Lydia's gowns and looked at her daughter. "What were you thinking when you agreed to that ridiculous wager? Offering yourself like that. It's pagan. I could hardly believe you would agree to such a thing. When your father first told me about it this morning, I was certain he was merely trying to goad me. When I realized he was quite serious . . . well, I don't think our discussion bears repeating. Suffice it to say that Samuel refuses to renege on his wager, so it will be up to you to put a stop to it."

At different times last night Lydia remembered she had wanted to put a stop to it, too. Today she remembered she had given her word and she found herself strangely reluctant to go back on it now. "Why, Mother? Why must I stop it? It's only an invitation to dine at the Cliff House. I've been there with Henry before and several times with James. It's perfectly acceptable, you've said so yourself."

"You're purposely being obtuse." Madeline laid a pale-green gown over the back of a chair and went to stand at the foot of Lydia's bed. Her carriage was stiff, and when she spoke, the aloofness of her posture became part of her tone. "You know this is a different matter entirely. You bartered yourself like a common dance-hall girl. Do you hear what I'm really saying?" She held up her hand as Lydia sucked in her breath and began to object. "I'm sure you think my judgment is harsh, yet how else can you describe what you've done? Those men were exchanging money for you. Any one of them could be forgiven for thinking you meant to offer more than your company."

"But—"

"And what do we know of Mr. Hunter? He's merely an acquaintance of your father's, a gambler and a foreigner. I found his manner a bit rough around the edges, his dancing abominable, and his conversation inadequate. He was only playing at being a gentleman. Indeed, a gentleman would not have accepted the wager."

"It was Mr. Moore who proposed the wager, Mother. He was your guest, remember?"

"Now you're being insolent. If Mr. Moore proposed the wager, which your father neglected to tell me, then it can only mean that you did something to command his attention in an unacceptable fashion. He would not have made such a bold wager if he didn't believe there was just cause for it. I think I know something about Brigham Moore's character. After all, he saved my life."

"I don't believe I did anything untoward, Mother. I danced with Mr. Moore and Mr. Hunter, spoke with both briefly about the orphanage, and conversed with them at dinner. In fact, our dinner conversation took place after the wager had been made and won, so I can't see that it matters in the least."

Madeline was undeterred. "If you did nothing to draw their attention to you, then you must ask yourself, where does their interest lie. If you reflect upon it, I'm certain you'll arrive at the same answer I have."

"My fortune," Lydia said dully. She had found herself thinking about it many times with Nathan Hunter, but she was uncharacteristically reluctant to believe it about Brigham. Lydia hugged her pillow tighter, and for one moment closed her eyes.

"Naturally, your fortune. I have every right to be concerned, Lydia, as you should be. Your friend James Early is many times more appropriate as a partner for you, yet you hardly spent any time with him last night. Mr. Moore and Mr. Hunter are nearer my age than yours."

"So old?" Lydia asked without thinking. Madeline was, after all, her mother, and that alone made her seem older than her years in Lydia's eyes.

Madeline's mouth flattened. "I can see that it's no good talking to you now. Perhaps once you've dressed and eaten something, you'll be more agreeable. I'm going for a fitting soon, but I'll be back before four. We'll discuss your plans for this evening then."

"Mother, I'm sor—" But Madeline had already given Lydia her back. The room seemed to shudder as Madeline closed the door, then Lydia realized it was only her reaction, not the room's.

Pei Ling glided into the bedroom moments after Madeline's exit. From Lydia's pained expression it was not difficult to imagine what had happened between mother and daughter in her absence. The maid drew Lydia a bath, brought her a light brunch, and set out a gown she deemed more appropriate than the one Madeline had chosen.

"You very late last evening," Pei Ling said as she combed through Lydia's damp hair. "I think perhaps I misjudge Nathan Hunter and he mean to do you harm."

"No," Lydia said. "You didn't misjudge him. He was very helpful." She told Pei Ling most of what happened the previous night. The bedroom in Nathan's suite was never mentioned.

"I sorry for Charlotte and baby. I know you sad and aching in heart. Poor Charlotte not so lucky as me. I not be here today if not for you, Miss Liddy. Please not to forget. And little children have no home if not for you. You do many good things. Only this thing not end so good."

"Thank you for that, Pei Ling," Lydia said softly, catching the girl's eyes in the mirror. "And for every-

111

thing else you did. Keeping Mother and Papa away from my room couldn't have been easy. I think it's a good thing you're so protective. Last night was very . . . difficult."

Pei Ling continued to comb and dress Lydia's hair. "I like to see you drunk, Miss Liddy. I think you must be very funny."

Lydia smiled. "Mr. Hunter would disagree."

"You like him?" Pei Ling asked, seeing her mistress's smile.

"No," she said quickly. She paused, then added, "I'm not certain. He's rude and rather arrogant actually. And he's not above threatening to get his own way. But if you had seen him with Charlotte, Pei Ling . . . the way he spoke to her, the way he held the baby . . . he seemed a different man entirely." And his hands, she thought, his strong, beautiful hands. "I don't think I could really ever understand him. Mother's probably right about him: he's too old for me and his interests are centered on my money. I should be thinking of some way to excuse myself from going to the Cliff House with him."

"You think same about Mr. Moore?" she asked.

"I don't know him very well." In the mirror Lydia saw that her color deepened.

Pei Ling saw it also. "I think you have fine opportunity to know him better. He downstairs now, waiting to take you for ride in carriage."

Lydia's cobalt-blue eyes widened. "He's here? Why didn't you say something before?"

"I say something now," Pei Ling said reasonably. "You not ready before now, so why say? No good rush, rush, rush. Mr. Moore come after Mother leave, while I get breakfast. He wait in front parlor. Mother always say not so bad keep man waiting. Only thing Mother say I like. Better than Chinese way, wait on man all the time."

Lydia stood up and smoothed the bodice and skirt of her rose gown. She frowned at her reflection, plucking at the short, puffed sleeves of the gown. "Do you know, Pei

112

Ling, I've been thinking I should go to Madame Simone's and choose some of my own things. That would please Mother. She's always wanting me to take notice of my appearance."

"Very good idea." Pei Ling did not add her thought aloud, for it would not please Madeline.

"I'll do it," Lydia decided suddenly. "We won't even tell Mother."

Pei Ling said nothing, her dark eyes fathomless.

Lydia accepted Brigham Moore's invitation to go riding with an alacrity she prayed was not forward or unbecoming. He was a comfortable companion, amusing, solicitous, and charming, so unlike Nathan Hunter that Lydia found herself resenting Nathan for extracting her promise. The air was cool, but the sun was shining, and Brigham's open carriage was the perfect conveyance for enjoying San Francisco's sites. The driver took them down Powell Street and into the noisy and lively center of Chinatown and Portsmouth Square. Lydia passed all the places she had the previous evening, yet in Brigham's company none seemed sinister or dangerous. Lydia felt as if her senses were heightened in Brig's presence, as if she could taste the color of the beautiful silks on display or touch the delicious odors coming from the kitchens all along Grant Avenue. People shouted in a language she barely understood, yet she heard music in the staccato speech and saw the artistry in the gracefully curved calligraphy of their written word.

She brightened under the attention Brigham paid her; his questions and interest warmed her. In turn he answered her questions, sharing his childhood in the workhouse, the hardships. He spoke of a farm in the country, his interests in mining and shipping. Knowledgeable and opinionated, Brig was also curious about Lydia's opinions. She believed she was heard.

It was only when the shadow of the Silver Lady Hotel

fell across their carriage that Lydia felt a coldness. Brigham mistook the reason for her shiver and generously offered a blanket.

"No, thank you," she said, "but it might be nice if we go to the park now. It's certain to be warmer there."

Brigham placed a blue plaid blanket over her legs anyway and secured the silken frog at the neck of her cape. His face was very close to hers, his breath warm and sweet. Then as he held her gaze, the smile left his green eyes momentarily, replaced by something more intimate, something nearer to passion than not. It was Lydia who turned away, a little frightened by the way he looked at her—and excited as well.

She groped for something to say as he sat back against the padded leather seat. "We raised a great deal of money last evening," she said.

Brigham was smiling again, the curve of his lips knowing. She was not unaffected by him, he thought, and that was good. The thread of tension he'd tugged on a moment ago would keep her wondering, thinking about him long after he left her. He wanted her to think of him this evening when she was with Nathan. "I would have liked to have been the one to win the poker game," he said. "For the pleasure of making the largest donation as well as for the pleasure of your company."

"You're very kind, but surely you can see by my presence here that it wasn't necessary. Mother says I shouldn't have accepted the terms of the wager, but I . . . I found it a rather lovely gesture." She surprised herself with her candid comment and glanced at him quickly to gauge his reaction. "I shouldn't have said that. I'm afraid I don't think sometimes."

"Nonsense," Brig said. "Your candor is refreshing. And, if I'm not mistaken, I believe there's a flattering comment in there for me. Can I hope that not only weren't you offended by my proposal, but perhaps you wish I'd won that hand?"

Beneath the blanket Lydia's fingers nervously plucked

114

at her gown. She nodded in response to Brig's question.

His expression satisfied and confident as they entered Golden Gate Park, Brigham Moore spent what remained of the afternoon chipping away at Lydia's heart.

By the time they returned to the house, it was after four. Mindful of the hour and her need to get ready, Lydia did not invite Brigham in for tea. Though she thought he was disappointed, he didn't press her, and his understanding lightened her heart all the more. She fairly ran up the walk to the house.

Madeline was standing in the foyer and made no effort to disguise the fact that she had been waiting for Lydia's return. "You were out," she said accusingly.

Lydia's smile vanished. "You can see that I was." She gave her cape to the butler and followed her mother into the front parlor. "Mr. Moore paid a call and I went riding with him. It was all perfectly respectable. He had a driver, the carriage was open, and our tour was most public. You can't find fault with that, Mother. You *did* introduce him to me."

"And I'm regretting it." Madeline's face softened, her vibrant emerald eyes were grave, the blue flame in their depths all but extinguished. "Darling," she entreated quietly, "don't you think I want only the best for you? I admit that I thought I had judged his character correctly, but I'm not above making a mistake. In light of his interest in you and yours in him, I thought it would be wise to make some inquiries. While I was out this afternoon I did just that.

"Has he told you, for instance, that although he's from London, Australia's been his home nearly a score of years? No, I can see by your face that he hasn't. Don't trouble yourself inventing excuses as to why he moved there. He was not a free settler. He was transported as punishment for stealing. He's a criminal, Lydia."

Madeline watched Lydia as she moved to one of the overstuffed armchairs. Her daughter did not so much sit as she did crumple. "Perhaps it's a curse passed from mother to daughter," Madeline went on as Lydia's complexion took on an ashen cast. "I remember being flattered by your father's attentions, taken in by his handsome face and beautiful smile. I knew from—"

"Please, Mother. You don't have to repeat the story." Lydia knew her mother was no longer referring to Samuel Chadwick. She was talking about Lydia's true father, Marcus O'Malley, a convict from Australia who came to San Francisco in search of gold in '49. He and others like him were called Sydney Ducks, a slur filled with contempt and loathing, but rarely said in their presence. The Sydney Ducks were wild and lawless, drunk on freedom and frustrated with dreams of gold that rarely materialized by digging mines and panning streams. They terrorized miners, shopkeepers, and women, moving about the city at night in gangs, looting stores and robbing casino patrons. "I understand how it was between you and Marcus," Lydia said. "It will only give you pain to dredge it up."

"I can bear my pain," her mother said. "But I cannot bear yours. Brigham Moore can't be trusted, Lydia. Don't repeat the mistake I made with your father, believing he was different from the others. His criminal leanings were evident in the end. Your birth was proof of that."

Lydia crossed her arms in front of her middle, feeling Madeline's words as a physical blow.

"Do you want to suffer as I suffered? You are the greatest joy in my life, yet you were born of my greatest pain. You're so vulnerable, Lydia. A man like Brigham Moore can sense that, take advantage of it. He would have you on his bed, under his—"

From the doorway Samuel Chadwick spoke. "That's enough, Madeline."

Madeline gave a start, surprised by Samuel's entrance and his tone. "You've interrupted me, Samuel," she said coolly. "I don't know that you've heard enough to pass judgment on my conversation with Lydia."

"I heard enough," he said tersely. "Leave her,

Madeline. Surely even you can see that your warnings have done more harm than good."

"I'm not going any—"

"Leave, Madeline," Samuel said, grinding out the words now. His hands were thrust in the pockets of his dark-gray jacket, but the shape of his fists was visible as a bulge in the line of the garment.

Madeline looked as if she were going to object again, thought better of it, and glided out of the room, her chin high.

Samuel did not even wait for his wife to leave. He went immediately to Lydia, sat at the ottoman in front of her and placed his hand on her shoulder as she slid to the floor and laid her head in his lap. Her sobs cut at his heart.

"I should never h-have been born," she stammered. "Every time M-Mother looks at me she remembers. She h-hates me. She must."

Samuel smoothed Lydia's hair, patting her gently. "No, darling, she doesn't hate you. Didn't you hear? She said you are her greatest joy." He marveled at his own ability to say the words so convincingly when he felt so little conviction. "Your mother doesn't know how to express her own fears, Lydia, so she hurts you without meaning to. Anyway, you're my greatest joy. Never doubt that." She turned her head slightly and he saw the faint smile that could always touch his heart. He handed her a handkerchief as she sat up and leaned against the apron of the chair behind her. "I really only heard the last of your conversation with your mother. I suspect it was about Nathan Hunter. Madeline was furious about that wager business last night."

"No," Lydia said, dabbing at her eyes. Her chin wobbled a bit as she forced a light-hearted mien. "We had that discussion at noon. This was about Mr. Moore. Mother's discovered he's English by way of Australia."

Samuel's dark brows lifted slightly and he stroked his graying handlebar mustache. "A convict?" When Lydia nodded, Samuel asked, "But how could your mother know that? It's not the sort of thing Mr. Moore would share as fodder for common knowledge. Unless, of course, there's more to the story than Madeline told you." Which was entirely likely, he thought. "Not everyone transported was guilty of murder, you know. Most of the men were there for crimes against property of a trifling nature. Not that I'm condoning theft, but it's hard not to be sympathetic to boys and men who were convicted for stealing umbrellas, lead from the tops of houses, or a pig or chicken to feed a starving family. Often it's a sickness in society that leads men to make a livelihood of crime, not a sickness in the men's souls."

"Do you think that may be the case with Mr. Moore?" she asked. "Mother did say he'd been in Australia almost twenty years. He would have been younger than me when he was transported. A child really."

"I don't know. But you could do no worse than to ask him. He might be happy to unburden himself to you."

"Even if he was a convict," she said, "he appears to have done well for himself, don't you think? Why, just look at the money he lost last night in your game." For a moment she was hopeful, envisioning Brigham Moore as a reformed criminal. A frown drew down the corners of her full mouth and knitted her brows. She worried her lower lip. "His money may have been stolen. I hadn't thought of that before. What if he's—"

"Now you're letting your imagination run and there's no good that can come of it." Samuel leaned toward Lydia and placed a light kiss on her furrowed brow. "Stop looking so fierce, darling. Smile. Unless I mistake the time, you should be preparing for your evening with Mr. Hunter."

Instead of smiling, Lydia's frown deepened. "But Mother doesn't—"

"Let me worry about your mother."

"Then you think it was all right to accept the wager?"

"Of course. Madeline is making too much of it. It was

118

made with complete respect for you, and even though Mr. Moore didn't win, Nathan is a good man." He laughed lightly, tapping Lydia on the end of her pared nose. "I admit I was looking forward to taking you to the Cliff House this evening, but some things were not meant to be. Still, who'd have thought they would both beat my full house?"

"Perhaps they cheated."

"In that case, Lydia, you'd do well to be terribly flattered. The only thing to be gained was your company."

"My money!" she countered.

"Now you sound like your mother. You place much too much importance on your fortune and not nearly enough on the other reasons a man may be interested in you."

Lydia did not fish for compliments. She simply looked at Samuel uncomprehendingly.

"You're beautiful, Daughter," he said sincerely. "A man can see it in your eyes."

He meant to be kind, Lydia thought, but he was talking about her on the inside. She longed to hear someone say she was beautiful on the outside, even if it was her own, prejudiced-in-her-favor, father.

Lydia took her time getting ready for Nathan Hunter. Instead of the quick dip and scrub she had had upon waking, Lydia soaked in scented rose water and allowed Pei Ling to manicure her nails. She ate a light repast that her maid prepared to tide her over until her late dinner with Nathan. She accepted Pei Ling's choice of a gown, thinking it was the least of all the evils in her wardrobe. The color was good for her, an ivory that accentuated the deep blue of her eyes and complemented her complexion, but the gown suffered from many of the same flaws as the yellow one: too much ornamentation in unflattering places, a draped skirt that made her waist look thick, and puffed sleeves that made her seem uncommonly broad in her upper arms. The total effect was one of disproportion. Lydia's critical examination in the mirror, minutes before she went downstairs to meet Nathan, focused on each flaw. Most troubling, she thought, was that her appearance mattered at all to her. It was Nathan Hunter who was waiting for her, not Brigham Moore.

"Here she is now," Samuel said, holding out his hand to Lydia as she entered the library. "And how lovely she looks. Don't you think so, Nathan?"

Lydia wanted to turn and run. Instead, she forced a smile, pretending to believe what Samuel said and what Nathan was going to say.

"I thought blue might be your color," said Nathan, purposely evoking remembrance of things past, "but I may have judged too quickly. Ivory suits you beautifully."

The compliment and the deliberate reference to last evening brought a flush to Lydia's face. He had a way of talking to her which breeched her defenses. Immediately she was annoyed with herself for believing anything he said, or wanting to.

The evening was clear and cool. The sun had dropped over the horizon hours ago, but dusk still lingered. Nathan covered Lydia's shoulders with the short satin cape she handed him. The beaded embroidery was cool beneath his fingers and his hands lingered on her shoulders for a moment. The inquiring glance she shot him over her shoulder made him realize what he was doing. He dropped his hands, and after bidding good-bye to Samuel Chadwick, Nathan escorted Lydia to the waiting carriage. The liveried driver gave them a jaunty salute with his whip and a tilt of his head.

Lydia sensed a change in Nathan's mood once they were alone and underway. "If you would rather not go," she said, "we could have the driver stop now, before we're completely down the hill."

Nathan didn't answer immediately. The blue-gray light filtering into the carriage was adequate to observe Lydia's face, and there was nothing in her features to suggest she was troubled by anything. Which meant she didn't know.

120

Nathan loosened one of the buttons on his jacket and reached inside to the vest pocket. He pulled out a slip of paper and held it out to Lydia. He was flattered when disappointment flashed briefly across her face. "It's not the wager," he said, correcting her assumption.

She took the paper, recognizing it now as a newspaper clipping. Pride demanded that she had never thought it was anything else. "I didn't think it was," she denied. "However, I can't read this in here. Is it so important?"

"I think it is. It's from the *Police Gazette.*"

"Mother doesn't allow that paper in our house," she said primly. "Most of what they report is lurid, sensationalist twaddle."

"So it is . . . some of it." He took the article back and tucked it away. "This isn't. A prostitute was murdered late last night. Very late. Which is why it didn't make the morning editions of a paper you might have read."

"I have no idea why you're telling me this."

"Her name was Virginia Flynt." Nathan watched Lydia carefully, saw her confusion, then knew the absolute moment of understanding as her mouth parted slightly and her eyes widened and stared at him unblinkingly.

"Ginny."

"Yes . . . Ginny."

"But how? When?"

Nathan's palms turned up in a gesture of confusion, and he leaned back against the velvet upholstery. "Sometime after I last left her with Charlotte and the baby and sometime before I returned with the gown you borrowed."

"She was dead then? You saw her?"

"I think I probably was the first one to discover her body." Because the blood was so fresh, he remembered, and her flesh was still warm. He did not tell Lydia these things, but he saw in her expression a certain understanding. Her imagination had filled in the gaps.

In her lap, Lydia's hands were trembling. Ginny.

Ginny dead. Murdered. Why would anyone want to hurt Ginny? "You alerted the others? Went for the police?"

"No."

"No? I don't understand."

"I don't expect you to." And he couldn't explain. How could she possibly understand what had gone through his mind when he'd seen Ginny's slashed wrists, the rope burns the wounds could not quite hide: a suicide that wasn't one at all. It mightn't have been Ginny he saw, but another woman all together, in another place, at an earlier time. Nathan had reacted with less presence of mind than he had at fourteen. He had so much more to lose now, and that thought guided his actions more than common sense.

The entry hall of Ida Bailey's brothel had been deserted when he came in. He did not find that unusual given the lateness of the hour. Even prostitutes eventually retired for the night, and he abandoned the idea that he might find some small comfort in the arms and thighs of a whore. He did look around for someone, but in the end no one saw him climb the stairs to Ginny's room to return the gown. He had rapped lightly on her door, and when there wasn't an answer he assumed she was on the floor above, keeping vigil in Charlotte's room. Opening the door quietly, he had walked in . . . and seen her.

She was dead. He knew it immediately. There was too much blood for it to be otherwise. The long, angry slashes on her wrists were fatal ones, yet Nathan found himself touching her, feeling for a pulse, some meager sign of beating life, before he allowed himself the luxury of panic.

There were voices on the stairs then, either above or below him—he couldn't tell—and the door to Ginny's room was not completely closed now. In mere seconds someone might come upon him, and their conclusion would be the obvious one. Dropping the borrowed gown,

122

Nathan threw open the window sash and unhesitatingly made his second leap of the night.

He might have broken his neck, or at least injured an arm or leg, but the full hedgerow below him cushioned his fall. He walked away with nothing more serious than a few scratches on the back of his hands.

"No one except you knows I was there," he told her. "Not yet. Perhaps you can understand why I would rather not be connected with any of this. Being linked to a murder—anyone's murder—will play hell with my business alliances."

"And that's important to you."

"As your reputation is to you. If you tell anyone I was there, I'll be forced to tell them the whole of our evening."

Lydia blanched. "All right," she said finally. "But Ida may say something."

"Ida Bailey has herself to protect—her business and her reputation. She's not going to say a word about her customers or anyone else who visited her house that night—including both of us. You saw for yourself how indifferent she was to Charlotte's death. I expect Ginny's murder is being observed with only slightly less callousness."

It was cold in the carriage now, although Lydia didn't think the temperature had dropped at all. The chill she was feeling worked its way from the inside out, finally prickling her skin so that even pulling her cape more closely about her shoulders didn't help. "Why tell me you went back there at all?" she asked. "I only told you to get rid of the gown, not to return it. I might never have known you were there."

"Yes, you would have. I dropped the gown on Ginny's bed before I left. The reporter mentions it lying there in his description of the murder scene, but he doesn't know what to make of it. It will be identified as Ginny's gown, but only you and I know why it's wet and soiled. Just as only you and I know which of us had it last." He leaned forward now, resting his forearms on his knees as the carriage swayed gently over the Point Lobos toll road. "When I saw the account in the paper I realized you might see it as well. The conclusion you would leap to was too obvious for me to ignore. You must know this: I did *not* murder Ginny Flynt."

Lydia's mouth was dry and her throat ached so that she could barely swallow. She wished it were darker so that she could not see Nathan's face quite so clearly, not feel the cool silver eyes cornering her as if she were indeed the wolf's prey. "Of course you didn't," she said at last.

And her tone convinced neither one of them that she believed he wasn't capable of it.

The Cliff House was built six years earlier not far from the western end of Golden Gate Park. Overlooking the ocean and a white sand beach, the tavern was a popular place with many of San Francisco's prominent citizens. Even the route to the Cliff house was considered a fashionable journey. The toll road was the sight of expensively tooled carriages making the circuit from the city to the Cliff House and back again. Style dictated that a dalmation dog follow the carriage, making the drive seem more of a procession than a mere pasttime. A mile-and-a-quarter-long speedway ran parallel to Point Lobos for use by horseback riders who still preferred speed to being seen.

Nathan and Lydia were seated in one corner of the tavern, and Nathan chose the chair at a right angle to Lydia instead of across the table from her. Her mood was quiet, more withdrawn than thoughtful. They spoke very little until their order was taken, and then only about the merits of the roast beef versus the lamb.

Nathan drank cold beer from a pewter mug. "I admit I was surprised to find you ready this evening."

"That's not a compliment, Mr. Hunter. I gave my

word. And it's only for this evening, isn't it? I'm not obligated to go anywhere with you ever again."

"Nathan," he said, reminding her. "My name is Nathan, Lydia."

That was that, she thought. He wasn't going to respond to anything else she'd said. Did he want to see her again or not? Conversation with him was so much more difficult than with Brigham. She felt as if Nathan only ever said the smallest part of what he was thinking.

"My mother didn't want me to come with you tonight," she said.

He noted the slight elevation of Lydia's chin, the subtle way she dared him to respond with the directness of her gaze. "Your mother has every reason to be wary of someone like me," he said.

That was not what she expected him to say at all. Lydia's eyes widened the smallest fraction. "She does?"

"Of course she does. What do you really know about me?" When Lydia didn't answer he went on. "My point precisely."

"My father likes you."

"The feeling is mutual."

"But I don't think he knows any more about you than I do," she said.

"Probably not. Is there something in particular I should tell you?"

Lydia did not ask her question at that time as the beginning of their meal was served. The waiter brought thick slices of hot bread and large bowls of golden mushroom soup. Lydia dragged a spoon through her soup, letting the steam escape and allowing the buttered broth a moment to cool. Nathan didn't wait and followed his first taste of the soup with a long swallow of beer. Lydia pretended she didn't notice and Nathan, who knew that she had, was once again reminded of her breeding, of good manners which seemed as natural to her as breathing. The differences between them were enormous.

"Where are you from?" Lydia asked. She took a slice

of bread, buttered it, and gave it to Nathan, then did the same for herself.

"Now that's something you *do* know," he said, beginning to wonder what effect the drinking had had on her memory. "I'm from London. I told you that last night."

"I know that's what you said. I had hoped you would be more honest this time, perhaps elaborate a little."

Nathan felt he was being led to a watering hole—and was going to discover the water was poisoned. His guard went up immediately. "I'm not certain what you mean."

She sighed, pausing in the act of lifting her spoon to her mouth, and glanced sideways at him. "Are you a digger?" she asked bluntly. A digger was an Australian, a term she had sometimes heard Madeline use to denigrate her real father. The brief hesitation as Nathan swallowed a bite of bread was all the confirmation that Lydia needed. "Never mind," she said. "I can see you know what a digger is, which is almost as good as admitting you are one."

"Is it important?" he asked, knowing that it was.

"It depends. Were you a free settler?"

"What you're really asking is if I'm a convict."

"Yes. That's exactly what I'm asking."

The waiter chose that moment to return with their main course: thin slices of rare roast beef, new potatoes, and golden carrots cut like pieces of eight. Lydia let him take her soup, her appetite waning rapidly as the knot in her stomach grew tighter.

"Is it because of Ginny?" Nathan asked when they had privacy again. "Is that what's brought on this inquiry?"

Lydia had to steady herself. She did not want to think about Ginny. "You said yourself that I don't know much about you. You even invited me to ask. If certain subjects were to be avoided, you should have said so at the beginning. I spent a pleasant afternoon with Brigham Moore only to arrive home and have my mother tell me he's a convict. You never said you were really acquainted

126

with Brigham, but neither did you deny it. In fact, you never addressed my question directly."

"Your point is . . ." Nathan prompted calmly.

"A trained ear is not required to know that you and Mr. Moore come from the same place. The flattened vowels, the way you sometimes lift a sentence at the end to make it a question. At first I thought it was a little bit of Cockney, which it may be, but there's something else there, too. So, I'm asking you again, are you a convict?"

"Yes."

Madeline Chadwick stood with her back to the tall, arched window in Brigham Moore's hotel room. Lamplight enriched the rich auburn color of her hair and lent her complexion a warmth that was noticeably absent in the hard set of her mouth.

"Don't look at me that way," she said to Brig. "If anyone has a right to be angry here, I do."

Her statement did nothing to lessen the tension in Brig's square jaw or the flared angle of his nostrils. He gripped the tumbler he was holding in one hand so tightly that it could have shattered in his hand. He wouldn't have felt it. His anger was a palpable thing and its target was Madeline. "I could kill you, you know," he said softly. "I could put my hands around your throat and deny you your very next breath."

Madeline's hand went to the hollow of her throat immediately, but she didn't retreat. "Just the sort of thing I might expect a digger convict to say," she said, dismissing his threat. "I knew what kind of man you were from the very first."

Brigham took a step toward her. His hold on the tumbler eased slightly. "And that's what attracted you to me."

"That's not true."

"Deny it all you want. It changes nothing." His white-hot anger was fractionally cooled. He dropped the tumbler over the back of the armchair behind him and approached Madeline, backing her against the window so that she could feel the fragility of the support behind her. "You told Lydia what I was because you were jealous."

"That's not true, either. I told her because I don't want you attending her. She's too young for someone like you. Far too inexperienced. You'll hurt her, and I won't have that. Better she should know you for what you are now than to find out after she's fallen in love."

"Is that the way it happened to you, Madeline?" he asked, his voice full of silky charm. "Are you certain you're not confusing me with someone else?"

"No," she snapped. Abruptly she pushed at Brig and started past him. He grabbed her arm just above the elbow and squeezed hard. "Let me go," she said through clenched teeth.

"Not until I tell you what I think, Madeline." Brigham yanked her toward him, and when she stumbled, he jerked her upright. He thought she would not dignify his manhandling with a struggle and he was proved correct. She stood toe-to-toe with him, the clean, cool angular lines of her face raised to his. Madeline's stance was frigid, aloof, but there was no mistaking that he had excited her interest. In the depths of her emerald eyes the blue flame pulsed.

"You told Lydia I was a convict because you thought I used you to get to her. You felt betrayed by my attentions to your daughter. You're quick to say she's young and inexperienced—and just as determined to keep her that way—because it helps you hide your years and your experience. You can't bear the thought that I might want your daughter when you want me all to yourself."

His smile was not the careless boyish one he so often wore in public. The placement of his lips created a knowing look, one of calculation and design. "Remember how we met, Madeline? How long after I pulled you away from that falling stone wall did we end up here?" Her eyes darted away. "Look at me," he ordered. "It was

128

twenty minutes. You know how I know that? Because I timed the walk from Market Street here one day. Twenty minutes to walk three blocks, climb four flights of stairs, and have you on my bed. We didn't even undress. The ground rolled with an aftershock and you didn't notice because your need for me was so great."

Madeline's breathing was quick and shallow. Brig's hand was at the small of her back, pressing her toward him. She could feel the hardness of his belly against her, knew the need he had in him now.

"I must have said something in those first few minutes that made you suspect my origins, but once you did, you wanted me then and there. You would have been disappointed if it turned out I wasn't a convict. Admit it."

"I admit to no such thing," she said huskily.

Brig's head bent and his warm whiskey breath was like a kiss on Madeline's face. "What is it that you like about us, I wonder," he said softly, raising one hand to her breast. He felt it swell in his palm. "Ahh, Madeline, do you know, right now I don't think it bloody well matters." Taking her hand, he led her into the bedroom.

Lydia set her fork down as the last vestige of her appetite vanished. He had admitted it. Nathan Hunter was a digger convict. She wanted to know what he had done and couldn't ask the question. When he didn't offer the information she asked, "How well do you know Brigham Moore?"

"We're old friends."

"I see." Though she didn't, not really.

"We're also partners. We have a stake in a gold mine and work a station together. That's what you would call a farm, or perhaps a ranch, only it's much larger than anything you have here. We raise jumbucks—sheep." He leaned back in his chair. Under the table his legs brushed her gown as he crossed his ankles and he expected her to move away, or at least shift in response. She did neither.

Something compelled him to goad her. "Sorry we're not in chains any longer?"

Her head jerked up. "No, I don't think that. I've never thought that. Only . . ."

"Only what?"

"Only I was thinking I was wrong to judge you so harshly yesterday. I didn't think you and Mr. Moore were so much alike."

"We're not," Nathan said. Then to ease the terseness of his words, he sat forward, nudged Lydia's plate toward her, and urged her to eat. Rather than wait for her questions, Nathan spoke to control the conversation.

"I followed Brig here on a business matter. I really can't tell you more than that it has to do with expanding our holdings and it's perfectly legal. We don't acknowledge one another publicly because we're attempting to make the best deal we can as individuals."

"You're selling something?"

"No—buying. Or trying to. We've both expressed interest in a particular property and now we're waiting to see which way the wind blows."

"Aren't you afraid your dual interest will drive the price up?"

"No. The owner doesn't think much of the property in the first place." He cut a sliver of roast beef and raised it to his mouth. "I met your father at the Silver Lady, just as I said I did, and he invited me some time later to your home."

"And Mr. Moore rescued my mother in the last shaker."

Nathan nodded, watching Lydia carefully as he chewed. "And she invited him." He swallowed and speared a small potato. "It was sheer coincidence that we were there together, and if you recall, I made your acquaintance a little earlier that evening."

"It was only yesterday," Lydia said, struck by that realization. "I've only known you since yesterday." Her large, solemn eyes were drawn to Nathan's strong, hard-edged profile as he laughed. He had a richer laugh than Brigham, more spontaneous for all that it was rare. And the thought bothered her because somehow it seemed a betrayal of Brig.

"Our brief acquaintance has been rather rich with experience, hasn't it?"

"Mmm." She felt a measure of her appetite returning and began to eat slowly. "How long will you stay in the United States?"

"Until I secure the property."

"Or until Brig secures it," she said.

"Yes," he said. "Or until Brig secures it."

Brig stretched lazily, smoothed the crown of Madeline's hair, then eased himself out from under her. Her long, elegantly curved legs were reluctant to give him up. He patted her naked behind and finally pinched her in order to get her to move. Reaching across her, he grabbed one corner of the sheet and dragged it across their bodies.

Madeline thought he meant to cover them both. She made a tiny sound of protest at the back of her throat when Brig threw his legs over the side of the bed, hitched the sheet around his waist, and padded into the sitting room. He returned with a glass of red wine.

"Nothing for me?" Madeline asked, pouting.

"I had planned to share."

"That's all right then." She sat up and fashioned a modest garment for herself out of the fringed coverlet. When she looked up from her task it was to find Brig watching her. Heat had returned to the dark center of his eyes. "Yes?" she said, her voice sultry. She raised her arms behind her and lifted her hair, held it up as if cooling her nape, then let it fall in a silky red cloud about her shoulders.

"Did you ever think, Madeline, that perhaps a man courts your daughter as an excuse to be close to you?" he asked. "My God, you have nothing to fear from her!"

131

"Is it true of you? Is that why you made that insane wager?"

"What do you think?" He sat on the bed and extended the glass of wine after he sipped from it. He turned it so Madeline's lips touched in the same place his had. When he withdrew the glass there was a drop of red wine on her mouth. He touched it with his tongue and the kiss began from there.

When Nathan and Lydia left the Cliff House it was after nine. A swirling wind brought nettles of salt air from the Pacific and sand from the white beach below them. At the horizon the stars alone distinguished the sky from the water. The sound of the tide was a steady roar in their ears and there was a discordant cry above it, a cacophony of sound Nathan could not identify.

"Sea lions," Lydia told him.

Nathan recalled seeing them in the daytime, basking in the sun on the rocks below. They were not any more beautiful than the sounds they made, but their antics were entertaining.

"Are there sea lions in Australia?" she asked.

"I've never seen them." They were standing near the edge of the cliff. Wind swept under Lydia's short cape and billowed the skirt of her gown. Nathan wondered what her reaction would be if he were to turn her slightly, draw her closer to his body, and shelter her against the wind. When he did turn her it was to escort her to their carriage. She accepted his arm naturally and he was again reminded of her graceful bearing as they walked across the pebble drive. "We have a queer sort of animal called a platypus, though. It lives in the ocean. Ever heard of it?"

"No."

"It's got something of the shape of one of your sea lions, but it has a large flat bill and webbed feet like a duck, a beaver's tail, and hair on its hide like a bear. It lays eggs like a turtle and feeds its pups with mother's milk.''

She looked at him sideways, her glance suspicious. ''You're making that up.''

''I couldn't,'' he said. ''Could you?''

Laughing, she shook her head. ''What a strange and wonderful place it must be.''

''It's hard and bleak is what it is.'' His description was reflected in his voice. ''The only thing more unforgiving than the land are the men who live on it. You'd do well to remember that, Liddy.''

It was all she thought about during the long silent ride back to Nob Hill. Nathan Hunter was an enigma. Just at the moment she found herself enjoying his company, he said or did something that made her wary of his attentions. His conversation was like his dancing: filled with fits and starts, drawing her close, then pushing her abruptly away.

When they arrived at Lydia's home it was she who suggested a walk through the gardens and down to the pond. She was embarrassed as Nathan checked his pocket watch. Did he have to be so obvious about wanting to leave her?

''It was a stupid idea,'' she said quickly, ducking her head. ''The wager said nothing about—''

''Damn the bloody wager,'' Nathan said. When Lydia's head shot up Nathan cupped the underside of her chin with his forefinger. ''I'd like to see your gardens. There's a gazebo by the pond, isn't there?''

''Yes.'' Confusion still clouded her eyes. ''But don't you have to go? You looked at your watch as if—''

''I looked at my watch because I want to make certain I get you inside by way of a door tonight, preferably the front one.''

''Oh.''

''Oh,'' he said, lightly mocking her. His hand dropped away from her chin and he offered his arm.

They stayed on the flagstone path as they walked, avoiding the damp grass they had trampled the previous evening. There was little they could see in the way of color, even with the bleached white half moon lighting their way, but the fragrances were rich and the night sounds of crickets in the hedges and fish leaping in the pond filled the strained breaks in their conversation.

Standing under the shelter of the gazebo Nathan drew Lydia into his arms. His silver-gray eyes held her motionless, and when he spoke his voice was a low, deep whisper. "Are you as curious as I am?" he asked.

Lydia's natural honesty kept her from pretending ignorance. She knew exactly what he was talking about and denying it served no purpose that she could see. He fascinated and frightened her. In that moment she really didn't care what his intentions were; she wanted to taste his mouth again.

Chapter Five

His lips were softer than she expected, his touch curiously respectful, even reticent. He made the kiss gentle in its seeking and Lydia was unafraid when he drew her still closer to him. She liked the way his mouth made contact with her for only a brief moment, just brushing her lips, urging them apart with only a suggestion of pressure.

Lydia's hands rose between them, not to push Nathan away as he first suspected she might, but to grasp the front of his jacket and hold on as she swayed dreamily. It made him smile.

Her eyes opened and stared straight up into his. "Have I done something wrong?" she whispered. She drew in her lower lip, uncertain now, and a tiny frown appeared between her brows. "You don't want to kiss me anymore?"

"The truth is, Lydia," he said lowly, "I'm not so sure I'll ever want to stop."

"That's all right then." Standing on tiptoe, it was she who initiated the kiss this time, touching him in the same manner he had touched her. It satisfied, then frustrated, and it was then that Nathan took control again.

At the first faint stirrings of passion he pressed for a more intimate response. Tilting his head, his mouth slanted across hers. They shared a breath, an indrawn gasp, and he tasted the sweetness of her mouth as she gave him what he sought.

Nathan's kiss excited her senses. Lydia knew the hard, angular planes of his body in contrast to hers, the beat of his heart through her fingertips, and heard the small sounds of her own passion rising. Behind her eyelids was a sunburst of color and in the center of her was another one of heat.

Backing Lydia against the gazebo's latticework, Nathan's hands slid from the small of her back to the underside of her breasts. Cornered, she stilled momentarily, aware and wary. He did nothing except wait, and when she swayed into him he knew she had accepted his touch.

His tongue traced the line of her upper lip, teasing a tiny shudder out of her. When the vibration was passed onto him he felt as though the kiss had come full circle. The innocence that was Lydia's, however, could never be his. The most he could hope for was that she would share his guilt.

Lydia stretched, sliding her arms around Nathan's shoulders, flattening herself against Nathan's chest. His thumb brushed the tip of her left breast and she sucked in her breath as she felt the tug of pleasure in the very soles of her feet. His lips were hard now; his tongue speared her mouth in a rhythm that was suggestive of another kind of intimacy.

"My God!"

The sharp, bitter invective drove a wedge between Lydia and Nathan. Nathan was surprised less by the interruption than by his own degree of disorientation. In spite of repeated warnings to himself, he hadn't kept his head, and a single glance at Lydia told him she had not done nearly as well as Nat. His hands dropped to Lydia's waist and he steadied her, drawing her away from the lattice. He took a half-step in front of her, partially shielding her from the censure of the intruders.

136

Madeline released Brig's arm, but she made no movement toward the gazebo steps. "That was an unbecoming display, Lydia," she said coldly. "Come out of there at once and go inside. We'll talk of this later."

Before Lydia could move, Nathan spoke. "Good evening, Mrs. Chadwick," he said with considerable civility. He nodded in Brig's direction. "Brigham. It's quite a pleasant evening for enjoying the gardens, don't you think?"

Madeline was not amused by Nathan's cool and unruffled tones. "The only thing that you were enjoying, Mr. Hunter, was my daughter. And she apparently had no qualms about letting you."

"Mother," said Lydia. The rush of heat to her face had scarcely lessened since she and Nathan had been interrupted, and some invisible pressure on her throat made it hurt to speak. "Please. It wasn't—"

"You can explain it all inside, Lydia," Madeline said, unwilling to listen. "Though how you shall explain it to Mr. Moore is beyond my comprehension. He dropped in to return a pair of gloves you left in his carriage this afternoon. You may as well have thrown them in his face."

Lydia found it difficult to meet her mother's eyes. She had not once ventured a look in Brig's direction. "Gloves?" she asked, grasping at the conversation to shield her complete humiliation. "I don't think I was wearing any. They must have fallen out of the pocket in my . . ."

Well acquainted with Lydia's tears, Nathan sensed her struggle to control them now. He turned his back on Brig and Madeline long enough to ask Lydia if she wanted his escort to the house.

"No, thank you. I'll be all right."

He searched her downcast face and wished that he might lift her chin and raise her eyes so he would know the truth. "Will you?"

She nodded. "I just shouldn't have let . . ." Lydia didn't finish her thought. She pushed past Nathan and fled the gazebo and then the garden.

Madeline stared hard at Nathan. "Once my husband hears of this, Mr. Hunter, I don't think you'll be welcome any longer." She thought that he would leave immediately, make an apology at the very least. Instead, he did neither of these things. He returned her look with an insolent half-smile and eyes that expressed contempt. Finally it was Madeline who turned away. "If you'll excuse me, Mr. Moore," she said.

"Of course," he said gallantly. "And please don't take Lydia to task on my account. I'd like to think she only wanted to make me jealous."

Madeline hurried up the walk to the house. Neither Brig nor Nathan spoke again until they heard the door close behind her. Brig was carrying a crystal-knobbed ebony cane. He tapped the silver tip against the flagstones and laughed softly as Nathan came toward him. "If you're going to throw a punch, Nath, at least let me move to the grass."

Nathan stopped in front of Brig, but he made no move to lift a hand against him. "She wasn't trying to make you jealous," he said, "because she didn't know you were there."

"Are you certain about that?" Brig asked good-naturedly. "After all, she was facing in the direction of the house when Madeline and I came out."

"You saw her?"

"Immediately."

Which meant, Nathan supposed, that she could have seen him. "I don't think jealousy was a motive." But he wasn't as certain as he had been a moment ago.

"Then perhaps she was just kissing you and thinking of me," said Brig. "She's halfway to being in love with me, you know."

Nathan started up the walk and Brig fell in step beside

him. "You can't be all that sure of her," Nathan said, "or you wouldn't have shown up here tonight."

Brig laughed again. "You know me too well, Nath. By God, you really do." Except for the light tapping of Brig's cane it was quiet as they passed the pond. "You may be interested to know," Brig said, "that Lydia knows I'm a convict. It's only a matter of time before she learns the same of you."

"She already knows. She asked me and I told her."

"Did she ask you what you'd done?"

"No. I think she was afraid to. And I didn't offer the information."

"Wise man. I don't think she'd have been kissing you like that if she'd known about . . . damn, what was her name?"

"Beth Ann Ondine."

"Not likely you'll ever forget, is it?"

"No not likely," Nathan said quietly. He wasn't just thinking of Beth Ann. He was thinking of Ginny Flynt. Who would ever believe he hadn't killed her? "Do you have a point?" he asked.

"Lydia's not going to have anything to do with either of us if she knows too much."

"The fact that she knows anything at all is your fault," Nathan whispered harshly. They were standing near the edge of the portico, not far from where he'd shimmied up to the balcony the night before. "She heard it first from her mother, and we both know how Madeline came by the information. She may have guessed a few things in the beginning, but I'll wager you confirmed most of her suspicions. You were insane to get involved with her. She's a bitch, Brig, and where you're concerned, she's a bitch in heat."

One corner of Brig's mouth lifted. "Perhaps that's where her daughter gets it from." He was curiously disappointed when Nathan didn't react. Had he misread Nathan's interest in Lydia? "What's she like, Nath?

I haven't even kissed her yet. You do plan to let me share in that pleasure, don't you? Assuming it's a pleasure."

"You're welcome to try your hand at her, Brig. I certainly don't have a claim. What you did this afternoon smacks of a little underhandedness, but as you pointed out before, there are no rules where Lydia is concerned."

"Underhanded?" asked Brig, his eys widening innocently. "What do you—oh, the gloves."

"Precisely. She didn't drop them and they didn't fall out of her cape. You lifted them and then you hid them and waited until tonight to return them. You knew Lydia was out with me, knew that I wouldn't keep her late, and you came to the house hoping we'd come in while you were still here. I'd say you probably saw our carriage arrive, never shared that information with Madeline, and got her out here on the pretense of seeing the gardens. I think her shock when she saw Lydia and me was quite real."

"It was."

"And everything else?"

Brig shrugged, no remorse in the gesture. "All true, I'm afraid. Yet it's hardly different than your timely intervention in the alley. Or should I say interference? And don't forget the card game. If it hadn't been for you, I'd have been with her tonight at the Cliff House, and quite possibly kissing her in the gazebo. Let's not discuss underhandedness, shall we."

Nathan sighed heavily, frustrated that Brig had outmaneuvered him. "Where's Samuel tonight?"

"I don't know. He's not at home, though."

Convenient, thought Nathan. "Let's go, Brig. I'd say today ended in a draw."

"A draw," he agreed. He put an arm around Nathan's shoulders as they rounded the corner of the house below Lydia's window. "Too bad we can't finish it that way. In the end there's just going to be one winner."

Nathan was only certain it would not be Lydia.

The mission that housed the orphans was a rabbit warren of rooms. Lydia hurried from one bedroom to the next looking for two of the youngest boys. She retraced her steps into the bedroom she had just left when she heard Richard's smothered giggle. A few minutes later, after fussing aloud that she'd *never* find them, she pulled them out from under a cot. John's hand was covering Richard's mouth, but that did little to silence the younger child's laughter. John's narrow, angular face was softened by large brown eyes and a gap-toothed smile. Richard was a slightly broader, rounder version of his older brother with the same dark chocolate eyes and heart-warming grin. That grin was finally uncovered when John let his hand drop.

Lydia tried to be stern. "Mrs. Finnegan is waiting for you boys in the kitchen. It's not a good idea to run off when there's work to be done."

Richard simply stared up at her soulfully and let his brother do the talking. "That's when it's the very best idea."

She remembered thinking the same thing at six. "All right," she said, pretending indifference, "but I heard her say there's raisin oatmeal cookies for the boys who clean her pantry shelves. I'll see who else—" She didn't have to go on. They rushed past her into the hallway and ran for the kitchen, their shoes clicking loudly on the red tile floor. Smiling to herself, Lydia pushed the cot back in place and straightened the pile of blankets at the foot. She looked at her handiwork and then at the other five cots and straightened each one of them in turn. The room the six smallest boys shared was painfully neat and barren, more like a cell than a bedroom. Their few personal possessions were kept in wooden crates at the base of each cot. The walls were whitewashed and showed nothing more interesting than a few cracks in the stucco. The new orphanage could not be built quickly enough to suit Lydia.

She backed out of the room, pulling the door shut, and bumped into Nathan Hunter. "Oh! What are you doing here?"

He noted she seemed more surprised to see him than unhappy. He took it as a good sign. "I came to see you, of course."

To give her hands something to do, Lydia smoothed the skirt of her soft gray gown. "I don't know why," she said with a credible amount of dignity. "It's been three weeks since the Cliff House. I thought you'd gone back to Australia."

"Not until Brig and I settle our deal."

She made to go past him, but Nathan blocked her path. "I have work to do, Mr. Hunter. Father Patrick's expecting me to help him in the classroom."

"No, he's not." There was something different about her, Nathan thought, though he was hard pressed to identify what it was. Her bearing was much the same—the chin still lifted when she felt threatened—but there was something else in her manner, an aloofness that suggested fear perhaps, or pain. He said nothing for a moment, studying her heart-shaped face. She was wearing her hair differently now, swept back lightly from her temples and coiled loosely at the back of her head. It was a dark, gloriously rich frame for her features and, looking at her, Nathan was struck again by her eyes, how deeply blue they were, how soft and fathomless they could be. "I spoke with Father Patrick when I came in," he told her. "He suggested I might find you back here and that you would be delighted to take me on a tour."

"Delighted?"

"His word exactly. I hoped it might be true." He

142

studied her face, aware that she had marshaled her defenses and was determined to be cool. "Well?"

Lydia avoided Nathan's light gray predator eyes. "Very well," she said, making little attempt to be gracious. "I suppose I can show you around. The sooner that's done, the sooner you can leave."

Since they were in the wing which housed the bedrooms, Lydia took Nathan from one to another, talking a little about the children and their backgrounds. Her conversation was hardly personal; she had conducted dozens of such tours when she was trying to raise money for the new building. Nathan listened politely and asked questions now and again.

"Didn't you get any of my messages?" he asked as they entered the chapel. Dust motes filled a row of sunbeams coming through the high, narrowly arched windows. Nathan shut the heavy oaken door behind him and leaned against it.

At the sound of the door closing, Lydia lost her train of thought. She dipped her fingers in the font and genuflected, then took a seat on the last rough-hewn pew. "What messages?" she asked when he sat beside her.

"I sent one every three or four days since I last saw you," he said. "You never got one? Or the flowers?"

"Nothing." She looked at him suspiciously. "You really tried to reach me? Sent me flowers?"

The chapel was still and peaceful and their voices were hushed respectfully. Nathan pointed to the golden cross on the altar. "This is not the sort of place where I'm likely to tell a lie."

She looked away quickly, trying to hide her smile. When she had composed herself she said, "Three weeks was a long time not to hear anything from you. I suppose it was my mother's doing. She wants to protect me."

"But she allows you to see Brigham."

"Yes. I've seen him twice since that night. How do you

143

know about it? Does he . . . does he talk to you about me?"

"No," Nathan said quickly. "It's not what you're thinking. I saw you with him at the theater one evening. Brigham and I rarely talk these days, we're not even staying in the same hotel any longer. He's moved to the Commodore."

"Have you had a falling out?" she asked, folding her hands in her lap. "Brigham doesn't talk about you, either."

Nathan placed his hand across both of hers. "What are your feelings for Brig, Lydia?"

She jerked her hands away. "Why would I tell you that? I haven't shared my feelings with Brigham. I'm certainly not going to share them with you."

"I suppose that answers my question." He stretched his legs out into the aisle and leaned back, resting his hands on the bench behind him. "If you had gotten my messages, would you have agreed to see me?"

"I'm seeing you now, aren't I?" she asked. "Anyway, why do you want to see me? Knowing that you and Brigham are partners, well, it makes me feel as if I'm some bone you're fighting over. I have no idea why you've both singled me out for your attention unless it's my money. There are hundreds of women in San Francisco, most of them better-looking than me and far more interesting."

"Do you ever tell Brig any of this?"

"Of course. He told me I was imagining it." Between softly teasing kisses Brig had told her that. "He said he didn't need my money." He had said that while his mouth was against her ear and when his tongue had traced the outer shell. "He said I was beautiful." He had kissed her eyes closed then, touched his lips to her temples, and followed the line of her jaw with his mouth. "And as interesting as a woman ought to be."

"You believed him?"

144

"Shouldn't I?"

"What if I said those things?"

"It's the *way* they were said," she admitted.

His imagination told him everything she had not. Nathan wondered what he could say that would turn her against Brig without turning her against him as well. The truth damned them both and lies could easily be undone. "Brig is an old friend," he said at last, "but that doesn't mean I'll give in easily. This has never happened to us before, Lydia. We've never shared any interest in the same woman so perhaps that's why you're feeling some rivalry between us. I can't speak to what Brig wants from you, but I know what I want."

"And that is . . . ?"

Marriage, he almost said. Yet something made him hold back the word and stop short of proposing. A chapel was not the place to discuss the type of marriage he had in mind. "Another opportunity to see you," he said instead. "Anywhere you want to go."

"Do you mean that?"

"Yes."

"Then let me think on it, Nathan," she said softly, raising her eyes to his. "I may have something in mind." Before he could reply Lydia stood up, stepped over his outstretched legs, and motioned for him to follow. "There's still the matter of your tour, I believe."

Lydia showed him the rooms they used for classes, the sitting and dining rooms, and finally the kitchen. John and Richard were sitting at a table in one corner, their legs dangling from stools much too high for them, eating raisin oatmeal cookies. They were also trying to kick each other under the table. Mrs. Finnegan was working at the large cast-iron stove while some of the older girls who lived in the orphanage snapped peas beside a butcher-block table. None of them paid the least attention to the two boys. It was Nathan who responded when John hit his brother's stool with his foot and tipped it backward.

145

Rushing ahead of Lydia, Nathan caught Richard a mere heartbeat before boy and floor collided.

Richard came up grinning in Nathan's arms until he tasted blood in his mouth. The screams that rent the air then caused Mrs. Finnegan to drop her spoon in the stew and the girls to overturn their pan of peas. Searching out the culprit, Mrs. Finnegan's eyes alighted on John and she started for the table, intending to box the boy's ears. He let out a shriek, slid off the stool, crawled under the table, and eluded the cook by running full tilt into Lydia's legs. He clutched at her skirt and begged her to save him.

Well aware of Mrs. Finnegan's keen and watchful eyes, Lydia caught John by the scruff of his neck and dragged him out of the kitchen. Nathan gave Richard a handkerchief for his bleeding lip and followed quickly, leaving a trail of smashed peas behind him. As soon as they were out of sight Lydia let go of John. She knelt in front of the boy. "I didn't hurt you, did I?" she asked anxiously. Behind her she heard Nathan chuckle.

John stuck out his bottom lip a little and rubbed the back of his neck. "Not much," he said, hoping she'd believe he'd been punished enough.

"All right," Lydia said. John's face brightened. She patted him on his bottom. "Now go tell Father Patrick what you did. And don't think I won't ask after you." His narrow face grew solemn and he turned away, dragging his feet with each step he took. Clearing her throat to quell the urge to laugh, Lydia turned to Richard. He was sitting comfortably in the crook of Nathan's arm, holding a handkerchief to his mouth.

"Let me see your lip," she said, suspicious that there might be a devilish smile behind it. There was. "Oh, Richard. You are an imp."

Nathan set the boy down. "That's why he's going to Father Patrick and tell him that he was stealing one of the other boy's cookies when the accident happened. Aren't you?"

Richard's lower lip trembled as his eyes grew round. "Must I?" he asked, looking to Lydia.

"Yes, you must."

Sucking on his injured lip, the boy returned the handkerchief to Nathan. "Thank you, sir," he said gravely.

Nathan and Lydia waited until he was out of sight and hearing before they shared their laughter. "Neither one of them will see the priest," said Nathan.

She sighed. "Probably not. They're counting on me not to inquire."

"Will you?"

Her expression was sheepish. "Probably not." Nathan smiled then, and Lydia felt the force of it slam against the barriers she had erected. She hated the fact that he had been kind to the children, that she had found it so easy to laugh with him, that he had found her in the place she had come to consider a kind of sanctuary. "I'll walk you out to your carriage," she said.

That was that, Nathan thought. He accepted her offer. When they were outside he pointed out the cinnamon mare posted at the rail. "I didn't hire a carriage today." They crossed the dusty yard. "How often do you come here?"

"Several times a week. Why?"

"I wondered when I might be able to see you again."

"Mrs. Newberry is having a party this evening to celebrate her husband's sixtieth birthday. Were you invited?"

"No. I don't know the Newberrys."

"I'm going with my parents and Brigham," she said. "If you want to attend, speak to my father. He's a good friend of the Newberrys and he can probably arrange something. I'm not sure I understand it, but my father seems to like you. At least he's asked after you these past few weeks."

"Actually, I saw Samuel last night at the Silver Lady. That's how I knew to come here today." Untethering the

147

mare, he mounted her in a swift, graceful motion. Looking down at Lydia, he saw she was still wearing a slightly confused, all-at-sea expression. He reached in his pocket and leaned toward her. "Here, Miss Liddy," he said, mimicking the solemn, penitent air of the boys, "have a cookie."

She stared at it for a moment, unbelieving of her own eyes. "Where did you—"

"Stole it, I'm afraid." The merest suggestion of a smile touched his mouth, and for an instant his eyes were warm. "I'll speak to Father Patrick about it later."

"And then he handed me a stolen oatmeal raisin cookie," said Lydia. "What do you think of that, Pei Ling?"

Pei Ling paused in brushing out Lydia's hair and caught her mistress's eye in the mirror. "I think Mr. Hunter want to see you smile. He know what I know. You beautiful when you smile."

Lydia's eyes dropped away from her reflection immediately and she busied herself collecting the hair pins Pei Ling would require. "I wonder if he'll be there tonight."

"He come. You have plenty young men admire you tonight. James be there. Also Henry Bell. Mr. Moore escort you and Mr. Hunter try to take you away. Wish Missus Newberry invite me to party."

Laughing, Lydia handed Pei Ling a hair pin. "I think it will be a dull affair."

"No. Not that." There was a knock at the door and Lydia and Pei Ling exchanged knowing glances before Lydia asked her mother to come in. Madeline's reaction to Lydia's gown was almost immediate. "Fireworks start now," Pei Ling murmured.

Lydia pretended she didn't hear. "Yes, Mother?"

"I came to see if you needed any help, but you seem to be almost ready." Madeline's emerald eyes were critical as they traveled over her daughter's bare shoulders and the severely cut lines of her midnight-blue gown. Tiny blue beads sparkled along the edge of the low-cut bodice. They were worked into the tight-fitting sleeves at the wrists and decorated the gown's hem and train. Lydia wore sapphire drop earrings, and when she turned her head to look at her mother inquiringly, they brushed against the smooth ivory stem of her neck. "Stand up, Lydia," she said. "I want a better look at what you're wearing."

"In a moment, Mother. When Pei Ling's finished with my hair."

Madeline opened her mouth to argue, then thought better of it. Whatever she said in front of the Chinese girl would get back to Samuel and he would not hesitate to confront her. She could do without her husband's criticisms these days.

Pei Ling took her time, winding Lydia's sable hair into an intricate knot at the back of her head. She anchored it with pins that she hid and a gold comb which she did not. Purposely freeing a few strands of hair at Lydia's temples and nape, Pei Ling created a softer look that contrasted beautifully with the severity of the gown. When she was finished she touched Lydia lightly on the shoulders, offering her silent support, and left the room.

Lydia stood and turned so that her mother could see the gown from all sides. She hoped that what she might hear would be different from what she expected. It wasn't.

"I don't think I approve, Lydia. Not at all." When Lydia stopped turning, Madeline walked around her. "Where did you get this? And when?"

After taking a calming breath, Lydia said, "I'd hoped you be pleased, Mother. After all, you've always wanted me to take more interest in my appearance. I had this made for me at Madame Simone's. It was just finished

149

yesterday." She almost bumped into Madeline as she started toward her wardrobe. Madeline stopped circling and Lydia excused herself. She opened the door of her wardrobe and pointed to the row of new purchases. "I had half a dozen made and there are three more on order."

"That was extravagant, Lydia. What's your father going to think when he gets the bill? You should have come to me and discussed it first."

"I discussed it with Papa," said Lydia. "He was agreeable."

"And you said nothing to me."

"I wanted to surprise you." Was Madeline hurt? Lydia wondered. Was that what she heard in her mother's voice?

Madeline indicated Lydia's gown with a dismissive wave of her hand. "*This* is a surprise."

"You hate it, don't you?"

"On the contrary. It's a lovely gown, but totally unsuited to you. You're too young to wear something like this, Lydia, which I would have told you had you had the grace to ask to me to accompany you to Simone's. You took Pei Ling, I suppose?" Lydia nodded, biting her lower lip. She felt herself shriveling inside her skin, becoming smaller and smaller as Madeline went on. "What on earth would she know about fashion? Someone your age requires pastels, or at the very least a printed fabric. And you've allowed Simone to neglect all the usual ornamentation. Oh, the beads are fine if you're planning to lead the opening number in a dance hall, but I don't know that they're suitable for Mr. Newberry's birthday party. The Newberrys are very circumspect, remember." She took Lydia by the elbow and escorted her to the full-length mirror. "Your shoulders aren't your best feature, darling," she said, running her palms across them. "The collarbones are very pronounced, aren't they? And the cut of this bodice . . . I'm not certain you want to expose this much . . . skin. What do you expect the men will think of you?"

Lydia ventured her thought softly. "Perhaps if I ask Papa what he thinks."

"Your father would never say anything against it," Madeline said truthfully. "He'd spare your feelings if you wore a sackcloth and ashes. Now, do what's best for all concerned, and find something else to wear. We still have enough time. I'll go and tell Samuel and Mr. Moore that you'll just be a little longer." She left the room without giving Lydia the opportunity to respond.

Still worrying her lower lip, Lydia stared dully at her reflection. She wanted to cry. She had been so certain she had made a good choice, and in less than two minutes Madeline had found all the flaws. If Madeline saw them so easily, then others would eventually. She had wanted to have admirers at the Newberrys' party, and instead she was going to embarrass herself. And she *would* embarrass herself, Lydia realized, because she was going to defy her mother and wear the gown anyway. It would be like wearing a sackcloth and ashes, she thought, remembering Madeline's phrase. Throughout the evening the gown would serve as a reminder that in all things she should learn to choose wisely.

Brigham Moore led Lydia onto the ballroom floor and took her into his arms. "My God but you're lovely this evening." He hoped he didn't sound as surprised as he felt. When he had first seen her coming down the staircase in her own home, he thought she was a guest, a friend of Lydia's perhaps, but certainly not Lydia. It *was* Lydia, though, and the entire time he watched her descend the steps, he felt Madeline's eyes on him. She was worried, he thought, and she had every right to be. Tonight Lydia would outshine her mother. For Madeline it must have felt like the end of the world.

151

"You always make such pretty compliments," Lydia said, smiling up at him. Her eyes were bright and her cheeks were flushed becomingly. "It's difficult to know how seriously to take them."

"Pretty compliments, Lydia?" He feigned a wounded look. "I speak the truth. I'm thankful you wrote me in on your dance card in three places before that crowd of young puppies descended on you."

"Mr. Newberry is sixty today, remember? Hardly a puppy. And I've written him in twice." She laughed gaily as he turned her several times in quick succession. "But it's kind of you to make jealous noises, Brig. It cannot help but flatter me."

"These aren't jealous noises. I *am* jealous. Look at my eyes."

"Your eyes are always green."

He pretended to be much struck by this observation and elicited another smile from her. "My point exactly," he said. "I was born to be jealous where you're concerned."

"Oh, Brig," she said softly, and gave herself up to the music and the moment.

Samuel excused himself from his circle of friends and walked to the edge of the ballroom when he saw Nathan arrive. He raised his hand slightly to catch Nathan's attention and motioned the younger man to join him. Nathan did so quickly, feeling every inch the intruder he was.

"Don't look guilty," Sam said, extending his hand in a warm, familiar greeting. "You have that invitation, don't you?"

"Thanks to you, sir."

"No thanks to me at all. I wouldn't have thought of it if Lydia hadn't put the notion in your mind. I'd say that things are looking up for you, Nath. She wouldn't have suggested you come this evening if she hadn't wanted to see you again."

"I hope that's what it means," he said, his tone

doubtful. "Are you giving Brig as much encouragement as you're giving me?"

"Brigham? That one doesn't need encouragement. But then you'd know that, wouldn't you? Lydia tells me you're business partners, though it's a damn odd way you diggers conduct business."

"This is a very special matter, Samuel. I'm assuming I can count on your discretion."

"As long as it's legal."

"It is."

"Good. The way you and Brigham work puts me in mind of confidence men. You'd be run out of town on your ear, and that's only if you're lucky. Most likely you'd be hanged."

Nathan restrained an urge to fiddle with his cravat. Samuel was liable to interpret the gesture as a guilty one.

"I'd hate to think that you were after Lydia's money," Samuel went on, then added significantly, "Or mine."

"Look at her, Samuel," Nathan said, tilting his chin in Lydia's direction. She was on the floor with James Early now, her head thrown back with laughter, the smooth curve of her throat exposed. She was as slender as a wraith, ephemeral in her beauty, and she fairly floated across the floor, as if she were held down by James's hand on her waist and nothing else. "Do you really think that when a man looks at her, he only sees her bloody money?" He didn't wait to hear Samuel's response. He was dodging the other dancing couples on the dance floor, thinking of what he would say to Lydia when he cut in.

James Early stepped aside for Nathan reluctantly. "Why haven't you married that boy?" Nathan asked, taking Lydia in his arms. He was careful not to hold her too tightly or draw her too close.

For a moment Lydia was too stunned to answer. Nathan had appeared from nowhere, summarily dismissed her partner, and now he was asking personal questions—all without so much as a greeting. She was hardly able to take it in, much less notice that his dancing form had improved immensely. He glided across the floor, turning her easily, and she didn't have to think to follow him, it came as simply and naturally as breathing. "It would be like marrying a brother," she said at last. "That's how I think of James."

"Have you told him that?"

"Several times. I think he feels the same way, but every so often he gets it in his mind that he should take a wife, and I'm as good a candidate as any. A better one, I suppose, than most of the girls he sees. At least James can talk to me."

"And what about that other young man I see hovering around you from time to time?"

"You must mean Henry Bell. Henry's fine, but definitely not for me." He'd also made the regrettable error of getting caught kissing Madeline in the Chadwick gallery. They both excused their behavior on the mistletoe above their head and the high spirit of the season, and as if to prove the innocence of the gesture, Madeline still pushed Henry at Lydia's head from time to time. "Henry's a pleasant enough escort, but that's all."

"He's proposed?"

"Once. I accepted once . . . and then I cried off. It all happened in the space of an evening, Mr. Hunter, so there's no wound to speak of." Her cobalt-blue eyes were grave as she studied his hard-edged features and tried to fathom his intentions. "Your questions are exceedingly personal. I wonder what you can mean by them."

"Only curious about the number of hearts you've broken," he said, his glance shuttered. A hundred, he thought, at least a hundred. The music drifted off and the orchestra picked up the strains of another waltz. Nathan had no choice but to give her up, but it cut him that he had to deliver her to Brigham.

"I'd like to go outside, if you don't mind," Lydia said

when Brig took her arm. "I've had quite enough dancing for the time being."

"Of course," he said, immediately solicitous. "I've been wanting to speak with you alone anyway." He glanced around the ballroom and saw Madeline standing with her back to them, occupied by her conversation with Samuel and several of their friends. It was the perfect time to approach Lydia.

The Newberrys had no gazebo or pond on their property, but they did have an immense marble fountain that Mr. Newberry had had shipped from Italy. Its three tiers consisted of ornate and fanciful sculptures of dolphins, water sprites, and, at the pinnacle, Neptune himself. Lydia thought the entire affair rather ghastly in daylight, but at night, as long as the moon was not too full, it looked rather pleasant and the steady spray of water was soothing to the ear. Though no word passed between her and Brig, they gravitated toward the fountain as if by mutual agreement.

White marble benches, just outside of the circle of mist, surrounded the fountain. Brig led Lydia to the one that put the fountain between them and the ballroom, thus giving them the illusion of complete privacy.

"My business in San Francisco is almost at an end, Lydia," Brig said, slipping his hand beneath hers. Their fingers intertwined. "When I came here I had no expectations of meeting someone like yourself, someone who would make me regret leaving California alone. I realize we have not known one another long, nor especially well, but I haven't the luxury of many more days in your city. Perhaps I am presenting this in a backward fashion, but I don't want you to think this is the impetuous proposal of a schoolboy. It's no infatuation that I feel, for I have enough experience to know otherwise. I'd like you to be my wife, Lydia. Come back to Sydney with me and the station at Ballaburn. We could be happy there, I know we could."

155

How beautiful this man was, Lydia thought. Strands of sandy hair gleamed silver in the pale moonlight and his green eyes were like precious stones. The boyish smile so often in evidence was absent now and the set of his mouth betrayed some of the anxiety he was feeling. There was the smallest tremor in the large, smooth hand that held hers.

Lydia's eyes darted over his face, the stillness with which he held himself betrayed by the faint muscle working in his cheek. "I'm not certain it's what I want," she said finally. "What you're asking . . . it's so much more than marriage for me. It would mean leaving my mother and father, leaving behind everything that is familiar, and taking up a way of life in a land I've heard described as bleak and unforgiving."

"But you're not saying no," Brig inserted quickly. "Is there reason for me to hope?"

Lydia eased her hand out from under his and stood up. "Of course you may hope, Brigham. In fact, I wish that you would. I shouldn't like it if you gave up so easily. I'd like to think about it . . . give you my answer later."

He also got to his feet and stood in front of her. "Later? You mean tonight?"

"Yes," she said, raising her eyes to him. Her thick lashes framed eyes that were almost black and her lips were fractionally parted, wet and inviting. "I mean tonight. But not here. There are too many things I still want to know." She hesitated, looking away.

"What is it, Lydia?" he asked gently.

She spoke in a rush. "Would you meet me later? Somewhere . . . I don't know—at my home perhaps. I could let you in after my parents go to bed and we could finally talk privately and with complete candor." She saw Brig's frown and immediately began to retract her statement. "I'm sorry. I've been forward again, haven't I? Oh, God." Despair was rife in her tone and she caught her bottom lip between her teeth. "I shouldn't have

156

suggested it. If you want to take back your proposal, I'll understand. I don't know what made me think that you'd—"

"Come," he finished for her. "I'll meet you, Lydia. You're an intriguing mixture of propriety and daring, aren't you?" In that dress she was a damned siren, he thought. His eyes darted to the curve of her naked shoulders. "Something else to love about you, darling."

Her eyes widened and darkened further at the center.

"I hadn't said it yet, but surely you've known. I'm in love with you, Lydia Chadwick. Quite hopelessly in love with you." He took her in his arms and kissed first her forehead, her closed eyes, then the tip of her nose before settling and lingering on the fullness of her ripe mouth. He kissed her deeply, almost drawing the air from her lungs, and didn't release her until he felt her sag helplessly against him. "I'm not above using everything at my disposal to win your hand," he said, lifting his head. He kissed her again, briefly this time, then left her to regain her composure before she entered the ballroom, certain he had sufficiently unbalanced her heart.

Nathan excused himself from the men he was talking to when he saw Brigham come back inside. More than a minute later Lydia followed. She looked as if she could use a drink, something more powerful than the party punch he eventually offered her.

"Thank you," said Lydia, holding the crystal cup between her palms. "You're very kind."

One of Nathan's dark brows kicked up. "I'm not," he said. "Not at all."

Over the rim of her cup she smiled. "Say whatever you like. I shall think what I like."

Frowning, Nathan slid his hand under Lydia's elbow and urged her toward the exit.

"Where are we going?" she asked. "I just came from outside."

"And I think you need to go back. It's obvious to me at

least that you need some fresh air. You haven't cooled
down sufficiently from Brigham's mauling."

Lydia laughed as they stepped onto the terrace.
"Mauling? Why, Mr. Hunter, you sound almost jealous."

His only response was to grip her arm a little tighter.
Glancing sideways at her face, Nathan could still make
out the high color in her cheeks and the swollen
sweetness of her mouth. She was full of herself this
evening, he thought, confident in a way he had never
seen before.

"May I at least put down my cup somewhere?" she
asked as they came upon the fountain. He didn't say anything, but paused long enough for her to set it down on
one of the stone benches before pulling her into the
shadowed recesses of the yard. Light from the house
could not reach them; strains of music could. When they
stopped walking, Lydia held up her hands, her face tilted
to one side in question.

Nathan didn't hesitate. When Lydia began to hum the
melody, he took her in his arms and led her in a waltz.
"How did you get out of the house in that gown?" he
asked baldly.

What confidence Lydia had was shattered. Her steps
faltered momentarily, and when she trounced his toes, it
was her fault, not his. "I didn't have anything else to
wear," she said softly. "Mother didn't like it, either."

"Either?" Of course Madeline hadn't liked it. "I didn't
say I didn't like it. In fact . . ." She was radiant,
luminous. Or she had been until she thought he'd been
expressing disapproval. ". . . you should always have
nothing else to wear."

The smile that had faltered on her lips brightened fractionally. "You don't think it's too . . . too . . ."

"I do." His eyes fell briefly on the hollow of her throat,
then came to rest on her mouth. "Indeed, I do."

Embarrassed by his regard, Lydia lowered her head.
She said the first thing that came to mind. "You're a

158

much better dancer than you were a few—" She cut herself off, appalled by her lack of good manners, and looked up at Nathan to see if he was offended. It seemed that he was. His jaw was clenched now. "I'm sorry. I shouldn't have—"

"It's all right," he said, his voice rough. He wasn't about to tell her he had been practicing, taking lessons from Miss Wilhemenia Gardner at her School of Dance.

It was the first time Lydia had sensed any vulnerability in Nathan Hunter and she wondered at it, wondered if she had been mistaken about the aura of confidence, even arrogance, that he showed most often. She wouldn't allow herself to think on it long, afraid it would sway her. After all, she already had Brig's proposal. "I'm glad you came this evening," she said. "I understand you have something to celebrate."

"I do?"

She nodded. "Certainly. Brigham tells me he's leaving for Australia soon. That can only mean the deal is close to being finalized. I assume you'll be going as well."

"Yes . . . yes, I suppose I will." What was she talking about? The deal closed? Nathan couldn't imagine that Brig had spoken of returning to Ballaburn without Lydia. In Nathan's mind that meant one thing: Brigham had proposed. Was it too late? he wondered. Had Lydia already given her answer? But, no, he thought, she couldn't have, because Brig would never have let her out of his sight. He'd have made the announcement tonight, before Lydia could think better of it. Nathan stopped dancing, never realizing the music had stopped sometime earlier.

"What is it?" Lydia asked.

Nathan's hands rested on the curve of Lydia's naked shoulders. His thumbs brushed her collarbones. "I want you to marry me, Lydia," he said tersely. "I want you to come back to Australia with me. I know you don't like me much, perhaps not at all, but I don't think it matters for what I have in mind."

Not matter? How could that be true? Since when didn't feelings matter in a marriage? "I'm not certain what you mean," she said quietly.

"Our marriage wouldn't have to be the usual kind," he said. "That is, it need never be consummated." He ignored her gasp, and when she tried to pull away he held her fast. "It would only be temporary anyway. I need a wife for a year, Lydia. A single year. Then you could leave me. I'd send you back to San Francisco if you liked, or anywhere else that you wanted to go. It would be up to you."

"Why?"

"Why what?"

"Why do you need a wife at all?" she asked. "And why for only a year? Why me?"

Why indeed. She was asking all the questions Nathan couldn't answer. It would have been easier to lie to her, tell her that he loved her, needed her, tell her all the things he imagined Brig had said. It would have been much, much easier, and still Nathan couldn't do it. Ultimately she would be betrayed, or feel as if she had been, and that was where Nathan's conscience had drawn the line. "It's difficult to explain," he said finally. Impossible, he thought. This time when Lydia tried to move out of his grasp, he let her. She didn't go far, only a few feet, and then she turned her back on him.

"You can't expect that I should answer you now," she said. "How could I? I've never had a proposal quite like yours before."

He came up to stand behind her. "I told you my intentions were so honorable you'd be insulted."

Lydia laughed mirthlessly. "Yes, you did. I had forgotten that. Your actions weren't always so honorable."

"Lydia?" He spoke her name softly, a question in the sound. "What are you saying?"

160

"Nothing."

He touched the nape of her neck with his fingertips, whispering across her sensitive skin and brushing aside a few loose strands of hair. He felt her shudder, not with distaste, he hoped, but with desire. "Lydia," he said again. This time his mouth was near her ear. His lips touched the pulse in her neck just below her lobe. Her response was to tilt her head away from him and offer the beautiful line of her neck. He kissed her again, nibbling, tasting. The curve of her shoulder was warm and sweet. Her fragrance filled his senses. She turned toward him with no more urging, raising her arms around his shoulders. Her lips were parted and her eyes searched his face.

He watched her the entire time he bent his head. It was only at the last moment that she closed her eyes and gave herself up to him. She let him kiss her lightly at first, taste her mouth, draw her lower lip between his teeth and tug gently. It was the tip of her tongue that touched him a moment later, tickling the underside of his lip, pushing at the barrier of his teeth, and finally urging itself into his mouth. He took up the sweet battle without protest, finding the sensual dance more to his liking. He had her backed against the reddish-brown fissured bark of a hollyleaf cherry tree without quite knowing how he'd done it. One hand rested on her waist, the other traced the edging of her gown, fingers dipping below the cool satin to touch the soft, warm skin beneath it. He wanted to push her bodice lower, cup her breast, and run his thumb across the nipple until it was hard and swollen. He thought she just might let him, but he didn't press.

"It wouldn't have to be a marriage without pleasure," he whispered against her mouth.

"Just without affection," she answered. She could have pushed him away then, but she didn't. She was greedy for the taste of him; the rough wetness of his tongue against hers was exciting. His fingers teasing the

161

curve of her breast was frustrating. She wanted to lay his hand completely over her naked breast, wanted to feel the moist heat of his mouth there. Instead her own fingers pulled impatiently at his shirt so that she could touch the flat hardness of his belly. Her hand splayed across his abdomen; the skin beneath her fingers was hot. The press of his mouth was hard and hungry now and his hand had moved to the small of her back.

He leaned into her, cradling her with his thighs, wishing that she would raise her skirt and let him come into her. In his mind he saw himself lifting her until she opened for him, wrapped her legs around his flanks and settled against him, taking him full inside, her back against the hollyleaf tree, her breasts against his chest, her tongue inside his mouth imitating the rhythm that she wanted between his thighs, stroking him, building a fire in his loins . . . in his heart.

Abruptly Nathan pushed away. His breathing was harsh, his voice only a little less so. His predator eyes bore into Lydia's dark ones. "There's something else you should know about me," he said, his jaw set, the tilt of his chin defiant, even angry.

She waited, frightened now, uncertain of anything except that things had somehow gone too far. The things she had been thinking, the things she had wanted from him, embarrassed her now. She didn't want to look at him, couldn't look away.

"My crime," he said bluntly.

Lydia continued to look at him warily. She nodded once.

"Murder." He didn't try to read her face in the darkness. Instead he began to walk away.

"Nathan."

He paused. Turned. "Yes."

"I want to think about your offer," she said calmly. "I also want to know more. Come to my house later tonight, after my parents have gone to bed. Two o'clock is good.

162

You can use the side door. I'll leave it open for you."

"I don't think—"

She raised her hand to stop his objection and regarded him steadily. The air was very still around her and there was expectancy in the stillness. "Come," she said.

"Where will you be waiting?"

There was only the smallest hesitation before Lydia answered. "My bedroom," she said. "I'll wait for you in my bedroom."

Chapter Six

"This way," Lydia said, opening the front door to Brigham. The grandfather clock in the foyer struck the half hour. They both glanced at it at the same time. One-thirty. Brigham was punctual.

He gave her his hat and coat, but when she started toward the staircase he hung back. "I thought we would talk down here," he said. "In the parlor."

Lydia shook her head, a faintly coy smile on her lips. "No. Someone may rise and see the lights here. No one will think anything about it in my room. I often stay awake reading."

"Your room? But your reputation . . . What if we're found out?"

She laughed lightly. "Then you'd have to marry me, wouldn't you?"

Brigham had little choice except to follow Lydia up the stairs. They didn't speak until she shut the door to her own room and turned to face him. Brigham trapped Lydia against the door, his arms braced on either side of her, and said, "I love you."

Lydia lowered her head at the last moment and his kiss caught her on the cheek and not her mouth. She ducked under his arms and walked to the sitting area of her bedroom. She gestured toward one of the armchairs and took the rocker herself. "We'll have to keep our voices low," she said, pointing to the fireplace. "My father's room is the one beside mine. We share a chimney; sometimes one can hear things."

"I don't think I care," he said, speaking in a normal tone. "As you said, if we're discovered, you'd simply have to marry me." He leaned forward and laid his forearms on his knees. His boyish smile was earnest, his green eyes frank and honest in their anticipation of Lydia. She was still wearing her dark blue evening gown, and the beadwork on the bodice caught the firelight, drawing Brig's attention to the fullness of her breasts. The line of her collarbone emphasized the shadowed hollow of her throat. It was difficult to look at her now and not think of taking her to bed, yet before this evening he had wondered how he was going to take her to bed while looking at her. "You'd make me a very happy man by agreeing to marry me, Lydia."

"Why?" she asked.

He was startled for a moment. A frown appeared between his brows and he brushed back a lock of sandy hair with his fingertips. "Because I love you."

"I know you've said that—and I hope you'll forgive me for speaking so baldly—but other men have said the same thing to me. What they really meant was: Lydia, I love your money."

"Have I given you the impression I need money?"

"No, but then neither did they."

"I see," he said slowly. "Perhaps you need to know that your money would not be unwelcome. I'm not so removed from the workhouse that I couldn't appreciate it. However, it's not necessary. I don't *need* it, Lydia. You can leave it all behind when we go to Ballaburn, let your mother spend it, give it to the orphanage, or your maid. I don't care. It's you I need, nothing else . . . no one else. Can you understand that?"

"It's difficult to believe."

"Would it help if I approached you on bended knee?" he asked.

"No, oh, no!" She started to laugh as he left his chair and fell on one knee in front of her. "Please don't." Then he was on both knees, his hands folded in a single fist, raised toward her in the posture of prayer. "Stop it, Brig, how am I ever to take you seriously?"

Brigham took Lydia's wrists and gently pulled her off the rocking chair and onto the floor. "How can you not?" he said softly, solemnly. His mouth was very near hers; his eyes were darkening. He saw Lydia's gaze drop to his mouth, raise to his eyes again, then back to his mouth. She didn't need to say what she wanted. Brig knew.

Lydia let him kiss her this time. Over his shoulder she watched the clock on her mantel. She suspected Nathan would be as punctual as Brigham, and that left her with fifteen minutes to fill. Brigham's kisses left her with no doubt how he would like to spend the next minutes. She pushed lightly at his shoulders, tilting her head back and taking a long draught of air. "Brig," she said. His mouth moved to her neck. She felt his tongue lick at the base of her throat. She said his name again, softly this time and with just a hint of breathlessness. "No, Brig, I can't think when you do that."

"I don't want you to think. I want you to feel."

Lydia inched away from him, batting his hands lightly and playfully when he made to reach for her. "I know what I feel when you touch me like that," she said. Revulsion. Pain. Disgust. None of that showed in her voice. She got to her feet. "Tell me about Banna . . . Bacca . . ."

"Ballaburn."

"Yes, Ballaburn. Is that the name of your estate?"

"Estate." He laughed, returning to his chair. "That's too grand a word. It's a station. A sheep ranch. Ballaburn raises some of the finest Merino sheep in the world. Our wool is prime."

"And can you make money doing that?"

"Back to the money, are we?"

"Well, yes." Lydia's attention was caught by a noise

167

somewhere down the hall. She pressed her hands to her middle. "Please, Brig, excuse me. I think I hear—" She broke off as she headed toward the door. "I'll only be a moment. Wait for me."

Brig's tawny eyebrows were drawn together. Something was not as it should be. Lydia's sudden attack of nerves alerted and alarmed him. Had she heard one of her parents? Madeline? Brig realized he was better prepared to face Samuel's censure than Madeline's. Samuel would want him to marry Lydia; Madeline would want to draw blood.

Lydia slipped into the hallway and hurried toward the back stairs that Nathan would be using. He was a third of the way up when she saw him. "You'll have to be more quiet," she whispered.

Nathan nearly laughed aloud at her admonishment. "I'm not near the sneaksman I used to be," he said softly. His hand slipped around her waist when he reached her. He was standing on the step below the landing and their faces were even. "Are you certain you want me here, Lydia? It's not too late. I could leave now and come back in the morning."

She shook her head and her fingertips found the side of his face. She touched his jaw, his cheek, the corner of his mouth. "The morning will be too late," she said. "I'll have come to my senses by then. You must know why I want you here." The look in his eyes was all the confirmation she required. He thought she asked him to come to finish what they began earlier in the evening. He didn't believe that she wanted answers to her questions, didn't believe that she deserved a better explanation for his incredible marriage proposal. He, like Brig, thought she wanted him in her bed.

Lydia kissed Nathan full on the mouth. "This way," she said, placing a finger to her lips. Taking his hand, she led him along the dark hallway to her bedroom. She paused at the door, opening it carefully and soundlessly. "You first."

The moment Nathan was inside Lydia slammed the door behind him, turned the key in the lock, and waited.

"Lydia?" Brig asked, turning away from the window.

"Lydia?" Nathan asked, turning toward the closed door.

"Nathan!"

"Brig!" Nathan spun on his heel and faced his old friend.

"Lydia!" They both shouted her name simultaneously, realizing they'd been had.

Nathan tried the door and found it locked. "Damn you, Lydia, open up. We'll wake the entire house."

"If you haven't already," she whispered harshly from the other side of the door. "Do you think I care? I'm quite safe on this side." She took the key from the lock, dropped it between her breasts, and went in search of her father's shotgun.

"She's gone," Nathan said, leaning against the door. His mouth curled to one side in self-deprecating humor. "I'd say the little baggage had this planned."

"Baggage?" repeated Brig. "Little bitch is more like it. What's she up to?"

"I'm certain we're going to find out."

"Can't you do something about the lock?"

Nathan bent, looked at the keyhole, and shook his head. "She's taken the key. By the time I get the door open, she'll be back. I don't think she plans to be gone long." He straightened. "Did you propose to her this evening?"

Brig nodded. "You?"

"Yes."

"Did she give you an answer?"

"No. What about you?"

"No."

Nathan sighed. "I'd say we've been found out, wouldn't you? She's more her father's daughter than I would ever have supposed."

"Too right she is." He was not amused by the revela-

169

tion. It was anger that brightened his eyes, nothing else. "Madeline whelped a blue-blooded bitch."

Jamming his hands in his pockets, Nathan moved away from the door when he heard Lydia's approach. "Have a care, Brig," Nathan said softly. "The least we can do is let her say her piece."

"Do you really think she might still choose one of us?"

Nathan shrugged. "She might." Behind him the key grated in the lock and the door opened. The first thing to enter the room was the barrel of a shotgun. He backed away respectfully.

Lydia kicked the door closed and waved the shotgun in the general direction of Nathan and Brig, indicating that they should move closer together. They complied without argument, both of them standing on the marble apron of the fireplace, backs to the mantel. "Thank you," she said calmly. "I shouldn't want to have to use this. You may as well know that I don't know much about a shotgun at all. I chose it because it sprays the shot. If I have to fire, I don't think I can miss."

"You know enough," Nathan said under his breath. She couldn't miss. Whether or not she had the will to shoot was another matter entirely. Nathan wasn't willing to put her to the test and he hoped Brigham felt the same way. "Are you going to tell us why you've brought both of us here?"

"It's not because I have any intention of marrying," she said. She saw the sharp look that Brig cast in Nathan's direction. She had never witnessed a more eloquent I-told-you-so. "That you think I could still consider it proves how depraved you both are. After tonight I want nothing to do with either one of you. I'm only sorry it's taken this long to bring you together in such a manner. I should have liked to settle this the day after I heard you both talking in the garden. Remember?" Her cobalt-blue eyes strayed to Nathan. "Mother chanced upon us in the gazebo."

"I remember."

"Only it wasn't chance." Now she directed her gaze at Brigham. "You made certain my mother was in the garden." Her eyes regarded both of them calmly. "Your mistake was in supposing you could talk freely beneath my window."

Nathan and Brigham tried to recall what had been said between them that night.

"Does it really matter?" she asked, divining their thoughts. "I learned enough to know that neither of you had any respect for me or cared anything about my feelings. I'm not certain I understand the nature of the game you're playing and therefore I know nothing of the rules. I had to invent my own, gentlemen. I suffered Brig's attentions these last three weeks while I waited for Nathan to try to see me again. I'm glad I wasn't wrong about you, Mr. Hunter. I had hoped so very much that you wouldn't give up. I'm only sorry Mother made it so difficult for you. Papa, however, righted the balance by directing you to the orphanage."

The shotgun was heavy in Lydia's arms and she lowered the barrel fractionally. "It happened just in time, I think, because Brigham was merely looking for the proper setting to make his proposal. The Newberrys' fountain, Brig?" she scoffed. "Really. How could I take you seriously there? All those gaping marble fish." She made a show of shuddering, oblivious to the anger flushing Brigham's features or the tension at the corners of Nathan's mouth. "And you, Nathan, so willing to follow suit when I let you believe that your friend had proposed. Your offer was a novel one, I must say. I admire you for not dressing it up with pretty speeches about love and desire. Brigham was not nearly so forthright. He wanted me to believe that our marriage was for an eternity. You were quite clear about needing me only for a year."

Brig turned his head sharply in Nathan's direction. "You told her that? Were you mad?"

Nathan didn't answer. He was watching the shotgun, watching it sag still lower in Lydia's arms.

171

"I think you're both mad," said Lydia. "Or so full of yourselves that you've lost all sense of good judgment. Coming here tonight, for instance. How easily you were convinced with a few kisses; how simply you were fooled into believing you were desired. You were fortunate I didn't vomit at your feet. God knows, I wanted to."

"Lydia," Nathan said, a note of caution in his voice. Beside him Brigham's fury was palpable.

She went on heedlessly. "If I was a fool in the beginning, you were fools at the end. My way is infinitely more satisfying."

Brigham looked as if he were ready to leap at her. Nathan knocked him aside and lunged sideways himself. The shot from Lydia's gun blasted harmlessly into the wall, mantelpiece, and hearth. She was so shocked by her own actions that she screamed and dropped the gun. Nathan scrambled to his feet, picked up the gun, and since it was useless after one firing, thrust it back in Lydia's shaking hands.

"You might have killed us," he said in a low voice. There was running in the hallway now, cries for Lydia, a call for the servants. He recognized Samuel's voice, then Pei Ling's. "You'd do well to think how your life might be different if that had happened."

Her entire body was trembling now, but she faced Nathan squarely. "You're supposing that your lives are worth something." Brigham was coming toward her and she spit on the floor at his feet. "What are two digger convicts more or less to the rest of the world?" Brigham's hand evaded the block that Nathan threw up and connected solidly with Lydia's face. She slammed against the door just as it was being opened from the other side.

"Lydia!" It was Samuel. "Lydia! Answer me! What's going on in there?"

"That was stupid, Brig," said Nathan. He held Brigham back when it looked as if he'd go after Lydia again. "Answer Samuel," he told Lydia. "He's liable to come in here shooting."

Samuel did indeed have a gun when he entered the room, a pearl-handled Colt that hadn't been used in recent years but was kept in primed condition nonetheless. Lydia leaned the shotgun against the wall. Her left cheek was stained red in the aftermath of Brig's slap. "These men were just leaving, Papa," she said calmly.

In the doorway, Pei Ling was brushed aside as Madeline stormed into the room. She yanked the belt of her satin wrapper closed and surveyed the occupants of the room and the damage.

"Samuel? What have you done? What does this mean?" she demanded.

Samuel's voice was as calm and even as Lydia's. "Lydia tells me these gentlemen were just leaving, Madeline."

"Leaving? Of course they're going to leave. But what are they doing here in the first place?"

"Lydia?" asked Samuel. He kept his revolver leveled on Nathan and Brigham, although he thought there was no danger. Neither of them appeared to be armed and neither appeared inclined to put forth an explanation. Brigham Moore was breathing a tad heavily and there was a coldness about his eyes that put Samuel in mind of Madeline when she was angry. Nathan, on the other hand, was much more difficult to comprehend. His wolf's eyes were implacable, his features shuttered by indifference. His shoulder was placed to the right and a little in front of Brigham, but Samuel couldn't tell if he was shielding Brigham or planning to hold him back. "Lydia," he said again, "answer your mother."

"They proposed to me tonight, Mother," she said.

"My God!" Madeline's hand went to her throat and her gaze was frozen on Brigham. "This is absolute madness! They proposed here? You invited them here to make their proposals?" Her anger was icy. Her mouth was set stiffly and the blue flame in the depths of her eyes added not a whit of heat.

"I invited them here *after* they made their offers," she explained simply.

"You mean you accepted both of them?"

"No, neither of them."

In the hallway, Pei Ling covered her mouth to smother a giggle. Her dark eyes darted from Lydia to her suitors to her parents. Other servants were crowding the corridor now and Pei Ling motioned them to be quiet else they would miss everything.

"You decided to shoot them instead?" asked Samuel. He plucked at his graying mustache thoughtfully. It was a damned French farce, he thought. He was standing about in his nightshirt, holding a gun on his daughter's suitors while his wife asked angry questions, his mistress giggled, and the servants gaped behind him. He wasn't even concerned about a scandal. Who would believe this of the Chadwicks? "Or perhaps they asked you to. Put them out of their misery, so to speak."

"Samuel," Madeline gasped. "How can you joke about this? Lydia's gone entirely too far this time. Not only is she dressing like a bawd, wearing gowns Madame Simone meant for a gambling-hall hostess, she's acting like one. And you can't say I didn't try to warn her. Didn't I tell her Mr. Moore was a convict and Mr. Hunter no gentleman? Yet you permitted her to entertain them both. At least I had the good sense to stop Mr. Hunter's messages and his flowers. *You* saw to it that he was invited to the Newberrys' party."

"A mistake," Samuel acknowledged softly. He noticed that Brigham seemed about to say something, but that an almost imperceptible nudge from Nathan stopped him. "Do you men have anything to say for yourselves? No? Lydia? There's more you want to say?"

"Only that I was the object of some rivalry between them, Papa. Whatever their interest, it wasn't me . . . not really."

Samuel indicated both men with a slight movement of his gun. "Well, since you seem to have worn out your welcome, if indeed you were welcomed at all, you had better take your leave." He raised his eyebrows in

174

question at Lydia. "You had something particular in mind, Daughter?"

Lydia nodded. "The window, Papa. I was going to ask them to leave by the window."

Now Brig spoke up. "I hardly think that's necessary, now that our presence is no secret. I'll leave the same way I came in—through the door Lydia *opened* for me."

Samuel raised his weapon and pulled back the hammer. "Not just yet, I think. Lydia, Mr. Moore's made a good point. Their presence is certainly no secret now. Was there some other reason you wanted these men to use the window?"

"Yes, Papa." Her features were serene, her smile beatific. "I asked Mr. Leeds to fertilize and mulch the flower beds today, especially the one just below my window."

From the hallway there was a burst of laughter. Samuel ignored it while Madeline slammed the door in the face of it. "You mean," Samuel said, "that just beneath your window is a load of fresh manure?"

"Very fresh. And lots of it. I specifically asked Mr. Leeds to see to it."

Brigham's anger exploded. Color mottled his complexion. The boyish features that were so handsome in repose were contorted with rage. "Damn you! I will not be humiliated at your whim."

"That's quite enough, Mr. Moore," Samuel said. "I think you'll gracefully take the exit my daughter's left you or you'll go out the door in a pine box. I won't have any trouble gathering witnesses to say I shot a thief. You are a convict, after all. I doubt there will be much of an inquiry."

"Damn all of you," Brig said softly. His eyes rested briefly on each of the Chadwicks; then he turned abruptly and stalked to the window Lydia indicated earlier. "You coming, Nath?"

"In a moment."

Brigham threw up the sash. The sweet pungent odor of

manure was like a slap in the face. Until that moment he had hoped Lydia was bluffing. He threw a quick glance over his shoulder as he climbed over the sill. Madeline's features were rigid, her face drained of all color. What he remembered most as he jumped was that she made no real protest to stop it from happening.

Inside the room the occupants heard a thud as Brig landed. His curses followed immediately. Nathan waited for Lydia's smile to fade before he spoke. "You've had your moment," he said. "I can even find it in me to applaud that lion's heart of yours, Lydia. I wish I could believe that you fully understood the nature of the enemy you've made this day."

Lydia shivered under the strength of his piercing glance and stepped closer to her father. "Are you threatening me?" she asked.

Nathan shook his head. "Warning you."

There was no scandal. None. Members of the household staff remarked on the events of that night among themselves, but never breathed a word beyond the granite walls of the mansion. Madeline took to her room for most of the day, but when she emerged it was as if nothing had ever happened. Lydia was confined to her room for three days—for her protection, her father said; for punishment, her mother said—and when she joined her parents again, not even marginally repentant for what she'd done, her father hired a bodyguard. Samuel alone dwelled on Nathan's parting words.

"You'll come with me, won't you, Pei Ling?" Lydia asked, getting up from the table where she'd eaten breakfast. "I don't want to go to Madame Simone's alone and Mother has a headache this morning."

Pei Ling began clearing away the dishes and handed them to the downstairs maid. "You not go alone," she said. "Mista Campbell go with you. You forget already you have company wherever you go?"

She thrust out her lower lip and sighed theatrically. "I wish I could forget. Papa has clearly taken a notion into his head and won't let it rest. Perhaps if you spoke to him."

Stricken, Pei Ling quickly shooed the other maid away. She could not meet Lydia's eyes.

Lydia was immediately contrite. They had never spoken of Pei Ling's relationship with Samuel, each preferring to believe the other did not know the exact nature of the liaison. "Of course you can't talk to him about it," Lydia said. "It was stupid of me to ask. I did not mean to presume on our friendship."

"I already speak to Samuel," Pei Ling said softly. She raised her dark, almond-shaped eyes to Lydia. They were very old eyes in a very young face. "I tell him I think he right. Mista Campbell good idea. You wound pride of men that night. Not so easy for men to forget. I happy Samuel hire man to watch you. I do most anything in world for you, Miss Liddy, but I not do this."

"I understand," Lydia said softly. She touched Pei Ling's satin sleeve. "Tell me, do you love my father?"

"Only one person I love more," she said. "You give me everything, Miss Liddy. My life and my love."

Lydia wondered if her father knew the depth of Pei Ling's feelings, and if he did, did he return them.

"You need anything else?" Pei Ling asked.

"What? Oh . . . no." She came out of her reverie. "No, there's nothing else. I suppose I shall go to my last fitting with Mr. Campbell in tow. I wonder if those spindle-legged chairs in Madame Simone's salon can hold him?"

George Campbell faced the prospect of going to Madame Simone's with admirable stoicism. At least that was Lydia's evaluation of his impassive demeanor. She did not find him particularly expressive in manner or conversation, and the ride to the salon was like every other time she was in his company: silent. She noticed his pale-blue eyes darted constantly, taking in everything around him and rarely lighting on her except to assure himself that she was still in his presence and unharmed.

Once they were at the salon Mr. Campbell stayed in the entrance hall and never gave Lydia the satisfaction of seeing him in one of Madame Simone's delicate chairs. Instead he leaned his massive shoulder against the door-jamb, occasionally glanced toward the street through the window, and sipped tea from a china cup that all but disappeared in the heart of his large palms.

Lydia forgot about him as she tried on two gowns for final alterations and leafed through pattern books and examined the latest Paris designs. She chose material for an evening gown, a riding skirt, and several day dresses while Madame Simone hovered near her shoulder, commenting on all of Lydia's choices. The salon's three seamstresses worked on the alterations while Lydia waited, and when the gowns were finished they were wrapped and boxed in the backroom, then handed to George Campbell to carry. Lydia enjoyed the sight of her giant protector carrying dress boxes to the carriage. Perhaps, she thought, he'd think twice before following her everywhere. What sort of danger had he thought Madame Simone's held?

Once she was home Lydia cut the parcel string and unwrapped her new gowns. Lying between them was a small, flat brown-paper package. She picked it up, turning it over in her hands, wondering if she should open it. It wasn't hers, of that she was certain. She hadn't ordered any trimming or fabric for herself. One of the seamstresses had put it with her things by mistake, she decided. She was about to toss it aside when she saw the faint writing in one corner. It was her name and it had been scrawled in pencil with an impatient hand.

"What's Madame Simone giving me?" she wondered aloud, sitting down on the edge of her bed. Lydia slid the string off the package and unfolded the paper. Her fingers

178

trembled when she saw the contents. She stared, suddenly grateful for her father's foresight and George Campbell's constant presence.

Lydia lifted the scrap of yellow bloodstained fabric between her fingertips, knowing full well what she held and still not wanting to believe it. Nathan's attempt at blackmail was obscene and she shook inwardly now, her skin cold and prickly. She had no difficulty recognizing the material for what it was: the bodice ruffle from her yellow ballgown. It was Charlotte's blood on the gown, but Lydia remembered it had been left in Ginny's room where she had changed her clothes.

Nathan had been quick to tell her about returning the borrowed blue gown to Ginny, but he had failed to mention that he was in possession of the hated yellow one. Lydia could think of only one reason for his failure. He had been holding the knowledge in reserve for an occasion such as this, waiting to see if he would need it to bend her to his will.

"Damn him," she said softly. "Damn him to hell." There was a note pinned to the ragged end of the ruffle where it had been torn free of the gown. The note was crisply folded into quarters and Lydia opened it carefully, afraid she might tear the sharp seams. *We need to discuss this. Silver Lady. Midnight Thursday.*

Lydia dropped the scrap of fabric back on the brown paper, wrapped it quickly, and stuffed it under her mattress. Today was Monday. She had three days to prepare for her meeting with Nathan, three days to decide how she was going to handle his ugly, underhanded attempt to make her accept his proposal. She walked briskly to the bellpull and rang for Pei Ling.

"I want you to go to the offices of the *Gazette* and *Herald*," she said without preamble when Pei Ling arrived. "Bring back every issue since the night of my charity ball. Get someone to help you carry them and try not to let Mother or Papa see you bring them into the

179

house." She thrust a gold piece into Pei Ling's hands. "I need them quickly, Pei Ling. I need your help and your silence."

Pei Ling's hesitation was so brief as to be nonexistent. She could not fathom why there should be any urgency regarding some old newspapers. It was an odd but harmless request, and Pei Ling never considered revealing it to Samuel or Mr. Campbell. She took one of the kitchen helpers with her and gave him change from Lydia's gold piece to buy his silence.

Lydia excused herself from the dinner table that evening after making a halfhearted attempt at eating. She pretended not to see the worried, puzzled glances that her mother and father exchanged. There was nothing she could share with them. They would be far more concerned if they knew why she was so anxious to return to her room.

Scissors in hand, Lydia cut out every article she found about Ginny Flynt's death, scouring the papers to make certain she missed nothing. There were only six of them. The longest, most detailed accounts were those in the *Gazette*, written a day and two days after Ginny's death. The *Herald*'s articles did not contain graphic descriptions. Each paper gave a separate notice in the obituaries. They all had one thing in common, however, and it was a surprise.

Ginny Flynt was not murdered, as Nathan had said. According to the newspapers, she had committed suicide.

Lydia leaned back against her intricately carved walnut headboard and closed her eyes. The clippings lay on her right, the newspapers were scattered all over the quilted bedspread. She held the sharp end of the scissors in her hand and tapped the other end against her knees as she tried to think, tried to make sense of what she had read.

It wasn't true, of course. Ginny had not committed suicide. Lydia refused to believe it. Certainly the death of Charlotte and the baby had been a hard blow, but Ginny had given no sign that she was hurting to the point of complete hopelessness. Ginny was not despondent.

How would she know? Lydia asked herself, recalling that she had hardly been in a state that night to be aware of another's feelings. But suicide? Ginny? No, it couldn't be true. Yet the papers were reporting it as a suicide. She had slashed her wrists, cutting them with a razor blade the police found lying on the floor by her bed. The *Gazette* reporter described the scene with adjectives like blood-soaked, sanguine, and crimson when referring to the bedsheets, and fair-haired, voluptuous, and naked when referring to Ginny. He re-created the grim events of that evening for the reader, using the facts as he interpreted them, making no apology when his imagination filled in the gaps of real knowledge. He related the deaths in the brothel earlier that evening and drew the conclusion that Ginny was grieving for her friend, for the baby, for herself, and suicide presented itself as a natural, even logical escape from the misery of her existence. He described how Ginny must have taken off the blue gown she was wearing so it would not be spattered with her own blood, how she wielded the razor with deliberate strokes, and how she must have lay there, fearful, curious, and somehow satisfied that life itself was leaving her body.

Lydia dropped the scissors and held her fingers to her temples, willing herself not to be sick. It didn't matter what the papers reported. Ginny hadn't killed herself; she would never believe it was true. Nathan hadn't believed it, either. He had never even hinted that the accounts called it anything but murder, and Lydia wondered about that now. Had he based his knowledge on his brief acquaintance with Ginny Flynt and his assessment of her character, or had he another reason for naming her death a murder? In spite of his words to the contrary, was he the murderer?

There was no mention in any account of a certain yellow ballgown, bloodied and crumpled, lying in one corner of Ginny's bedroom. There was only one reason the *Gazette* reporter had failed to make something of it and that was because it hadn't been there when he was. Nathan had dropped the blue gown when he left, but he had obviously seen the yellow one and taken it. Instead of destroying it, he'd kept it. Perhaps he had never really considered how it might be of use to him. Indeed, if Lydia had agreed to his marriage offer, she might never have known he had it. But she had humiliated him, made an enemy, and he was showing her now what that meant.

Dazed by her discovery, Lydia slid off the bed and built a fire in her fireplace. She put the clippings in the drawer of her nightstand, but she burned the newspapers and eventually the package Nathan had sent her. The damning reminder that she had also been in Ginny's room the evening of her death disappeared in light and heat and a curl of smoke. She went to bed then, wondering if she should meet Nathan, wondering if she dared.

In the end, she felt as if she had no choice. She bought a gun. George Campbell helped her choose one, a nickel-plated derringer that she could hold easily in the palm of her hand and keep concealed in her reticule. Lydia couldn't tell if he was secretly amused by her purchase or a little bit hurt that she thought he couldn't protect her. Lydia decided it was best she didn't know. She had no intention of telling him that she was plotting her escape from Nob Hill.

"Where to now, Miss Chadwick?" he asked as they walked out of the gunsmith's. He opened the door to the carriage and helped her inside.

"The cemetery on Russian Hill," she said.

Campbell's craggy features were perfectly still. He gave the driver directions and followed Lydia inside the cab. "The cemetery?" he asked when they were beyond the driver's hearing. He glanced at the roses on the seat beside her. "That's why you took those from the garden?"

182

"Yes."

"If you don't mind me asking . . . the gun, the flowers, the cemetery . . . it's not my funeral you're planning, is it?"

Lydia was so startled by his unexpected conclusion that she burst out laughing.

George Campbell was not particularly comforted that she didn't answer his question. He received his answer at the cemetery itself. Lydia walked up and down the rows of headstones until she came across the ones she was looking for. They were side by side, just beyond the umbrella shade of a weeping willow. The ground on top of the graves hadn't settled yet and the tufts of grass were uneven in their sprouting. George looked at the headstones as Lydia bent to arrange the flowers at the base of the first. *Charlotte Adams and Child. At Peace.* And the second: *Virginia Flynt. She Touches Heaven's Gate.* The stones were newer than even the graves, unmarked by last night's rain. He wondered about the women she was mourning, why, if they were close friends or relatives, she wasn't wearing black and why she had difficulty finding the graves. He wondered why there were no dates on the stones.

Lydia straightened and stepped back from the graves. "We can go now, Mr. Campbell. I've made my peace." The stones were exactly as she had requested and she silently thanked Pei Ling for taking care of the things she could not. She felt George Campbell move closer to her back as another carriage wound its way up the hill and a man on horseback appeared above them at the crest. Lydia found his precaution disconcerting when there was nothing remotely sinister about the presence of other mourners in a cemetery. The horse and rider disappeared and the carriage stopped long before it reached them. Lydia wanted to chide her bearish protector, but didn't. She remembered how simple Nathan had found it to reach out to her through Madame Simone. This very

183

night she would be on her own and perhaps she would have reason to regret incautious words.

Leaving the house was not terribly difficult. Mr. Campbell had gone to his own home hours earlier once Lydia assured him she was not going out for the rest of the evening. It was not strictly a lie, she told herself, since it was now Thursday morning, or at least it was after midnight. Nathan had chosen a poor time to request the meeting since Lydia's father was only just retiring at that hour. She would be late for her appointment at the Silver Lady, but she would be there.

She had no choice but to walk, but she did have the foresight to wear clothes she lifted from her father's wardrobe. A pair of his mining dungarees that should have been given to the rag picker long ago were belted around her waist with a cord from her drapes. She wore a baggy flannel shirt, three pairs of woolen socks to fill out the shoes which were already stuffed with paper, and a slouch hat low over her forehead. Her hair had been pulled into a tight knot on the crown of her head and stuffed under the hat. She also wore a navy-blue woolen jacket with large pockets to hide her hands, the derringer, and the check she had drafted from her own account at the Bank of America.

Keeping her head low, she walked through Chinatown and Portsmouth Square unmolested and sauntered through the lobby of the Silver Lady as if she had every right to be there. She knocked briskly on the door of Nathan's suite and barely heard the sound above her heart knocking against her ribs.

The door opened quickly, without warning that anyone was approaching it, and Lydia was unceremoniously hauled inside. She found little comfort in the knowledge that Brigham was as stunned by her appearance as she was by his.

"You!" she said, yanking her wrist free of his grasp.

184

"What are you doing here?" He was wearing evening clothes, a black-tailed coat, white satin vest and shirt, and black trousers. His sandy hair was touseled and his face a bit flushed as if he had been exerting himself moments earlier.

Brigham made no attempt to retake her arm. His green eyes darted over her, taking in her odd attire. Her shape-lessness didn't fool him now. He had touched her breasts, had felt their fullness. He knew the smallness of her waist and the silky thickness of her sable hair. Anyone could be forgiven for thinking her plain, as he had once upon a time, but he knew better. Her grave cobalt-blue eyes drew his attention. He smiled. "My, you are resourceful, aren't you? There are unexpected depths to you, I'm thinking. May I have your hat? Take your coat?"

Lydia shook her head. "Is it both of you then? Is that why you're here?"

"Both of us?" Brig reached behind Lydia, turned the key in the lock and pocketed it.

She tried not show the confusion his action caused her. "Both of you," she repeated, looking around the suite for Nathan. "The note . . . the gown . . . never mind." Had she said too much? Brigham was studying her with a cool, remote glance, his tawny brows slightly raised. "It doesn't matter. I'm here to see Nathan. Where is he?"

Brigham pointed to the bedroom. "Nath won't be much company," he said. "He's passed out, I'm afraid. Almost drowned in his bath water. I only just put him to bed. We've been out this evening, drinking since after dinner, but I stopped a half dozen shy of Nath."

Lydia frowned. Brig didn't smell as if he'd been drinking and she was standing close enough that she should have been able to tell. She glanced uncertainly in the direction of the bedroom.

"Go on," Brig said. He laughed shortly. "You can stop looking at me as if you expect to get tossed on your head—out the window." He followed her in. A lamp was burning on the bedside table. "If I'm going to toss you at all, it'll be on that bed."

Her head snapped up. Brig's tone held not a whit of humor. His voice was low, resonant with suppressed anger and echoing danger. She tried to duck under his arm and go back to the sitting room, but he blocked her path easily.

"I think you said you wanted to see Nathan," he said. This time his smile did not reach his eyes. He caught her shoulders, spun her around, and pushed her further into the room.

Nathan was there. He was lying on his side in the bed and deeply asleep. A sheet was tangled around the length of his bare legs. It covered his buttocks and the lower half of his chest, preserving modesty but leaving no doubt that he was naked beneath it. He didn't stir as Brig prodded Lydia forward by placing a hand at the small of her back.

"I've seen enough," said Lydia. "There's no reason for me to stay. I must have been mistaken about tonight."

"No mistake," Brig said, blocking her way again. "Why don't you sit there . . . on the corner of the bed?"

"No." The single word was drawn out, more of a protest than a flat refusal. "Please let me pass."

"Aaaah," he said gently, as if making a discovery. "The lady pleads prettily."

Lydia's chin came up. The brim of the slouch hat shaded her face. "I'm not pleading. I'm merely being polite." She was standing toe-to-toe with him, and inside her pockets her hands were curled into fists. The knuckles of one hand brushed the derringer, the knuckles of the other, the check. She was frightened of Brig, of the anger that more closely resembled a young boy's petulance and peevish willfulness than a rational man's temper. When he would not move aside she asked, "Do you know why I'm here?"

"Of course. Nathan told me what he had planned.

Really, Lydia, hasn't experience taught you that we don't have many secrets? Why don't you sit down and we'll talk about it?"

Lydia finally accepted Brig was not going to let her back in the sitting room until it served his purpose. She sat heavily, hoping to jog Nathan into wakefulness though she had no clear idea what she expected from him. He flopped onto his belly and lay motionless. Lydia withdrew the check. "I haven't filled in an amount," she said, smoothing the paper over her knee. "Here, take it. Fill in any amount you like."

Brig kicked the bedroom door closed with the heel of his shoe. Leaning back against it, he crossed his arms. "You must have a great deal of money to make an offer like that. How do you know I won't bankrupt you?"

"I'm hoping you'll be reasonable about this."

"Yes, of course. Reasonable." His lips flattened and one corner of his mouth lifted in disgust. "You forced me out a window, remember? I was ankle-deep in manure. Was that reasonable?"

Lydia held out the check. "Here. Take it."

Brig reached for it, caught it in his fingertips, and resumed his position at the door. "You've made it out to Nathan," he said. He folded it neatly into quarters, creasing each fold with his fingernails to make the lines sharp and clean. He fiddled with the paper absently, studying Lydia with a remote, impartial gaze.

Unable to help it, Lydia shivered, and looked away from what he was doing. The sound of his nails skimming across the paper may as well have been a cat scratching slate, her reaction was the same. Her skin prickled and she gritted her teeth. She didn't look at him again until he finished. "What are you going to do with it?" she asked as he dropped it into his vest pocket and smoothed the slight bulge with the flat of his hand.

"It's no good to me, is it? You've made it out to Nathan."

"That's because I didn't know you were his partner in this as well," she said. "I'd have made it out to you both otherwise."

"Are you really so naive?" he asked. "Do you think either one of us can simply take this to your bank and get the money? You're likely to have all manner of police waiting for us in that event, to say nothing of that fellow who follows you everywhere. Nath and I won't be taken in so easily. We have too much to lose—Nathan especially."

"Then you'll want cash." She should have realized they wouldn't trust her. She didn't trust them.

Brigham shrugged.

"I want the gown," Lydia went on. "All of it. Every scrap and furbelow. I don't want to be at your beck and call the rest of my life."

"Quite understandable. But we're at an impasse, don't you think? The gown's here, but your money isn't." He went to Nathan's wardrobe, opened it, and showed her the yellow gown hanging on the inside of the door. "See? The way Nathan tells it, this gown puts you in Miss Bailey's brothel the night two women died. Not the sort of thing you'd want common knowledge." He took the gown off its hook, fingered the fabric idly, then tossed it under the bed. "Your parents would be horrified. Nob Hill would be talking about it for years."

"That's why I've come," she said quietly, then added more forcefully, "But don't think I care overmuch for my reputation. My conscience is clear. I did nothing to cause the deaths of either Charlotte or Ginny."

"You didn't? I understand you threw the doctor out when Charlotte was giving birth."

Lydia gasped softly. "Nathan told you that?"

Brigham smiled. "I told you there weren't many secrets." He struck a casual pose, resting his arm against the mantel. There was a decanter of liquor and a tumbler half filled with the same liquid near his fingertips. He circled the rim of the tumbler with his forefinger. "Anyway, it's Nathan's reputation I'm more concerned about than yours. He's the one in need of protection. This is not the first time he's been involved in a murder like this."

"The newspapers say Ginny's death was a suicide," she said, struggling for calm.

"Nathan says he knows differently. He says it was murder. You can forgive him for tying one on tonight, can't you? He's been afraid for weeks that you'd go to the police. That's why we decided it was necessary to confront you with the gown. Nathan wants to be certain you'll maintain your silence."

"Then you don't want money for the gown."

Brigham shook his head. "No, I'm afraid the gown was merely the bait to get you here, Lydia, and get you here alone. We can't give it up, or what's to keep you silent then?"

"My word."

"Not good enough. But I've thought of something."

Lydia knew what was coming, had suspected it all along. The only surprise was that it was coming from Brigham and not Nathan. She stood. "You'll have to believe I'm not going to say anything." She started to go, dodging Brig's arm as he stuck it out to stop her. He caught her easily, drawing her arm up and behind her. Her struggle was brief, and when it was over Brigham was holding her derringer. She hadn't even felt his hand inside her pocket.

He let her go and examined the gun. "You should have used this immediately. Else why carry it?" He aimed it at her. "There's only one agreeable solution short of killing you," he said. "And that's to take you out of the country. It wouldn't be abduction, not in the strictest sense, not if you were my wife."

"*Your* wife?" she asked. "Not Nathan's?"

"I'm not *that* concerned about his protection. I still want you for myself."

Lydia glanced toward the bed again. "He didn't pass

189

out, did he? You drugged him." She called herself all manner of fool for not realizing it immediately. "You two have a peculiar sort of partnership. Each with your eye toward the main chance. You'll work together when it suits you, work alone when it suits you more."

"That's always been our nature. We've been friends for a long time, Lydia. This won't change anything."

"Why am I so important to either one of you?" she demanded. Her voice broke and she fought back agitation and fear in order to have control again. "Is it all for the sake of some ridiculous wager set between you?"

Brigham didn't answer her question. He asked one of his own instead. "Are you in agreement, Lydia? Will you freely marry me?"

"Not you. Not Nathan. You're insane to think I would."

He sighed, dropped the derringer in his pocket, and backed Lydia against the bed. The mattress caught her knees and she sat down abruptly. "You're going to make things difficult, aren't you?"

She stared at him, unable to look away.

Brigham took off her hat and tossed it aside. "Undo your hair," he said flatly. She shied away when his fingertips brushed her cheek. "Don't do that again." Lydia opened her mouth to scream, but the sound was cut off by the hand he clamped across her lips. "That's something else you should have done right away. It's too late for that now." Hauling her up in his arms, Brig pushed her toward the mantel. He lifted the tumbler of liquor he had fiddled with earlier and didn't waste a moment telling her what he expected her to do, or ask her permission. The hand that covered her mouth shifted quickly to pinch off her nose. It didn't matter if Lydia's lips parted to scream or draw a breath, the end was the same: Brig poured the liquor down her throat. She coughed and sputtered, tried to spit it out, but was forced to swallow most of it. "It will take a little while to feel the full effects," he told her, easing his grip slightly. "Nathan

190

fought it, but you can see that it did no good. And he had even less of the stuff than you." The hand at her waist slipped under her baggy flannel shirt and cotton camisole and slid upward to her breast. Her skin was cool to the touch. "What we do until you pass out is up to you. Afterward, it will be up to me. You could take down your hair now and save me the trouble later."

"I don't think so," she said, pressing the barrel of her derringer against his ribs. "Feel that? You're not the only one with light fingers."

Brig's eyes widened slightly but he didn't remove his hand from her breast. His thumb brushed her nipple, raising it to pearl-like hardness. There was amusement in his voice, not anger, not fear. "You don't think much of my marriage proposal, do you?"

"And you don't think much of my threat."

"You're right. I don't." His smile faded slowly. "Put the gun away, Lydia. I plan to do the honorable thing by you. Does it matter so much if I have you now or after the wedding?"

"You're not going to have me at all. Take your hand away."

His fingers merely tightened, and he caught her nipple between his knuckles. "Makes you want to scream, doesn't it?" he asked softly, bending his head a fraction. "I could make you like it, Lydia. You know that? I could make you want me, want more. Put the gun away. Let me show you what I mean. Go on, Lydia . . . do it . . ."

Lydia reared back as the pressure of his hand became unbearably painful. Her breath caught on a sob and a gasp. Tears came to her eyes and Brigham's features dissolved in a blur. Her finger convulsed on the trigger of the derringer, more in reaction to the pain than out of an intentional desire to hurt him.

The gun went off between them. The report was surprisingly quiet, muffled in part by Brigham's flesh pressed against the barrel. Lydia jumped back and this time Brig let her go. Blood flowered on his vest, and when he covered the wound with his palm it stained his fingers. He looked, first at his bloody hand, then at Lydia, and his eyes were glassy, dazed. He meant to go forward; he wanted nothing so much as to wrest the gun from her hand and shove the barrel in the soft hollow of her throat. His feet carried him sideways and he stumbled, falling against the mantelpiece and striking it with his shoulder, then his head. His body folded unevenly, at the ankles, the knees, finally at the hips and waist, and Lydia watched, thinking of how he had folded her check earlier, and how he would not be pleased that his dying was not so crisp and clean.

The gun slipped through Lydia's nerveless fingers and fell to the floor at the same time Brigham did. "Oh, God," she whispered, dropping to her knees beside him. She felt for a pulse in his neck and found a faint one. His hand had fallen away from the wound and blood covered his shirt and vest in an ever-widening circle. Lydia stood on trembling legs and pressed her fingers to her temples, trying to think clearly in the face of a raging headache. The tears had long since dried from her eyes, but her vision was still hazy, her sense of balance uneven. She made it to the bed and sat down hard.

"Nathan." Lydia leaned toward him and shook his shoulder. If only she could rest, she thought. If only she could close her eyes for a few minutes, give herself time to think about what she should do. It was impossible, of course. She had as good as killed Brigham Moore if she didn't get help. "Nathan. Wake up. I need you." Lydia started to cry. She crawled toward him and shook him this time with both her hands placed firmly on either side of his neck. "Damn you, Nathan. You've got to w-wake up. I don't know what to d-do." Tears dripped over her cheeks and splashed on Nathan's back. Her entreaties met with no response. "Please, Nathan. I'd marry you . . . I would. I'd do whatever you wanted. Don't let me be a murderer. H-help me."

He lay there unmoving, oblivious to Lydia's fear, to

Brig's danger, to the small hands that pounded his back. Lydia slid off the bed again and directly onto the floor. She fought waves of dizziness and nausea and, after what seemed an eternity to her but was nothing longer than a few seconds, she reached Brigham. She searched his pockets and found the key that would get her out of the suite. She'd have to get help, she thought, even if it meant incriminating herself. It was self-defense after all. The authorities would understand that. "Wouldn't they?" she asked aloud, stumbling forward into the sitting room. She braced herself against the outer door with her shoulder and fumbled for the knob with her hand. Unable to make the key fit the lock after several tries, Lydia tiredly slipped down the length of the door and met the keyhole at eye level. She raised the key and made a stabbing motion with it at the lock.

Her eyes closed.

Her head sagged.

Lydia crumpled and the key fell out of her outstretched and upturned palm.

Part Two

Pacific Interlude

Chapter Seven

Nathan nudged open the cabin door with the toe of his shoe. He dropped the valises he held in each hand and behind him he heard the captain's men set down the trunk they were carrying. He turned to Lydia and lifted his hands slightly, palms upward and asked, "Shall I carry you across the threshold, Mrs. Hunter?"

Lydia's smile was shy, her nod barely perceptible. Out of the corner of her eye she saw the two crewmen exchange knowing glances and grin widely. She realized she didn't care. Holding out her arms, she slid them naturally around Nathan's neck as he scooped her off the deck and carried her into their cabin. The crewmen followed with the trunk, then the valises, and left with hardly a snicker between them, shutting the door as they went.

Nathan let Lydia down slowly so that her body slid against his. They stood in the middle of their cabin, the place that would be their home for the next five weeks, and held each other in a loose embrace. Placing the back of his hand against Lydia's cheek, Nathan rubbed gently, deepening the flush that had come to her face.

"You're warm," he said. "Perhaps you should lie down. The doctor said—" He stopped because she was shaking her head, completely uninterested in anything the doctor had recommended.

"I didn't much care for that doctor," she said, easing from the circle of Nathan's arms. "I think he drank. Did you notice?"

"I noticed." Nathan doubted that Dr. Franklin went anywhere without his flask. Lydia had known that once; now it was a revelation to her. "I should have found a better man to care for you," he said.

Lydia raised her hand and placed a forefinger on Nathan's lips to silence him. "I had a better man," she said softly. He had been at her bedside day and night. "I had you."

Nathan didn't say anything. He kissed the tip of her finger, and when it fell away he missed the warmth and gentle pressure. What would she be saying, he wondered, if she could remember the kind of man he was?

Since the night of the shooting nearly a week ago, there was little Lydia recalled. What she knew now consisted primarily of the things Nathan had told her, a mixture of half-truths, slightly skewed stories, and outright lies. There were truths as well, things he realized she had to know because she would find them out when they reached Ballaburn, but he was cautious about sharing them. Nathan found Lydia's loss of memory both a bane and a blessing. He had rewritten her personal history to suit his needs and now he had the wife he had set out to get months ago. It wouldn't have been possible if she could remember, and while he marveled at her willingness to accept anything he told her, he also knew the reason. Lydia's thinking was simple and straightforward: she couldn't fathom having married someone she didn't love, and she couldn't imagine someone she loved lying to her.

When Nathan wasn't counting his blessings, he was hating himself.

Unaware of the tenor of Nathan's thoughts, Lydia was blithely investigating the cabin. It was sparsely furnished, with few amenities beyond the utilitarian. There was a small table for dining and writing, two chairs, an upholstered storage bench below the porthole, a cupboard which held a basin, pitcher, and chamber pot, a small Franklin stove, an armoire firmly bolted to the wall, and finally, a three-quarter bunk covered with a brightly patterned piece quilt.

"Not quite what you're used to, is it?" he asked. He came up behind her and placed his hands lightly on her shoulders.

Lydia turned her head just enough to show him a cheeky grin. "I don't remember what I'm used to," she said. She removed his hands from her shoulders and drew them around her waist. She leaned backward and rested against him. "And I'm thinking this is just fine."

His chin rested on the silky crown of her dark sable hair. His eyes wandered over their room. "You had a fireplace in your bedroom," he said. "The mantel was cluttered with jade figurines and photographs and a vanity with ivory combs, perfumes, and powder. There were fresh flowers in a cut-glass vase by your bed and your rugs were from the Orient. You had an enormous walnut wardrobe, an armchair and a rocker, and a bed that was half again larger than this one."

It was as if he were talking about another person. Lydia felt no ownership of the things he described. She couldn't have told him the color of her comforter, the pattern of the rugs, or the kind of flowers that filled the vase. She didn't even try to remember. Those things seemed of minor importance when she compared them to what Nathan had inadvertently told her.

"You've been in my bedroom?" she asked.

"Twice."

"Oh."

He gave her a little squeeze and pressed a smile against her hair. Her thoughts were plainly clear to him. "Are you going to ask why I was there, or would you rather assume I've already had my evil way with you."

"Evil way?" she said, realizing she was being teased. She turned in his arms and raised her face to him.

"There's nothing evil about your way. That's the problem. Looking at you, I can believe that I might have done anything for you . . . or *to* you. That's the sort of way you have about you." Dangerous, she wanted to say, but not evil. He was darkly attractive in a manner that captured her attention and her imagination, and even frightened her a little because of her response to it. She was intrigued by the light gray eyes with their dark blue rings, the penetrating predator eyes that often seemed to look through her rather than at her.

Although she remembered little of her past there were two things of which she was certain. In spite of the fact that Nathan Hunter was a convict, he was not an evil man, and she loved him absolutely.

"So," she said, "if I didn't let you ravish me in my bedroom, why did I let you in at all?"

Nathan laughed softly and immediately felt her attention drop to his mouth. His smile vanished. "I don't think I'm going to tell you," he said softly. "The doctor said there are some things you should remember for yourself."

Her voice was husky, matching his, and all she could think about was his mouth. "How convenient for you."

"Yes." He bent his head and his lips hovered above hers. "Yes," he repeated. His mouth slanted across hers, hard and hungry and wanting. He held her close so that she seemed a part of him rather than apart from him. And all the while he pleasured himself with her kiss he knew that what he was doing to Lydia was his greatest crime. He never once considered turning back.

They broke apart rather shakily as the deck beneath them jerked suddenly, then rolled and swayed with a greater pitch than before. The *Avonlei* was underway. Lydia went to the padded storage bench, knelt on it, and peered out the porthole. Moonlight was reflected on each crest wave, breaking and scattering every time a wave unfolded on shore. Outside the line of her vision was the city. She craned her neck to catch a glimpse.

200

"Would you like to go on deck?" Nathan asked. "You could bid farewell there."

She shook her head and moved away. Her place was with her husband now. "There's no one I want to see, nothing I want to say."

Only because she couldn't remember, Nathan thought. She knew she had parents because Nathan had told her. She knew they didn't approve of Nathan because he had shared that as well. But Lydia thought she had left her family behind to marry him. There was no memory of Brigham Moore, the shooting, or the sleeping powder that had nearly killed her.

She didn't know that Nathan had awakened at dawn, groggy and disoriented, discovered Brigham lying on the marble apron of the fireplace and her on the floor of the sitting room, her body blocking the door and the key lying beside her open palm. Like Brigham, she had barely been breathing, but there was no blood to explain it. Nathan put Lydia in his bed and went in search of Dr. Franklin, the only physician he knew in San Francisco whose silence could be bought.

It was more than twenty-four hours before Lydia came out of her deep sleep, and by that time Nathan had moved her to the orphanage. Using the confidentiality of the confessional, Nathan shared Lydia's crime with the priest as well as his plan to protect her. While Samuel Chadwick had a troop of men, including George Campbell, searching the city for Lydia and Nathan, they were receiving sanctuary, if not a blessing, from Father Patrick.

Nathan did not know what to expect when Lydia woke. He considered a number of scenarios during those critical twenty-four hours when he thought she might die and prayed that she wouldn't. In the end, everything he imagined fell far short of the mark because Lydia hadn't even known her own name. That's when Nathan understood he had been given another chance. The lies were told, one after another, until there was no turning back without losing her forever.

Dr. Franklin warned Nathan that Lydia might recover her memory any time or never. Nathan didn't dwell on either possibility. He made arrangements to leave the country with her on the *Avonlei*. At his insistence Lydia penned a brief note to her mother and Samuel, telling them that she had married Nathan, that she was safe and happy, and that she hoped they could be happy for her. He gave that note, and one he had written to Pei Ling, to Father Patrick to be delivered upon their departure. Nathan suspected that in a few hours Samuel Chadwick would understand everything, and perhaps forgive him a little. The other possibility, that Sam would send someone to kill him for abducting his daughter, Nathan preferred not to think about. He did not want to spend the remainder of his life jumping at shadows. His eyes fell on Lydia.

Not when there were so many other things he wanted to do. "Would you like a bath?" he asked.

"Really? I could have one here?"

Nathan smiled because her pleasure was so evident, her eyes so guileless. "I think it can be managed." He had paid a great deal for their passage so Lydia could have every amenity, and there weren't many to be had on a Pacific voyage. Surely this small request could be arranged. The captain of the *Avonlei* was amiable in a gruff, bearish sort of way. He took on passengers to help defer a few costs. The *Avonlei* was first and foremost a cargo ship and Nathan suspected she did a profitable business in the opium trade in addition to carrying silks and tea from the Orient, and wool and lumber from Australia.

A copper-rimmed tub arrived in just under ten minutes. It required ten more minutes to fill. The captain sent along a white linen tablecloth to line the inside of the tub and a jar of lavender-scented bath salts. Lydia knelt beside the tub and added the salts, swirling them in the water with a lazy circling motion. "Do you think this belonged to the captain's wife?" she asked, setting the jar on the floor.

"I don't think he's married."

"A mistress then," she said with a worldly air. It was at odds with the heat in her cheeks. Nathan laughed and she glanced over her shoulder at the sound. There was a dimple at each corner of his mouth and she imagined that she must have fallen in love with him very easily. "I wish I might always make you laugh. I can't think of a better purpose for my life right now."

Her very words erased Nathan's smile, but Lydia had turned back to her bath and didn't see. "Would you mind terribly if I had the cabin to myself for a little while?" she asked. "I'm feeling a bit nervous about . . . about—"

He hunkered down beside her. "I know," he said. "I confess I'm feeling a bit nervous myself."

"Oh." Her arm stopped circling in the water. "But you've done it before."

His eyes widened slightly. "Well, yes," he admitted slowly. "But not with you."

She looked at him shyly, her eyes not quite able to hold his gaze. "I might disappoint you."

Nathan tipped her chin upward and kissed the corners of her mouth. "The only way you can disappoint me is by not being up to your neck in water when I return. I'll give you ten minutes, then I'm coming in to scrub your back." His mouth lingered a moment longer on hers and then he was gone.

Lydia placed a chair beside the tub and laid her nightdress and towel over the back of it, a washcloth and soap on the seat. She undressed quickly, glad that Nathan had left because she had no idea how to go about undressing in front of him. How could she manage any sort of delicacy and grace when she felt only eagerness and trepidation? Was one supposed to pull the gown over one's head or let it fall over the hips? Did one remove shoes

203

and stockings before the dress, or after? And then there were all those horrible red stripes left on her flesh by her corset.

Under the water Lydia's palms smoothed the skin from the underside of her breasts to the tops of her thighs. Would he touch her this way? she wondered. Would her husband be a gentle lover?

She leaned her head back against the rim, closed her eyes, and touched her mouth with the tips of her fingers. His last kiss had been gentle, respectful, yet Lydia sensed he had been holding himself back, or at least she hoped that he had. She wanted him to want her as fiercely as she wanted him. It had been an undercurrent in all her thoughts since he carried her into their cabin.

She heard the rattle of the door handle, then the scrape of the bolt being thrown. She felt, rather than heard, Nathan's approach.

Lydia was not, as Nathan requested, up to her neck in water, but Nathan wasn't disappointed. Her breasts gleamed whitely just below the waterline, and the curve of her arched neck glistened with beads of water, a string of yellow diamonds in the lamplight.

He knelt beside the tub, took the face cloth, and wet it, then rubbed the sliver of scented soap over it. "Where should I start?"

Her eyes opened then, darkly anxious. "I thought you would know."

"Another first," he admitted softly. "But if you'll lean forward, I'll start with your back as promised."

She did, resting her cheek on her drawn-up knees. Nathan began at the back of her neck and very lightly traveled across her shoulder, then lower, beneath the water and down the length of her spine to her buttocks. He lingered, then leaned forward and kissed her shoulder. She hummed her pleasure.

Nathan had never set out to give a woman pleasure before. The whores he knew didn't expect it, some may

204

not have known it was possible. Occasionally it happened, more by accident than design, but Nathan wanted it to happen this time. He wanted Lydia's pleasure more than his own. If she never remembered anything else, he wanted her to remember this. And if she regained her memory he wanted her to know she had been dealt with gently by him, that he had cared enough to want to make her happy.

"Lean back now," he said.

Her limbs were heavy, her mind cloudy with the infusion of pleasure at Nathan's hands. She unfolded her body slowly, leaning against the tub and languidly raised her arm for Nathan to take. She realized she wanted him to look at her, touch her, and where she had been apprehensive before, she was deliciously anxious now, curious and wanting.

Nathan soaped her arm, running the cloth from her wrist to her shoulder, soaping the soft inside of her elbow, kissing her just above the pulse in her wrist. The other arm received the same treatment and then her legs, from ankle to hip. Each time his hand disappeared under the water his touch became a little more intimate, his washing a caress.

He abandoned the washcloth altogether when he washed her breasts. Palming the soap, Nathan's hand fell to the hollow between her full breasts and circled lazily in a figure eight.

Lydia wanted to rest her head against the rim again, close her eyes, and pray that he never stopped touching her the way he was now. Her prayer didn't change, but she watched him, fascinated by the beautiful lean-fingered hand that caressed her with such gentleness and raised such a burning between her thighs. His hand was dark against her skin, and the calluses on the pads of his fingers were deliciously abrasive as they spiraled toward her nipples.

He dropped the soap and made no attempt to recover it.

The pretense of washing her was put aside. It had only been an excuse to touch her and they both knew it. Their eyes met, held. His hand moved against her breast a little harder than it had before. Her eyes darkened as pleasure shot through her.

"You fit my hand," he said, moving it to her other breast. He caressed and cupped her and she swelled slightly under his attention. "You like that?"

She bit her lower lip and nodded quickly.

Nathan smiled.

"You have dimples," she said, watching his mouth, fascinated.

"I don't."

When the smile disappeared so did the dimples. Lydia raised one hand and touched each corner of his mouth with her forefinger. "Here . . . and here," she said. "Only when you smile. And only sometimes."

"Only sometimes?"

"It depends on the smile, I think," she said. There were cold smiles, forced ones that were almost aggressive, more a baring of teeth than a welcome. She might have told him about the smiles she didn't understand, the ones that made her think she didn't know her husband very well at all, but his hand was drifting across the flat of her abdomen and lower, and she couldn't think what she wanted to say anymore.

The tips of Nathan's fingers caressed the inside of her thighs, parting her legs with their gently insistent pressure. His fingers dipped lower and touched the tuft of dark silky curls between her legs. He looked at her and saw that she was watching him. "Close your eyes," he said. "Just feel, Lydia. I want you to just feel."

His husky urging closed her heavy-lidded eyes. Her long dark lashes fluttered once, then lay still. He kissed her lids and she held her breath, waiting, not knowing quite what to expect, only certain that she wanted to learn.

The sensations that Nathan caused to build inside her were extremes. The hot, white fire at the center of her made her flush and shiver, feverish and cold at the same time. He was stroking her now, touching her with deft purpose, so that she lifted against him as the pressure and intimacy increased, and then his finger was inside her, and even when she gasped he did not release her.

He kissed her on the mouth and whispered against her lips, "Feel, Liddy."

She felt. Pleasure spiraled through her, a pinwheel of sparks fired each thread of tension that pulled at her limbs. Her breath came in short, shallow bursts, forced out of her by his touch. She held the sides of the tub, her fingers pressed whitely against the rim. There was the soft sound of pleasure rising at the back of her throat. Nathan felt it on her lips and smothered it with his kiss.

He felt her begin to shudder a moment before she knew what was happening herself. He drew back and let the cry come to her lips and took his own pleasure in the sound. His wolf's eyes were narrowed, watching every fleeting expression of Lydia's passion. There was a flush that rose from her breasts, across her shoulders, and finally colored her cheeks. Lydia's lips were cherry-red, parted, dewy. Her eyes were heavy-lidded, slumberous, deeply blue, and she was staring at him wonderingly.

Nathan took her wrist and raised it as he stood, bringing her with him. Rivulets of water ran over Lydia's shoulders and between her breasts. She shivered, but it had the heat of Nathan's eyes as the source, not the chilled air. He wrapped a towel around her, and when she looked at him oddly, he said, "So I can have the pleasure of taking it off." Her eyes dropped away shyly but her faint smile was pleased. Nathan led her to the bed, sat down, then brought her down on his lap. Her arms went naturally around his neck, and beneath her thigh she could feel his arousal. Their foreheads touched and her eyes were wide, searching. She shifted slightly and he

207

sucked in his breath. "Don't move," he said. His mouth was very close to hers. She could almost taste his words. "Can you feel me, know how much I want you?"

"Yes," she whispered.

"I've never had a virgin before. I'm not sure I've ever known one."

A little thrill shot through Lydia. She could offer something to this beautiful man that no other woman had.

"This first time," he said, "I may hurt you."

"I don't mind." Her lips touched one corner of his mouth. "You've already given me pleasure." Lydia's fingers threaded in the fine dark hair at the back of Nathan's neck. She held him immobile as she pressed her mouth to the opposite corner of his lips, then to his cheek, his jaw, and finally to his ear where her teeth caught his lobe and tugged gently. She felt his lips on the curve of her neck and she offered it up, kissing his temples, his brow, and the bridge of his nose.

Nathan caught her mouth with his own. It was a tasting at first. A whisper of flesh, a teasing of tongues. Neither was satisfied with that. Their mouths parted and clung and the kiss became a seeking. His tongue glided across her lips, probed, sought a match with hers, and found sweet pleasure in her response. Their desire had an energy of its own, feeding on itself, making the kiss harder and deeper so that it foreshadowed the thrustings of their bodies.

Lydia was toppled backward onto the bed. Her fingers worked quickly on the buttons of Nathan's shirt. He stopped her, rose from the bed, and turned back the lamps so that only the narrowest shaft of moonlight and starshine entered the cabin. She wondered about him extinguishing the lamps, wondered if it was unseemly, even wanton, that she wanted to look at him and be seen by him in turn. Perhaps she wasn't a virgin at all, she worried. Perhaps she had made love hundreds of times except with the man who was her husband now. Oh, God, she thought, what if she had lied to him? How would she explain?

Then he was in bed with her, tugging at her towel under the sheet, and he pulled her hips close, seeking for the natural cradle of her thighs for his hard arousal, and Lydia accepted that she had worried needlessly. She had never felt anything like this before, had never known this aching need he was creating in her at this moment. It was not something she could have forgotten.

Her hands fluttered to Nathan's shoulders, smoothing his flesh from the curve of his neck to his arms. His skin was warm and taut and her fingers danced over it. She felt a ridge across his back, a raised line of flesh that should not have been there, and she paused in her exploration. Lydia would have asked about the scar, for surely, she thought, that was what she felt, but Nathan redirected her curiosity, taking her by the wrists and bringing her palms flush to his chest. Her thumbs brushed his nipples, raising them, and bringing a small moan of satisfaction to Nathan's lips.

He found the pins that anchored her beautiful hair and tugged at them. Burying his face against the curve of her neck, Nathan's senses were filled with the fragrance of her, lavender and musk. He kissed the hollow of her throat, traced the line of her collarbone, then his body slipped lower, and while his hands learned the shape of her body, his mouth suckled her breast, sipping, laving, drawing the tip into his mouth and pulling the threads of pleasure that radiated to every other part of her.

Her fingers clutched his buttocks, and she pressed against him, rubbing, wanting him to satisfy the ache between her thighs and unable to say the words aloud. Her legs slid against his. Her toes curled as his mouth moved slowly to her other breast, circled, teased, and finally licked the shell-pink nipple with his tongue. She said his name then, while all her other thoughts remained unspoken, but it was as if he heard the things she couldn't say.

One of his hands moved from the curve of her waist, over the flat plane of her belly, and when his knee slipped between her legs, parting her thighs, Nathan's fingers began an intimate caress, touching, stroking the budding center of her pleasure. He found her wet and hot, ready for him, unafraid in her eagerness and innocence.

"Touch me, Liddy," he said huskily. "Help me."

She did as he asked, hesitant at first, then at his urging, with more confidence. She held his aroused member, stroking, making a caress of her exploration. They shifted. She raised her knees and the soles of her feet slid along his calves as he knelt between her thighs. Her buttocks were lifted; her hand reached out blindly, searching, finding, guiding.

He came inside her slowly, watching her all the while, listening for some sound that warned him he was hurting her. She moved beneath him, trying to accommodate his entry and not let him know about the pain because she didn't want him to stop. He felt her stiffen anyway and started to withdraw. Lydia's legs curled around him and she held his forearms.

"No," she whispered. "Come into me. I was meant to fit more than your hand. I was meant to fit all of you."

"Oh, God, Lydia." And even more quietly, "Forgive me." He thrust inside her fully, covering her with his body. She was tight around him, and hot. He wanted to move in her right away and forced himself to hold back, waiting for her to adjust to the hard length of him. He kissed her long and deeply and sometime during the kiss they began to rock in unison, their limbs locked, their bodies sliding.

Everything he had made her feel before he made her feel again, this time more powerfully. Knowing what was awaiting her, Lydia was an eager participant, moving against Nathan, tightening around him. Her fingers

210

tripped along his forearms and then fell to the mattress and curled in the sheets. She wanted to see his face, know that he was sharing in the pleasure as he was sharing in the passion.

Lydia cried out her need and his name as Nathan's strokes quickened. The tension dissolved in her while it continued to build in Nathan, tightening the muscles across his back and in his thighs. Her hands were on him now, caressing him, clutching him, urging him toward finding his own release. And when he did, she held him in her arms and stroked his hair, her fingers a whisper against his neck, the tenderness that was so much a part of her nature inherent in her touch.

Nathan had never wanted to cry after making love to a woman before. He did now and barely understood it. Lydia made him ache in ways that had nothing to do with wanting her and everything to do with needing her. He had never been frightened of a woman before. Lydia scared him to death. He came close to telling her the truth then, just so she would hate him and never let him near her again. It was almost a physical blow to realize that that scared him just as much.

"Do you know what I regret?" Lydia asked quietly. Except for the gentle stroking of her hand, she was still. Nathan's weight was comforting, somehow reassuring, and she didn't wait for his response to her question. She knew he was awake because his thumb was making a pass across the inward curve of her waist. "I regret not remembering our wedding."

He raised his head, kissed her on the tip of her nose. "As long as you don't regret the wedding."

"No. Not that." She smiled to herself as Nathan's head rested on her shoulder again and one of his legs trapped both of hers. "Actually, I do think I remember something of it. Father Patrick said the service, didn't he?"

"Yes."

"I thought so."

She sounded pleased with her capture of an elusive memory, Nathan thought. "Do you recall anything else?" he asked calmly, as if his future did not depend on her answer.

"No," she said. "Nothing. But I'm never going to forget our wedding night." There was another wedding night, the first one, though, that she could not bring to consciousness no matter how hard she tried. Nathan told her that after the ceremony in the orphanage's chapel, they had taken a room above a tavern outside the city. She had been tired, he said, worried about the manner in which she'd left her parents. Going against their wishes had been hard on her. Lydia appreciated his honesty. He could have led her to believe differently and not risked as much, but he didn't. That evening, when her weariness had become a relentless and pounding ache in her head, Nathan, instead of pressing her with his attentions, had given her his own mix of powder to help her sleep. Her first real memory was of waking up and finding Nathan kneeling at her bedside, sleeping, his cheek lying against the mattress, and his hand curled around hers.

"Do you know?" she asked, still thinking about the moment when her fingers had tightened in his and he came awake. "I sensed that I belonged with you as soon as I saw you."

A fancy of her part, Nathan thought. Their first meeting had been in an alley and she hadn't had a good look at him until he'd coerced her into his hotel suite. Far from thinking she belonged with him, she had run the other way. Humoring her, Nathan asked, "How could you be so certain?"

How could she? she wondered. It had seemed so clear to her at the time, knowledge that she had in her fingertips, a sense of knowing that could hardly be defined in plain words, more certain than intuition, more rational than instinct. "I can't explain it," she said finally, "but it's real. I feel it now. I couldn't belong to anyone else . . . ever."

"Liddy," he said softly. He wanted to say that she shouldn't think of being his forever, that things could change, and that he was not everything she imagined him to be. But he couldn't tell her. However briefly, she believed he was kind and good, patient, generous, and loving, and Nathan was reluctant to let her see he was none of those things. "Liddy," he said again, helplessly, inadequately, and kissed her full on the mouth.

The taste of him lingered long after he withdrew. Lydia snuggled against him as he turned on his side and pulled her close. She fell asleep almost immediately, lulled by the ship's constant rocking, peaceful in *Avonlei*'s cradle. Nathan finally slept because he was exhausted.

He came awake hard, wanting her. He wasn't sure what he would do if she didn't let him have her. Take her anyway probably. He wanted her that much.

It didn't come to that. Coming awake by slow degrees, Lydia turned in his arms naturally and moved with sinuous grace against him, a sleek cat with her eye on the cream, circling her master's leg. Lydia did everything but purr as she took him inside her. His thrust was powerful, deep. Her back arched, her nails pressed white crescents into the taut, warm flesh of his shoulders. Throwing back her head, Lydia felt the driving force of his body become hotter and harder. She wrapped her legs around his flanks and matched the rhythm of his desire.

Nathan felt her all around him, her hands, her arms, her legs, and more intimately, the velvet center of her, and still it was not enough. He had her heart, her trust, her love, and he had none of it fairly. Suddenly he was angry, blindly, irrationally angry, and his only outlet had already been set in motion.

He ignored her wimper, thrusting in her deeply, touching her womb. His mouth was hard on her skin. He drew hotly on her slick and salty flesh, bruising her with kisses. He said her name like a curse, spilling into her, the

213

planes of his face rigid with tension as he gave Lydia his seed.

In the aftermath he was silent except for his harsh breathing, motionless except for the hand that caressed her hip.

Lydia lay on her back and turned only her head toward him. She stared, trying to fathom his expressionless, implacable eyes.

"Did I hurt you?" he asked to fill the silent void.

She wondered why he asked the question when he didn't seem to care about her answer. He hadn't hurt her, but it was almost as if he had wanted to. Finally she said, "No."

Nathan turned on his side and propped himself on one elbow. The hand at her hip moved to her hair. He drew strands of it across her shoulder. "Yes," he said. "I did."

But he didn't apologize, Lydia noticed, or explain his actions; yet there was an expression that briefly entered his eyes and she thought it was regret. She would have to be satisfied with that for now. Beyond the certainty that she belonged with him, Lydia realized she knew little about Nathan Hunter. And before? she wondered. What had she known about him before she lost her memory? Nathan told her himself that their courtship had been brief, spanning only a few months. "Have I ever known you well?" she asked.

Nathan's fingertips smoothed her brows and traced the graceful arch of her cheekbone. His knuckle pressed lightly against her chin, brushed her bottom lip. He felt her beautiful dark blue eyes on him, curious and expectant. "As well as most," he said. "Better than some."

His flippancy made her frown. Had she angered him in some way? "That's no answer."

"No, it's not." He hesitated, and finally the question was pulled from him, as if against his will. "What is it you want to know?"

Lydia evaded his exploring hand while she sat up. She

drew part of the sheet with her and leaned against the wall. Brushing back a lock of hair that had fallen across her cheek, she asked, "You told me you were a convict," she said. "Why didn't you tell me about the scars?"

So she *had* felt them. Nathan followed Lydia's lead and sat up, hitching a blanket around his waist. He started to reach for his shirt, which was hanging on the corner post of their bunk, then stopped. Shrugging, he withdrew his hand. What did it matter? She knew they were there. He had hoped in the dark she wouldn't learn about them. He remembered trying to stop her from touching him there, but he hadn't been quick enough. Her hands had felt so good on his back—tender, gentle. Lydia's hands were healing, her touch a balm.

"How should I have brought the matter up?" he asked. "I turned back the lamps so you wouldn't be offended."

"Offended? Do you really think I'm as delicate as all that?" She pulled the sheet aside and pointed to her knee. "Here. I have a scar. An ugly one, too." It was the shape of a half moon, almost two inches long, and raised above the smooth skin around it. "I wanted to be so beautiful for you, and I saw this, and—"

Seeing it, Nathan smiled. He leaned toward her, bent his head, and brushed the scar with his lips. "You are beautiful for me," he said.

Lydia looked up at him as he raised his head, not quite believing what she heard.

"Don't cry," he said as she blinked back tears. "Why are you crying? What did I—" But she had launched herself into his arms and he stopped questioning and simply held her.

She hardly knew why she was crying herself. Lydia couldn't have explained it to Nathan. He gave her one corner of the sheet to wipe her eyes as her muffled, hiccuping sobs gradually stopped. "I love you," she said, her voice hushed. "I may not remember falling in love, but I *know* about this feeling I have for you."

Nathan's arms tightened around her. His cheek rested

215

against her hair. "There has never been anyone in my life like you, Lydia. No one so gentle or giving, honest and innocent. Sometimes . . . sometimes I think it's all been a mistake, that you can't possibly love me, and I . . ." He fell silent.

"Yes?"

"Nothing." He didn't tell her that he got scared when he thought of her not loving him, not needing or wanting him. Nathan could not make himself that vulnerable, not for anyone, not even for Lydia. "You wondered about the scars," he said.

He would tell her about the ones on his back, of course, but Lydia knew now that there were other wounds that had never quite healed, and she knew he would not speak of those. She would have to be patient if she hoped to understand the man she loved. Laying her palm against his chest, Lydia waited.

"I got these stripes while working Van Dieman's Land," Nathan told her. "Tasmania they call it now. As if changing the name could change the bloody stink of hell's own island. I labored near Hobart, felling Huon pine for ship timber. Sixty and seventy feet tall, some of it was, and so large around that three men could barely ring the trunk. All-day labor, sixteen hours in the summer, twelve in the winter, was the schedule we kept most times. I cut myrtle that the wheelwrights needed and celery-top pine for masts and spars for the shipbuilders. Van Dieman's Land was rich in resources and, God knows, the labor was cheap.

"The guards were ruthless. Ofttimes they used convicts as guards and they were worse. No man's life was valued beyond the work he could do. Death was an escape, looked forward to more often than not. On the mainland gold had been discovered and men scrambled for tickets-of-leave to take up a pickax and shovel for themselves rather than work the government land. I waited ten years for mine and by then I had these stripes.

"Twenty-five for tampering with my leg irons. It didn't

216

matter that I couldn't walk in them. Twenty-five for losing the shirt of my uniform, even though it was stolen from me. Fifty for fighting with a convict who tried to rape me." He felt Lydia's shudder, and knew her well enough to understand that it wasn't revulsion that made her shiver, but pain. She felt it for him, shared it. There was nothing in her life remotely similar to anything he had suffered, yet her capacity for empathy and acceptance made Nathan feel as if he must protect her from herself. "By the time I left Van Dieman's Land for Sydney I had spent over two hundred days in solitary confinement. Don't dwell on that," he cautioned. "I don't. For ten years' time it was not such a bad record."

She didn't believe he didn't think about it. It was part of him, part of the anger that seethed just below his consciousness. He couldn't talk about the fear, the loneliness, or the deprivation. But he could be angry. It was so much easier. "Did you ever tell me why you were sentenced to the penal colony?"

"Yes."

Lydia didn't want to make him repeat it, but she had to know. "Ten years is a long time to be sentenced," she said. His crime could not have been a trifling one.

"I was sentenced for twenty."

"But you said you had a ticket . . . a ticket-of—"

"A ticket-of-leave. But it's not a pardon, and it doesn't mean one's sentence is over. It's simply a method of allowing convicts to work for someone else, a system of providing laborers and servants to men who can pay them. It decreases the government's burden of caring for the convicts. All that's required is accounting for them. A ticket-of-leave does not permit unrestricted travel."

"Yet you came to San Francisco."

"An arrangement with my employer." *The bribing of a number of officials,* he added silently. "I couldn't have done it otherwise. I'm not a free man yet."

Lydia frowned. "Nathan, you must have been a child when you were sentenced. How can that be?"

"I was fourteen. Not so young, Lydia." He paused as her arms circled his back and she felt the uneven ridges of his scars, the thin white lines of his suffering. "I was convicted of murder," he told her without inflection. "There are some who say I was fortunate not to get the gallows." It was only recently that he had begun to believe that sentiment may have been true. Holding Lydia, he could accept Van Dieman's Land as the only path that could have taken him to her.

"Did you do it?" she asked.

"Not many people ask me that question. You didn't, you know. Not the first time I told you."

"Then I married you without knowing." She shook her head. "No, I must have known the truth somehow."

Nathan caught her by the shoulders and held her away from him. His eyes were grave, his features set hard. "Don't make me into something I'm not," he warned her. "I didn't kill at fourteen, but I've killed since. That's the legacy of Van Dieman's Land, the price of living there, sometimes the price of getting out alive. Get rid of your foolish, romantic notions, Lydia, because they can't last where we're going. I'd rather not crush them, but I will if it means you'll survive."

His hands dropped away. He slid his legs over the side of the bed and stood. Crossing their cabin, he poured water into the blue-and-white spongeware basin, rinsed his face, and began shaving. The small mirror above the stand reflected Lydia's pale face, the stunned hurt in her cobalt-blue eyes. He did not look at her long, but when he dressed he made certain his back was to her so that she could see his scars and know a little better the kind of man he was.

Nathan could protect her from everyone but himself.

When he was gone Lydia rose from the bed. There was an ache between her thighs that was not precisely unpleasant. She could still feel the shape of Nathan inside her, the heat and hardness of him, and in spite of how he had parted from her, she wanted him again. If he had walked in their cabin right now, Lydia would have opened her sheet and drawn him inside. She did not think she had much pride where Nathan Hunter was concerned.

Kneeling beside the tub, Lydia washed quickly with the cool water, then rinsed the sheets clean of the stain of her virgin's blood. There were six gowns in her wardrobe, including the one she had worn on board, and a riding habit. Lydia chose a hunter-green dress with mother-of-pearl buttons trimming the bodice and a high collar that banded her slender throat like a choker. She found a green grosgrain ribbon that nearly matched her gown and used it to loosely pull her hair back.

She was ravenously hungry, but was not free to roam the ship as Nathan was. To pass the time until someone remembered she needed to be fed, Lydia finished unpacking the trunk and valises. Like her own things, Nathan's clothes were finely made. Nathan told her she came from a wealthy family, but looking at his clothes, Lydia realized she had not married a pauper. She remembered something about gold mining. Was that her family's fortune or his? She frowned, a furrow between her brows, trying to recall what he had said, and, more important, when.

After struggling a few moments, Lydia went back to her task. She found embroidery hoops, silver-gray thread the exact shade of Nathan's eyes, and white linen napkins stenciled lightly with an ornate H. Aaah, she thought, smiling now, she was most definitely a woman in love if she had set herself this task. Embroidering was not her long suit and she didn't question how she knew that. Nathan could think what he liked, but some things she just *knew*.

Scattered among the clothes she also found a deck of cards, two books, one of Shakespeare's sonnets, the other a dry account of sheep farming, and at the very bottom of one of the valises Lydia's hand closed around a nickle-plated derringer.

She was holding it in her open palm, staring at it,

219

completely unaware that her hand was shaking, when Nathan walked into the cabin. He stopped in his tracks and held onto the tray he carried with white-knuckled pressure.

"Put the gun down, Lydia," he said, forcing calm.

Until he spoke Lydia hadn't known Nathan was in the room. Surprised, she looked at him over her shoulder. "Why do you have a gun?" she asked.

He tried not to show his relief because surely she would wonder at it. The first thing he thought when he saw her holding the derringer was that she had somehow remembered everything. It could happen that suddenly, Dr. Franklin had told him, and though Nathan had little respect for the doctor, he also had no other information to contradict him.

Setting down the breakfast tray, Nathan went to Lydia and took the gun from her hand. "Why does anyone carry a gun?" he asked, putting it back in the valise. He shoved the valise and its companion under their bed and dragged the empty trunk to the foot of it. "For protection," he said when she didn't respond.

"A derringer? It's a lady's weapon."

"How is it that you can recall such odd things and can't remember important ones?" It was strictly a rhetorical question. "It's a weapon that can be easily concealed and that suits a man as well as a woman."

"I don't like it, Nathan. Can't you get rid of it?"

He went to the table and began unloading the tray, setting two places. There were orange slices, biscuits, butter and honey, link sausages, and hard-boiled eggs. "Did you take a good look at the men on this ship last night, Lydia? We're not taking a voyage to do the Grand Tour of Europe, remember. This is a trader's vessel and there are only six other paying passengers on board. Besides the missionary's wife, you're the only woman. Mrs. Wilson, by the way, is nearing sixty, hatchet-faced, and skinny as a sixpence standing on edge." He poured black coffee into two mugs while focusing most of his attention on Lydia. "You understand what I'm saying? We'll *keep* the derringer."

"All right," she said. Picking and choosing her battles, this was not one she cared to fight. And there was also the matter of breakfast. Nathan held out a chair for her and she sat down, thanking him. She waited until he was seated opposite her to begin eating, unfolding her napkin first and smoothing it on her lap. After the first few bites of his food, she noticed Nathan did the same. The napkin was an afterthought.

"How is that a convict on Van Dieman's Land knows the niceties of laying a table?" she asked. "I wouldn't think that sort of life was conducive to refinement or such fastidiousness."

"It wasn't. And don't start thinking I was the scion of some titled family in Britain, or the bastard son of a landed lord before I was transported." Her expressive eyes, wide and startled now, gave her away. "Before I was named a murderer I was a sneaksman."

"Sneaksman?"

"A thief. You'll learn the language. Most of the men you'll meet at Ballaburn were thieves of one sort or another. Star-glazers. Till friskers. Area sneaks. Some were poachers, poor sods down on their luck and trying to feed their families."

"And your employer? What sort of thief was he?"

"Mad Irish?" Nathan paused in buttering his biscuit. "None at all. He was a political prisoner in the early forties, hence the moniker. He served out a sentence in Sydney, struck gold on the banks of the Turon River, in an outcropping not much above one hundred and fifty miles from where he had labored for his crimes, and bought the land at Ballaburn. His station is ten times larger than the estate that was confiscated from him in Ireland. Mad Irish appreciates the irony."

Nathan broke off a piece of his biscuit and put it in his mouth, chewing thoughtfully. "But you were asking about my manners, weren't you? All Mad Irish's doing.

221

He's one for a plan. Plotting runs in his blood, I think, and he saw something in me he either liked, or thought he could use. I was as rough and ill-bred as a dingo before he took me in." He held Lydia's fascinated glance and said softly, "And I still haven't smoothed all the edges."

She smiled, understanding that it was his apology for this morning.

"God, Liddy. When you look at me like that . . ." Like he was adored. Worshiped. It took his breath away, and it made him want to sweep the table clean and take her right there.

Lydia's glance dropped away from his darkening one, but she felt her nipples harden as if he had brushed them with his thumbs, and between her thighs the ache was insistent. Her fingers trembled ever so slightly as she began to peel her orange.

"What sort of things did Mad Irish teach you?" she asked.

"More reading than I knew. Writing. Enough ciphering so I couldn't be cheated by the freemen traders. I learned how to talk to the aristocracy without revealing my stain, and how to converse with a woman who wasn't a whore. He taught me how to dance, though I never took to it well."

"Perhaps Mad Irish wasn't the right partner."

"I've danced with you," he said. "I didn't do well then, either."

Lydia's features tensed as she tried to remember. "It's no good," she said finally. "I can't bring it to mind."

Nathan reached across the table and took the orange from her fingers. Lifting her hand as he stood, Nathan skirted the table and drew Lydia into his arms. "There are memories best left in the past, I think," he said. His smile was beautiful, and when Lydia's gaze dropped to his mouth he knew she was looking for his dimples. He did not think he disappointed. "But some things you have to learn for yourself. You choose the tune."

Lydia began humming a waltz, unwittingly the last

melody she and Nathan had danced to at the Newberrys. She was sublimely unaware of the floodgate of memories she had opened for Nathan as he turned her in elegant circles about their cabin. He was remembering a certain beaded blue dress with a bodice that cut across her breasts at an almost indecent depth. She had mesmerized him wearing that gown. Blinking, lifting the veil of the past from his eyes, Nathan realized she had captured him again wearing one of Madame Simone's severest creations. He was glad he had gone to the salon and picked up the gowns she had ordered; it was well worth the risk to be able to look at her now and bask in the warmth of the artless smile.

"You lied to me, Nathan," she said, interrupting her humming.

He was momentarily disoriented. He had told so many lies. Which one was she going to take him to task for? "Lied?" he asked.

"You dance beautifully."

His steps faltered and she trod on his toes.

"Or at least you did," she said.

She was laughing at him and Nathan surprised himself by not minding. He pulled her closer and bent his head. "You have a mouth that should be kissed thoroughly and often, Liddy."

"I'm glad you think so." Her arms went around his neck and she pressed her body flush to his. She raised her face and felt the warmth of his breath. "I'm very glad you think so."

His kiss was a heady nectar of coffee and honey, a bittersweet taste that Lydia savored and held precious among her new memories. The breakfast kiss, she called it, and the thought made her smile because of all the breakfasts they would share and all the kisses just like this they would exchange.

It might have become something more if it hadn't been for the knock that intruded on their privacy. Nathan broke the embrace reluctantly and set Lydia from him.

223

"That will be Mrs. Wilson," he told her. "The hatchet-faced missionary's wife. She's come to take her morning constitutional with you." He couldn't help but be flattered by her disappointment. "I didn't know you intended to ravish me after breakfast," he said. "I would have told Mrs. Wilson to wait until lunch."

Reigning in her frustration, she said cheekily, "Now you'll have to wait."

Nathan was well aware of that. "I know," he said huskily, thinking of the swelling in his trousers. "Lord, how I know."

Chapter Eight

Samoans called them *papalagi*. Sky-burster. The first clipper ship, with its sails spread wide, swelled by the tropical winds, must have looked very much like an albatross or some other enormous white bird as it pierced the horizon where heaven and ocean met. Many ships had come since that time, bringing strange customs and influences to the islands that made up Samoa: Tutuila, Upolu, and Savai'i. Now *papalagi* had come to describe the white man and took on all shades of meaning when contrasted with *fa'a Samoa*—the Samoan way.

Forty years ago Reverend John Williams of the London Missionary Society had traveled half the world to bring Christianity to the Samoans. His memory was still regarded with great respect and the message that he brought had long since been incorporated into *fa'a Samoa*.

Merrily Wilson hardly possessed the hatched-faced features that Nathan purported her to have, but neither was she aptly named. Her disposition was best described as solemn and serious, though words like puritanical, dour, and grave also came easily to mind. She was almost four inches taller than her husband, large-boned and angular. Lydia spent a fair amount of time with her on deck each day, taking part in the constitutional ritual, or in her cabin, embroidering the linens that Nathan had given her while Merrily read from the Bible or told her stories about the Samoa Islands. Lydia managed not to disgrace herself by falling asleep when Merrily read in her somber monotone, but she had come to enjoy listening to the missionary talk about the Samoans themselves. It was clear to Lydia that while Merrily did not always understand the people she ministered to, she clearly loved them.

Hugh Wilson was opposite his wife in appearance, but not in effect. Balding, bespectacled, and bandy-legged, Hugh was round where Merrily was sharp. Though his features lent him a certain joviality on first acquaintance, it soon faded as one came to know him. Lydia had as little to do with him as was politely possible, and strove not to be too critical of Hugh. He, like his wife, would never be anything but *papalagi*, but he loved his calling.

The *Avonlei* had followed the northeast trade winds since leaving San Francisco. Equipped with an auxiliary steam engine, the clipper ship easily passed through the breezeless doldrums when her sails failed her. The captain of the *Avonlei* planned a two-day stop in Apia harbour on the island of Upolu. The delayed departure was first and foremost an opportunity for trade; the *Avonlei* took on bananas, copra, green coconuts for non-intoxicating refreshment, and cacao. An alternate reason for the delay, one that was only whispered about among the crew because of the presence of Mr. and Mrs. Wilson, was the island women. Zealously guarded by their men, shy and retiring, each sailor hoped he might be the lucky fellow who could entice one girl from her *aiga*—her extended family group, upon whom she depended for protection. Nathan paid little attention to the stories. He suspected the women on Upolu had long since learned to be wary of the *papalagi* who traveled on the wings of the great white birds.

Rushing water was a steady, somehow soothing, roar in his ears. Nathan barely noticed it, his attention fully caught by Lydia's play in the blue crystalline pool below him. She ducked beneath the water and came up with her dark hair sleekly pulled back over the crown of her head. Turning her head sharply from side to side, her hair whipped back and forth, showering the pool with beads of water as clear and brilliant as diamonds. For a brief moment, each bead that caught in a ray of sunlight scattered a rainbow of color that delighted Lydia and took Nathan's breath away.

She closed her eyes, head tilted to one side, and combed her hair with her fingers. The ends of it floated on the surface of the pool. She hummed softly to herself.

Her expression was serene and sensual, and Nathan kept watching her, drawn by her pleasure, fascinated by her calm. Water glistened on her face and shoulders and the exposed cord of her neck. Her eyelids were fringed by dark, spiky lashes and a pale rose wash of color heightened the arc of her cheeks. Without warning, she raised her slender arms above her, stretched, and dove backward. Nathan had a glimpse of her breasts, her hips, before she disappeared under the water. She stayed under for a long time, gliding to deeper parts of the pool so that Nathan all but lost sight of her, then she shot up suddenly, spraying water in all directions and smiling and laughing happily with the sheer force of her abandon.

The pool was a sanctuary of sorts, circled by a lush growth of ferns. Except for the outcropping of lava rock where Nathan sat and the waterfall which fed the pool, the greenery was unbroken in any place. The dense rain forest had grown right to the water's edge, powerful and oppressive, then yielded to the placid pool.

The single most beautiful thing in nature's setting of emerald ferns, diamond and crystal water, ruby petals, and amethyst blossoms, the jewel that caused the others to sparkle less brightly, was Lydia. Even when she moved out of the sunlight into the cool shadows of a canopy of ferns, Lydia was radiant. Her wet hair was like polished ebony, her skin as smooth and warm as ivory. And yet it was more than the cobalt-blue eyes that were centered on him now, or the soft smile that invited him to join her. In the passage of time since leaving San Francisco, Lydia's spirit had been set free. It touched him now, enfolded him, and drew Nathan to her as surely as if she had taken him by the hand.

He stood and tugged at the brightly colored *lava-lava* that was hitched at his waist. The wraparound skirt fell on the rock beside the one Lydia had taken off earlier. Naked, he waded into the pool. The water lapped at his waist almost immediately. It was cool against his heated skin. He dove under and came up in front of Lydia, his flesh sliding smoothly and wetly against hers. He felt all of her, knew the contours of her body as she was pressed to him: the lush curves of her breasts, the taut plane of her belly, the inviting line of her thighs as they cradled him.

Her arms circled his neck and she raised her face, eyes wide, guileless, and open in the expression of her need, her desire. Her mouth was damp, parted. Her breath was sweet. Nathan lowered his head as his hands rested lightly on her waist and his mouth touched hers lightly, briefly, in a tantalizing promise of passion. It was Lydia who pressed for more and Nathan who slipped away, ducking below the water and out of her reach.

She was a much better swimmer than he. Lydia caught him easily, grabbing him by the ankle and pulling him back. He came to the surface sputtering and Lydia landed him a hard kiss on his mouth that stole the last of the breath from his lungs. They gulped air simultaneously, and when he dipped below the water this time it was by mutual agreement. Lydia held on, her tongue spearing his mouth, greedy for the rough pleasure of his kiss. They surfaced closer to the falls, where the water churned and frothed with more force, bubbling up around them and rising in a mist above their heads. Standing in the middle of it, it was as if they had created the steamy turbulence. Seeing Lydia's sultry smile, feeling the heat of her body,

Nathan found it easier to believe in her life force than the rushing cascade of water at his back.

"Liddy." He said her name softly, as if tasting the preciousness of it on his tongue. "Come with me."

She thought he was going to lead her to the densely carpeted forest floor and make love to her on a blanket of fallen ferns. Instead, he took her to where the water was calmer and a few inches less deep. He kissed her then, his mouth sliding over her cheeks, her forehead, and her temples. His fingers threaded in her hair and held her still while his lips slipped damply along her jaw and down her throat. At the curve of her neck and shoulder he paused, sipping lightly on her skin, tasting her, and raising a whimper born of wanting from Lydia.

He thwarted her efforts to return his kisses until desire had welled so forcefully inside her it could not be held back. She tore away from his hands and stopped offering her neck for his pleasure. She became the aggressor, wrapping her arms about Nathan's shoulders. Bouyed by the water, Lydia lifted herself easily to his height, met the impassioned look in his darkening gray eyes, and kissed him full on the mouth. Her lips touched his dimples, or rather, touched his skin where she sometimes saw them emerge. The tip of her tongue traced his upper lip, then the lower one, and pressed inward to the slightly uneven ridge of his teeth. He frustrated her entry, and Lydia smiled because she knew what he wanted. Retreating, her mouth caressed his face: the bridge of his nose, his cheeks, the underside of his jaw. Her tongue teased the edge of his earlobe, flicking, and her teeth nipped him gently.

His mouth opened to call her a name. Siren, perhaps. Or beautiful temptress. It remained unspoken, a thought unshared, as Lydia's mouth covered his and gained the sweet entry she had sought earlier. Her hands tightened on his shoulders, each caress harder and more deliberate than the last. Their mouths held tight, tongues engaged in delicious conflict. Water lapped at their skin, supported and caressed them.

Nathan's hands slid along her rib cage and cupped her breasts. The shell-pink tips were hard, her breasts slightly swollen. His thumbs brushed her tender, sensitive nipples once. Twice. Then he stopped and waited, anticipating the moment when she would move sinuously against him, rubbing, desiring the pleasure of his flesh against hers. Her hands dropped to cover his, then she moved his hands slowly against her breasts in the motion she wanted him to imitate, and she watched him all the while with eyes that were darkening to obsidian.

He surprised her, lifting her easily, raising her breasts to the hot suck of his mouth. She gasped as he took one nipple, laved it with his tongue, and worried it gently with his lips and teeth. His face was pressed briefly in the valley of her damp flesh as he moved to the other breast. He kissed the spot where her heartbeat fluttered against his mouth, then he suckled her breast, drawing on Lydia's responsive flesh until she cried out.

Lowering her, Nathan's eyes darted over her face, his features tense with concern, not passion. "Did I hurt you?"

His question caught her off guard. Didn't he know? In the weeks they had been together, shared the same bed on the *Avonlei*, shared every carnal intimacy, Lydia thought he had come to know her body, her every response, better than she. Hurt her? He couldn't have been farther from the mark. "God, no," Lydia said softly. "No, you didn't hurt me. I love what you do to me, everything you do. When you touch me . . ."

His brows lifted, waiting. There was the brightness of unshed tears in her eyes and against his will he was moved by it.

"When you touch me," she began again, "I feel you tug on something inside me, something powerful and primitive, and it tingles and pulls at me and makes me want you all the more. It only hurts when you don't."

230

"Don't?"

"Don't touch me," she said. There was something else that hurt, but not physically, not the way he meant, and she kept it to herself as she had from the first moment she realized her husband had never once said he loved her. "Only when you don't touch me."

Nathan felt Lydia's legs wrap around him as she lifted herself. Her hand slid between them as he cupped her buttocks and she held his hard arousal, poised above it, making him wait this time, making him anticipate the pleasure of being inside her, surrounded by her. Her face flushed and her eyes closed as she lowered herself onto him, and this time it was Nathan who sucked in his breath at the sheer pleasure of the sensations.

She moved slowly, savoring the control, enjoying a heady sense of power in making love to Nathan in just this manner. Her mouth touched his shoulder, kissing him in a dozen different places, her lips as light as a whisper across his flesh. Her hands caressed his back and he didn't stop her, even when her fingers ran swiftly across the thin, ridged scars that laddered his skin. He was smooth and warm, tautly muscled where tension rippled through his shoulder blades and down his arms. Her breasts slid slickly against his chest and she felt the arousal of his nipples. Smiling, Lydia buried her face against the curve of his neck and shoulder and bit him very, very gently.

Nathan had enjoyed the slow, teasing tempo of Lydia's lovemaking until he glimpsed her siren's smile and felt her savage little love bite. Growling deeply at the back of his throat, Nathan's fingers pressed harder against her buttocks and he thrust hard, pushing deep inside her, and repeated the motion again, urging her to catch his rhythm now. She held him with her arms and legs, and more intimately with the feminine center of her. The roles of captor and captive were reversed and reversed again. Pleasure gathered force between them as they gave freely and took greedily.

231

Lydia was rising on a swelling tide of excitement. The water around her, the dense forest just beyond it, the air redolent with exotic fragrances as well the familiar one she associated only with Nathan, Lydia felt as if all her senses were fired for this moment. When he made her come, she would shatter into rainbow colors like the water prisms, only her colors would be more vibrant, she thought, magenta instead of pink, emerald instead of green, gold for yellow. Her colors would be hot and liquid, like the molten center of Nathan's eyes where onyx ran to silver.

It happened in just that fashion. The colors were brilliant behind Lydia's closed eyes as she shuddered in Nathan's embrace. Her back arched, her head was thrown back, her nails made small white crescents in his upper arms. This time she bit her lower lip to keep from crying her pleasure aloud. She heard it in the rushing fall of water, in the rustle of ferns, and in the keening cry of alien birds in the treetops.

Pleasure coursed through Nathan then. Every spring of tension spun wildly out of control and he filled her with his seed, holding her so tightly that she was a mere extension of him. He held her for just that way for a long time after, his face pressed to the damp curve of her neck, tendrils of her wet hair flicking his cheek. His eyes were closed and what she couldn't see were the tears that scalded his lids and swelled his throat almost shut. Words were superfluous now, and for that Nathan was thankful. He couldn't have given sound to anything he was thinking.

He let Lydia down gently, watching her lovely breasts vanish beneath the water. Drawing a line with his forefinger from the hollow of her throat to her navel, Nathan's knuckles brushed her breast and he felt a frisson of pleasure shake her slender frame. He raised his eyes to hers and realized she had been watching him, too, waiting, her expression expectant and somehow wary at the same time. What did she want? he wondered. What had he done to make her wary of him?

Lydia blinked. When she opened her eyes again the smile that touched her moist lips touched her eyes, too. She stood on tiptoe, kissed Nathan lightly, then took his wrist and led him to the rocky outcropping where their colorful *lava-lavas* had been discarded. Nathan fastened his around his waist, the hem coming to midcalf. Lydia wrapped her mauve one around her middle, knotting it to the left of her breasts so that it split along the length of her thigh when she walked. Nathan placed a lei of island orchids around her neck and realized that he was staring at her only when she turned aside, embarrassed by his attention.

They sat down together where the rocks were flat and smooth. Lydia's bare toes dipped in the water as it splashed against her perch. She pulled all of her hair over one shoulder and sifted through it with her fingers. When it was combed out she began to braid it in a thick plait that would fall in a single line down the center of her back.

Nathan sat beside her, his long legs stretched out across the warm rocks, his arms braced behind him. He studied her profile, the touch of the aristocrat in the shape of her nose, in the tilt of her head and chin, the fairness of her skin. What was he doing with her? he asked himself silently and not for the first time. He knew the answer, but the answer didn't make sense anymore. She should have been completely out of his reach, someone he might desire but would never have. He was a bastard, the son of a whore, a sneaksman, convict, and murderer. On reflection he added abductor and liar.

In so many ways they were opposites. His soul was black. Sometimes the pure white light of Lydia's blinded him. He wasn't particularly kind. Lydia had a giving heart and a gentle soul; she felt things deeply when often he could feel nothing at all. It was more than his back that

233

was scarred, more than his flesh that bore the wounds of his past.

Most mornings she was hard to wake; most mornings he woke hard. She cut her food in tiny pieces and ate slowly, savoring the taste of each morsel put in front of her. There were moments he forgot he wasn't hungry anymore, forgot the food wasn't going to be stolen from his plate if he didn't shovel it in. There were times he was midway through his second helping before he realized Lydia had barely made a dent in her first. With so much of her past erased from her memory, Lydia lived almost exclusively in the present—desiring, discovering, loving, wanting. Nathan lived there as well, but for different reasons. He hated the past and dreaded the future. There was no other place for him.

Perhaps it was the reason they practically ignited when they touched, Nathan thought. He had no other explanation. Nothing in his experience had prepared him for Lydia or the things she was capable of doing to him. And here, on this verdant tropical island in the middle of the South Pacific, hours away from the date line and sailing into tomorrow, Lydia had come to him with incredible abandon and sensuality and shown him a depth of sensation and pleasure that he had never known. She was making love to him, he realized. Making love.

What the bloody hell, then, was he doing to her?

Lydia dropped her braid down her back and laid a hand on Nathan's thigh. She stared out over the pool toward the crystalline curtain of the waterfall. A bird swooped low, cut behind the steady shower of water, then reappeared on the other side, crying gleefully, triumphantly, at this superb flight of daring. Lydia smiled widely and turned the full force of it on Nathan at the moment he was most vulnerable.

"There must be no more beautiful place than this on earth," she said, a hint of reverence in her voice.

"No," said Nathan. But he wasn't thinking of where

they were. He was only thinking of her. "You don't want to leave, do you?"

"Do *you?*"

Did he? "Not as soon as we must," he said finally. "But eventually, yes, I'd want to leave. I'm just the sort of man God drove out of paradise, Liddy. I don't belong here—not for long."

It hurt her when he talked that way, as if he were still the man he had been with no hope of expecting better, as if the scars that lashed his back had made the same indelible impressions on his soul.

"But you," he said quietly, turning away from her. "You don't belong anywhere else."

Lydia leaned against him and was immediately enfolded in the secure circle of his arms. She hugged her knees to her chest. "I belong with you," she said. "Don't you ever forget that." She grinned then, shooting him a quick glance. "Just in case I do."

They walked for several miles in the dense forest before they came to the place where they'd left their *papalagi* clothes. Sometimes Nathan carried Lydia along the path that had been beaten out and tramped down by the Samoans before them. Lydia's tender feet weren't always up to the task of traveling the rough terrain.

Lydia smiled ruefully of her own reluctance to shed the *lava-lava* and trade it for the conventional and proper gown she had worn that morning. "What do you think Mrs. Wilson would say if we both arrived in Apia village wearing these?"

"She wouldn't say anything," said Nathan. "But only because she'd have fainted dead away. Mr. Wilson, however, would point out that while it is quite proper for the Samoans to adopt the *papalagi* way, we must not adopt the *fa'a Samoa*—and that includes the wearing of a sheet."

Lydia laughed at Nathan's mocking piety. He had caught Mr. Wilson's tone precisely. She dropped the *lava-lava* and picked up her undergarments, including her stiff whalebone corset, and began to dress. When she turned her back to Nathan for help with lacing the corset, he simply removed it and flung it into the trees. Rounding on him, Lydia said his name in shocked accents.

Mimicking her inflated outrage, Nathan repeated his name. "Did you really want to wear it, Liddy?" he asked, taking his own voice back. "If you're that bent on being tortured by your own clothing, I'll get it for you."

Lydia looked over her shoulder to where Nathan had pitched the corset. It was hanging rather precariously from the end of a palm frond, its strings caught neatly in the fringed leaves. Her eyes traveled the length of the long, slender tree trunk. She had seen village children shinny up the trees, retrieve a green coconut, and slither back down, all of it accomplished in a mere heartbeat, most of it while Lydia's heart was in her mouth. She didn't think she could ask Nathan to climb that palm. Even if he could do it, she couldn't stand it.

"It can stay just where it is," she said, slipping her chemise over her head. "No corset's worth a broken neck."

Nathan grinned at her reasoning. He didn't point out that he could have shaken the tree or thrown a shoe at the palm frond to knock it down. She probably wouldn't thank him for presenting those options.

When they finished dressing, Nathan slipped his arms around Lydia's middle from behind. He drew her back against him while his palms smoothed the material of her plain gray gown from her waist to the high-collared bodice. "Much better," he murmured against her ear. He placed a light kiss on her temple. "I can feel you under here, not whale skeleton." To prove his point, his thumbs passed over the tips of her breasts and Lydia's nipples hardened immediately.

Looking down at herself, Lydia could see the faint

236

outline of her arousal. She pushed his hands out of the way and raised her arms to cover herself. "Everyone will know," she practically wailed.

Nathan's dark eyebrows lifted. He raked back his hair with his fingers, feigning complete puzzlement. "What? That you have breasts? Honestly, Lydia, I can't think of anyone who doesn't know that already." He scooped up their native garments with one hand and took Lydia's wrist in the other. "Come along. We did say we'd be back in the village by sunset. If we don't hurry, they'll all come looking for us."

Shaking her head all the while, Lydia let herself be hustled along the path before she had a change of heart.

Nathan and Lydia spent the first part of the evening— their last on Upolu—with Mr. and Mrs. Wilson in their small thatched home beside the church they had come to serve. Though the building materials differed significantly, the Wilsons' house was familiar in that it was built to model the *papalagi* idea of a suitable dwelling. Rectangular in shape, their home had a sloping roof, four walls for securing privacy, open squares at eye level meant to be windows but which held no glass, and a door. Mrs. Wilson had her house servant, a lovely young girl with blue-black hair and copper-colored skin, prepare a European-style dinner with chicken and rice that they had taken from the stores of the *Avonlei*. They sat at a table, on rough-hewn chairs, used all the proper utensils with their meal, and made excruciatingly correct and boring conversation.

As soon as they could politely excuse themselves, Nathan and Lydia did so. They were hardly a stone's throw from the missionary's home when Fa'amusami, the girl who had served their dinner, darted out from behind a palm and blocked their path. Her almond-shaped eyes fairly danced with the laughter she just managed to smother with the back of her hand.

"Come," she said. "I make special treat for you. This way."

Fa'amusami led them along the white coral sand, through a grove of palms, to her *fale*, the airy, beehive-like structure that the islanders called home. Oval in shape, the *fale* was constructed with the trunks of palms which were driven vertically into the sand at wide intervals, some as large as five feet. The *fale* then was entirely open at ground level and the trunks supported an impressive dome of thatch. Steady ocean breezes swept through the dwelling and when it rained, mats were lowered from their position near the ceiling to keep it out. It was beautifully simplistic, perfectly functional, and so suited to the environment of the island that the Wilsons' house seemed hopelessly out of place.

Fa'amusami introduced Lydia and Nathan to her father and mother, three younger sisters, and two brothers. Lydia's tongue tripped over the names but they were scrupulously polite not to laugh at her. She and Nathan were served *palusami* and ate it with their hands, licking the thick coconut cream from their fingertips and the corner of their lips as even the youngest children did. The baked *taro* on which it was served had a flavor unlike anything Lydia had tasted. Nathan watched her eat it delicately, learning each nuance of its succulent and strangely sweet and starchy flavor, and he thought about her kisses, how she touched his mouth in the same manner, learning the taste of him. He looked away quickly and caught Fa'amusami's father, Fiame, watching him, an approving, knowing look in his dark eyes.

They sat on mats on the floor and drank sparingly of *kava*, an intoxicating drink made from pepper plants native to the islands. Fiame shared stories about the islands that had been passed to him. He spoke with great skill, for he was a *matai*, a chief of lesser rank who specialized in oratory and who, on occasions of great importance, spoke for the highest-ranking village chiefs. They learned no *papalagi* man, excepting Hugh Wilson, had ever been invited to their dwelling. Fiame did not trust the *papalagi* with his daughters, he told them, but since Nathan clearly had eyes for no one but his wife, Fiame made an exception of Fa'amusami's request.

"One of *papalagi* kill woman on Savai'i," Fa'amusami explained to Nathan and Lydia as she walked with them to the harbor. "Father very careful after he hear of death. Very horrible. Wrists cut with shell used like knife. Stupid. No woman here take her life like that. Not *fa'a Samoa.*"

"Then it was a great honor you gave us tonight," Lydia said. She took Fa'amusami's slim brown hand in hers. "Thank you so much." She glanced at Nathan, expecting him to echo her thanks to their hostess. He was frowning deeply, his silver-gray eyes perfectly impenetrable.

"Excuse me," he said abruptly, dropping his hand from Lydia's waist. "I won't be long." With no explanation, he walked briskly back to the *fale* and sought out Fiame.

"She reminded me of someone," Lydia told Nathan much later that evening. They had been rowed back to the *Avonlei,* not in one of the ship's crafts, but in the native *fautasi,* a many-oared boat that skimmed the ocean's surface like a waterspider. In the morning, perhaps before they even woke, the *Avonlei* would be sailing out of Apia Harbour, on the last leg of its journey to Sydney. They had only just left the island and already it seemed that her memories were more dreamlike than not.

"Who?" he asked. He was standing at the shaving basin, wiping the last bit of lather from his face. He had gotten into the habit of shaving at night when he knew how he was going to spend his time in bed with Lydia. The ritual was so imprinted in Lydia's mind that color suffused her face whenever she happened to glance at his shaving mug.

Nathan looked in her direction and realized Lydia was

paying absolutely no attention to what he was doing. Not only wasn't she blushing, she had done nothing about getting out of her day dress. The collar was still modestly buttoned to her throat and she hadn't undone her braid. She was sitting on the edge of the bunk, her hands folded quietly in her lap, while her very busy thoughts caused a furrow to form between the gentle arc of her brows.

Nathan tossed the towel he'd been using on top of the washstand and went to sit beside her. "What's this all about?" he asked. "Have you remembered something?"

"I don't know . . . I'm not sure. Fa'amusami. I keep thinking I've met her before. But that's impossible, isn't it?" She looked at Nathan now, her frown still in place. "I've certainly never been to Samoa before."

"Not as far as I know. Here, let me play the lady's maid." He raised Lydia's feet, first one, then the other, taking off each shoe in turn. She didn't even protest as he reached under her gown and rolled down her stockings. "You used to have a personal maid, someone who did this sort of thing for you, I suspect. Or at least helped you with your clothes. Do you recall anything about her?"

Lydia shook her head. "Nothing."

"The case could be made that she and Fa'amusami share some of the same features. Almond-shaped sloe eyes, dark hair, a softness in the way they speak. Perhaps it's Pei Ling you're thinking of."

"Pei Ling." Lydia said the name slowly, trying it out. It was completely unfamiliar. "She was my maid?"

"Your maid and something more. I think she was your greatest protector, save Samuel." Nathan was a little surprised to discover that in all he had told Lydia about her past, he had never mentioned Pei Ling. Had he done it purposely, afraid that she would remember everything if he spoke of her? Knowing Lydia's nature, and the things Samuel had shared offhandedly one time about how Lydia had met Pei Ling, Nathan suspected the Chinese girl was more friend than servant.

"Did she like you?" asked Lydia. She pushed at her

gown, covering her bare calves, while Nathan massaged her feet.

Nathan raised a single brow at her display of modesty. It was really too bad, he thought, that the *fa'a Samoa* did not have a more far-reaching influence. "Like me?" he repeated. "That's an odd query."

"You said she was my protector. I wondered if she helped me elope with you."

"No. She didn't do that. But I think she trusted me." At least she had. Nathan couldn't imagine what Pei Ling might think of him now. The letter he had written her, the explanation he had hoped she would share with Samuel, was it enough to make him less offensive in Pei Ling's eyes? He wished he knew. Pei Ling's thinking could very well be a hint of what he might expect from Lydia some day. "She was dedicated to you," he said. "If she liked me, then I'm not so certain she likes me now."

"But then she doesn't know you as I do," said Lydia.

Nathan didn't say anything to that. Moving Lydia's feet to one side, he unfastened the buttons at her throat and eased the gown over her shoulders. Her complexion had pinkened from her time in the sun and there were freckles across her collarbones. He leaned forward and kissed each one.

Lydia let him push her back gently on the bed. She raised her hips to allow Nathan to take her gown off over her hips and down her legs. He kissed the dark shadow of her navel through her chemise as he worked the dress off her. "Tell me about Pei Ling," she said. "Perhaps it will help me recall something."

Nathan dropped Lydia's gown on the floor and, a moment later, her pantalettes. He sighed and sat up fully. Only one of them was engaged in the task at hand and it was a most unsatisfactory arrangement. "I suppose I must," he said. His voice hinted at regret, though whether it was because of what he had to give up immediately or what he could lose in the future was unclear to him.

241

"I really don't know very much about her, not from anything you've said, but Samuel once told me something about you and Pei Ling . . ."

"Yes?" she prompted when he fell silent. She sat up a little, supporting herself on bent elbows.

"Pei Ling is fiercely loyal to you with good reason," Nathan explained. "Samuel says it's because you saved her life."

"You must have heard it wrong."

"No, I don't think so. At the very least you saved Pei Ling from *a* life, that much I know. She was being offered up to sailors as they bounded off their ships in San Francisco Harbor. She was tied to the man at her side as if she were his pet, and he was selling the right to take her leash for two bits. You must not have been standing very far away, waiting with your friend James Early to take a shipment for delivery at his warehouse. Right in front of your eyes, a sailor bought Pei Ling, leading her behind a stack of crates in the nearest waterfront alley. Apparently you rushed to her rescue, paying the sailor twenty dollars in gold to give her up and fifty more to the man who was selling her."

"I can't imagine it."

"I can." Nathan could just see Lydia marching up to a sailor probably twice her size and demanding the release of his whore. All along he thought she had the sense of a Jackaroo. He had come to realize she also had the spirit of a lioness.

"My," she said softly, trying to see it in her own mind. "I suppose I acted that way because James was there."

Nathan was not going to let that pass. "I believe you acted entirely on your own, though your father did mention that once James realized you were not leaving the wharf without Pei Ling, he helped you come up with the money. James was not as eager to enter the fray as you."

"Perhaps he was not so impulsive."

"Probably not," Nathan said. "But neither was he so

courageous. Then or now. It happened three years ago, Lydia. You were only seventeen, Pei Ling even younger than that." He did not mention that she had saved Pei Ling from the cribs only to have Samuel eventually choose the girl for his own bed. The marriage problems of Samuel and Madeline were something that Lydia would have to learn about entirely on her own. He had no intention of explaining what he barely understood himself. "James Early was never a proper match for you."

She smiled, liking the proprietary tone he used. "And you are?" she asked, giving him a look that was both sly and mischievous.

He didn't want to think about her question too deeply. Nathan answered as he knew she expected him to. He pounced on her, pinning her to the mattress with her arms above her head. His face was just inches above her and his light-gray predator eyes captured her attention. "You know I am," he said with husky menace. "Say it."

Lydia shook her head and dropped the gauntlet. "Make me."

He kissed her first. Not on her mouth as she expected, but on her shoulder. His lips were warm, her skin warmer. His teeth caught the wide strap of her chemise and tugged, easing it over her shoulder. Taking advantage of her bare flesh, Nathan feasted. Starting with her collarbone, his mouth placed tiny, tasting kisses along its length. The curve of her neck and the hollow of her throat held the fragrance of the lei she had worn on their trek from the falls. His lips tickled her skin, making her shiver and shift a little restlessly as he moved closer.

Nathan's knee nudged the hem of her chemise. It traveled upward, over her calves, her knees, and came to rest just at the top of her thighs. Nathan bent once and kissed the silly, insignificant scar on her knee with such reverence that in that moment Lydia knew she was absolutely adored. He stripped off his shirt, his trousers, and drawers. It was not often that he was entirely naked when she was still clothed. It was exciting in a way. She kept thinking the next thing he would do would be to remove her shift. It never was. The anticipation was deliciously maddening.

He kissed her breasts through the thin cotton shift. His tongue made a wet circle on the cloth and the extra abrasion of the material made her nipples stand up hard and stiff. He took his time arousing her, pressing his mouth to her breasts again and again, drawing the fabric through his lips, then her nipple, worrying both with his teeth. When he heard her whimper, he stopped.

Lydia's fingers dug into his thick dark hair and tried to force him back to her breast. He smiled. The dimples that melted her heart appeared briefly. He was also shaking his head, refusing to budge.

"Say it," he said.

Though Nathan's methods were especially persuasive, Lydia wasn't ready to give in just yet. It was a matter of pride—and pleasure. "You'll have to do better than this," she said. But her voice was very, *very* husky.

Nathan reacted swiftly, turning Lydia over on her stomach and straddling her thighs. "I can do much better," he assured her. His voice was momentarily near her ear. His breath was hot on her flushed cheek.

She tried to raise her head and see him, but she couldn't. He was already leaning back, his hands reaching behind him to stroke her calves. The backs of her knees were incredibly sensitive to the light caress of his fingertips. She bit the underside of her lip to keep from crying out this time and swallowed the other sounds of her desire.

Pushing the hem of Lydia's shift upward to the small of her back, Nathan cupped her buttocks in his palms and gently kneaded, gradually working lower to the tops of her thighs. There were two small indentations at the base of her spine. He touched a knuckle to each in turn, then kissed them both, flicking his tongue in the tiny depressions.

His hands slipped under her shift, up her back. His

thumbs traced the ridged length of her spine, then across her shoulder blades and along her folded arms, stopping where her wrists cradled her head. His hands caressed the tender and sensitive inside of her arms, then slid under her and held her breasts in the heart of his palms.

Lydia said his name softly, pleadingly. Nathan bent close to her mouth and she said it again, breathlessly this time.

"Is that all?" he asked softly. "Just my name?"

She nodded quickly, squeezing her eyes shut before she changed her mind and said the words he wanted to hear.

Nathan moved off her thighs. At first Lydia was bereft by the loss of him, but then he was lifting her so that they were both kneeling on the bed, her back flush to his chest. He supported her with one arm beneath her breasts; the other cut diagonally across the flat of her abdomen. From behind her he pushed her thighs apart with his knee. She was open to him now, vulnerable in her wanting.

She turned her head slightly, wanting to give him her mouth. Instead it was her neck she inadvertantly offered up to him. His mouth did not sip her skin now. Like the rest of him, his kisses were hard and hot. The hand on her hip moved to the inside of her thigh, stroking, caressing. His fingers slipped into the downy tuft of hair between her thighs at the same time his tongue speared her mouth. Lydia cried out this time. Nathan smothered the sound.

She felt the strength of his arousal against the cleft of her buttocks. She rested her weight against him and felt him suck in his breath, taking the air from her lungs. He broke the kiss. She gasped. Nathan made his husky demand. "Say it."

"You're . . . you're a proper match."

Nathan laughed. It was more of a growl, the sound coming from deep in his throat and slightly raspy, definitely triumphant. It was enough to prickle her skin.

Lydia made a small protesting movement when he didn't lay her down, but except for a gentle reassurance, he paid her little heed. "This way," he said lowly, lifting her hips. "Lean forward now."

"But—" She didn't finish because it would have been a senseless gesture. She was already doing as he asked, and Nathan was entering her from behind. Her cheek rested against the back of her hands at the foot of the bunk. Lydia's sable hair spilled over her shoulder. Her eyes were closed, her lips parted. Nathan's every thrust filled her, his every withdrawal left her aching. His hands stroked her from breast to thigh, pressing, molding, learning the shape of her. The position he held her in was novel and exciting and highly pleasurable. He rocked her body and she met his thrusts, surging against him until she felt the tempo change, his penetration become quick and shallow, and then his entire body tightened. He found his release in her.

Nathan drew her on her side and they lay together spoon-fashion, his hand resting on Lydia's hip. He caressed her, sometimes dipping to her inner thigh. His breathing slowed while hers quickened in anticipation of his touch. Nathan did not tease her long. He wanted her to feel the same pleasure she had given him and she was almost there, just skimming the surface of her climax, every sense heightened to him. He whispered her name and pressed more deeply, intimately.

She felt as if she would shatter if he didn't hold her and he seemed to know how it was for her. When pleasure shuddered through her, Nathan's embrace secured her and his body absorbed her trembling excitement. Her name became a softly spoken litany on his lips and his gentleness in that moment touched her deeply.

When she turned toward him as he lay on his back, Nathan glimpsed the sheen of tears in her eyes. Before he could question her or raise his concern, she was pressing her mouth to his in a remarkably chaste kiss. "You make me so happy," she said quietly, then Lydia rested her cheek against the curve of his shoulder and fell asleep.

Nathan was sitting on the padded bench beneath the porthole when Lydia woke. His knees were drawn up to his chest, his back pressed in the corner. He was wearing his trousers and nothing else. A band of moonshine slanted across his folded hands, but his face was in shadow. Deep in thought, his eyes focused vaguely on some point across the room, Nathan was unaware that Lydia had wakened, or that she was watching him.

She was glad he didn't know. He might have moved or come to her or said something and she didn't want anything from Nathan except the pleasure of looking at him.

It was his hands that she noticed first. She could hardly look at them without thinking of how they felt on her body, how the beautiful shape of them, the long fingers, the slightly rough pads of his palms, could make her feel beautiful in turn or give her such pleasure.

Her eyes made out the outline of his arms and shoulders in the darkness. His skin was smooth, pulled taut over defined muscles. She could almost feel the embrace of those arms, the circle of safety and security, the crook of the shoulder that pillowed her head. She raised her eyes fractionally, searching out the sharp lines of Nathan's profile, the Roman nose, the lean jaw, and the cleanly cut angle of his cheek.

He moved then and his face was briefly illuminated in the beam of moonlight. The predator eyes, those silver-grey, implacable, no-quarter eyes were turned in her direction. Their glance was piercing, almost savage, and then it was shuttered, shadowed again as he grimaced, as though in pain, and rested his head against the wall, his eyes closed.

Lydia sat up, wrapping the bedsheet around her like a

lava-lava. She approached him quietly, the only sound the whisper of the fabric against her skin. She stood beside him, not touching, not speaking, and waited for some sign from him that she was welcome in his thoughts, or a relief from them. It came a moment later when he reached for her wrist, drawn to her by the fragrance that would always remind him of the island, but which was Lydia's own. Nathan made room for her on the bench, slipping his arms around her as she leaned into him. His cheek rested against her hair.

"I'm sorry I fell asleep," she said. She turned her head a little and his chin nudged her temple. He kissed her lightly and the simplicity of the gesture, the warmth of it, curled Lydia's toes.

"I'm not," he said. He had watched her for a long time before he moved from the bed. Those moments had been the single most peaceful moments of his life. He would never regret them. "Have you been awake long?"

"Not long."

They were quiet. Outside, waves slapped rhythmically against the *Avonlei* and above them, on deck, a seaman on nightwatch played a wooden flute. There were footsteps, someone dancing, and then deep laughter and sporadic applause. Lydia found herself smiling and Nathan's arms tightened fractionally.

"They're having a good time tonight," she said.

"Hmm."

"They must be as reluctant to leave the island as we are."

"Probably."

"Fa'amusami said something tonight that bothered you."

"She did?" he asked, pretending ignorance.

"About that murder on the other island. You went back to see her father."

"Weren't you bothered by it?"

"Of course, but . . ."

"Yes?"

248

She shrugged. "I don't know. I just thought . . ."

He waited. Did she know? Could she remember?

"Nothing," she said finally, softly. "It was nothing."

Nathan was glad she could not see his relief. It could only make her wonder all the more. He did not want to discuss his conversation with Fiame and he did not want to think any more about the island girl's violent death. Did death follow or precede him? He could not admit to Lydia what he had no proof of himself.

Raising one hand, Nathan shifted Lydia's hair over her left shoulder. His fingers played in it, stroking, sifting. It was almost as peaceful as watching her sleep.

His voice was low and resonant when he spoke. "You should have another wedding," he said.

"What?" Surely she hadn't heard him correctly.

"Another wedding," he repeated, his hand stilling momentarily. "I've been thinking about what you said our first night on the *Avonlei,* about not remembering our wedding. We should get married again before we go to Ballaburn. There's a church in Sydney I think you'd like and I know the priest. Father Colgan has been a good friend to Mad Irish, and Mad Irish to the church. He would do the ceremony for us."

Lydia was moved to silence. His gesture touched her so deeply that she felt tears prick her eyes. Against her back she could feel Nathan's heart pounding in his chest.

He cleared his throat, uncomfortable with her stillness, her quiet. "I haven't said it very well, have I?" he said self-consciously. "I don't suppose you remember me asking you to marry me the first time, either."

She only shook her head. Even the smallest words were stuck firmly in her throat.

"I see."

For a long time he didn't say anything else, and Lydia began to think he wouldn't.

"Will you marry me?" he asked.

He put forth the question abruptly, a shade defensively, as if the answer were not a foregone conclusion.

His uncertainty was precious to her, and with it came Lydia's realization that her husband was not entirely confident of her affection, of the place he held in her heart.

"I should like to be your wife," she said, finding his hand and placing hers over it. "I should like it above everything."

She didn't mean what she was saying, he thought. She couldn't, not when she didn't know him for the man he really was, the man who had tricked her, lied to her, and was doing both those things to her now, almost without compunction. Almost. It eased his mind that the feelings of regret and pity were there. They meant he was not totally beyond redemption.

God but he wanted her to say those words and know what she was saying.

"Did you hear me?" she asked when he didn't make a reply.

He squeezed her hand. Above her, his eyes closed momentarily. "I heard you."

She thought he might say that he loved her. He didn't. Lydia said them instead. She turned in his arms and kissed his face and thought she tasted the wet saltiness of tears, but she was never sure that they weren't her own.

He made love to her then and Lydia forgot about everything except for the moment.

They stood arm in arm at the taffrail of the *Avonlei* as the ship was made ready to sail out of Apia Harbour. On shore a group of islanders waved and children chased one another along the beach, laughing with the clear tones and unfettered joy of youth. One of the boys tossed something white into the air and they all scrambled to catch it. It fluttered to the ground just out of their reach.

"Is it a kite?" Lydia asked, intrigued by the antics of the children. "I could have shown them how to make a better kite."

"I don't think that's what it is," he said, following the children's play with narrowed eyes. "In fact . . . No, it couldn't be . . ." He disengaged hmself from Lydia's arm and hurried away, returning in less than a minute with the captain's spyglass. He held it up, adjusted the focus. "I'll be damned," he said softly, lowering the glass and passing it to Lydia. He was smiling now. "See for yourself, Lydia."

Puzzled, she lifted the small telescope. "Oh, Lord," she said, mortified. "Where did they . . ." Her voice trailed off. She remembered where. Her cheeks were deeply flushed as she gave the glass back to Nathan. "It's all your fault."

He was trying to look innocent, but there was the unmistakable glint of laughter in his eyes. The object the children were tossing and chasing with complete abandon was Lydia's corset.

Part Three

Ballaburn

Chapter Nine

The *Avonlei* left San Francisco in spring and in just over four weeks, sailed into winter. It was late on the night of June 28 when the *Avonlei*'s lookout spotted light from Macquarie Tower's single oil lamp at South Head. Sydney Harbor was just beyond. Lydia and Nathan stood on deck with their fellow passengers and watched the beacon of light, still some twenty miles away, grow infinitesimally brighter as they neared it. Lydia was glad for the lined cape that had hung uselessly in her wardrobe until now. Her breath misted in front of her as the temperature nudged the low forties and the southeast trade winds no longer seemed warm.

They stayed on board the *Avonlei* that evening while the ship was anchored in Watson's Bay, waiting for dawn to ease its passage to Sydney Cove. Lydia was up before Nathan. She had all their belongings packed and was sitting on one of their trunks, anxious and expectant, hopelessly incapable of containing her excitement.

Looking at her, it was impossible for Nathan not to smile. She had his clothes laid out for him, his shaving soap lathered, and fresh water in the basin. Whenever he performed his morning rituals with less speed than Lydia thought was warranted, she sighed audibly and dramatically.

Their trunks and valises were finally placed on a

carriage bound for Sydney along the South Head Road. Lydia would have ridden on top with the luggage if Nathan had let her. She wanted to see everything, know everything, about her new home. The other passengers were indulgent, giving her the window seat on the right so she could enjoy the best view on their journey.

What she saw delighted and mystified her. It also frightened her a little as well. She could not put a name to most of what she saw. Nathan saw her distress and intuitively understood the cause.

"It's not your memory," he whispered in her ear. "You've never seen the like before, because there's none like it. Imagine what the men on the First Fleet must have thought when they sighted Botany Bay."

"It was another world."

"It was hell." The words were not said angrily but simply as a statement of fact. "This whole area is sandstone," he said. "You saw the beaches on the ocean side, how beautifully golden they are. That's from the wearing away of the sandstone. Where you can't see it outright in the ridges and gullies, it's only covered with a shallow bed of humus. It won't support market crops and it won't support a garden."

What it did support, however, was remarkably diverse and hardy. There were trees, some as high as fifty feet, with gnarled trunks and a thick hide of bark, narrow, silvery leaves, surviving in the sandy soil by grit and determination that seemed wholly Australian. There was the red gum, growing quite impossibly where a tree should not have been, sprouting from the head of bare sandstone rock and inviting the sun's caress on its smooth and satiny bark, shining with a hint of pink and white. There were fragrant eucalypts with their bluish-green leaves and groves of cabbage palms with slender, graceful trunks, and a headdress of fan-shaped leaves.

The billowing sails of clipper ships dotted Port Jackson and the port itself was shaped by dozens of inlets and bays. The route their carriage took closely followed Rose Bay at one point, then passed near Double Bay and Woolloomooloo Bay. It seemed fitting that such an alien place should have its share of equally alien names.

Sydney had much in common with the vegetation surrounding it. The city was a battler and a survivor as well, settled by people who had put down roots in spite of the long odds against them. Nearly one hundred years after the First Fleet landed, Sydney was not merely surviving anymore. She had come into her own, flourishing with industry and trade, deserving of the hardearned reputation as the mother city of the Continent.

Petty's Hotel, on the western side of York Street, was where Nathan and Lydia finally alighted. It was a grand and stylish building, with three floors, wide verandas, and wrought-iron railings. On the perimeter of the property was a spiked iron fence. Stone pillars flanked the main gate.

Lydia looked around the lobby while Nathan registered them at the front desk and the clerk sent out two boys to bring in the luggage from the sidewalk.

"Does Mad Irish know you've returned?" the clerk asked, making a notation in the heavy registration book. He squinted over the top of his spectacles rather than push them up his nose.

"Not unless rumor travels even faster than I think it does," said Nathan. "We've only just arrived."

The clerk looked beyond Nathan's shoulder, his brows raised slightly as his eyes darted over Lydia. She was examining the small collection of native oil paintings on either side of the fireplace. "That's her, then?" he asked, his voice dropping to a conspiratorial whisper. "Who'd have thought Mad Irish would—" He broke off because Nathan had closed the registration book over his hand and was pressing on it hard. "So that's the way of it," he said, trying to ease his hand out. "She doesn't know."

"I swear I'll break your hand, Henry. But I'll do it one

finger at a time, perhaps one knuckle at a time."

Henry smiled nervously. His high forehead was instantly shiny with sweat. "Of course," he said. "I don't know a thing about the wager. Not a thing."

Nathan didn't release the clerk's hand right away. He leaned his elbow casually on the book and called to Lydia to join him. "Lydia, this is Henry Tucker. Henry, my wife. Henry's been at Petty's about four years now. Isn't that right, Henry?" Henry's smile was fulsome, but he didn't do more than nod. "And he'll see that we get the best treatment while we're here."

"Yes, ma'am," Henry was moved to say.

"How very kind you are, Mr. Tucker," said Lydia. "I'm certain I'll enjoy my stay."

Nathan leaned away from the desk. Henry removed his hand surreptitiously and got the keys to Nathan's suite. "Your room opens on the veranda," he told them. "Anything wrong at all, come to me. I'll put it right again, just see if I don't."

On the stairs to their room, Lydia said, "Mr. Tucker was very accommodating. You must know him well."

Nathan shrugged. "He used to work for Mad Irish at Ballaburn. Now he caters to the Squattocracy."

"The what?"

"The Squattocracy. The aristocracy of the bush. Graziers. Stockmen. Farmers. Men who got their claim on the land by squatter's rights and now have some money in their pockets to spread in the city. Generally a squatter is a large landholder."

"I see. Then it was your money and position that made Mr. Tucker so pleasant."

"I suppose so."

"Oh," she said softly. "And I thought it was because you had his hand slammed in that book."

Saint Benedict's Church was one of the oldest Roman Catholic churches in the country. Built of stone in the

258

Gothic style, it had a spire that towered over its neighbors on Abercrombie and George Streets. The chapel was used on weekdays as a school, and that's where Nathan found Father Colgan.

"We shouldn't interrupt their instruction," Lydia said, pulling Nathan by the sleeve in an attempt to hold him back. "Oh, look, we've already distracted them from their lessons."

Nathan felt the press of two score of eyes turned suddenly in his direction. The youngest children were already talking out loud and shifting in their seats. Father Colgan clapped his hands once to regain their attention, gave his book to the oldest child in the classroom, and bid them all to recite multiplication tables in unison.

"Nathan, my boy!" he said happily when they were outside the classroom. "What a sight you are! And Mad Irish himself wonderin' if you'd ever return to Ballaburn. I told him you were as good as your word—and so you've proved me right." His large hands clasped Nathan by the shoulders and gave him a small shake, beaming widely. Father Colgan had fiery red hair and eyebrows only a shade darker. His green eyes were open and friendly and his nose was slightly flat and misshapen, the result of three rounds of fisticuffs with a street bully in his youth. "Mad Irish has seen you, hasn't he? You've only just come from Ballaburn?"

Nathan shook his head. "We've only just come from Petty's Hotel and before that from the *Avonlei*. Mad Irish is certain to hear I'm back before the day's out."

Father Colgan turned his hearty smile on Lydia. "And it's a pleasure to make your acquaintance, dear child. I've been wanting to meet the woman who could lay claim to—"

"My heart," Nathan interrupted. He had no idea where Father Colgan's statement might end, but he was not prepared to take any chances. It worked. The priest was distracted.

"Love, is it?" Father Colgan laughed. "Sure, and I can

259

see for myself that it is. Who would have thought? I wasn't certain there was a colleen who would have you. And what a fair lass she is, too." He poked Nathan lightly in the ribs. "What a wager it's been, eh? Make the introductions, boyo."

When Nathan was done, Lydia was warmly embraced by Father Colgan. His obvious affection surprised her, for she had done nothing to earn it save become the wife of Nathan Hunter. Perhaps that counted for something more than Nathan had led her to believe. Squattocracy indeed.

"Lydia and I want to be married here, Father," Nathan said.

"Married? But you said . . . it's Lydia Hunter, isn't it?"

"Oh, yes," Lydia assured him. "But I don't remember that, you see, and Nathan thought I might like to have another ceremony. One I *can* remember. You'll do it for us, won't you?"

Father Colgan's smile was fixed now and his eyes were sharply questioning as he turned to Nathan.

"Lydia," Nathan said quickly, "would you mind terribly if I spoke to Father Colgan in private?"

She was gracious, though bewildered. "I wouldn't mind at all. Perhaps I could stay with the children. Their recitation requires a little work. Seven times eight is *not* sixty-three." She slipped inside the classroom and in a matter of minutes the droning voices became a lively chorus.

Father Colgan listened and nodded his approval. "She's a fine one. You were fortunate it turned out so well for you. How's Brig taking it and what's this folderol about her not remembering your wedding?"

"Let's go to your office," Nathan said. "Lydia will be fine with the children. She loves them—the more urchin-like, the better."

The priest listened without comment for twenty

mintues as Nathan explained the situation more fully. Even then he knew there were some things the younger man was keeping to himself. He wanted to press with questions but counseled himself to tread lightly. He leaned back in his chair, supporting the back of his head in the cradle of his palms. "It was a mad scheme from the beginning," he said finally. "And didn't I say that very thing to Irish? Oh, well, I'll take it up with him when I see him again. He's not been to church above three or four times since you and Brig left for California. As things turned out, praying wouldn't have come amiss."

Perhaps that was so. Nathan wasn't sure, and what he didn't need from Father Colgan was yet another lecture on the sheer folly of Mad Irish's plotting. "Will you marry us?" he asked.

"It's what she wants?"

"Yes. You can ask Lydia yourself."

"I believe you. It's clear as my lumpy nose that she loves you."

"She thinks she does."

Father Colgan had no reply for that. Nathan would not believe anything he said to the contrary. "Very well, Nath." He sighed. "I'll do it. Mad Irish would like to see this marriage, though. Can it wait a day or so? Give him time to come in from Ballaburn?"

"No. Lydia and I want to be married today."

"All right. We'll have the ceremony in the chapel. I'll excuse the children for the afternoon. Let me get the proper vestments and find Sister Isabel and Sister Anne. They'll be very pleased to act as your witnesses and Mad Irish would never dare doubt them."

Nathan's lips were cool and dry as they touched Lydia's mouth at the end of the ceremony. Her hands were enfolded in his, protected and warm. There was a faint reassurance as he squeezed them gently. Lydia's

261

dark blue eyes were bright, her smile radiant, both of them lighted from the inside as if she were the source.

Father Colgan offered his congratulations and kissed Lydia on the cheek. He turned to Nathan. "There was never a wager like it," he said, shaking his head. "And, God willing, there never will be again. Here, sign your names in the book so the marriage can be recorded."

Lydia wrote first, signing her name Lydia Chadwick Hunter. There was a space to record her occupation. "What do I put here?" she asked.

"American free settler," the priest told her. "It means you're not a convict."

Lydia finished quickly, then gave the pen to Nathan. He had to produce his ticket-of-leave and dutifully record his crime and his sentence. For the first time Lydia had a sense of the burden Nathan carried and she understood the bitterness she sometimes glimpsed in his eyes. When he straightened she saw the anger that was not quite shuttered, the embarrassment at having to record his convict status in front of her. She took the pen from his hand, then took his hand, and now it was she who offered reassurance.

They did not return to their hotel immediately after the ceremony. Nathan took Lydia to eat at the Royal Hotel, which boasted a polygonal bar and two grand saloons, each one hundred feet long. They dined on clams and wild rice, sweetly buttered peas, and drank champagne from delicately fluted crystal goblets.

"People know you here, too," she said, a little awed by the fact.

One corner of Nathan's mouth lifted in a self-mocking smile. "If we were in San Francisco it would be much the same thing, only it was *your* family that was known. It's really Mad Irish they know, and me by association. And if you're carefully observant, you'll notice that the Sterling don't pay much heed at all, only the Currency."

"Sterling? Currency? What does that mean?" Hon-

262

estly, she thought, they spoke English in two different languages. At various times today she had heard herself described as a sheila, a cliner, a sninny, and most, disturbingly, as trouble and strife—the wife. Tea was supper, dinner was lunch, and supper was a light repast in the late evening. Bluey was a man with red hair and bloody was an interjection that turned inoffensive statements embarrassingly blue. "What does money have to do with anything we were discussing?" she asked.

"Everything and nothing. Sterling are the children of the English free settlers. The coin of the realm. No convict stain. Currency, though, refers to the paper script used here before there was a gold strike and a mint. It means the offspring of convicts." His mouth flattened fractionally. "What our children will be."

"Will you mind?" she asked.

"I should be asking you that question." In truth, Nathan had spoken without thinking. He had never given much thought to having children, none at all to having children with Lydia. She could be pregnant now, he realized, and he had never even considered what that would mean to her, to him. God, but he was a selfish man. "I don't think I've adequately prepared you for life here, Liddy. It's not what you were used to."

"I don't remember what I was used to."

"So you've told me."

Lydia looked around the dining room. None of the other patrons were paying them the least attention. Her hand slipped under the table and touched Nathan lightly on his leg. "Our children will be quite proud to call you Father."

Nathan held Lydia's glance over the rim of his goblet. Her hand had traveled stealthily to his inner thigh, and though her features were serenely innocent, her thoughts were not. "Keep your hand there a second longer, Mrs. Hunter, and I'll put you over this table, toss up your skirts, and see if I can't start our family right now, right here."

Her face flamed. She removed her hand quickly. "Nathan!"

"Try not to affect such shock, Lydia. The matrons are looking now."

Ducking her head, Lydia applied herself to her meal. In her secret heart of hearts, though, she was pleased.

The first industries of Australia, and therefore the first industries of Sydney, were brickmaking, flourmilling, shipbuilding, and distilling and brewing. George Street was a wide and busy thoroughfare, opening up Sydney south toward Victoria and west to the Blue Mountains. Carriages and horses kicked up plumes of dust in their wake. Women lifted their skirts when they left the sidewalks and took their chances among the coaches, wagons, and carts in the street. Toohey's Brewery offered ale and porter in bulk or bottled, and from the size of the warehouse, Lydia concluded they turned a handy profit.

Lydia thought they were strolling aimlessly, without any particular destination in mind, simply taking in the sights, when Nathan steered her into David Jones, Ltd., an emporium with the latest in fashion as well as the practical. A visit there, and a later one to Anthony Hordern and Sons in the Haymarket district, yielded Lydia two riding skirts, five cotton blouses, undergarments, stockings, nightdresses, three day gowns that needed only minor alterations, and two evening gowns for which she was measured, poked, and stuck with pins. Nathan chose the fabric and the color and Lydia forgave him his arrogance because he chose so well. He bought her riding gloves and boots, delicate slippers for parties, sturdy walking shoes, and plain leather ankle boots for daily wear. The drapers and haberdashers fitted her with hats for riding in the bush and bonnets for the city.

Nathan approached shopping, she heard one clerk

whisper, like a willy-willy—a dry storm tornado. Indeed, he swept up most everything in his path. By the end of the afternoon, Lydia was exhausted. She fell asleep in their carriage, her head resting heavily on Nathan's shoulder on the journey back to Petty's Hotel.

When Lydia awoke it was dark. She stretched languidly, shaking off the dregs of sleep slowly. It was lighter outside than it was in the room, thanks to street-lamps and moonlight, and Lydia could see Nathan on the veranda, leaning against the iron railing, his arms braced stiffly in front of him. His posture was of a man deep in thought, of pain, perhaps, certainly of tension. She would have gone to him, but she did not think he would thank her for it. There were times, and surely this was one of them, when Lydia suspected her husband wanted nothing so much as his aloneness. She let him have it.

It wasn't until he pushed away from the railing, shaking off the tension that made his spine rigid, that Lydia sat up and moved to the edge of the bed. Her dress was hanging over the back of an overstuffed armchair near the fireplace. Lydia didn't bother with it, pulling her fur-lined cape over her shift instead. She slipped her feet into a pair of flat shoes and opened the French doors to the balcony.

Nathan held out his hand to her and she took it eagerly, allowing herself to be pulled into the warmth of his loose embrace. His arms slid around her from behind and his hands slipped into the opening of her cape, under her breasts.

"Still sleepy?" he asked, kissing the crown of her head.

"A little. Your generosity wore me out today."

He nipped her ear and his smile and tone were wicked. "That's too bad. I had planned on being more generous this evening. My God, Lydia, what are you wearing under this cape?"

"You should know. You took my dress off."

265

So he had. Not that he hadn't expected her to put it on again. The circle of his arms tightened and his chin nuzzled her thick sable hair.

"Even the sky is different here," Lydia said.

"Hmm?"

"The sky. You must have noticed before. Where's the Big Dipper?"

He didn't comment on the fact that she could recall an arrangement of stars and not the faces of Samuel or Madeline. The tenacious hold she had on some parts of her memory still fascinated him, but he was becoming used to it. "There is no dipper Down Under," he said. "But there, high in the sky to your right. That's Crux, the Southern Cross."

Her eyes followed the path of the stars making up the small but brilliant constellation. "It's beautiful. All of it is, actually. Just different. I'll grow accustomed."

Nathan wasn't so sure. She was determined now, but circumstances could change . . . *would* change. Before the end of one year, Lydia might very well change her mind and choose to take a clipper back to California. Nathan wondered what he would do then.

"I have something for you," he said.

Lydia could tell by the way he spoke that he wasn't sure of her response. There was just an edge of little-boy bravado to cover his uncertainty. "You've already given me so much," she said, "what could you possibly have for me now?"

"While you were being fitted at Hordern's I had this taken care of." He released her long enough to reach into his pocket; then he placed a small, velvet-covered box in her hand. "If you don't like it . . ."

Lydia fumbled with the tiny button and string clasp on the side of the box. When she released the fastener she opened the box quickly, prepared to love whatever it was that Nathan had wanted her to have. There was no pretending involved, however. The opal ring was breathtakingly beautiful.

Taking Nathan by the hand, Lydia pulled him into their suite. She lit an oil lamp on the nightstand and took the ring out of its velvet bed. Mounted in a yellow gold setting, the stone was iridescent, reflecting light in a pyrotechnic play of color. Tiny veins of green and blue fire flashed as Lydia turned it. She could see pink turning to red, a hint of violet, and mother-of-pearl white on the translucent, polished surface.

"Oh, Nathan," Lydia said softly, wonderingly. She couldn't think of anything else to say. Words were inadequate to describe her pleasure.

"Here, let me put it on for you." She gave him the ring and held out her left hand. He slipped it on her ring finger, watching her all the while. "You really like it?"

"Like it? Nathan, you've dazzled me."

He breathed a little easier then. "You could still have a diamond if you wanted it."

"What would I want with an ordinary diamond? You chose this."

"I chose it because it's Australian," he said. "I found that fire opal years ago at Ballaburn. "I've never told anyone where it came from. It's been a talisman for me."

"Then I'll treasure it all the more," she said sincerely. Rising on tiptoe, Lydia kissed him. "How could you think I wouldn't like this?"

Had he been so obvious, or did she simply know him that well? Both questions were unsettling. "The jeweler told me most women would prefer a diamond."

"I would take you as the worst sort of man to lump me with *most women*."

"Then there was something he said about an opal being bad luck if it wasn't your birthstone. That would be October."

"It's settled then. I say I was born in October. Choose a day."

He smiled at the blithe way which she settled the problem. "The twenty-third."

"Close," she laughed. "It was the twenty-first."

"All right. The twenty-first." Because she had laid her cheek against his shoulder, Nathan did not see confusion cloud her eyes or the troubled frown that touched her mouth. "You can have a birthday once each month if you like."

"No, thank you. I should be older than you in no time at all."

He gave her a gentle push away from him. Her smile was teasing and her dark lashes fluttered coyly. The effect was spoiled when her stomach growled. "I suppose I'd better feed you, hadn't I? Here, or the dining room?"

"Here, please."

They ate a light meal with cheese and fruit for dessert. Nathan fell asleep afterward, his head lying in Lydia's lap in front of the fireplace. She stroked his dark hair, feathering the silky tuft of the nape of his neck. The back of her fingers caressed his cheek, resting briefly in the faint hollow. She traced the line of his black brows and swept back the lock of hair that had fallen across his forehead.

It was after midnight when he woke. Lydia hadn't moved, even when the fire went out. He helped her to her feet and they stumbled rather stiffly to the bed, collapsed, and were deeply asleep in moments, hands linked under the covers.

Lydia left Nathan a note on the mantel when she went out the next morning. She had no intention of being gone long, she only knew that she needed to be alone, to think. She had no particular direction in mind as she walked out onto York Street. The metallic call of a loose flock of honeyeaters caught her attention. The small songbirds pranced in the hotel garden, nervously active and noisy as they gleaned the ground for insects and the flowers for nectar. Lydia noticed her presence did not disturb them in the least.

She walked aimlessly, turning left, turning right, taking no real note of her surroundings after the songbirds. Lydia was remembering things, she was sure of it, and while the realization could have been a comfort, it was not. Lydia began to consider whether she really *wanted* to recall the past. The thought that she might not was a slightly chilling one.

The return of vague memories had really begun in Samoa. The threads of the past were so elusive, so gossamer-like, that Lydia held a memory for only a moment, felt it brush her, then slip out of her grasp. Faint recognitions had happened first on Upolu. Fa'-amusami had seemed familiar to her and Nathan had confirmed her suspicion, likening the native girl to someone Lydia had known before. Yet whenever Lydia struggled to gain a clear picture of Pei Ling, she saw only Fa'amusami. Now was no different. It was frustrating and annoying, this state of knowing and not knowing.

Last night, sitting in front of the fireplace with Nathan's head in her lap, Lydia's legs had gone to sleep. The numbness itself was not uncomfortable; she had barely noticed it until she wanted to stand. Then blood circulated quickly, tingling, pricking her skin in a hundred different places, and it was then that she really understood how numb she had been.

It was like that now. Her mind was prickly, exploding with tiny sparks that meant she was struggling to wakefulness. She wanted to be blessedly numb again. She wanted to stand. She could not have both.

On the white coral sands of Upolu a second silk thread tugged at her memory when Fa'amusami spoke of the murder of a Samoan woman. It fit with no other fact that she knew about herself, yet Lydia had felt a frisson of awareness then. There had been confusion, a measure of alarm, and when she mentioned Fa'amusami's words to Nathan, he dismissed them, but he did not ease her mind.

The children in Saint Benedict's school were wholly unfamiliar as individuals, but collectively they struck a chord, as though the situation itself was not a novel one.

There was a sense of comfort as she had worked with the students. More than that, there was a sense of competence that made her wonder how often she had done the very same thing in the past. She knew about the orphanage in San Francisco, knew about her work in raising money for St. Andrew's, because Nathan had told her. But this was something different.

Among the sea of faces in that classroom she had a fleeting impression of other young faces, as though a photograph had been waved in front of her and then quickly withdrawn. The picture in her mind was of two boys, alike in enough ways that they could have been brothers. They were grinning at her, one of them gap-toothed, both of them with dark chocolate eyes. She had thought it was their laughter she heard, but it wasn't. Caught daydreaming, the schoolchildren were giggling because she had stopped reciting. She went on with the lesson as though nothing had shaken her.

Lydia tried to recapture the images of the young boys, or put a name to either one of their impish faces. She could do neither.

So why had she known beyond any doubt that her birthday was October twenty-first? It was a startling revelation when she had chanced upon it. It might not have happened at all without the opal and a silly superstition. Yet when she airily demanded that Nathan pick a date, she knew immediately that he had chosen the wrong one. He had not understood when she corrected him that she had briefly stumbled upon the past, that she had recalled a birthday fourteen years earlier when she had been given a porcelain bisque doll in a starched gingham dress. She even remembered the doll's name: Emmaline.

Lydia became forcefully aware of her surroundings when a driver bearing down on her in his carriage called out to her. She jumped back on the sidewalk, her face hot with embarrassment, only due in part to what the coachman had called her. Behind her a man chuckled, and when Lydia turned to give him a cold stare, she saw his eyes running over her with an interest that was appreciative in a base, sexual way. Turning her head quickly to avoid the impending proposition, Lydia glanced to either side of her and hurriedly crossed the street.

She did not recognize anything around her. The community was poor. The houses were clustered, the wooden construction sagging. The narrow roads and footpaths were badly in need of repair and generally filthy. Sailors lolled in the doorways of pubs with names like the Cat & Fiddle, Brown Bear, and The World Turned Upside Down. They watched her go by, leering, calling out to her, but their interest was not attached for long as more amenable young ladies strolled in front of them.

There was a large population of Chinese in the area. Except to try to sell her something in their open-air markets, they paid her little attention. She attempted to speak to two vendors on different occasions, but in each instance their knowledge of English was so poor that she could not make herself understood.

Lydia sensed that she was taking a circular route and that her attempt to regain her bearings had come to nothing. Her suspicions were confirmed when she confronted the wooden sign above a pub named the Roo's Rest for the second time.

Adjusting the wide ribbon on her bonnet and clutching her reticule a bit more tightly, Lydia looked along the street for someone who might be trusted to give her the directions she required back to Petty's Hotel.

Nathan sat up in bed and threw his legs over the side. He looked around for Lydia, and not seeing her, assumed she had gone to the dining room for breakfast. He had already washed his face, shaved, and combed his hair when he found her neatly folded note on the mantel.

"Bloody hell!" he swore under his breath. Dressing

271

quickly, Nathan went to the front desk to see Henry Tucker. "Did you see my wife this morning?" he demanded without preamble.

Henry blinked widely. Here was the anger Nathan kept tightly leashed given full rein. There had always been a suspicion among the men at Ballaburn that Nathan Hunter was madder than Mad Irish himself. Brigham Moore used to make a joke of it and the graziers would laugh. Seeing it now, Henry could not raise a smile; laughing was out of the question.

"She walked out a little over an hour ago," he said uneasily. "A stroll, I think. Or shopping. She didn't say what her intentions were."

"Did she ask for a direction, mention anything she wanted to see?"

"No." Henry fidgeted with the register book.

"Did you see which way she went when she left?"

Henry shook his head.

Nathan's hand on top of the desk clenched in a tight fist. His mouth took the shape of grimness and his angry eyes narrowed. Somewhat to Henry's amazement, he pushed away from the desk without banging on the top of it.

"Where will you look for her?" asked Henry as Nathan stalked toward the door.

"Wherever there's trouble."

The door to the Roo's Rest banged open and the barrel-chested owner, his broad features ruddy with anger, hefted a small boy into the street. The boy fell on his hands and knees in front of Lydia, yelping as he scraped his palms and shins on the ground.

The pub owner may have been satisfied with throwing out the urchin, but the boy hadn't the good sense to know what to do with his freedom. He scrambled to his feet and raised his arm in an obscene salute and yelled, "Bloody barstud!"

272

Accent aside, Lydia realized the boy had called the owner a bastard. She was knocked aside as the owner came roaring out of the pub, looking angry enough to kill, and made to grab the boy. Lydia managed to keep her balance, and just as the owner's thick fingers caught his prey by the scruff of the neck, Lydia pelted him with her beaded reticule.

She may as well have swatted him with a pillow for all the good it did. He was startled by the intrusion, but he brushed her off as if she were nothing more threatening or annoying than a blowfly. He shook the boy like a ragdoll so the child's head flopped one way, then the other, and though the boy kicked and flailed, his strength was pitifully slight compared to his assailant.

Lydia increased her efforts, abandoning the reticule altogether and using her fists. She pounded the man's back, calling all the while for him to let the child go. The altercation had gathered a small crowd, but no one stepped forward to help her. In fact, Lydia thought she heard wagers being placed on the outcome and the odds-makers were not giving her even chances. Thoroughly appalled, Lydia increased her efforts, using the sharp point of her leather shoe to inflict damage.

The Roo's Rest owner took her seriously now. He released his hold on the boy and took Lydia by the upper arm. She fully expected the boy to run the moment he was loose. Instead, he turned on the owner, scratching the ground and jerking his head like a banty rooster, his fists clenched and raised.

"Leave her be, Bill!" He charged forward with two quick punches to Bill's middle, retreated, and came back again, butting Bill with his head this time. "D'ye hear me, Bill? Leave her be!"

Lydia thought it was doubtful that Bill responded to anything the boy said. Her heel grinding into the toe of his foot probably had more of an effect. He pushed her away hard. She stumbled, twisted her ankle in one of the ruts in the street, and fell down. Pain was instantaneous and sickening. She blinked back tears and sucked in her lower lip.

Boy and man were both distracted for a moment, but the man recovered more quickly, cuffing the boy on the side of his head and knocking him flat to the ground. Bill considered the moaning child dispassionately, shook out his hand, and rolled down both sleeves of his shirt. Money exchanged hands as people in the crowd collected on their wagers. There was a shift in the circle as Bill pushed his way through and went back into the pub. The door swung loudly shut behind him and the crowd slowly moved away, some of the winners following Bill's path to the Roo's Rest.

The crowd had cleared before someone offered her a hand. It belonged to the urchin. He was little more than half her height with dusty blond hair and a thin solemn face. Poverty clung to him. It was in more than the ragged, mismatched clothes that he wore, or the dirt that was like a bruise on his fair skin. There was a certain vacant look in his eyes, an absence of hope, a wariness that came from expecting the worst and receiving it. It was a terrible thing to look upon in one so young. Even when he smiled, as he was doing now, it had no substance.

Lydia accepted the hand, careful not to pull him down as she got to her feet. "I thought I would be helping *you* up," she said, pointing to the spot where he had been lying. She brushed off her dress and righted her bonnet. "Thank you. Are you certain you're all right?"

"Me?" He jabbed himself with his thumb. "I'm all of a piece. Don't worry 'bout me none. Ol' Bill gets that way once in a while. Saw that he was goin' to cuff me and I just took a little clobber on the chin. Laid there moanin' like for effect. No sense in him taking another jab at me."

"That was very wise of you," Lydia said. She tried to put a little weight on her ankle but the effort made her pale. Her smile was gritty. "Could you help me onto the

274

sidewalk there—" She broke off, wanting a name to put to the child's face.

"M'name's Kit. Christopher really, but Bill don't like the name much." He slipped an arm around Lydia's waist and let her lean on his bony shoulder for support.

"Bill is a relative?" she asked, beginning to form a better understanding of the fight.

Kit shrugged. "M'sister's husband. Only m'sister's been dead these past six months. Bill's got the pub and he got me. Only he didn't want me. We have a regular blue, like the one we just had, every three or four days—whenever Bill gets shikkered. The grog's no good for that one. Bound to feel crook later. How about you, Miss? You're looking pretty crook yourself. What did you hurt when you fell?"

"I've twisted my ankle."

"Here now," he said solicitously. "I'll get a carriage for you. Send you to the infirmary over on Macquarie. Some quack there will set you right again." He started to run off, stopped, and backpedaled to where he left Lydia standing. "I'll need some coin, miss. No driver will give me a second look if I can't show him some coin."

Lydia smiled faintly. She knew she was being robbed and she still gave up two golden sovereigns willingly. She closed Kit's grimy hands over the money and bid him take it. He disappeared around a corner and into an alley and Lydia limped to a stone retaining wall farther down the street and leaned against it.

She had no idea how long she stood there, her ankle swollen and throbbing, her head aching with pain only slightly less than what she felt in her foot. Nathan saw her first. He stood on the opposite corner, watching her, forcing back the anger that had driven him up and down Sydney's streets looking for her. He had imagined all manner of trouble that she could have found. That she was even in The Rocks without an escort was excuse enough to turn her over his knee. Couldn't she see the

275

place was a haven for harpies and sailors who had just crawled up from Sydney Cove, fresh from a month or more at sea? Didn't she have the sense to know she could have been accosted, even in daylight?

Lydia didn't see Nathan until he was less than ten feet in front of her. His wolf's eyes pinned her to the wall and it didn't matter in the least. She couldn't have moved anyway.

"You have some explaining to do," he said softly when he came to stand directly in front of her.

She nodded, but didn't say anything.

Her silence lit Nathan's short fuse. He placed his hands on either side of her shoulders and gave her a hard shake. "Look at me, Liddy! Are you ever inclined to act as if you have cotton between your ears? Have you taken notice where your feet have led you? This is The Rocks, Lydia. There's no part of Sydney more squalid or dangerous. It's like Portsmouth Square, only the dangers are real this time! If you wanted to explore this morning, you should have wakened me, or taken a carriage, or asked Henry where you might walk safely. Instead, you cast aside all manner of good sense and walk straight into a den of larrikins. These men would as soon throw up your skirts as look at you. Do you understand what I'm saying?"

Lydia bit her lower lip, her eyes downcast. Her face was the pale gray color of ash. "I understand," she said quietly. "Will you take me home now, Nathan? I don't feel well."

The haze of anger cleared and Nathan realized she did not look well, either. His hands no longer gripped, but supported. "What is it? What's wrong?"

"Just a small sprain, I think. It's nothing. Can we go back to the hotel?" Out of the corner of her eye she saw the slow approach of a carriage.

"So something *did* happen," Nathan said, disgusted. "Here, let me see. Which foot is it?" He hunkered down

276

and lifted the hem of Lydia's gown. His fingers were a mere fraction of an inch away from her ankle when he was attacked from behind.

Nathan toppled, set off balance by a pair of thin arms wrapped tightly around his neck and a pair of bony knees jammed hard into his waist. He tried to twist, grab at his assailant, but when he moved, so did his attacker. He did manage to reach over his shoulder and get a handful of hair. For his plans he was bitten on the side of his neck.

"What the bloody hell?" he said, grinding out the words between clenched teeth.

A clear, high-pitched voice answered him. "You ain't fit to kiss her foot! Can't you see she's not some harpy?"

Lydia's hands covered most of her face. She watched the scene played out through splayed fingers. The carriage driver had a good view from his perch and there were faces in all the windows across the street.

Kit screeched on, rolling onto the street with Nathan still in his clutches. "She's probably got some rich sod for a husband who would tear your eyes out for looking at her!"

"Whose eyes do you think you're tearing out?" Nathan demanded tightly. He rolled on his back and pinned Kit under him, making the boy's fight quite ineffective. "Take your bloody knees out of my side and your rum daddles out of my pockets!"

Rather than giving up, Kit looked to Lydia for help. "I've got him now, miss. Hit him with your bag!"

Lydia's hands slipped from her face. Kit's large eyes appealed to her while Nathan simply glared. She spoke to the urchin. "He *is* my husband, Kit."

"Good of you to tell him," Nathan said as the grip on his neck was eased. He got up, brushed himself off, and surveyed the onlookers who had paused in their steps to see what was going on. The look on Nathan's face sent them hurrying away and the faces in the windows dis-

277

appeared behind yellowing curtains. Only the driver remained with his carriage.

Nathan held out a hand to the boy and pulled him to his feet. "Kit, is it?" he asked. The boy nodded. "Well then, Kit, let's suppose you give me back the ten-pound note you took out of my pocket, the platinum watch fob, and—" Nathan checked his vest, "—the sovereign."

Hearing all of that, Lydia looked down at her hand to make certain she still had her ring. It was there, though she realized now she had been fortunate. She watched Kit hand his booty back to Nathan and thought about the pain in her ankle so she wouldn't disgrace Kit or Nathan by laughing.

"I thought you were going to hurt her," Kit explained with youthful bravado.

"I gathered that," Nathan said dryly.

Lydia limped a few steps forward. Nathan was immediately at her side and she leaned on his arm. "It was very gallant of you, Kit, to want to protect me, but as you can see, Nathan intended me no harm."

Kit thrust his hands in his pockets. His forefinger poked through one of them. He rocked on the balls of his feet as he looked from Nathan to Lydia and finally to Nathan again. He spoke in adult tones, man to man. "I'd wail her good when I got her home, sir. That's how m'dad did me mum and Ol' Bill did me sis. Kept them in line, too. You never saw one of them going off where they weren't allowed. Worse could have happened here today." Kit plucked one of the sovereigns Lydia had given him out of his shoe and gave it back to her. "Here you are, miss. Don't hate him when he wails you. It's for your own good."

Lydia was perfectly speechless, but Nathan was asking seriously, "Did your father use a switch or the flat of his hand?"

"Just his hands, sir. 'Course they were big as paddles. And now and again he'd use his fist, but that's not

278

sportin'. Not with a lady. Mum could hold her own, wallop him right back, she did. But your lady wouldn't take to that."

"I might," Lydia said under her breath.

"I see," said Nathan. "You've been quite helpful, young man. I'll consider your suggestion." He motioned to the driver, who hopped down from his seat and opened the carriage door. Nathan helped Lydia inside and tossed his sovereign back at Kit. "Get yourself some flash clothes and look the gentleman you are."

Kit clasped the gold coin tightly. "Yes, sir. Thank you, sir. G'day, miss." The carriage started to pull away. Kit ran after it briefly, waving. Just as it was turning the corner, he felt a beefy hand take him by the trousers and lift him off the ground. Bill shook him down for the sovereign, then returned to Roo's Rest.

Lydia wanted Nathan to stop the carriage. "Did you see that?" she asked. The tears in her eyes were only in part for her own pain. Mostly they were for Kit. "His brother-in-law took the money you gave him! We have to go back, Nathan. I'm not going to let that man bully that child."

"And what do you propose to do about it? Think you can be by that boy's side for the rest of his life? As soon as you leave, that bully will only take out his anger on Kit again and it will be worse for your interference."

Lydia didn't want to hear a rational argument then. She wanted Nathan to be as angry as she was over the injustice of it. Turning away, she stared blindly out the carriage window.

"Anyway, Liddy, it's likely the boy will steal the money from the pub's till."

"That's no answer." Still, it made her feel a little better that Kit might get some of his own back.

"It's part of life here in The Rocks." His tone was not callous, but matter of fact. He slipped his hand in Lydia's and squeezed gently. "Suppose you tell me what

279

happened here this morning. Is this the sort of thing I can expect often—a nipper attacking me to defend my lady's honor?"

Lydia shook her head and gave him a watery smile. Tears were an uncomfortable lump in her throat. She took a lace-edged handkerchief from her reticule and pressed it at the corners of her eyes. She told the story haltingly, without exaggeration, leaving out only the reason she had gone walking alone in the first place.

"So you see," she said, coming to the end. "Kit surprised me. I really didn't expect him to return with a carriage and change from the money I gave him. I didn't expect him to return at all. I thought I would just stand there until someone offered help or I could walk again."

"God," Nathan said softly. "What a wait that might have been."

"Do you know what people were doing while Kit and Bill were fighting?" she demanded, angry again at the thought of it. "They were making wagers on the outcome! No one lifted a finger to help or summon the police. They simply watched. I had to do something!"

"And what did it get you except a twisted ankle? Bill's in his pub. Kit's with Bill. Nothing has changed, not even your understanding of the people here. This isn't San Francisco, Lydia. No one's going to summon the police if they can avoid it, especially in The Rocks. The police are mostly despised; they're too much like the guards who controlled the prisons. Our past dies hard here. We do what we can without interference from others, and in the main that means the government authorities. There's still widespread sympathy for men on the outside of the law. They're seen as rebels, an embarrassment to the government who can't catch them all.

"No man here tells on his brother. Learn that, Lydia. It's the honor code of a criminal community. Learn it, or die for breaking it."

Lydia's breath caught at the end of Nathan's speech.

He was gripping her hand so tightly her knuckles were ground together. He seemed totally unaware of what he was doing. "Please, Nathan," she gasped shortly, trying to ease out of his bruising clasp. "You're hurting me."

Nathan felt the pull on his hand and looked down at what he was doing. He released her abruptly. He turned away, but not before Lydia had glimpsed the stricken look in his gray eyes. None of that could be heard in his voice. "I'm sorry," he said tersely.

She laid her hand gently over his. They rode back to the hotel in silence.

Chapter Ten

Lydia's foot was propped on an ottoman, supported by two pillows and ice wrapped in a linen towel. Her ankle was frozen, immobile, and still throbbing, but Lydia refused to complain. She was not giving Nathan another opening to lecture on her morning's folly. He looked as if he were just waiting to say something. She could tell by the way he beat the pillows when he fluffed them.

"Would you like something to eat?" he asked.

"No, I'm really not very hungry. But if you want to go to the dining room . . ."

He leaned back in his chair. "No. I can wait."

"Oh." Her smile flattened. She picked up the embroidery in her lap and began to work. She relaxed a little more when Nathan picked up a newspaper. They sat without speaking while Lydia's mind wandered back to the morning. She went over everything, but most especially the things Nathan said to her in the heat of anger, and she kept coming back to the one thing that didn't make any sense. Portsmouth Square. What had he meant by that? What had happened in the San Francisco rough quarter that wasn't a real danger?

Lydia bit off a thread with her teeth and critically examined her work. There was an ache behind her eyes that wasn't there because of strain. Did she really want to know about Portsmouth Square? No, probably not . . . but there was something else.

"What sort of wager did you make with Mad Irish?" she asked casually.

The newspaper stayed precisely where it was. "Wager?"

She nodded. "Father Colgan said something about it. Remember?"

"Actually, I don't."

"Well, he did . . . or I thought he did. And Henry, he mentioned it this morning as I was leaving. I just smiled and pretended to understand. I know I didn't imagine what Henry said."

"I never said you did." The paper was lowered slowly. "About Henry or Father Colgan. I simply said I didn't remember."

"But there was a wager, wasn't there?" Something about it nagged at her. She could feel the prickling, the sparks and static. "What was it about?"

"We're always making wagers. Will it rain on Tuesday? How many pounds of wool can Bob Hardy shear in a day? Who will win the next Melbourne Cup? It doesn't mean anything in particular."

"Yes, I'm sure it doesn't. I was just curious. What was this one?"

Nathan's face was impassive, his tone devoid of inflection. "Mad Irish wagered I'd never find anyone who'd have me."

"Then you've won."

He didn't say anything immediately, then, "Yes. I won."

Lydia's sprained ankle delayed their trip to Ballaburn by seventy-two hours. Nathan half expected to see Mad Irish storm Petty's Hotel in search of them. It was hard to imagine that word of their arrival in Sydney hadn't reached the station. He wondered if his employer had been gripped by cold feet after all this time. Mad Irish afraid? It was something to think about. He certainly had good reason to be.

Hobbling over to the bed, Lydia sat on the edge closest to Nathan. He was reading the *Sydney Morning Herald,* or at least pretending to read. The pages hadn't been turned or folded in the last ten minutes. Lydia pulled on the bottom corner of the paper, lowering it, and peered over the top. "I've finished trying on the dresses from Hordern's. They fit and they're packed. Are we leaving today or have you changed your mind?" *Again,* she wanted to say. Have you changed your mind again? Lydia found her husband strangely reluctant to leave Sydney for Ballaburn. Packed with ice, her ankle had presented a problem only on the first day. She had been willing and able to travel after that, but Nathan professed to be more cautious. Lastly he used the excuse of waiting for her gowns to be finished. Now that was taken from him, too.

Nathan closed the paper and let it slip over the side of the bed. "Do I detect a bit of censure in my wife's voice?" he asked blandly.

"Anxiousness," she said. "Impatience. Eagerness."

"No censure?"

"None." She crossed her heart.

Looping his arms around her neck and shoulders, Nathan brought her close so that their foreheads touched. "Only one of us is dressed for traveling."

"That would be me."

"I noticed." His fingers started to unfasten the long line of tiny buttons at Lydia's back.

Lydia gave him a playful shove and danced away from the bed, closing the difficult buttons. "Oh, no. I only just got out of bed. I'm not going back in again."

Nathan's dark eyebrows curved upward. "It wasn't meant as a punishment. You make it sound like some horrible sentence."

"Do I?" She paused in her task. "Well, I suppose it was in a way. You've been out and about these past three days while I've been confined here. My ankle's just fine."

She raised her skirt and turned her left foot in a series of circles. "See?" There was a fine blush to her complexion as she added, "I thought I proved that earlier this morning."

One corner of Nathan's mouth was raised in a half smile. "So you did." She had indeed. Lydia had been playful this morning, creative in her loving. They had used every inch of bed space, rolling from the scrolled mahogany headboard to the fretwork in the footrest. Was it any wonder that he wanted her again? "All right," he said, sighing. "But think about tonight at Ballaburn. I have a bed there half again this size."

"Oh, my," Lydia said softly. "I'll need a map to find you."

A Cobb & Co. coach, as popular in Australia as Wells-Fargo was in the States, took them from Sydney via the Parramatta Road. The coach was gaily painted, hung on leather springs to take the worst jarring out of the journey. Each one of the matched roans was carefully groomed. They wore blue saddle cloths, silver mountings, and their harnesses, oiled and polished, were decorated with blue rosettes.

Lydia and Nathan shared the coach with twelve other passengers, their luggage, and the mail. The coach could have held more people but not with the trunks and valises that Lydia brought. She was more than a little embarrassed by her excess of riches though Nathan seemed completely unperturbed and none of the passengers commented.

They traveled toward the Blue Mountains, the barrier along the Great Dividing Range. Evaporating oil from the forest of eucalypts caused a thick, distant haze and the play of light on the haze gave the mountains their color and their name. For years the dark and rugged terrain had held back the settlers with its dead-end valleys and steep sandstone cliffs. It had taken intrepid explorers to follow the mountain ridges, not the valleys, and discover the rich grassland beyond.

The Cobb & Co. coach rattled over the mountain roads, making surprisingly good speed. Watching from the window, Lydia held her breath as the ground seemed to drop away from them into deep, rocky gullies. Where trees grew they were most always the fragrant eucalypts. The spreading crowns of coolabahs and snow gums, the giant mountain ash, and river red gums, shaded the road in some places. Scrubby brushwood littered it in others.

Nathan tried to gauge Lydia's reaction to what she saw. Could she see the beauty in the land or was it too foreign to her? Looking from the great height of the ridges, the country below often looked brown and barren, yet when the coach approached one could see there were meadows and streams, grass and water enough to support sheep and cattle and fertile enough to support crops.

"Will we soon be at Ballaburn?" she asked. Some of the other passengers laughed. Lydia looked to Nathan quickly, wondering what she had said.

"We've been crossing Ballaburn land this last half hour," he told her.

"Did you ever tell me how beautiful it would be?"

Had he? No, he had told her about the bleakness, the unforgiving nature of the land when one didn't know how to work with it, how to irrigate it, how to find water in the barren outback and food in the bush. "I wanted you to make up your own mind."

The main house at Ballaburn sat on a gentle rolling hill, surrounded by green-and-gold terraced grassland. A stream of blue water, a clear meandering tributary of the Macquarie River, mirrored sunlight and the eucalypt forests in the foothills framed the stone manor.

Ballaburn was thousands of acres of land. Ballaburn was the livestock, the shearing sheds, the windmills and bores for water, the paddocks, the dams and fences, and the stables. It was a changing station for Cobb & Co. coaches and a place for passengers to take refreshment. It was the stockmen who worked in the far reaches of the station, protecting the property from bushrangers and the vagaries of nature. But first and foremost, the house was Ballaburn.

Mad Irish had not designed or built the house himself. It had first belonged to the Shaws. In the gold strike of 1851 they lost it when their freed convict labor fled to mines near Bathurst and south to Melbourne. Their livestock was ravaged by bushrangers who viewed them as easy targets and parts of the property were lost to diggers in search of gold and squatters who demanded a share of the wealth. Quincy Shaw sold his property to Mad Irish that year and packed up his wife and five unmarried daughters and returned to England.

Ballaburn's style was in the tradition of great English homes, though on a much smaller scale. It had two floors, a sweeping veranda on the second, and a terrace on the first. The entrance was flanked by white columns and led up to by a circular stone drive. The windows were large and rectangular, set deeply in the stone with broad sills and no shutters. Smoke curled from three of the four chimneys and a brightly colored fairy wren, his tail cocked, strutted across the edge of the sloping slate roof.

Crossing the stream on a sturdy narrow bridge, the coach slowed as it approached the house, stopping sharply in front of the terrace. From somewhere in the house there was a great cry as Nathan jumped out of the carriage. He held out his hand to Lydia and helped her down while their trunks and valises were being lowered to the ground. The other passengers alighted, milling around and stretching their legs while the coach and driver moved off to the stable to exchange worn horses for fresh ones.

Ballaburn's door was flung open and out came an apple-cheeked woman with a cupid's mouth and two chins. She stood just under five feet, had deep-set blue eyes, dimpled hands, and fine silver-blond hair that curled away from the coil at the nape of her neck. She did not look like she commanded an army, but Lydia swore she saw several men straighten to attention when they saw her, Nathan among them. Then again, perhaps it was the duster she wielded with such authority that made them jump.

"Refreshments will be out directly," she announced. "I've got shandy for you and biscuits if you've a mind to have some."

Lydia knew from her stay at Petty's that shandy was a mixture of lemonade and light ale. She nearly blanched at the thought of drinking it again.

Molly Adams saw Lydia's look and shook her head. "Not for you, ma'am. I've got fresh tea brewing if your husband would take it in his head to bring you inside now." Molly turned on her heel and marched back into the house.

Lydia glanced at Nathan for an explanation. "Is she always so . . . so—"

He shook his head. "Only when she's furious." He took Lydia's arm and crossed the terrace into the house, stopping just at the door to let a serving girl pass with a pitcher of shandy and glasses. "Don't pay it any heed. I don't. Didn't you hear her shout when the carriage stopped? It has something to do with our wedding, I'm sure, and the fact that she wasn't at it."

"Tea's in here," Molly said, wiping her hands on her apron. She opened the second door leading from the wide entrance hall and gave a quick jerk toward it with her thumb. "Just brewed a cuppa for Mad Irish. He's waiting for you, same as he has been since he got your letter from San Francisco, same as he has been since the *Avonlei* arrived, same as he—"

A stentorian voice boomed from the parlor. "That's enough, Molly. Show them in."

She winced. "Don't say I didn't warn you," she whispered, shaking the duster at Nathan. Molly smiled suddenly. "Ah, but it's good to have you back, Nath." She pushed open the door a little wider and ushered Nathan and Lydia into the parlor.

Mad Irish was a robust man in his fifty-eighth year. At first glance he was not a handsome man, but there was something about him that commanded a second look and then a third, and finally caused one to revise the first opinion. There was a certain ruggedness to his features that was attractive to women and forbidding to men. His dark-blue eyes were set wide and he sported a thick iron-gray mustache that covered part of his upper lip. He had a square, tight jaw and a chin that jutted forward. Broad-shouldered and thickly muscled, with a ruddy outdoor complexion, Mad Irish gave the impression of power and strength.

He was sitting in a large wing chair turned halfway between the open door and the fireplace, a wool lap blanket covering his legs. He did not rise upon their entrance, but held out his hand to Nathan instead.

Nathan accepted the near bruising handshake from his employer without comment. He took a step backward from the chair and motioned Lydia to come to his side. He put an arm around her waist when she did so.

"This is she, then," Irish said, not waiting for introductions to be performed.

Lydia felt herself being assessed by eyes that were very much like her own and found herself keeping back the hand she would have extended in any other circumstance. She held herself proudly, refusing to be intimidated by such an obviously rude man. It was difficult to believe Nathan had been taught anything in the way of good manners from Mad Irish. Her host's silence went on so long that she came close to telling him just that.

"She has the look of her mother about her," Irish said, turning to Nathan. "Haughty."

"I was inclined to believe that was your influence, Irish."

There was a slight furrow between Lydia's brows as she

looked to her husband. "Nathan? I don't understand." But she did. Or she was beginning to. She was coming to wakefulness faster and faster, aware suddenly of things she had not known before. The numbness in her mind was fading and the pain was hot, sharp, and intense.

Irish frowned. "You haven't told her?"

"That was your condition, remember? She wasn't to know."

"Nathan?" Lydia asked again. Her legs felt weak and she realized she was leaning more heavily against him. She closed her eyes briefly.

"There's no easy way to explain, Liddy," he said quietly, staring hard at Mad Irish. "This fellow is being a stiff, rude bastard right now because he doesn't know what to say to you, and that's the truth of it. So it's up to me to make the introductions." And pay the consequences, he added silently, for surely he would be made to pay. "Mad Irish, this is Lydia Chadwick Hunter, my wife. Lydia, this is—"

"Your da," Irish interrupted. "I'm your father, Lydia."

Lydia stared at him blankly. There was a blinding white light behind her eyes. "Marcus O'Malley." Someone said the name aloud but she wasn't certain if it was her own voice or Nathan's or Marcus himself. Lydia's hands went to her head and she held them there, trying to keep back the pain, trying to force back the memories.

Nathan caught her as she slipped to the floor in a dead faint.

San Francisco

Brigham Moore found his trousers at the foot of the bed and put them on. He eased into his shirt, careful not to pull at the bandages that still swathed his chest. Compounded by Brig's battle with pneumonia, his bullet wound had been slow to heal.

"You've got some of your color back," Madeline said. She slipped into her silk wrapper and belted it securely around her slim waist. "Dare I hope that I put a little of it there?"

He despised her coyness, her constant need for reassurance. He answered as expected. "You know you did. You, my dear Madeline, have the most amazing mouth." His eyes grazed her and settled briefly on her lips, letting her know that he was thinking of the things she had just done to him. "Shouldn't you be getting dressed?" he asked, glancing at the clock on the mantel. "Samuel will be here soon."

Madeline sashayed to the window and looked out. "He's coming up from the stables now," she said casually. "Better hurry if you don't want him to find you with me."

"Bitch!" Brigham's fingers flew over the buttons of his shirt. He yanked his suspenders over his shoulders. "You'd like that, wouldn't you? It's what you've been trying to accomplish all along."

"Yes!" Madeline swiveled her head like a striking cobra. "Yes, if it means keeping you here! Why do you have to go after Lydia? She chose her own path. Let her suffer for it—the way I did."

"I don't have time to argue this now," he said tiredly. "We've been over it before. Let me handle Samuel first, then we'll see." He ducked into the hallway carrying his shoes, shutting the door on the glass figurine Madeline hurled at his head. He hurried to the guest bedroom he had been using since the beginning of his recuperation and finished dressing. He brushed his hair quickly and took a last critical look at himself in the mirror. He couldn't tell he'd spent the last hour in Madeline's bed, how could her husband?

God, but the jealous bitch was going to ruin everything for him. Brig started downstairs. He'd have to think seriously about what he was going to do with her.

Brig was waiting for Samuel in the study. He had a

tumbler of Scotch poured for each of them. "I thought you might want this," he said as Samuel entered. The older man was looking preoccupied and careworn of late. His hair had grown remarkably grayer since Lydia's disappearance. Brigham knew that, like Madeline, Samuel did not trust him entirely. Unlike his wife, however, he suffered Brig's presence in the house as a means to an end. In Madeline's view Brig was an end to himself. She was miserable when she thought about him leaving.

Samuel took the tumbler, thanked Brig shortly, and sat down. "George Campbell tells me that he's booked passage for both of you on the *Falworth*."

"Yes, sir. Just this afternoon. We'll be leaving in two days time." Brigham sipped his drink. "You know, it's not strictly necessary that George accompany me. I could do this just as well on my own."

"It's more to the point that you're accompanying my man," Samuel said, speaking his mind plainly. "If it weren't for the fact that you know precisely how to find Nathan Hunter, I would be sending George on his own. I don't know where your truths end and your lies begin, or where you mix the two, but I do believe you're telling the truth when you say no one will give Nathan Hunter up. You see, I knew a few of the Sydney Ducks from the old days, and I remember what a tight gang they were, quite willing to cut one another's throats but just as unwilling to give up any one of their number."

"No, sir. You're right. We're not a very trusting lot."

A gross understatement, Samuel thought. He put down his drink and picked up his pipe. Opening a tin of sweet, dark tobacco, he began to pack the bowl. "Which is why you will be going with George Campbell. I don't criticize George when I say honestly that he would meet a dozen brick walls in his search for Nathan and my daughter. If I thought differently I would have dispatched him weeks ago, long before you were well enough to travel. I didn't—for one reason: I expect you to find Lydia and George to bring her home."

"I know what your expectations are," Brigham said. "I share them."

"Yes," Samuel said, giving Brig a hard look, unconvinced of the other man's sincerity in his own mind. "See that you do."

Brigham finished off his drink and sat down opposite Samuel, his long legs stretched in front of him. His handsome features were relaxed and a smile played at the corners of his mouth. "I have a score to settle with Nathan."

"Just so you don't have one to settle with my daughter."

"She was an innocent pawn."

Samuel nodded. "O'Malley's plotting again. Nathan's bullet would have been better spent in Marcus's chest than in yours."

"There were times I felt the same way. Like when that doctor brought me here from the hotel in his carriage. I swear Franklin found every blessed rut in the road between the Silver Lady and here."

"You were fortunate that Nathan sent Franklin to you at all. You could have bled to death in the room. It's always intrigued me, though, that Franklin was instructed to bring you here."

"I suppose, since I saved your wife's life in that quake, Nathan thought I'd get the best care here."

"His actions are altogether puzzling," Samuel said thoughtfully. "You say he sent a note to Lydia, asking her to meet him. She goes and he attempts to abduct her. You find out about his plan, intervene, and end up with a bullet in the chest."

"That's the jist of it. I couldn't stop him from leaving with Lydia."

"I'm surprised she agreed to meet him at all. I thought she made her feelings quite clear to the both of you when she tossed you out of her bedroom window."

That incident still rankled, but Brigham didn't show it.

"She did, Mr. Chadwick. At least to me she did. I had quite given up on Marcus's mad wager. I even told Nathan it was a draw—we both lost. But Nath doesn't give in so easily. You've seen the proof of that. Lydia made an enemy that night."

Samuel remembered Nathan saying almost those very words. At the time he thought Nathan was referring to Brigham. Now he had reason to understand how wrong he had been.

"My mistake," Brig went on, "was in thinking I could reason with him. I should have brought help with me. I was trying to avert embroiling your daughter in a scandal. I'm sorry I couldn't do more for her."

"She was fine when you saw her, though?" Samuel asked anxiously.

Brig had told him so repeatedly, but the older man needed to hear it again. "She was fine. Frightened, but physically well. You must believe that Marcus never intended any harm should come to his daughter. He only wanted to see her."

Samuel snorted, puffing on his pipe a little harder. "You're speaking of physical harm. Lydia could be hurt in a thousand other ways. Her note to me said she was eloping with Nathan."

"She was forced to write it, I'm sure. He meant that she should give the impression of willingness in a play for time. He had to be concerned that you would find them before he could leave the country." Samuel had never seen the second note meant for him, the one written by Nathan that explained more of the situation than Brigham ever intended to explain. Nathan had meant his missive for Pei Ling's hands and then Samuel's, but Madeline intercepted it quite by accident. It had been destroyed long ago and she, perhaps, would have to carry its secrets to her grave.

"He chose a good place to hide in the meantime," Samuel said, sighing. He had been able to trace Lydia's

295

message back to the orphanage through the person who delivered it. By then Lydia and Nathan were gone and Father Patrick was unable to tell him anything, bound by his vows at first, then by a stroke that left him paralyzed and speechless. Thus, Samuel was dependent upon Brigham Moore for answers, a situation he approached cautiously and with some repugnance.

"Nathan might have tried to take your life," he said, "but he also tried to save it."

"Nothing puzzling in that. That's the kind of mates we are." He sat up and leaned forward, resting his forearms on his knees. "I don't expect you to understand. We go way back, Nathan and me. I took him in, taught him how to live by his wits on streets meaner than anything you have here. He was my protégé and I was his mentor. I looked out for him for years. It was as much a part of my nature as breathing. Even sentenced to Van Dieman's Land, I looked out for him until I was released and then I didn't stop thinking about what would become of him. I traveled to Sydney, took a job in a printing shop, and met Mad Irish through some people there.

"He wanted a son and I made myself one to him. I did everything that man ever asked of me, and I came to love him like a father, but I would have given him the short shrift if he hadn't taken Nathan in when the time came. Irish had no need for two sons, he said, but he hired Nathan on and let Nath prove himself. And Nathan did what I knew he could. Eventually he was moved from the outbuilding where he stayed with the other jackaroos and stockmen to the main house where I lived with Irish. I wouldn't have thought then that anything could come between us."

A ring of blue gray smoke circled Samuel's head. His eyes were hooded as he took Brigham's measure. The things he was being told now were all new to him. "My daughter came between you."

Brig shook his head. He stood and poured himself another drink, leaning against the sideboard when he turned to face Samuel again. "Not your daughter. Marcus's daughter."

Ballaburn

"She asleep?" Marcus asked as soon as Nathan entered the parlor.

Nathan nodded. "Molly's staying with her now."

"Here, help me into my chair," he snapped. "Never felt so damn helpless as I did when she fainted like that. What was it all about anyway? Or doesn't she have any spine?"

Nathan didn't answer right away. He crossed the room and took Irish's wheelchair from where it had been relegated to the shadows. Pushing it over, he put it in front of Irish and took the blanket from his lap. Irish braced his powerful arms on the arms of the chair and hauled himself into it while Nathan held it steady. Beads of perspiration dotted his wide brow and he mopped them away impatiently.

"Give me that blanket. Can't stand looking at these pin legs of mine."

Nathan handed it over silently and poured whiskey into his tea while Irish tucked it in. Behind him he heard Irish wheel around sharply. "Your daughter has a great deal of spirit, Irish," he said finally. He stirred his tea, dropped the spoon, and turned around. "Don't crush it because you're afraid of her."

Irish practically sputtered. The expression in his cobalt-blue eyes was indignant. "Afraid?" he demanded. "Of her? You're not thinking clearly, Nath."

Nathan shrugged. "Have it your way. You'll lose her, too. She's got spirit sure enough, but she won't stand for your abuse. She'll leave Ballaburn and you'll never get to know her."

"She's your wife," Irish argued sourly. "She'll stay."

"I don't know how seriously Lydia will take our vows

now that she knows she's been tricked."

"You'll make her stay. Or you'll lose the land. It's a year, remember? We agreed that she had to stay in the country a year."

"In the country. Not at Ballaburn."

"Don't split hairs. That's not in the spirit of the wager and you know it! She must stay at Ballaburn."

Nathan's cup and saucer rattled as he set them down hard. "Word for word," he gritted, "the wager with Brig and me was this: Find my child. If Madeline had a son Ballaburn will be split equally among the three of you. But if she's a daughter, and she's unmarried, the man who brings her to Ballaburn wedded to him and can keep her in the country a full year after the marriage will receive the lion's share of the land. The other will receive only the lion." He raked back his hair, reined in his temper, and proceeded more softly. "The lion, as we both know, is that plot of land extending down from Lion's Ridge to Willaroo Valley. It's—"

"A thousand acres," Irish interjected.

"Of scrub and sand and treacherous gullies. The only part of Ballaburn that amounts to less than nothing. It's been mined and bored and it's yielded neither gold nor water. You knew what you were about when you offered it as the loser's prize. Well, I've won, Irish. I've brought your daughter to Ballaburn. I can keep her Down Under. But if you want to keep her at Ballaburn that's your affair." He started to walk away, going four steps before Irish called out to him.

"Don't you leave me, damn you!" Irish yelled. "The land isn't yours yet. The year's not up and I'm not dead! I don't even know that she *is* my daughter. You haven't offered me proof of that!"

Nathan halted in his tracks and turned slowly. "It's Nathan you're talking to. Not Brig. He entertained the idea of bringing a fake, not me."

Irish's smile was smug. "That's why I sent both of you. Knew that together you'd keep each other honest in your own fashion." He waved Nathan over to the chair he had vacated. "Now sit down and tell me what's happened. Your letter of two months ago was short on detail and Lord knows I can't believe half of what I've heard since you've arrived in Sydney."

Nathan hesitated. Mad Irish certainly had a way about him. Domineering. Demanding. Impatient. He was also one of the finest men Nathan had ever known. With a self-mocking grin, Nathan sat down and began answering the questions Irish fired at him.

It was at the end of the lengthy interrogation that Molly Adams poked her head through the open doorway. "I'm taking some tea and biscuits to Lydia now," Molly said. "She's awake and asking to see you, Nathan."

Nathan nodded. "Get her whatever else she wants, Molly, and tell her I'll be right there."

"She didn't ask for me?" Irish asked. Though he was unaware of it, Molly and Nathan both heard the thread of hope in his request, the need and anxiety he would not admit.

"Just Nathan," said Molly. "And you're lucky, Irish. Unless I miss my guess, she plans to tear a strip into him."

"I'm coming," Nathan repeated. Molly disappeared and he heard her heavy tread on the stairs. "Molly's probably right about what Lydia wants. You can hardly appreciate what you set in motion, Irish, and God damn me for wanting what you offered. Ten years ago I would have been satisfied with the lion."

Lydia was out of bed when Nathan entered the room. The covers on the large four-poster were disheveled as though it had been recently and hastily vacated. On either side of the bed was a large window with cream-colored curtains that were drawn back. Sunlight fell on the hardwood floor in two long rectangular patches. The room itself was exactly the way Nathan remembered it.

There was an armoire situated at an angle in one corner, a highboy dresser, oval tables beneath each window, one with a pitcher and basin and linens, the other with a lamp and a stack of books. A rocker which was rarely used for anything but a pants rack sat facing the fireplace. The mantel was bare. Their trunks and valises littered the floor but only some of the luggage was open and no attempt had been made to find a place for any of their belongings.

Lydia was standing in the stream of sunlight. There was a penumbra of soft golden color about her head and wisps of sable hair took on a fiery brilliance. Light glanced off her white shoulders and sifted through the cotton shift she was wearing. She dropped the gown she had been holding over the back of the rocker and her hands fell straight to her sides. She stood there, still and proud and silent, tearing a strip into Nathan with nothing more than her dignity.

Nathan shut the door behind him and leaned against it, waiting. When Lydia stepped out of the sunlight he could see the path of dried tears on her pale face. Her eyelids looked tender and swollen and the expression in her dark-blue eyes was not accusing, but grieving.

"I've remembered everything," she said quietly.

His eyes closed briefly and behind him his hands folded into tight fists. There was a deeply felt ache inside him that was only hinted at in his voice. "I thought that you had."

"I can't even think how to say how much I despise you." She raised her arms and crossed them in front of her protectively. "It's all been a lie."

Nathan didn't say anything.

Lydia looked away quickly and forced back the sob that hovered on her lips. After a moment she said, "Tell me about Brigham. Did I really shoot him?"

"Yes."

She nodded slowly, as if she expected the answer but had hoped it might be different. "I thought perhaps it was part of the game you both were playing with me, some sort of trickery to make me think I had killed him."

"No trickery," said Nathan. He pointed to the open valises. "You were looking for the gun?" She nodded again. "I got rid of it shortly after you found it on the *Avonlei*. I didn't want you to hurt yourself with it."

"Or hurt you."

"That had also occurred to me."

Unable to meet his eyes, Lydia stared at a point just over Nathan's left shoulder. "Father Patrick didn't marry us."

"No, he didn't. He wouldn't."

"And all that time on board the *Avonlei* . . ."

"It was as if we were married."

"As if." Lydia laughed shortly, without humor. "We *weren't* married."

"No," he said. "We weren't. Not then."

Lydia hugged herself tighter. "God, that I could be so foolish."

Nathan pushed away from the door and took a step toward her. "Lydia."

She shook her head furiously, withdrawing into herself to keep him at bay. "No, don't touch me. I don't think I could bear it if you touched me." Her eyes felt gritty and her mouth was dry. "I wanted to believe, I suppose. It could only have happened because I wanted to believe in it so much. There were moments when I thought I was remembering something, moments when I was only a hairsbreadth from awareness, and I beat them down. I know that now. In some small dark corner of my mind I must have been afraid the truth would look like this." Lydia's smile was self-deprecating. "Thank you for never saying that you loved me," she said. "That would have been the worst lie of all."

She turned away then and went to the window. There were sheep grazing in the meadow and a stockman was currying a horse outside the stable. Lydia fingered the curtains with a hand that trembled. "I want to go home,

Nathan. Please say that you'll help me go home."

"I can't do that."

"Can't? Or won't?"

"All right," he said heavily. "I won't do that. Have you thought what it would mean? There'd be an inquiry into Brig's shooting and possibly a trial. Do you want to face that?"

Lydia blanched, but her voice remained composed. "It happened in your hotel room, Nathan. I was there at your behest. The note, remember? You wanted to see me about Ginny Flynn's murder. I went there hoping to get back more of my yellow ballgown than the scrap you enclosed in the note." She glanced over her shoulder at Nathan. There was a line between his brows and his eyes were remote, thoughtful. "No one saw me come and I'm willing to bet no one saw you take me out of there. You're a far more likely suspect in Brig's shooting than I'll ever be."

"Except for one thing," Nathan said. "I didn't do it, Lydia, and you won't let any believe that I did. That's not your way. You'd never let anyone take responsibility for something you'd done."

He was right about her, she thought miserably. She had always thought honesty was a virtue and it hurt to have it wielded against her in a mean, back-handed fashion. She remembered the night Brigham had confronted her with such startling clarity that it seemed impossible now to have forgotten it. She could see the events unfold as though she were a spectator and not a participant, and hear her own voice begging Nathan to help her, swearing that she would do anything—even marry him—if only she would not be named a murderer. Had he heard her through his drugged sleep? Had she somehow forced his response?

"It was self-defense," she said.

Nathan nodded. "I know. I told Irish the same." When he had mounted the stairs earlier on his way to face Lydia, Nathan vowed that she would only hear the truth from him. She deserved at least that much. Now, faced with the prospect of her leaving, Nathan was sorely tempted to break his vow and beg no one's forgiveness for it. He had no idea whether Brigham Moore was alive or dead, but he knew what Lydia thought and he could have used it. He didn't. "I don't think you killed him, Lydia."

"I tried to reason with Brig," she went on, lost in her own thoughts. "He didn't want to hear anything I had to say."

Nathan crossed the room and came to stand at Lydia's back. She had nowhere to go, trapped by his body and the window in front of her. His hands hovered near her shoulders for a moment, then fell back to his sides. "Did you hear what I said?" he asked. "I don't think you killed him."

Lydia turned suddenly. She stared at Nathan, her eyes wide. "What? How can that be? His pulse . . . I couldn't feel a pulse . . . and there was so much blood."

"But he was alive when I took you out. And I sent Doc Franklin to see him, gave him instructions to take Brig to your home when he was well enough to travel." His tone became dry. "Your mother, I believe, will care for him."

Lydia's lips parted slightly on a tiny sound of pain. "He was having an affair with my mother, wasn't he?"

"Yes."

Her stare was frank. "Were you?"

"God, no."

She believed him. "That's something, at least," she said with bitter sarcasm. "So, the last you know of Brigham Moore is that he is settled on Nob Hill making a cuckold of my father."

"I don't know that at all. I told Doc Franklin to take him there. I don't know if he made it."

Lydia sidestepped Nathan and sat down on the edge of the bed, drawing her knees up to her chest. Her bare toes peeked out from beneath the hem of her shift. "You could have let me think I murdered him."

"You may have."

"I know. And I'll find out when I write to my father. But you could have let me think it now, when quite the opposite may be true. Why didn't you?"

"I didn't want you to stay here for the wrong reasons," he said finally. He nudged one of the trunk lids closed with his knee and sat on it. "You shouldn't be afraid to go back. Even if you killed Brig, even if there is a trial, no jury's going to convict you. And if he *is* alive, you shouldn't have to live one day thinking differently."

Lydia's eyes held Nathan's for several long moments. She was the first to look away. "I'd like to be alone now, if you don't mind."

"There's only one coach in and out of Ballaburn," he told her. "It's already gone."

She nodded. "I know I'm not going anywhere today, but I'd still like to be alone to think about tomorrow."

The dining room at Ballaburn had a western exposure. The brilliant white sun of the early afternoon had lowered and washed the foothills with pink-and-gold light. Flames crackled in the fireplace behind Irish's place at the head of the large table. He looked up at Lydia's entrance and set down his water glass. His head bowed slightly in acknowledgment of her presence.

Nathan stood, skirted the table, and held out a chair for Lydia on Irish's left. He felt her infinitesimal start of surprise when she saw Irish's wheelchair, but her fixed, gentle smile did not falter. He returned to his own seat across from her and struggled for distance in the way he was seeing her and feeling about what he saw.

He was not even certain she would join them for the evening meal, and here she was, freshly bathed and coiffed, every last vestige of traveling dust and weariness washed away. Except for the heavy, faintly slumberous look of her eyelids, there was no evidence that she had ever cried. She was wearing a deep lavender silk gown with piping, fringe, and buttons all just a shade lighter.

304

The collar was high and the tight bodice buttoned down the front well below her waist, making her seem breakably slender. She wore gold-and-pearl earrings which swung delicately when she turned her head.

Nathan glanced at her hands and felt a chill creep under his skin that eventually reached his eyes. Lydia was not wearing her ring.

"I'm pleased you decided to join us," Irish said. "Molly thought you might. She wants you to especially try her bread. It's just fresh from the oven."

Lydia looked over the table. There was a steaming leg of lamb, roast chicken, boiled buttered potatoes, mint jelly and gravy, corn and beans, and a covered basket bulging with hot rolls. "Everything smells delicious. May I?" she asked.

Irish nodded. He expected her to fill her own plate. Instead, she bowed her head and said a blessing. Afterward she served him, then Nathan, and finally herself and missed the look that passed from Irish to Nathan, the look that expressed surprise, confusion, and a certain softness of feeling.

"What should I call you?" she asked, turning to Irish as she raised a slice of meat to her mouth. His hesitation almost made her regret the question, for in that moment she saw what he really wanted and it was impossible for her to comply. "I can't call you Father," she said gently. "My father's in San Francisco. I hope you can understand."

"Samuel Chadwick," Irish said.

She nodded. "Mother calls you Marcus. Nathan's always called you Mad Irish."

Nathan grinned. "I don't call him Mad Irish to his face, Lydia. No one does. I'd prefer we forget what I call him behind his back."

"As if I didn't know," Irish scoffed, wagging his fork at Nathan. To Lydia, he said, "I'd be pleased to have you call me Irish. I probably wouldn't answer to anything else anyway."

305

"Irish it is."

"Does this mean you're staying at Ballaburn?" he asked.

Lydia looked from Irish to Nathan. "I honestly haven't decided. I've written to Mother and Papa, explaining as much as I know of what's happened, and I've asked Papa to send money for my passage. I may stay here or in Sydney until then."

"Sydney!" Ruddy color rushed to Irish's face and he made a blustery protest. "Where would you go? What would you do? You don't know anyone in Sydney."

Still looking at Nathan, Lydia said quietly, "I don't know anyone here, either." She lowered her eyes then and continued eating.

Irish opened his mouth to say more but closed it again when Nathan caught his eye with a quick warning to stop. Not used to being told what to do, Irish took the advice without much good humor, stabbing at his food when he returned to his meal.

"You wrote a letter once before to your parents," Nathan said to Lydia. "At the orphanage, remember? Just after you recovered from your fever."

"I wrote what you told me to write," she said. "And it was a lie. We didn't elope. I doubt that Papa believed it anyway. It had to have confused him. He was there when I sent you and Brig jumping from my bedroom window. He *knew* how I felt about the both of you."

"Jumping out of windows?" Irish interjected, his iron-gray brows making a single thick line above his eyes. "What's this about? Nathan?"

"Later," Nathan said shortly. "I also wrote a letter, Lydia. One to Pei Ling to be given to your father. I told him all about Marcus and the wager and my part in it."

"Did you?" she asked, clearly disbelieving.

"Yes."

Lydia hesitated. The way he spit out the single word it was like a slap. "Then you told him more than I know," she said, refusing to be baited. "I've heard about this

306

wager, of course, but I don't think I've ever been told the truth about it. Have I?" Nathan started to say something, but Lydia held up her hand, cutting him off. "No, I'd like to hear it from Irish."

"Nath was right," Irish said. He wheeled away from the table to the liquor cabinet and poured himself three fingers of whiskey. "You do have spirit. Scratch the surface of that serene Madonna face and one can see right away that you don't back down. Do you get that from Madeline, I wonder, or from me?"

He came back to the table. "I suppose you think you've been the one wronged here, the one who's had everything done *to* her and *against* her. You've probably never considered you're the person everything's been done *for*." His fingers pressed whitely on the tumbler and he stared at his drink, not at Lydia. "This afternoon before you fainted you said my name. I was surprised that you knew about me at all. I'd have thought Madeline would have kept it a secret from you."

"She did for many years. She told me when I was fourteen."

"And what did she tell you?"

Lydia was suddenly uncomfortable. Quite unconsciously she sought out Nathan, mutely appealing to him for help.

"Irish . . ." Nathan began. "She doesn't—"

Irish slammed his empty hand against the arm of his chair causing Lydia to jerk in surprised reaction. He spoke roughly to Nathan. "She asked me to tell her about the wager and I will—in my words, in my way. You can leave if you want."

"No, I'll stay." After all, he thought, he was one of the people something had been done *to*.

"What did your mother say about me?" Irish asked Lydia again.

Lydia laid down her fork. "She said you were a rapist . . . that you had raped her and that I was the child of your violence. She said you were a dirty Sydney Duck

307

and that you had committed unspeakable crimes before you were transported. She told me once that there had been a time when she trusted you, thought you were different from the others you ran with, and then you proved to her how wrong she was by taking her by force."

Irish's grip on his tumbler eased gradually. "And what would you say if I told you that it was all lies?"

"I'd say *you* were the liar."

Irish nodded, expecting that answer. "Then you're not ready to hear about the wager. You wouldn't understand and you wouldn't believe."

"You expect me to believe you?" She snapped her fingers. "Just like that? Ignore everything my mother's ever told me about you when I have all kinds of evidence to support what she's said? Nothing you've done has been for me. It's all been for *you*. You've acted ruthlessly and without feeling. I may not understand this stupid, childish wager of yours, but I know enough to realize you never once acted on my behalf or on the behalf of anyone besides yourself."

Lydia swept the napkin from her lap, folded it neatly, and dropped it beside her plate. She stood, her silk gown whispering softly in the oppressively silent room as she pushed back her chair and walked out.

Nathan watched her go, appreciation in his silver, blue-ringed eyes. The faint smile that hovered on his lips applauded her. He uncovered the rolls, chose one, and began to butter it.

Irish shot him a sour glance and finished his drink in two long swallows. "You approve, I suppose."

"Of Lydia? Yes, I approve. And so should you, Irish. She's your daughter through and through."

Setting down his tumbler, Irish said heavily. "No, she's not. She's Samuel Chadwick's daughter. She just reminded me how much."

There was a lot of truth in that statement and Nathan didn't respond to it. "What is it that you expect from her?"

"An open mind. If she'd just hear me out with an open mind, I'd be satisfied with that. What chance do I have of being heard when Madeline's filled her head with those foul lies?"

"You weren't really asking for an open mind, though," said Nathan. "You wanted her to believe you outright and she's not going to do that. She needs time, Irish. You have to let her come to know you, learn to trust you a little. She's not going to respect you simply because you say you're her father. Her feelings aren't attached."

"Can't you talk to her?"

"No. Not about this. You said you wanted it in your words, your way. I'm not interfering. Besides, she was very clear about her feelings toward me this afternoon. I don't have any influence."

"But she's your wife." His tone suggested there should be no problem.

"She doesn't think like convict women, Irish, or their daughters. She doesn't expect to be treated with indifference except in the bedroom, and in there she doesn't expect to be treated like a whore. Lydia has a heart and mind of her own and you'd do well not to try to stuff her with your opinions because she'll reject them all. You've got to give her time."

"Time," Irish said softly, "is the one thing I don't have."

Chapter Eleven

"I brought you this," Nathan said, nudging the bedroom door closed with his boot heel. He carried a tray filled with a helping of everything from their meal. "You left the table without eating much. I thought you might be hungry."

"I am." She put down her embroidery and cleared the side table ladened with books so Nathan would have a place to put the tray.

"We'll have to get another table for you here if you're going to eat many meals in this room." He pushed the table and tray close to the bed where Lydia was perched on the edge.

Prickles of warmth touched Lydia's cheeks and she stared at her hands in her lap momentarily, sighing. "Yes, well, I'm surprised you've brought me anything at all, or more than bread and water. I was unconscionably rude to your employer."

"Don't let my relationship with Irish stop you from speaking your mind. He and I have muddled through for years. It was quite something to see him set back on his heels."

"Still, I was rude."

"You were baited." Nathan sat down in the rocker and stretched out his legs, using his heels as a brake to keep from moving. He glanced around the large room and realized some other furniture was in order. Odd, he thought, how it had all seemed adequate before Lydia. Now he wanted a place where he could sit beside her while she embroidered, a desk where she could write, and a small table where they could have a meal alone when Irish was in one of his black moods. "You won a measure of Irish's respect this evening."

"I don't know if I want his respect," she said honestly. "I'm not certain I like him or care to. He's not a very kind man."

"Kind? No, that's not Irish. He's not cut from the same cloth as Samuel Chadwick and you'd do well not to compare them. There's no competition here for your affection. At least Irish doesn't mean for there to be. He only wants to come to know his daughter."

Lydia dabbed a tiny slice of lamb in mint jelly, pausing as she lifted it to her mouth. "As to that," she said. "How do I know he's Marcus O'Malley? How do I know I'm really his daughter?"

Nathan laughed softly, a half smile on his lips. "He asked a similar question. You only have to look at his eyes to know the truth. They're your own, Lydia, and you know it."

She didn't respond to that, but ate in thoughtful silence. "What happened to Irish's legs?" she asked. "Would he mind if you told me?"

"He probably thinks I already have. You barely reacted when you saw him in his chair at dinner."

"I was shocked. And you noticed."

"I was touching you," he said softly. "I notice when you tremble."

For a moment Lydia forgot how to swallow. She simply stared at Nathan and felt heat blossom in the pit of her stomach. "Don't," she said suddenly, angrily. "Don't say things like that and don't look at me that way."

One of Nathan's brows arched, his features both amused and mocking. "You wanted to know about Mad

Irish's legs," he said calmly, as if her outburst had never been.

Lydia began to eat again. "Yes. Has he been in the chair very long?"

"A little more than three years. We'd had a run of bad luck with the bushrangers. They were taking sheep, knocking down fences, and breaking dams. One of Ballaburn's stockmen was killed defending the property. There was a time when the rangers left Ballaburn alone, in deference I suppose to the fact that Mad Irish was a convict himself. But that changed as he got richer and the size of his holdings grew. In general, there's quite a bit of sympathy for the bushrangers, but not here at Ballaburn, not when we've seen firsthand what they're capable of doing.

"Brig and Irish and I set out with a plan to stop them. We left a few men to defend the house while everyone else mounted to drive the bushrangers out. Irish and I were riding together near Nillaburra ridge, heading south toward the gully. God, I can even remember what we were talking about when it happened."

San Francisco, Nathan thought. They had been talking about the wager even then. Irish had had something like it in mind for years. Long before Nathan arrived at Ballaburn, Irish had been tutoring Brigham, preparing him to make the voyage to California and bring back his son or daughter from the rarefied air of Frisco's social elite. But Irish had hedged his bets, bringing in Nathan at Brig's request and tutoring him in the same vein. While Nathan proved to be a quick study, Brigham still had years of a jump on him, and was prepared to leave Ballaburn long before his friend. Irish, however, was only willing to send them in tandem, and that meant Brigham was forced to wait until Irish decided Nathan was ready.

"I was trying to convince Irish to let Brig leave Ballaburn," Nathan said, his head tilted to the right as he retrieved old memories. "He wouldn't hear of it.

313

Wouldn't consider giving Brig the money for his passage and wouldn't think of letting me go with Brig then. Brig had been bending his ear in a like vein for weeks with a similar lack of success." He realized that he was coming perilously close to telling Lydia about the wager and shifted his focus. "I've always wondered if we'd been paying more attention to what was around us, whether we could have heard the bushrangers taking up positions along the ridge."

"Oh, God," Lydia said softly as her thoughts leapt ahead of Nathan's story, knowing precisely where it would lead.

"We didn't have any time to get to our guns as the shots were fired. Our horses reared, scrambled, and lost their footing on the steep hill. Mine was shot out from under me and I slid fifty yards to the gully floor. I had a broken leg and a dislocated shoulder. Irish wasn't so lucky. He took a bullet in the back."

"And hasn't walked since."

Nathan sat up straighter. He nodded. "We were left for dead. Would have been, too, if it hadn't been for Brig. When we didn't return to the house that night he took a few men with him and tracked us down. They found us in the morning and brought us both back on a sledge."

Brig again, Lydia thought. Did Nathan hate her for what she had done to his best friend? And Irish? What must he think? "Don't you wonder what's happened to Brig?" she asked. "You've never expressed the least concern."

"How would you know my concerns? I couldn't talk to you about him the entire voyage because you didn't recall his existence. Isn't your question a trifle hypocritical anyway? You're the one who shot him."

"He was trying to—"

Holding up his hand, Nathan stopped her. "You don't have to defend yourself to me. I didn't mean to sound accusing. I know Brig." He wanted to win at all costs, Nathan added silently. "I've often thought that if it

314

hadn't been for your memory loss, you might have shot me as well."

"I still may." She blinked widely, covering her hand with her mouth as she realized she had spoken her thoughts aloud.

Nathan leveled her with a hard, chilling glance. "Don't try it, Lydia. You wouldn't like the consequences."

"I didn't mean—"

"As for Brig," he said, ignoring her protest. "If he's recovered, we'll know it soon enough because he'll come to Ballaburn. And if he's dead, well, there's nothing much I can do about it, is there?"

"My God, you're a hard man."

"Those are the realities, Lydia. They don't make me hard, only practical. You've never had a mate like Brigham Moore so I don't expect you to understand. Just accept it."

"I only thought—"

"Don't." He stood. "Don't think. I've already told you I don't blame you for what happened. If anything, I have you to thank for removing Brig from the picture. You helped me win." He turned on his heel then, not waiting for her to demand that he leave, and strode out of the room.

A few minutes later Lydia watched him from her bedroom window as he took a horse from the stable and charged hell bent for leather into the darkening hills.

It was after midnight when Nathan returned to the room. Lydia had been drifting in and out of sleep for the better part of two hours. As quiet as Nathan was, Lydia bolted upright when she heard the door click into place.

"Who's there?"

The question stopped Nathan in his tracks. He swayed a little, his imperfect balance the result of lifting too many beers with Irish. "It's Nathan," he said. "Who were you expecting?"

Lydia leaned across the bed toward the nightstand, fumbled for the matches, and lit the oil lamp. She replaced the glass globe carefully and adjusted the wick. "I wasn't expecting anyone," she said. She drew the covers more securely around her, but it wasn't only because the room was chilled.

Nathan sat heavily in the rocker and began removing his boots and socks. His grin was a trifle lopsided and a dimple appeared at one corner of his mouth. "But then I'm not just anyone."

"I wasn't expecting you, either," she said. "What are you doing here?"

He held up a shoe with the tip of his forefinger. It slipped off and thundered to the floor. "Should be perfectly obvious. I'm undressing."

"I can see that. But why here?"

Shrugging out of his jacket, Nathan frowned. "I know I'm a bit tiddley, but not so much that I don't know it would cause considerable comment if I undressed anywhere else. Where did you have in mind? One of the shearing sheds? The entrance hall? The kitchen?"

"Your bedroom," she answered.

"This *is* my bedroom." He got up and went to the armoire, opening it with an exaggerated flourish. "See? My clothes are—" He stopped, brows drawn together in perfect puzzlement. "—are not here." He remembered the trunks and valises and swiveled around, looking for them. They weren't in the room. "What have you done?"

Lydia drew a deep, calming breath. "What I've done is unpack my belongings. I had yours removed to another room, not without some protest from the housekeeper, but I persevered. You'll find them at the end of the hall, in the room that once was Irish's before his accident kept him to the first floor. It looked very satisfactory."

"The hell it is." He sloughed off his alcoholic haze as if he were molting a too tight skin. He suddenly felt very sober.

316

Lydia watched as he disappeared into the hallway, a little shaken by the cold resolve she had seen in his predator eyes and in the hard set of his features. He was back in less than a minute, carrying two valises stuffed haphazardly with his clothes. He left again, and this time his return was announced by the bumping and scraping of one of the trunks as he dragged it along the hallway.

Lydia ran to the door, trying to shut it before he and the trunk came through. Nathan stopped her, bracing his shoulder against it. He held it there, pushing back against her strength, proving that she couldn't shut him out. "I don't want you here," she said, yielding the entrance to him.

"You've made that clear." He dropped the trunk and caught her by the waist as she made to go past him into the hall. "I, on the other hand, want to be here, and I want you with me."

Lydia's movement was not so much a struggle as it was a wriggle frought with frustration. "Let me go."

"Certainly." He kicked the door shut.

At her sides Lydia's hands clenched. She was about to say something, thought better of it when Nathan's glance gave no quarter, and marched back to the bed. She scooted to the side farthest away from him and sat there stiffly, the covers tucked thickly around her. Lydia made every effort to address him calmly. "I suppose there's no chance of you sleeping anywhere but in this bed?"

"Hardly."

"Turn back the lamp then when you've finished unpacking." Lydia lay down and curled on her side, giving Nathan her back and forcing an even cadence to her breathing.

He had no intention of emptying either the trunk or the valises tonight. He had wanted to make a point and he'd made it. Nathan finished undressing, put out the light, and crawled into bed naked. Stretching his arm across the wide mattress, he could feel the warmth left by Lydia's body on the flat of his palm. Reaching further, his fingers could almost touch the curve of her back.

"You don't have to sleep there, Lydia," he said, a certain husky weariness in his voice. He withdrew his hand and tucked it under his pillow. "I'm not going to touch you." She said nothing for so long that Nathan thought she was ignoring him or had fallen asleep.

Lydia had done neither. She was thinking. "Why are you doing this, Nathan?" she asked at last.

"You're my wife, Liddy." He stared at the faint outline of her in the darkness. It was the only explanation he was prepared to offer.

San Francisco

Madeline was pouting. "I don't want you to leave."

Brigham removed her arms from around his neck. "Lower your voice. Samuel will hear you."

"I doubt that. He's got his Chinese whore with him tonight."

"You really hate Pei Ling, don't you?"

"Why shouldn't I? Until Lydia brought her into this house Samuel was faithful to me."

"Somehow I doubt the reverse was true," Brigham said. He gave the silk belt around Madeline's waist a little tug, tightening it, and stepped away from her. "Why he ever put up with your infidelities is beyond me."

Madeline sucked in her sulky lower lip and abandoned her seductive posture. She moved to her vanity, sat down, and began brushing her hair with hard, quick strokes. "Samuel knows I married him to get a name for my baby. There was never any pretense about it."

"The way I understood it, you could have had O'Malley's name."

"As if I'd have wanted it," she said coldly. Her hair swirled around her shoulders as Madeline swiveled on her stool. "I don't want you to go tomorrow."

"So you've said. The passage's been booked though

and I have every intention of leaving in the morning."

"Why is it so important to you? Does it mean so much that Nathan's won?"

It means everything, Brigham thought. What he said was, "He hasn't won yet. Not if I can persuade your daughter to come with me."

"Her note said she was married to him."

"We both know he made her write that. There's no record of their marriage anywhere in San Francisco." He slanted her a considering look. "What difference would marriage make? You'd come with me if I asked you."

"Ask me."

Brigham didn't hesitate. "Take George's place on the ship tomorrow."

Madeline blinked. "You're really serious, aren't you?"

"Deadly." He smiled. "Well?"

"You're mad. Why would I travel to that miserable country when I have everything I want here?"

Brigham walked over to Madeline. Placing his hands on her shoulders, he gave her a light push and turned her on the stool to face the mirror. Standing behind her, his eyes caught hers in reflection. "Do you really have everything?" he asked. "Think you'll find another lover like I've been to you?"

"Don't be absurd," she said coolly. Pride dictated her response. "Of course I will. You think too much of yourself. You always have."

"A moment ago you were begging me to stay."

"Hardly begging. Begging would be writing it down in an impassioned love letter: *I can't live without you.* Or some other sort of drivel like that."

Brigham went to her escritoire and took out a sheet of notepaper and a pen. He brought it back and laid it on the vanity in front of her. "Write it down. I like impassioned love letters."

"You have a dozen, I suppose."

"Not a one." Madeline picked up the pen and wrote *I can't live with* before Brigham stayed her hand. "It's

319

enough," he said. He raised her hand and kissed it.

"If I really wanted you to stay," she said, removing her hand from his, "I'd tell Samuel what was in Nathan's letter that we destroyed. My husband would see that you'd spend the next ten years in jail."

"Threatening me, Madeline?" The way his fingers whispered across her collarbone took the hard edge off his voice. Reaching over her, Brig opened the middle drawer of her vanity and pulled out a silk scarf. He pushed aside one shoulder of Madeline's robe and trailed the scarf lightly over her skin, watching her reaction in the mirror.

Madeline caught the end of the scarf and twisted her hand, wrapping the scraf around her wrist. Brigham still held the other end. She stood, the blue flame leaping in her darkening eyes, and used the scarf as a leading ribbon to make him follow her to the bed. She lay down, pulling him with her, and kissed him hotly on the lips, loosening the belt of her robe with her free hand. The robe opened. Brigham's hand closed over her breast, kneading it, brushing the nipple so it stood up hard and stiff. She cried out when his mouth replaced his hand.

"Sshh," he said, rising above her. His smile was gentle. "Quietly, darling." He kissed her until there was only the soft moaning sound of her hunger.

Madeline's hands slipped under his open shirt, her fingers curling like talons. She scratched his back as her body moved sinuously under his.

Brigham caught her by the silken wrist and brought her hand around. "None of that," he said softly. Raising her wrist to the spindles in the headboard of her bed, Brig fastened the scarf tightly to one of them.

"What are you doing?" she whispered. Her leg stroked his and her knee nudged his arousal. She was more excited than alarmed.

"Something I like to do when a woman wants to put more scratches on my back." He spread kisses across her face and neck while he worked the silken belt free of her

320

robe. When he had the belt he used it to secure her other wrist. He sat up, straddling her thighs. "You like it, don't you?"

Madeline didn't answer. She twisted under him, struggling in the way she imagined he wanted. His eyes were incredibly hot and dark. Her tongue came out to wet her lips as Brigham stroked the underside of her outstretched arms.

"I think you should come with me," he said softly. "Do you know what it's like to make love on a ship?" His hands neared her breasts, circling, brushing her with his knuckles. "Come with me, Madeline."

It was difficult to talk. Her skin leaped in anticipation of his touch. "George is going with you."

"Do you really think I'm going to let him follow me all the way to Sydney?" he asked pleasantly.

Madeline couldn't think for a moment through the haze of her excitement. What was Brig saying?

"He's not welcome where I'm going." He bent over Madeline and placed his mouth on hers. His tongue traced the line of her lips. "You're welcome, though. The voyage will be very lonely if you don't take my offer."

Madeline averted her face. "What will you do with George?"

Brig's hands caressed her breasts, her rib cage, and the taut plane of her abdomen. He could feel the excited flutter of her heart and hear the quickness of her breathing. "You don't really care about George, do you?"

She shook her head, closing her eyes as Brig's touch forced a wave of pleasure through her.

"I didn't think so," he said softly. He kissed her mouth again, deeply this time. His hands left her briefly, long enough to pick up the pillow that was lying near her head.

He raised it and his mouth at the same time. This time when Madeline cried out, the sound was smothered by the pillow. He held it there long after her body had gone still. "You shouldn't have threatened me," he said finally, easing himself off her. "I was undecided until then."

Moving quickly, with the rote precision of a task long since refined, Brigham took the ebony-handled letter opener from Madeline's escritoire and cut her wrists. He removed the bloody scarf and belt from her wrists, stuffed them in his trouser pocket, and arranged her body on the bed to suit his fancy. Practicing Madeline's handwriting for several minutes at her desk, Brigham finally finished the note she had begun for him. It now read: *I can't live with this ache in my soul.* He locked the door to her room and left via the window and the balcony, entering the house again from the side entrance on the ground floor.

He slept deeply that night, fully aware that no one expected Madeline up at dawn to see him off. He would be hours at sea before her body was discovered and even then Brigham doubted he would be a suspect. The suicide note had been a masterstroke.

She really shouldn't have turned him down, he thought. He might have been able to let her live until they reached Sydney.

Lydia sat in the kitchen with Molly, spooning nut and raisin filling onto pastry squares. Every few minutes she would glance out the kitchen window, see the bright winter sunlight, and sigh. She hadn't been out of doors for longer than a few minutes since coming to Ballaburn. After the first day a steady rain had misted the valley, swollen the stream, and driven most everything toward shelter except the sheep and Nathan Hunter. He had been gone for four days and three nights, riding out to the far reaches of the station, taking inventory of the work that had gone undone in his absence.

Irish had kept to himself most of that time. Lydia saw him at meals, but their conversation was stilted and superficial, so uncomfortable that they were both

322

relieved to get away from the table. Lydia was many times more at ease with Molly Adams, the housekeeper and cook at Ballaburn for a dozen years, confiding in her almost without being aware that she had. No one at the station knew more about what Lydia thought and felt than Molly, and Molly would have sooner been burnt at the stake than break a confidence.

"You don't have to stay in here and do this," Molly said. She wrapped a towel around her hand and opened the hot oven door a crack, checking her pastries. "I've been doing it alone these past twelve years and I'm not the worse for it. If I need help I'll find Tess. She's not had anything to do this morning besides a little dusting."

"There's no coach today?" Lydia asked. It was Tess who served the refreshments to the passengers. The girl lived for the arrival of the coach with its surfeit of male travelers. She flirted and teased, all of it fairly harmless as far as Lydia could tell, and made each weary passenger feel welcome at Ballaburn while the horses were being changed.

"No coach. And it's a good thing, too. Jack's not going to put up with much more of her antics. He's been trying to catch her eye since Brig left and she's having none of him. She needs to be plonked on the head with a waddy and dragged off to a minister. That shiela's always wanting what she can't have or doesn't need."

A dollop of filling slipped off the end of Lydia's spoon and splattered thickly on the tabletop. She scooped it up with her finger and destroyed the evidence of her surprised reaction by eating it. "Tess and Brig?" she asked casually, still sucking on the end of her finger.

"I shouldn't have said that," Molly said. She dusted her bread board with more flour, slapped the dough down hard, and began rolling it out with more energy than was strictly necessary. "Forget you ever heard it—or at least that you heard it from me."

"It's forgotten."

"Go on with you," she said, jerking both her chins in

the direction of the door. "The boys will fix you up with something in the stables. It's about time you're seeing more of Ballaburn than the inside of this house."

Lydia laid down the spoon. "I don't know my way around," she said, a little uncertain about going off on her own. It was not the same as riding along the Pacific shore or cantering through Golden Gate Park. "Tess says that—"

"Tess is it now?" Molly scoffed. "Probably filled your ears full of tales about the blackfellows and God knows what else. Well, if you're really worried, then take someone with you." She paused and caught Lydia's line of vision squarely. "Take Irish."

"Irish?"

"Who else?" Molly went back to her rolling. "It's his station. Knows every inch of it. He can't go everywhere these days, not that he doesn't want to, but that contraption he rides in will take him most places."

"You mean his wheelchair?"

"I mean his buggy."

Irish was surprised by Lydia's request to accompany her. He also accepted with such alacrity that Lydia knew Molly had been right to suggest it. Lydia's mount was a ginger mare, sure-footed, the men in the stable said, and responsive to light handling. Jack and Pooley saddled the mare for her, tripping over each other in their eagerness to help. Harnessing Irish's gray gelding and hitching the specially made, one-seater buggy was accomplished with much less fanfare. He was lifted easily into his seat and given his buggy whip. There was no fussing, a situation he would have abhorred, as a wool rug was placed over his legs.

"It's not a bad way to travel," Irish told Lydia as they rode over the bridge, "but I get a little tired of staring at Horatio's hindquarters, if you take my meaning."

Lydia took his meaning very well. His buggy was low to the ground, more like a racing sulky. It was supported by two large narrow wheels at the rear and tilted backward

324

so that Irish sat a restful angle rather than stiffly upright. In order to see precisely where he was going he had to look to the left or right of his horse; mostly he just gave Horatio a general direction and relied on the horse to get him there.

"Nathan never let on that Ballaburn was so grand," Lydia said. Although Irish shrugged as if it were a matter of indifference to him, Lydia thought she glimpsed a smile on his craggy, weather-worn face. "He said it was big, but not grand."

"He probably thought you wouldn't think so. He told me the kind of place you lived in. Ballaburn can't be half the size of it."

"I didn't live in a palace, Irish. It was huge, yes, but not that enormous."

"But bigger than Ballaburn," he said.

"Yes. Why does it matter so much?"

"It doesn't."

Lydia knew he was lying, yet she couldn't fathom the reason. She looked back over her shoulder at the house and saw an inviting warmth there in the gold-and-brown stone that was never any part of her home on Nob Hill. "Your property is much bigger," she said.

"It has to be. Samuel isn't a grazier. I am."

She didn't know what to say to that. Irish was bent on making comparisons and still he undervaluated the breadth and beauty of what he had. Who did he think he had to impress? "I'm not my mother," Lydia said with sudden insight.

"God forbid," said Irish, raising his eyes heavenward. "As if I'd want that she-devil here."

She persisted, slowing her mare to a walk and coming immediately abreast of Irish's buggy. "You know what I mean. I don't understand why, but you're gauging all you're showing me by her standards. Quite honestly, Irish, she'd hate it—all of it. The isolation alone would drive her to madness. She needs to be in the heart of the city and Sydney wouldn't do at all for her. The house is too rustic, too small, inadequately staffed, and, worst of all, serves as a way station for the Cobb & Co. line. You may be rich as Croesus, Irish, but my mother would still turn her nose up at what you've built here."

"I didn't bloody well build anything for your mother." He gave his horse a flick with his whip. The buggy rattled ahead of Lydia. "I built it for you," he muttered.

"What?" Lydia kicked her mount to follow. "What did you say?"

"I said I built it for you," he snapped. "Now, do you want to learn something about your heritage or carry on about your mother?"

Lydia's mouth closed abruptly and she hung back again, stunned by what he had to say and by the way he said it. When she caught up to him on the rise of a hillock she said, "You're a thorough boor, Irish, but I want to hear about Ballaburn." This time she was certain she saw his thick mustache lift to one side as he smiled.

Ballaburn's landscape was dotted with sheep. Four thousand, she learned, were scattered all over the station, some grazing in loose flocks where the vegetation was rich, others foraging singly where food and water was sparse. Most of them were Merino, a breed with a heavily wooled head and excellent soft fleeces that brought Ballaburn its largest return pound for pound. Hornless Southdown sheep, with their small round bodies and short fleece, were raised mainly for mutton. The medium-sized, white-faced Dorset yielded milk, and the ewes had a tendency toward birthing twins which kept their number high. All the sheep had especially thick fleeces now. Come September and springtime, when the worst of the cold nights had passed, the Merinos would be mustered in mobs to the shearing sheds and relieved of their coats.

There was cattle also, but just what the station needed to supply the men with an alternative to mutton. Horses were raised strictly for working; no one had any dreams of entering one in the Melbourne Cup. A garden behind

the kitchen supplied tomatoes and maize and other vege-
tables, and wild blackberries grew in abundance on
thorny bushes in the hills. What Ballaburn didn't have
naturally was delivered from town on one of the coaches
or done without. Molly and an entourage of helpers and
hell-raisers only went to Sydney three times a year for
supplies.

Lydia and Irish sat in the spotted sunlight under a
coolabah tree, she on a blanket, he in his buggy which she
unhitched from Horatio and swung around to face her.
They chose food from the basket Molly had packed for
them—cold meat, fresh fruit, her sweet and gooey raisin
and nut tarts, and drank warm beer from a jug.

Replete, Lydia leaned back against the dense trunk of
the coolabah. "I like your land, Irish. I like your smelly
sheep and your blue ribbon streams. The sky is almost
impossibly wide here and the light . . . the light touches
everything. What did you call those birds? The ones that
were laughing when we rode near them."

"Kookaburras."

"Yes, kookaburras. Well, I even like them."

His dark blue eyes narrowed, watching her, and Irish
felt the light from her gentle smile touch him as sunlight
never could. "You're more beautiful than your mother
ever was," he said.

Lydia's response was immediately to begin packing the
basket. "We should be getting back," she said flatly.

Irish swore because he could not get out of his buggy
and shake her and make her stop what she was doing.
"What did I say?" he demanded.

"Nothing. You didn't mean anything by it." She
hooked the basket on her arm and folded the blanket.

"Stop right there," he growled. He tapped her wrist
with the end of the buggy whip, in no way that would hurt
her but that *would* get her attention. "Stop. That's better.
Now tell me what I've said that has you so riled."

"You must not remember my mother very well,
because you'd never mistake me for being beautiful. I

327

don't like those sort of comparisons. People, men especially, mean to be kind by it, but it doesn't endear me to them and never has. They always want something in return for their pretty, empty compliments. Mother was right about that."

Irish retracted the buggy whip. "I thought you had already concluded for yourself that kindness is not among my short list of virtues. Also, I can't think of one thing that I want from you that a pretty, empty compliment would get. And finally, I remember your mother quite well and she was younger than you are now when I knew her. If you would but take all those points into consideration, you'd realize I said nothing more than I believed to be the truth." He let that sink in for several moments, then he said, "Hitch up my buggy, will you, Lydia. It's time we were heading back."

That evening after dinner Lydia sat with Irish in his study. He was cataloguing his books, the collection of which was an indication of his wealth as much as the size of his holdings. When Irish asked if she would help, she heard herself accepting in a voice that was almost painfully eager.

"When do you think Nathan will be back?" she asked. Dusty volumes surrounded her on the floor. She picked one up, blew loose dust from the top edge and spine, and began to shine the leather binding with an oiled cloth.

"It's hard to say. I think he probably means to stay out a week."

She sighed. Three more days.

"You miss him?" Irish asked shrewdly.

Lydia didn't look up, but her dusting became a little more hurried. "He left without anything being settled between us."

"Settled?" Irish frowned. "What isn't settled?"

"Whether I'm to stay or go, for one thing. The conditions of our marriage for another. An annulment may be

328

possible. At least it's something we have to consider."

"Annulment?" Irish set down his pen and peered down at Lydia from over his desk. "There will be no annulment."

"That's not your decision, Irish," she said calmly. "Nathan and I will discuss it."

Irish wheeled around the desk and rolled himself right up to the circle of books surrounding Lydia. "You should know about the wager, then," he said evenly. "If it's an annulment you're thinking of asking Nathan for, you need to know what it will cost him to give it to you."

When it was put before her that way Lydia wasn't certain she wanted to hear. Some part of her knew she would regret it, and still she faced Irish with clear, open eyes and said, "I'm listening."

"The wager involves three of us: Nathan, Brig, and myself. The prize is Ballaburn itself, divided equally among Nathan and Brig and my child if he was a boy, but going almost totally to the husband of my daughter if my child was a girl. If you had been a boy, Lydia, you would have had to settle here for one year to inherit your third of my holdings. That includes shares in my gold mines northwest of here and the properties I own in Sydney.

"I didn't have much faith that a daughter, on the other hand, would elect to come here, much less agree to stay—especially not a daughter who had been raised by Madeline. Therefore, in the event my child was a girl—which you certainly are—I told Nathan and Brig the only way they could have the land was to bring you to Ballaburn as a wife. Since Nathan was the one who succeeded, he must now keep you here a year if he's to take over the land. I would prefer you stayed at Ballaburn, but Nathan pointed out that our agreement only said you should stay in the country a year. That could mean Sydney or Melbourne or some humpy in the outback. A humpy's a shack, by the way, and I don't suggest you live in one."

Irish's hands folded over the curved arms of his chair. "Have I been clear enough, Lydia? There's no part of this

329

wager that makes any allowance for an annulment. Nathan can only take the property through marriage. Where you live is negotiable. Marriage is not."

Lydia set down the book she had been holding like a shield. She regarded Irish steadily. "So you're saying that Nathan won't agree to an annulment."

"He won't. He wants Ballaburn more than anything. You'd have to have known the deprivation and torture Nathan's suffered to understand what this place means to him."

"You used him," she said quietly. "You knew how hungry he was for something this fine and beautiful and you used him."

"I make no apologies for it. He knew he was being used. So did Brig. He was a good choice, too, not because he loves Ballaburn particularly, but because he's greedy."

"I might have married him."

"Sure, you might have," he said, his brogue surfacing. "And if you were more your mother's daughter and less your father's, you would have. A pity it would have been, I know that now, but I didn't know it when I set them up with passage, clothes, and enough money to stake their venture in San Francisco. I even gave Brig the advantage of a month's head start because he had waited so long for the opportunity to go. Nathan could well have arrived and found the matter settled. Apparently it wasn't."

"No," she said. "Nothing was settled. I met them both the same day."

"And chose between them fairly."

Lydia's dark brows arched in question. "Chose? I had no choice. Fair? There was no fairness to me. I don't know what Nathan told you about what transpired, but our marriage could not have occurred without Brig's attempt to drug me and Nathan's lies. That's the sort of men you sent to find your child, Irish." Her shoulders slumped tiredly, no anger in her voice, merely a certain

330

sense of hopelessness and rejection. "To treat me with so little regard, you must have regretted my conception more than my mother."

Irish frowned deeply, marking his high forehead with ridges. "Madeline told you that? That she regretted your conception?"

"Not in so many words," Lydia answered, looking at her folded hands in her lap. "But it was always clear. I don't blame her. It stands to reason that she should regret my very existence."

"Because I raped Madeline."

Lydia winced but said softly, "Because of that."

"I see." Irish looked at his daughter, regarded the bowed head, the slope of her shoulders that spoke of her weariness, the full line of her lower lip that quivered in spite of her best attempts at controlling it. She seemed vulnerable to him in a way that she had not before and he realized he might never have a better chance to be heard. "I loved Madeline Hart," he told her. "I was thirty-eight when I threw my luck in with some other convicts and went to San Francisco. I had gold fever like the rest of them, dreams of a rich strike that would buy me back the dignity of my birthright. The bloody Brits had taken everything from me and this was my chance to turn the world right again.

"I panned the streams, worked the hills, and never found so much as a fingernail's worth of gold. I did find Madeline, though. She was a flame-haired witch at eighteen, all flashing green eyes and a smile that turned this old man's heart over. I should have known better, I suppose. I had a score of years on her, had seen and done things she couldn't even imagine. Perhaps that was part of the attraction I held for her. I don't know."

He eased back slightly in his chair, looking older than his years now as a lightning flash of pain shot down his spine and disappeared in the part of his body that could not feel anymore. "Madeline and I were only together—intimate—three times." He saw Lydia's deep flush and went on. "On none of those occasions was it rape. You could have been conceived at any time because I did nothing to protect your mother. I wanted her to have my child and I wanted her to be my wife. Whatever you might choose to disbelieve, Lydia, know that I wanted you."

Lydia had raised her face. She was looking at him now, listening.

"Your grandfather, Madeline's father, surprised your mother and me in the hardware store he owned hours after he had closed it for the night. Madeline was naturally embarrassed and frightened and she said the first thing that came to her mind. She accused me of breaking into the store and raping her. I didn't even try to deny it. Madeline was too hysterical to reason with and her father had a shotgun leveled at my belly."

"So you ran," Lydia said.

"Your mother told you that much, I see."

She nodded.

"Too right I ran, and kept on running. I was a Sydney Duck, despised by every proper Yank, and I could feel the noose tightening around my neck. But I didn't leave California. I waited Madeline out, giving her time to think about her situation and realize she didn't have to lie to her father. After six weeks I met her in secret and proposed." Irish shook his head as though still incredulous about events more than twenty years in the past. "She refused me, Lydia. More to the point, she laughed at me. Her father was already a wealthy man; his store went from bust to boom with the discovery of gold. Pickaxes at forty dollars. Canvas tents at a hundred. What could I possibly offer her? Nothing, she said, so she turned me down.

"I waited another two weeks and went back to her, hoping I could make her reconsider. She knew she was pregnant then—with *my* child—and she hated me for that. There was no chance of making her listen to anything I had to say. I tried to tell her about the con-

332

versation I overheard in one of the pubs, about the land west of the Blue Mountains being a lot like the land where gold had been discovered in California. A drunken Duck named Hargraves made the boast within earshot. He swore he'd find gold back in Australia if Frisco wouldn't give any of it up.

"I'll be rich, I told her. Richer than she could imagine. And I'd have a fine home and land enough to support a dozen children."

"She didn't believe you," Lydia said.

"No," he sighed. "Madeline didn't believe *in* me. She didn't love me—probably couldn't love me, or anyone else for that matter. She clung resolutely to her rape story, no matter that it was bound to force me out of the country. Days before I sailed I heard she had plans to marry Samuel Chadwick. I knew him by reputation, not by acquaintance, and I knew he had come across one of the richest strikes in California. I remember thinking I wanted to kill him for his good fortune."

"Papa is a fine man, Irish," Lydia said. "He deserved more happiness than my mother ever gave him."

"So Nathan tells me. He says my escape was most fortuitous."

Lydia's smile was soft with regret. "She's still my mother. I won't sit here and say word after word against her. She can't help being the kind of person she is any more than you can help being who you are."

"What sort of person am I?" he asked.

"Cross and hard and resentful. Still angry at her, I think. A manipulator. Hurtful and mean-spirited."

Irish sucked in his breath at her hard appraisal. "Don't forget boorish."

"And boorish," she said. "But there are people here at Ballaburn who think you walk on water. Molly says you're generous. Tess says you're kind. Jack says you're fair, and I've never heard Nathan, for all that you've used him for your own needs, say a word against you." Lydia pushed aside the stacks of books in front of her and moved closer to Irish's chair. She sat up on her knees, placing her hands on his lap, and because he couldn't feel them there, she took his hands in hers. "Which leads me to believe that you're either exacting your revenge on Madeline through me, or you're so frightened I may not like you that you don't know how to act." She looked at him earnestly with eyes that were as a deeply blue as his own. "Which is it, Irish?"

He blinked hard, forcing back the veil of tears that blurred his vision. "Scared to death, I'm afraid."

Lydia raised his hands to her lips and kissed the thick knuckles. "That's all right, then. There's no shame in being scared."

Nathan had a rough scrub of beard on his jaw and above his upper lip whe he returned to the house. His hair needed cutting, especially at his nape where the dark strands brushed his collar. A well-worn hat, broken in over years of time, fit the shape of his head exactly and had protected his complexion from the hardening edge of the elements. His clothes smelled of the bush and the meadow, of eucalypt oil and sheep dung, of campfires and cattle. He caught his reflection in the clear smooth water of Balbilla Creek as he crossed the bridge and wondered what Lydia would think when she saw him now.

It was certain his appearance would do nothing to improve her opinion.

Raising the brim of his hat with the back of his hand, Nathan reined in his mount and sat staring at the house, as if something on the face of it might hint at what he could expect. How had she fared these last days? Was she even there? he wondered, or had Irish managed to drive her away? He couldn't imagine Lydia spending all her time in her room, but what would she have done? She must have sickened of her embroidery by now and Molly and Tess had most things in the house well in hand.

Where was Lydia's place at Ballaburn as the daughter of the owner and wife of the heir?

Nathan stabled his horse, brushing the animal down himself to delay going to the house that much longer. Eight days in the bush and not a single one of them passing without missing Lydia. He would find himself turning, wanting to point out the koala in the gum tree or the roo springing powerfully on his hind legs through the scrub, and there was no one there to be delighted or confounded. She wasn't there to share his shelter in the rain or the warmth of his fire in the inky cloudless evenings. He missed her questions, missed her making him think about things he took for granted.

He turned to her during the day and reached for her in the night. His saddle roll was small comfort when he wanted to be pillowed against Lydia's breasts and feel her fingers sift through his hair. He ached to touch her as well, recall the sweet fragrance that touched the curve of her neck and the soft underside of her elbow. He wanted to caress her with his hands, his lips, his tongue, and make the loving warm and sweet and lingering.

Nathan's horse whinnied, bringing Nathan back to the present. He finished filling the feed bag, straightened, and jammed his hands in the deep pockets of his wool-and-leather jacket. Striding from the paddock to the house, he felt the taut strain of his body against the button fly of his jeans. What he wanted now was Lydia arching under him, crying out as he took her hot, hard, and fast.

On the threshold of the kitchen he stopped. Lydia was pouring hot water into a large copper tub. Steam rose from the surface of the water and lent her flushed complexion a damp glistening sheen. She dipped her fingers into the water, pulled them back abruptly, swearing under her breath, and added a pan of cool water from the kitchen pump.

Nathan's eyes wandered over the slender line of her

back, the narrow waist belted by a plain white apron, and the hips which curved so gently as she bent over her work. He leaned against the jamb, letting the door swing closed behind him. "Dare I hope that's for me?"

Lydia jumped and spun around, holding the empty bucket in front of her protectively. Her heart thundered along after her initial fright was over. "You startled me," she said obviously and inadequately.

"I see that." He studied her with a lazy, hooded glance. Her heart-shaped face was tilted toward him. She was all dark blue eyes and a wide inviting mouth.

"It is for you," she said.

For a moment Nathan couldn't think what she was saying. What was for him? Her eyes? Her mouth? Then he remembered what he looked like. The bath was for him. He rubbed his jaw with the back of his hand and his smile was rueful. He wasn't even fit to kiss her. Nathan pushed away from the jamb and began shrugging out of his coat.

Lydia unconsciously moved to the far side of the tub as Nathan entered the room. He seemed to fill every available space with his presence, leaving her little room to maneuver or protect herself. Although his appearance now was the polar opposite of how he had looked on their first meeting, Lydia felt as she had then, drawn to the dangerous appeal of his remote eyes and the mouth that merely hinted at a smile. She wanted to respond as she had that first time and run as far and as fast as she could.

She lowered the bucket in front of her. "I saw you from one of the upstairs windows when you were crossing the bridge. I thought you might welcome a bath."

"I looked bad even at that distance?"

"No," she said quickly, looking away. "Oh, no . . . I mean . . ." He had looked so weary, she thought, pausing on the bridge as he had, reluctant to journey the last hundred yards to the house and equally reluctant to set

336

out in the bush again. "I just thought it might be a small comfort," she said.

He paused in unbuttoning his shirt. "Thank you."

Lydia glanced up, smiling. "If you'll put your things over that chair, I'll come back for them when you're in the tub. I have fresh clothes laid out for you upstairs. I'll get them now."

Nathan watched her go. He was also reminded of how their first encounter at the Silver Lady ended, and his words, spoken softly to himself were an echo of that occasion. "Oh, Liddy, I think you've only postponed the inevitable."

Chapter Twelve

"You and Irish are getting on," Nathan said. He wiped the last bit of lather from his face and tossed the towel on top of the washing stand. On the pretense of checking his shaven jaw for the ravages of the straight razor, Nathan glanced in the mirror again. His eyes, however, focused on Lydia's reflection. She was sitting in the rocker, her hands folded calmly in her lap and her attention drawn inward to her own thoughts. There was not the least hint of rose color in her cheeks. The fact that he was finished shaving and what that act had previously signified made no impact on her that Nathan could see.

His eyes wandered over her. Her beautiful hair had been loosely plaited in a thick braid. It curved around her neck and fell over her shoulder. The curling tip brushed her breast. The modest collar of her nightgown was buttoned to the hollow of her slender throat and the robe she wore was tightly cinched at her waist. Her feet were bare. Lydia's heels rested on a rung on the rocker below the seat and the chair swayed back and forth slowly. She looked demur, untouchable, and in spite of that, or perhaps because of it, she was desirable.

Nathan repeated his earlier observation and added, "It was quite evident at dinner this evening. Irish was enjoying himself immensely."

Lydia suddenly realized Nathan was speaking to her.

Her head snapped up and she stopped worrying the inside of her lip. "We've managed a truce of sorts," she admitted.

"It's more than that." He turned away from the mirror and leaned back against the washstand.

"Perhaps it is. I suppose you're congratulating yourself for whatever progress has been made."

Nathan begun unbuttoning his shirt. "What do you mean?"

"You know very well. You're not going to deny that your leaving for the bush was planned, are you?"

"Not at all. But you seem to suspect some ulterior motive. My conversation with Irish should have put those thoughts to rest. Didn't you hear anything I told him at dinner? I thought you were interested."

"Of course I heard, and of course I was interested, but you're deliberately misunderstanding me." Nathan was trying to avoid the very subjects she wanted to discuss and had been almost since the moment he arrived at the house. She could admit to herself that she had hoped the bath and fresh clothes, the solicitous attention paid to him, would soften Nathan to the point where she could venture with her concerns.

Her plan had not worked nearly so well as his own. He had managed to avoid being alone with her until now, giving her no opportunity to say what was on her mind. During dinner the conversation centered on the station, with Nathan reporting to Irish what work needed to be done. There were squatters to roust, a dam in need of extensive repair, and stray livestock to be brought back from neighboring stations. He estimated twenty sheep lost only recently in the northwest to dingos and another hundred gone to bushrangers.

"You know I mean your plan to leave Irish and me in each other's pockets for a week," Lydia said. "I'm quite sure you needed to go, and Irish found your report valuable, but it was more important to you that Irish and I make some sort of headway."

Nathan's look was considering. His fingers paused on the buttons of his shirt. "Wasn't it important to you?"

"Stop doing that!" Frustrated, Lydia tightened her folded hands into a single fist. "Stop making it seem as if you did what you did for me. Yes, Irish and I are getting on as you said. I'll even admit to you that I've arrived at a certain fondness for him and that I enjoy his company as much as he enjoys mine. The opportunity you arranged for Irish and me to come to know each other has been well used, but it doesn't alter what's between you and me, Nathan. Nothing's changed there."

Nathan shrugged out of his shirt and hung it on a hook near the armoire, then he sat down on the bed and began taking off his shoes and socks. "I hope you'll forgive me for being obtuse again," he said, "but to what 'nothing' in particular are you referring? From my perspective everything's changed. Or have you forgotten our voyage on the *Avonlei*? Have you forgotten Samoa? Tonight at dinner I brushed your hand. You reacted as if I were diseased. If that's an indication of how nothing's changed then you and I see things very differently."

In spite of her nearness to the fireplace and the crackling red-orange flames, Lydia felt warmth seeping out of her flesh and bone. "That's not fair," she said softly, staring at her clasped hands now. "You know I haven't forgotten anything about the time we spent together. But it was all a lie, Nathan. It was based on the fact that I couldn't remember anything else. I think we need to discuss how we mean to go on from here."

Go on from here, he thought. Her words echoed eerily in his head. It sounded ominous. He unfastened the top button of his trousers. "Apparently you've given it a great deal of thought these last days. I take it you have some idea of how you intend us to proceed with our lives. Why don't you tell me what you've decided?"

Lydia didn't like the edge of sarcasm she heard in his voice, the tone that was gritty and soft and fluid and infinitely dangerous. She drew her bare feet onto the seat

341

of the rocker, hugging her knees to her chest. "Well, I *have* given it a lot of thought," she said quietly, "and it seems to me there is but one solution to serve us both: a marriage in name only."

"A marriage in name only," Nathan repeated consideringly. His palm rested on the flat of his abdomen. He tapped himself lightly on the belly as he thought it over. "No," he said at last, his icy gray eyes settling again on Lydia. "I don't think so."

"You only pretended to think it over," she said accusingly.

He shrugged, unconcerned. "True. Do you know why? Because it's madder than any bloody thing Irish has ever proposed, that's why. Do you really think I'm going to lie beside you night after night and never lay a hand on you again—or that you're not going to want me to? I'm not a monk, Lydia, and I won't be treated like one. You don't remember our voyage the way I do if you can think you can live like that, either."

Lydia's skin went from cold to hot as he stirred memories she would have preferred to keep buried. "I told you I remember," she said. "That's why I believe separate bedrooms is the most reasonable solution. You wouldn't hear of it the night before you left and, quite frankly, I can't force you out of here, but I *can* take another room."

"And I can drag you back."

She nodded, catching the underside of her lip again. Why must he make a difficult situation even more strained? "I realize that," she said. "That's why I didn't move my things. I thought it should be a mutual decision for one of us to go elsewhere."

Nathan leaned forward, resting his forearms on his knees. "We both stay here," he said. "That's the way I want it."

Agitated by his high-handedness, Lydia stood. "And what of what I want?" she demanded. "Do my wants mean so little to you?"

He shot to his feet and crossed to stand in front of her

in a few strides. His fingers hooked one of her wrists to keep her from retreating. "Your wants?" he asked. "They mean a great deal to me. But I don't think you know what they are."

"Please, Nathan, let me go." She pulled her wrist lightly, hardly believing he would hold her against her will. His grasp only became tighter.

"Shall I tell you?"

"Nathan."

He ignored her. He dragged her hand to the taut front of his trousers and forced her to feel the heat and strength of his arousal. "You want this," he said. "You want it inside you, filling you, touching you so deeply that you'll cry out with the pleasure of it."

Now Lydia tried to pull back in earnest. Her cheeks were flushed hotly and the expression in her dark eyes was rebellious. "Don't be crude. If *this* was all I wanted, then any man would do."

"What are you saying?" he asked, letting her go. "That any man won't? That you want me?"

"Yes . . . no . . ." She threw up her hands to ward him off. "You're only trying to confuse me."

"You're already confused, Lydia. You've mistaken me for some man who is not your husband. Vows were exchanged, promises of honor and obedience were made. *With my body I thee worship.*"

"And what of love, Nathan? I made that vow, too." Lydia turned away from him quickly, blinking hard to stem the flow of hot tears. She had promised herself she wouldn't cry in front of him, wouldn't let him see how deeply felt the hurt was.

"You didn't know what you were saying then," he said, "so I won't hold you to it."

She laughed shortly, humorlessly. "How very gallant of you."

"But the other things we promised to each other," he went on, "I expect will be kept."

"Of course. They serve you."

343

"Serve me?" he asked. He placed his hands on her shoulders and turned her around. Raising one hand, he cupped Lydia's chin with his thumb and forefinger and lifted her face toward him. "Do you really think I'm the only one served? I'm offering you fidelity and respect and the comfort of these surroundings. In the bed behind us I'm offering you pleasure. Are you really going to be so proud and stubborn that you won't accept what you want the most?"

"You don't know what I want," she said, pulling her chin away from his touch. Her cobalt blue eyes were sad now. She pitied him because he could not understand or chose not to. "You don't know what it's like for me."

"Don't I?" When she had jerked aside, Nathan's hand had remained in midair momentarily. Now he lowered it to the curve of her neck. It lay lightly against her skin and the collar of her gown. His thumb flicked at the button at the base of her throat. He felt her pulse racing just beneath his fingertips. "How can I not? I see and feel things when I touch you that you only sense. Did you know that your beautiful eyes are darkening now? They're so expressive, Lydia. They captivated me at our first meeting, so wide and deep, cautious and curious at the same time. And even when you hold my gaze defiantly as you're doing now, I've already glimpsed the excitement you want to shield."

"You're wrong."

"I'm not." The button he was flicking slid through the fastening loop. His hand drifted lower and began the same casual manipulation. "Your heart is beating hard. I can feel it with the heel of my hand." His other hand had moved between their bodies and was tugging on the belt of her robe. When he released it his fingers splayed wide across her abdomen. "Your skin is warm," he said. "It's almost as if you're not wearing this nightgown. If I were to touch your breasts right now they would swell in my palms and the nipples would stiffen. It wouldn't be because you're cold, Lydia. We both know that. It would be because you like it when I touch you there. You like my hands on your breasts, my fingers teasing. You like it when I put my mouth there and suck."

She gasped. His hands had not moved. He was still only touching her throat and her stomach and yet it was as if he were doing the very things he described. She could feel her breasts swelling and the tips of her nipples hardening. The thought of his mouth there created a tug inside her that went from her breasts to her thighs. His words were powerful, the ache immediate and intolerable. Closing her eyes did not help; the vision was clearer.

Nathan undid another button and went resolutely to the next. "Your skin is so sweet, Lydia. Warm and silky. The fragrance is elusive, perhaps it's not even there, but I always think of flowers, of lilac and lavender and tropical orchids. I think you like it when I taste your skin, when I touch my mouth to your bare shoulder or raise the flesh of your neck with my teeth. My tongue on your breast, Lydia. What about that?"

His voice was a husky whisper and his words lay across her like a silken net. The entrapment was seductive and appealing. Inside she was liquid. Her knees threatened to give way. Another fastener was undone and this time Nathan's fingers slipped past the lace piping and brushed her skin. She could barely draw a breath.

"Open your mouth, Lydia." He bent his head toward her and she could taste his words on her lips. "Let me kiss you the way you want to be kissed."

Lydia's entire body trembled violently and then was still. "No." She dragged her eyes away from Nathan's, breaking the spell, and eluded his hands as he made to grab her. Putting the rocker between them, Lydia knotted her belt again. Her palms were perspiring. She pretended to smooth her robe to wipe away the evidence of panic. "Leave me alone, Nathan. I don't want you to touch me at all. Go to Tess if you need a woman. She'd be happy to oblige you."

Nathan's brows arched. "Tess? You're mistaking me for Brig. She's never been in my bed."

"She'd have you though."

"Probably." He hooked his thumbs in the pockets of his trousers. "But she's not the woman I want. She's not my wife. You are."

Lydia simply stared at him.

"Do you know that I spent most of my time in the bush thinking of you?" he asked. "I regretted that I had to leave so quickly after we arrived, and yes, you were right that I left to give you and Irish time alone together. At least you were partially right. I also left because I'd hoped that bloody nonsense about absence making the heart grow fonder was true. I see now that it isn't. But if you didn't miss me here"—he pointed to his temple—"or here"—he touched his heart—"I think you did miss me here."

Lydia squeezed her eyes shut, not wanting to see where he pointed but knowing just the same.

"If I ever entertained any doubts, your response a few minutes ago put them to rest."

Peeking at him through the thick fan of her lashes, Lydia saw his hands had returned to his pockets. She glared at him. "I don't care what you saw a few minutes ago," she said, "or what you *thought* you saw, but I don't want you, Nathan Hunter. Do you understand? I don't want you!"

Nathan kicked aside the rocker. It tipped on its side and thudded heavily to the floor. Lydia flinched, startled, and her eyes darted toward the door.

"No one's going to interfere," he told her. "Irish can't come up here and Molly and Tess wouldn't dare. Don't think of bolting, Lydia. We're going to settle what's between us once and for all."

"Fine." She folded her arms in front of her, under her breasts, and thrust out her chin. Her stance dared him to touch her.

Nathan accepted the challenge. If she had been a man

346

he might have hit her, but he knew she was bracing for the touch of another kind. He did not disappoint. Closing the distance between them, Nathan's hand snaked around her neck and after an initial, futile resistance on Lydia's part he brought her face to within a hairsbreadth of his own.

"Can you really say you don't want me?" he asked.

Lydia averted her eyes. His breath was warm and sweet on her face. "I don't want you."

"We'll see, Liddy." His lips brushed the closed and mutinous line of her mouth. "We'll see."

Nathan slid one arm around her stiff back and another under her knees. He picked her up. She did nothing to stop him; neither did she place her arms around his neck to help him. Her slight body was deadweight in his arms. Dropping Lydia on the bed, Nathan followed her down and lay beside her. She didn't struggle, but lay still and quiet. Though she gave no indication that she intended to fight, Nathan trapped Lydia's legs beneath one of his own. He propped himself on one elbow and stared at her while she stared at the ceiling.

"You've set me quite a task, Liddy," he said softly. His fingertips played with the wisps of silky hair at her temple. "You'd do better to give in now gracefully than have compliance dragged from you almost against your will. Pleasure will be yours either way, but one will leave you with the bitter aftertaste of guilt. It doesn't have to be like that."

"You could admit that I know what I want and leave me alone," she said. "You could allow me to choose freely how I give my body."

"And to whom?" he asked. "Not as long as you're my wife, Liddy. You belong to me."

He recalled his approach to the house, his thinking then that he wanted to take her fast and hard, and how it had changed again. His desire for her was the same, his need just as deep as it had been, but Lydia, whether she understood it or not, controlled the tempo of his loving.

347

He wanted to be inside her, wanted to be sheathed by her, but he needed to hear her admit it was what she wanted too.

He bent his head and nuzzled her neck, nibbling her skin with his warm, dry lips. The tip of his tongue traced the outline of her ear. His teeth tugged on her lobe. He knew precisely where to touch to wring a response from her and what he engaged in was not foreplay, but an assault.

Nathan's lips touched the corner of Lydia's mouth. His nose brushed her cheek. He kissed her chin, the underside of her jaw, and the crinkle just between her brows. Her lids closed as his mouth drew near her eyes and he kissed them gently in turn, in no hurry to force her response quickly.

His free hand slid under her robe and cupped her breast through the nightgown. His fingers made a slow spiral path toward the nipple. He heard her suck in her breath sharply as his thumb hovered over the sensitive flesh. The anticipation aroused her as much as the touch.

Nathan's knee nudged the hem of Lydia's nightgown upward. She pushed at the material, trying to lower it again, until Nathan captured her wrists and pinned her to the bed. His grip was loose, but Lydia would not struggle against it. Instead she glared at him.

"Have done with it, Nathan," she said tightly, marshaling her defenses.

"No," he said. "Not like that."

Lydia averted her face as his mouth tried to capture hers. He accepted the line of her neck and touched her skin lightly with his mouth. She moved restlessly against him, wanting and not wanting, and when she turned her head to tell him what she thought he was waiting for, his lips closed over hers and he pressed the opening she gave him. The kiss was deep and hot and the contact of their mouths was punishing.

Nathan felt the change in Lydia's response. Her anger transformed her and she wanted him to know it. She arched against him, breaking the hold he had on her wrists. Her arms curved around his back and she brought his weight full against her.

"You want me?" he asked. His voice was whiskey smooth.

"I *want*," she said.

Lydia's fingers curled like talons and she felt Nathan's shudder as her nails caressed his back. Her movement under him was graceful and feline, the sound at the back of her throat part seduction, part contentment.

Nathan sat up. His hands were impatient as he parted Lydia's robe and pushed up her gown. He knelt between her thighs and leaned forward, kissing her first on the lips, then between her breasts where the last button on her nightgown had been opened. His mouth moved lower as the gown inched upward. She felt his lips on her skin just above her navel, then his tongue making a damp trail across the taut plane of her belly, and finally his mouth was exploring her intimately, touching and tasting her with such sweet purpose that Lydia's fingers stopped clutching the sheet and threaded in Nathan's hair.

She was moist and hot, ready for him, but Nathan's attention remained unrelenting, forcing another response from Lydia so that while she was urged closer to the edge she was never quite allowed to reach it. She raised her knees, pressing her heels into the mattress, and just when she thought he only meant to torture her with his touch, he raised himself up and unfastened his trousers.

Lydia wanted to deny him, deny herself. She did neither. When he thrust into her she met him and when he began to withdraw her long legs wrapped around him, holding him to her. She moved with him, her body arching almost violently as he came into her deeply and drew out her hunger and her need.

She marked his back with her nails as he came at her harder and harder, as if he were angry, too. The set of his features was harder than his thrusts. His skin was pulled taut over the bones of his face, and his eyes were silver and piercing, dark mirrors at the center and like shields at the outer edge. A cord in his neck stood out as his throat was arched. He closed his eyes and his entire body shuddered release. Lydia felt it, thought it was passing from him into her, then realized it was her body that was shattering, her senses that were igniting and sparking and exploding.

Her eyes were dry and gritty, which was odd, she thought, since she had never felt more like crying. She turned her head aside as Nathan moved away from her and shoved her nightgown back over her legs while Nathan fastened his trousers. Reaching to the bedside table, she turned back the wick so the room's muted yellow light was extinguished, then shifted completely to her side so that Nathan's piercing eyes couldn't see any part of her face.

Nathan sighed. He lay on his back, his head cradled in his palms, and stared at the ceiling much as Lydia had done earlier. What had any of it proved? He'd forced a response from her but not for him. He hadn't been able to make her say she wanted him. How had it been possible on the *Avonlei?* Until the end, when frustration and anger at her denial had overridden his good sense, he had touched her just as he had on the *Avonlei.* He had caressed her in the manner he knew she enjoyed, kissed her in just the way that gave her the greatest pleasure. He knew every inch of her body, delighted in it, worshiped it, and yet he hadn't been able to make her say she wanted *him.*

He turned on his side and drew the bedcovers over himself and Lydia. She remained stiff and motionless beside him, flinching only momentarily when he laid his hand over her hip. He let it rest there, allowing her to get used to it rather than remove it.

He had no clear idea of what he wanted to say to her, only that he couldn't let things stand as they were. "Lydia?"

She didn't answer. She forced her breathing to be even and calm.

"I know you're not sleeping."

"I'd like to," she said.

He hesitated. "I could promise you now that this won't happen again," he said softly, "but I think it would probably be a lie."

There was such a long pause before he continued that Lydia thought it was all he intended to say. "I'm listening."

Nathan drew in a deep breath and let it out slowly. "I know you thought it was your money that brought us together. I suppose there's even some truth to that because it was as Irish's daughter that you were important to me. But all that was ever required was that you take my name, and I've known almost from the beginning that it wasn't going to be enough. I find you very desirable, Lydia. I always have. You're so beautiful to me that I ache when I look at you."

The tears that would not come before fell now. They dripped out of the corners of Lydia's dark eyes and splattered silently on her pillow. How long had she wanted to hear someone say she was beautiful and mean it? All her life it seemed. And now, hearing it, she understood at last how unimportant it was. She did not know if she was crying for herself, or for Nathan, or from the pain of this new awareness. Lydia jammed her fist against her mouth to keep from sobbing aloud.

Nathan was saying quietly, "I don't want a marriage in name only. I can't live like that. Not with you here in this house. Not even for a year."

She nodded once and when she had control she whispered, "I understand."

It was the middle of the night when Lydia turned to him. She had been lying there, her buttocks cradled against his thighs, and she could feel the hardness of him pressing against her. He was naked now, in both his body and his need, but he made no move to touch her. She thought he was sleeping until she turned and saw that his eyes were open. The silver-blue veil of moonlight caressed the planes of his face and his shoulder. His eyes darted over her, grazing her mouth once, then again, longer the second time, before lifting to hold her gaze.

"I'm not going to do anything about it," he said, thinking of how much he wanted her right now.

"Even if I asked you to?"

Nathan's entire body jerked in reaction as her hands disappeared under the covers and sought out his arousal. She stroked him the way he had taught her to and when it wasn't enough for either of them her mouth replaced her hands. She loved him as she had on the *Avonlei*, with the tenderness of feeling that had engaged her heart and soul, and only one of them understood that everything she did for him was in the way of a good-bye.

When Nathan woke in the morning he found the space in the bed beside him was cold. It was a cruel way to greet the day, he thought, turning over sleepily. Lydia should have been there next to him. Her fragrance was still in the pillow. He smiled, burying his face against it. Memories of her middle-of-the-night loving assailed him. God, how sweet she had been, how giving. Her hands gliding over him . . . the caress of her mouth . . .

Nathan's groan was muffled by the pillow. He shook his head, laughed at himself for such torturous thoughts on himself, and sat up. Tossing the pillow behind him, he threw his legs over the side and stretched his arms wide. Naked, he padded to the washstand and poured fresh water into the basin. He washed quickly, shaved, and dressed, eager to join Lydia at the breakfast table. He would tease her about letting him sleep so long, but he would make certain neither Irish nor Molly heard him.

He would whisper it in her ear and they would have to wonder at the cause of the beautiful peach blush. It would be a secret, his and Lydia's alone.

He was still smiling when he entered the dining room. Lydia wasn't there. Irish was. Nathan felt an immediate pang of disappointment. Nodding briefly at Irish, he filled his plate at the sideboard and sat down.

"Lydia's already eaten breakfast?" he asked.

Irish's reply was short, his humor black. "Apparently."

Nathan's brows lifted a little. "Are you in pain this morning?"

"Why the bloody hell should you care?"

"All right, Irish," Nathan said. He put down his fork and leaned back in his chair. "Suppose you tell me right now what's going on. I'm sure I don't have any idea."

"Oh, no? Perhaps this will help." Irish reached in his vest pocket and pulled out Lydia's opal wedding ring. It lay in the flat of his calloused palm, smooth and iridescent and delicate, in startling contrast to the hand that held it. "I found it in my strongbox this morning. There was a note with it, addressed to you. I read it."

Nathan imagined he could feel the color draining from his face. His stomach knotted. There was nothing in his experience that hurt as badly as what he felt now. He'd been beaten and starved and exhausted and flogged and he would have accepted any of those things, or all four, in order to take away the white-hot tangle of pain inside him. He reached for the ring, surprised that his hand didn't tremble when he felt as if he were shaking all over.

Irish snatched his hand back, concealing the ring in a tight fist. "It's mine," he said coldly. "She left it in exchange for the money she took out of the box and the horse she took from the stable."

"May I see her note? You said it was meant for me."

Putting the ring back in his pocket, Irish pulled out a square of paper that had been neatly folded in half. He flicked it at Nathan. "How the hell did you manage it?" he

353

demanded angrily. "One evening back from the bush and you undo everything I've worked for these past twenty years, everything I shared with my daughter this past week. She would have stayed at Ballaburn if it wasn't for you!"

Nathan felt as if he had been struck, then struck again. His chair scraped noisily against the floor as he pushed away from the table. Clutching the note in his hand he stood and strode out of the room, slamming the door behind him as he left.

Without having any direction in mind, Nathan turned his back on the house and walked. And kept on walking. The morning was briskly cool and he wasn't wearing a coat, but he hardly noticed the chill, he was that numb.

He stopped when he reached the crest of Wallaroo Hill. He sat in a sliver of sunlight beneath a red gum tree. The house at Ballaburn was far below him, a gemstone set on a bed of emerald velvet. As far as he could see was the land that was promised him, the broad fields and meadows, the blackberry thickets, the ice-blue water and endless sky. All his. Nathan laughed and the taste and sound of it was bitter.

He stared at Lydia's note for a long time before he unfolded it and smoothed it over his drawn-up knee. In spite of that precaution, the words blurred. He read:

"I did indeed understand the import of your words last evening. You see, Nathan, I do not think I am suited to a marriage such as I suggested. You proved that to me and then I proved it to myself. Knowing your feelings, knowing my own, and sharing a conviction, I hope, that divorce is out of the question, it is apparent that leaving Ballaburn presents itself as the only satisfactory answer.

I wish you would not follow me, for I have no intention of fleeing the country. Irish has explained the whole of the wager to me and I mean to stay a full year from the date of our legal marriage.

I go first to Bathurst, for, I understand the way is well marked and not far, and should not present a problem to a woman traveling alone. I will take a coach directly to Sydney. When I am settled I will write for my belongings as I could only travel with a few things.

I do not undertake this leaving without much thought. My decision was not made impulsively or without some knowledge of the consequences. I ask you to consider this when you entertain the notion of forcing my return, especially if it is your pride which demands that action. I have to appreciate the depth of your feeling for Ballaburn and why you would accept all the conditions of the wager to own her. Irish has been unfair to both of us, but perhaps more so to you. He used your desire for the land and your great respect and affection for him and turned them against you. I pray you will not let him threaten you with losing Ballaburn. You've won it; it's yours. I will do my part to see that you keep it.

I trust you will see that I have done the proper thing. It would serve no purpose for me to remain. If it matters at all to you, I do not despise you, as I wish I might, and I permit myself to believe that you no longer think of me only as a means to an end.

Lydia"

Nathan's shoulders heaved once. He caught his breath on a dry, aching sob and tears burned his eyes but would not fall. Refolding the note, he slipped it into his shirt pocket, leaned back on his elbows, and squinted as he raised his face to the sky. A kookaburra's raucous laughter mocked him.

His head moved slowly from side to side in denial and overwhelming futility. Lydia gone. It seemed he had been dreading it forever, so long in fact that beneath the layers

355

of pain there was a sense of guilty relief that it had finally happened.

He sat up, shivered, and hugged his knees to his chest. How deliberate had he been, he wondered, in driving her away from Ballaburn before she suspected the truth? What had he done to make the very thing he feared happen as if it were determined by fate? And then, what hadn't he done?

"I love you, Liddy," he murmured to the sky.

Father Colgan peered at Lydia over the wire rims of his spectacles. His hands were folded on top of his neatly ordered desk and he was leaning forward in his chair. The expression in his green eyes was one of grave concern and he listened patiently, without interruption, as Lydia explained her situation.

"So you see," she said, "I thought you might be able to help me, if not directly, then by pointing me to someone who can give me a proper position." The dust of travel was still on her clothes. Lydia tried not to fidget with the wrinkles in her gown but she found herself nervously smoothing the fabric in her lap. It was clear that Father Colgan was interested in her problem and he wouldn't turn her away cold, but it was just as patently obvious that he was shocked by her defection from Ballaburn. "I've promised Nathan I will stay in Sydney for one year and I intend to keep my word. There's a matter of a living to be earned, though."

"Yes," Father Colgan said thoughtfully. "Yes, yes. Well, you've quite given me something to think about, haven't you? I don't recall coming across the like before. And you say you don't want to take money from your father?"

"No," Lydia said firmly. "Even if Papa could make arrangements to have money sent to me quickly, I've already decided to do this on my own. Foolish pride, perhaps, but there you have it. I've always been able to

depend on Papa's money to get me anything I wanted—
or get out of any difficulty. I think it's time I managed on
my own. Papa will understand."

Dark-red brows arching above his eyes, Father Colgan
absently pushed his spectacles up his bent nose. "Do you
really think so? Irish has waited a long time to support
you. I'm not certain what you mean by being able to
depend on his money."

"I'm not speaking of Irish, Father. I'm talking of my
papa—Samuel Chadwick."

"I see . . . I think."

"I don't want anything from Papa *or* Irish."

"And your husband?"

Lydia's smile was gentle. "No, Father, nothing from
Nathan. I would never ask."

"Your mind's set on independence, then."

"Yes. As near to it as I can achieve. Will you help
me?"

Father Colgan took off his spectacles, folded them, and
set them gently on the desk, glass up. He rubbed his wide
brow with a thumb and forefinger. "Your place is with
your husband, Mrs. Hunter. I believe that strongly."

"I've explained—"

He held up a hand to stop her. "And I've listened. It's
only because I've known Irish and Nathan as well as any
man can that I understand what's brought you to this
pass. I still say you belong at Ballaburn with Nathan. You
loved him when you married him."

"Things have changed—"

"So most of them have," he agreed, "but not that one.
Unless these eyes of mine are much worse than I suspect,
you're still in love with your husband. It's all right. You
don't have to deny or confirm it. Let this old man believe
what he will. In spite of what I think, in spite of what you
think, I'm going to help you, Mrs. Hunter."

Lydia stopped fidgeting. Her eyes closed briefly as she
said a silent thank you. "I lit four candles before I came
to your office," she said.

The priest smiled. "I know. I saw you." He clapped his hands together and leaned back in his chair. "Have you an idea of what sort of proper position you would like? Something in a store? A clerk, perhaps? If you have some skill with a needle, then I know a woman who is always looking for seamstresses for her shop."

"Actually I was thinking of something here, Father. At Saint Benedict's."

"Here?" He thought about that. "I already have a housekeeper and the sisters see to the church. The heavy work is done by our male parishioners."

"I was thinking of the school."

"The sisters help me with the school as well," he said. "Why? Do you have some training there?"

"Not training, but experience." She described her work at St. Andrew's Orphanage to Father Colgan and he listened attentively. "I'd work very hard for you, Father. I did for Father Patrick and he was very happy with what I could do in the classroom."

"I imagine he was," he said noncommittally. "Tell me, have you given any thought to where you're going to live?"

"I have enough money to stay at Petty's Hotel for a few months even if I don't find a position. I exchanged my . . . umm . . . my wedding ring for some money."

"I see."

Lydia hurried on. "I know a position at the school wouldn't pay very much, but eventually I'll find another place to live. There aren't many things I need, Father. Food and shelter, a few books, and a purpose. I can manage with those."

"Sister Anne *is* going to a mission on Fiji soon," he said, thinking aloud. "And Sister Isabel has many other duties. I suppose there might be a place for—"

"Oh *thank you!* I promise you won't regret this. Shall I start this afternoon? I can, you know. I think I even remember some of the names of the children from the one time I helped them. I'm quick at that sort of thing."

Lydia was on the edge of her chair now, her excitement bubbling. "Or would you rather I go to Petty's first and change out of these dusty clothes? That might be better. The children are used to you and the sisters, all perfectly neat and pressed. I probably look shockingly disreputable. I wonder if they may call me Miss Chadwick? If I'm to use my married name it's bound to raise questions and eyebrows. I really think it would be—"

Father Colgan held up both hands this time, in part to halt Lydia's rush of words, in part as a symbol of surrender. He was grinning widely. "Enough, Lydia. Enough. Your enthusiasm does you credit, but let us try to temper it a bit. You will start your duties in the classroom on Monday next. The children will return to school then. We had a small, er, altercation among the students yesterday and I've dismissed them all until I can speak to each of the parents."

"Altercation?"

"Boyish high spirits." He felt her skepticism. "All right. It was a veritable riot. One of the newest boys is having a hard time of it. You'll see for yourself come Monday."

"You're not expelling him then?"

"No. I promised his sponsor I'd do what I could, and I'm not giving in yet. I may lose two or three other students in the process, but I'm not giving up on this nipper. I've got a streak of stubbornness to rival any."

That pleased Lydia. "I think we'll get on very well, Father." She stood and extended her hand. "Monday next. I'll be looking forward to it. May I have some books so I might prepare lessons?"

Father Colgan released Lydia's hand. If there had been any bargain made he believed he'd got the better of it. "Follow me. I'll show you where everything is."

Irish wheeled his chair around sharply. The footrest caught one of the legs on an end table and the chair and

Irish came to an abrupt halt. Nathan did not move to offer assistance, knowing it would only make Irish angrier. He stayed where he was, one hip resting on the edge of Irish's desk, his arms folded casually in front of him, and said nothing while Irish tried to extricate himself and the chair.

"Bloody hell," Irish swore sourly, pushing the table over. Free now, he completed his turn, faced Nathan, and went on without missing a beat. "You're going after her, of course."

"You said you read what she wrote to me," Nathan said. "There is no 'of course' about it. You know what Lydia's wishes are. I'm staying here at Ballaburn."

"She doesn't know what she wants."

Nathan didn't argue the point. He had spent all morning thinking about that very thing and had come to the opposite conclusion. Lydia *did* know what she wanted. "What did her letter to you say?" he asked. "I assume she didn't leave without writing you as well."

"She wrote. Told me she regards me affectionately. Says she'll miss me but that I'm welcome to visit her in Sydney. *Regards me with affection!* Hah! *Visit her!* As if that's satisfactory. I want her here, Nathan. I've only known her a week. A week!"

"You've had longer with her than I have, Irish."

"What do you mean? You were with her for the entire voyage."

"Never mind," he said. "It's not important." Irish wouldn't understand. The voyage was something that happened out of time, something that should never have been. Her memory loss altered the way she responded to him. Lydia had trusted him then, loved him, all because she hadn't really understood the man he was. Now she remembered and now she was gone. There was no one around to force him and Lydia into each other's pockets as he had done for Irish. "She said you could visit her," Nathan went on. "That's more invitation than I received. I would not treat the affection you've earned so

360

cavalierly. I know. Lydia thought she loved me once."

The bluster drained out of Irish. He couldn't intimidate Nathan or threaten him. He refused to plead. "What do you suggest I do?"

"Wait to hear from her. Once she's settled, take her belongings to her personally. If she wrote that she wanted you to visit, she meant it. Lydia's resourceful, Irish. She'll be writing soon."

He nodded, sighing. Calmer now, he felt not only his own sadness but had a sense of Nathan's as well. He poured himself a drink, offered Nathan something, and recapped the decanter. "What about you?" he asked.

Nathan shrugged. "I'll be here if she changes her mind."

Irish was not deceived by Nathan's practiced indifference. He rolled his tumbler of whiskey back and forth in his palms, watching the amber liquid slosh gently against the rim but never overflow. "What about your feelings for my daughter?" he asked.

"What about them?"

"Does she know you're in love with her?"

Nathan levered himself away from the desk. His hands settled at his side. "I have work to do, Irish. I've neglected things all morning." He started to walk to the library door.

"She was going to ask you for an annulment," Irish said. Out of the corner of his eye he saw his words stop Nathan cold. "That's when I told her about the conditions for you to take control of Ballaburn. I told her you'd never agree to an annulment. Was I right?"

"It's a moot point," Nathan said heavily. "No one will ever know because she didn't raise the issue. That isn't what we argued about last night. Annulment was never mentioned."

"Ask yourself why. I don't think it's because she was worried that you'd turn her down. She'd take that risk. She had nothing to lose."

"What are you getting at, Irish? Say it plainly so I can

disagree and get on with my work."

Irish's glance was assessing and shrewd. "Just this: she didn't broach the subject because she was afraid you'd *accept* the offer. That's how much she wants you to have Ballaburn. If you can't see that it's a measure of her love, then you, my friend, need to get a better ruler."

Nathan laughed shortly. One corner of his mouth lifted in a mocking smile. "You keep trying to write a better ending to your ill-conceived wager. Be satisfied that it worked as well as it has. You've got Lydia here for a year and passed on the scepter at Ballaburn. There was never a word mentioned about anyone's happiness. Not Brig's, not mine, certainly not Lydia's. You can't make things right between Lydia and me so don't interfere. You're only guessing as to how each of us feels. You don't know anything about it, Irish. Not a thing." He turned on his heel and left.

Irish pursed his lips and brushed his thick mustache with a forefinger. He stared thoughtfully at the open doorway long after Nathan had gone through it. "Don't I though?" he said to himself. "That I could have given Ballaburn to one fool and sired another. It doesn't do a dying man credit."

In spite of Lydia's doubts that it would ever arrive, Monday morning was eventually upon her. Her room at Petty's Hotel was small compared to the suite she had shared with Nathan, but it was adequate for her needs, reasonably priced, and Lydia was comfortable there. She could walk to St. Benedict's, thus saving cab fare, and Henry Tucker treated her as if she were royalty. She had already written to Nathan and expected a trunk of clothes to arrive any day. The missive enclosed her best wishes to Irish, another invitation to visit her in Sydney, and Father Colgan's reminder that Mass was at ten on Sundays.

Anticipating the lessons at Saint Benedict diverted

362

Lydia's thoughts from Ballaburn and Nathan during the day. At night there was no help for it. She thought about Nathan when she was awake and dreamed about him when she was asleep. Lydia was only astonished that her grief wasn't immediately evident to everyone, for grief exactly described what she was feeling. It wasn't logical or rational since she could list—and often did—the reasons she was better off in Sydney. None of those reasons kept her from hugging her pillow when she reached for Nathan and didn't find him. She missed looking up from her embroidery to catch him watching her thoughtfully. She missed surprising a smile from him and spying the elusive dimples. She managed each day because there was simply no alternative, but time had done nothing to ease the pain. She wondered if it ever would.

There were seventeen children in the chapel schoolroom ranging in age from six to fourteen. Ten of them were boys, most of them high-spirited, talkative, and curious. One child sat apart from the others, alone in a seat he might have shared with a classmate if he had been so inclined—or been invited. Lydia gave him only a cursory glance as she walked into the classroom behind Father Colgan but she noted his aloneness and wondered at it. Was this the child that had caused last week's riot?

The priest had only introduced her to the class when he was called away by Sister Isabel. He apologized to her and the students, gave the class instructions, and whispered to Lydia that she was on her own. She estimated that she was alone forty-five seconds and only halfway through the roll when the first spit wad was thrown.

As near as she could tell the lone boy in the back hadn't done anything to instigate the initial attack or the barrage that followed, but once he was hit he didn't hesitate to retaliate. Before Lydia could get down the aisle the child had jumped on top of his desk and flew across the aisle and three desks to get at the ringleader. His fists flailed in the air and he let loose a string of curses that opened Lydia's eyes wide.

She knew then precisely who the boy was and where she'd seen him before.

Clapping her hands together smartly, she directed all the interested observers into the hallway and shut the door; then she pushed aside the chairs and desks so there were no unintentional bruises, and let the two boys clobber away.

Kit's adversary was not nearly the size of his burly brother-in-law, but the battle was heading toward the same end. Kit was a head shorter, twenty pounds lighter, and so angry he wasn't thinking how to get the better of his opponent. He did display a remarkable degree of tenacity, though. His arms worked like windwills, connecting just a third of the time but never letting up, and he came back each time Daniel Flaugherty put him on the floor. He'd spring to his feet and start jabbing and jumping all over again.

"Get him *away* from me!" Daniel yelled, swatting at Kit. "Or I'm going to really hurt him."

The challenge came back. "As if you could!"

Lydia's only response was to push aside another desk as the combatants widened their arena. The movement of both boys slowed a little; they both glanced in her direction, anticipating her interference. She shrugged and held up her hands, palms out, in a gesture of innocence and impartiality.

The boys continued to circle, but the punches they threw lacked any real menace. After a minute of posturing and threatening they stopped altogether and turned simultaneously, wary and puzzled, in Lydia's direction.

"Aren't you going to stop me from killing him?" Daniel asked.

"Aren't you going to stop him from killing me?" Kit asked.

Lydia answered both questions with a gentle, enigmatic smile. "Put the desks back where they belong,

364

boys." Her voice was quiet and firm. "I'll let the other children in."

The classroom was restored to order as the students marched in single file. There were curious glances at the two subdued warriors and Lydia heard one child ask in a stage whisper, "Who won?" She didn't hear the reply, but when she turned around to face the class, she saw Kit and Daniel were both pointing at her.

She felt very good about that.

Chapter Thirteen

"What did you do then?" Irish asked. He was chuckling around a mouthful of grog, trying to swallow and laugh at the same time. Across the table from him Lydia's smile was innocent and demur, as if she could not understand what he found so amusing.

"I began the lesson, of course," she said simply. She put a hand over her glass when the waiter came by to pour more wine and ordered another glass of beer for Irish. "And then I kept Kit and Daniel after school when the other children left for the day."

"They cleaned for you?"

She shook her head. "A dirty classroom wasn't the problem. When I talked to them I discovered that Kit was being teased constantly because he was so far behind in his work. He was doing sums and reading that the youngest children were doing, and not doing it as well. He'd never been to school before, but the other students didn't care about that. You know how children can be."

"No," he said. "I don't. But you seem to understand them."

Lydia blushed, embarrassed and pleased by Irish's genuine admiration. "Daniel, on the other hand, is one of the biggest boys in the class. His size alone would have made him a natural leader at his age, but he's also smart as a whip. He was counting on the interference of some adult to stop the battle. The riot he helped cause the week before got everyone out of a few days of school. He was a hero." She laughed, shaking her head as she recalled their stunned expressions when they learned their punishment. "Daniel is tutoring Kit every day after school for one half hour. In the evening Kit comes here to the hotel and I help him with more lessons. He's making fine progress and Daniel is satisfied with helping."

Irish was fairly beaming with pride. "It's a wonderful thing you're doing. Father Colgan must be pleased."

"I think he is," said Lydia. "I've already been given more responsibility in the month I've been there."

"A month," Irish said softly. "It's hard to believe it's only been a month. We've missed you at Ballaburn, Lydia."

"You could have visited before now," she admonished. "I thought you might bring my trunks yourself."

"That's what Nathan suggested, but I . . ." He hadn't been able to travel then. With almost no warning the pain in his upper back had become excruciating, so much so that Irish had found himself confined to bed, unable to sit up for any length of time. The bullet in his spine was shifting. He knew it, had been warned by a surgeon it could happen, and now it was. ". . . But I thought it would be better if you had the opportunity to settle here. I hope you don't think I didn't *want* to see you."

"I never thought it for a moment." Her eyes darted over Irish's face. A faint gray tint colored his complexion. He was thinner than when she had last seen him and there were new creases at the corners of his eyes and forehead. Even when he laughed there was a suggestion of tension around his mouth. "Have you been feeling well, Irish?"

He raised both iron-gray brows in astonishment. "Me?

I've got no complaints." He waved to the waiter and had another beer sent to his table. "Except that I'd like to have my daughter at Ballaburn again."

"That's not possible. Not now. Perhaps in a few months."

A few months, Irish thought. It might not be too late. "You're going to stay at Petty's then?"

"A while longer. Mr. and Mrs. Garrison have offered to rent me a room. Those are the people who have taken Kit in. Do you know anything about that, Irish?"

"Garrison." He said the name thoughtfully. "Don't they make shoes in a shop over on Elizabeth Street? Good work as I recall. They've been part of Saint Benedict's Parish as long as I've been there."

"That's the Garrisons. But I wasn't really referring to them. I meant about Kit finding a place with them."

"I would assume that's Colgan's doing."

"Yes, but Kit has a sponsor. Someone who helps pay for his schooling and clothing, the extra bills the Garrisons have incurred. Do you know anything about that?"

"How would I?"

Lydia sighed. "I'd thought perhaps that Nathan had said something to you about it."

"Nathan? You mean . . . *Nathan* is the child's sponsor?"

"Your astonishment isn't very flattering to him. Of course he's Kit's sponsor. I just wondered if he ever said anything to you. He kept it a secret from me."

"My, my, my." Irish was grinning. "Just who is this rapscallion anyway?"

Lydia related the incident in The Rocks. "Nathan told me there was nothing to be done for the child and then I stumble upon him again, clean and pressed, a brightness in his eyes that wasn't there before, and I almost didn't recognize him. Nathan's responsible for giving Kit this opportunity and I would never have known if I hadn't come back to Saint Benedict's."

"Why do you think he kept it to himself?" Irish asked. "He could have gained a little ground in your eyes if he had said something earlier."

"Don't you see? He didn't do it to impress me."

"He impressed the hell out of you anyway."

"He'd done that a long time ago," she said softly. She raised earnest eyes to Irish. "Don't tell him I said that."

Irish shook his head. "Not a word."

Lydia hesitated, absently pushing some food around on her plate. "Nathan told me once that a murder conviction led to his transportation. Is that true?"

"As far as it goes."

"What does that mean?"

"Nathan didn't murder any whore. I believe that. I always have. Has he ever told you about it?"

"He only told me he hadn't done it. I believed him, too."

Irish briefly described the murder for which Nathan was convicted. "Nath doesn't say much about it," he continued. "Brig told me most of what I know."

"And Brigham? How was it that he was transported?"

"The damn fool wanted to be with his friend. Tried to come to Nathan's rescue and ended up on the same ship with him. Later, when he was able to leave Van Dieman's Land, he traveled to Sydney. That's where I found him and through him, Nathan. He always made it clear that when I took him on that I was taking on his mate."

"They're very close then."

Irish shrugged. "In an odd sort of way. It always struck me how Brig wanted Nathan close so he could protect him and . . ."

"Yes?"

"Well, it doesn't make much sense," Irish said, "but I got the impression that Nathan stayed close so he could protect everyone else." He laughed. "An old man's fanciful notions, I'm afraid. Can't give you an example to

370

explain it clearly, but it was always there at the back of my mind when I'd see them together: Brig taking charge and Nathan letting him, but Nath always watchful."

Lydia thought about that. Striving for nonchalance, she asked, "Did Nathan ever tell you about Ginny Flynt?"

"Ginny Flynt? No, I don't— Oh, you mean the whore who was murdered in San Francisco. Yes, Nath mentioned it. Ugly business, that." He frowned, his cobalt-blue eyes clouding. "You don't think . . . you're not suggesting it was Nathan who did it?"

"Not at all," Lydia said. "I've been thinking about it off and on since my memory returned. It wasn't Nathan. It never was. Brigham Moore's the killer."

Lydia collected her books from the desktop and her reticule from a side drawer. She glanced around the classroom, saw that everything was in order, and stood up. "You can go on home, Kit," she said. "You don't have to walk me to the hotel."

"I don't mind," he said. Kit was sporting a yellow-and-purple bruise under his left eye, the result of an after-school altercation. Walking Lydia back to Petty's was more for his own protection than it was for hers though he would never come right out and say so. He'd got the shiner for defending Lydia against an insult. She would never know that, either.

"Well, if you're sure." Lydia dropped her books in his outstretched arms. "Would you like to stay for dinner with me at the hotel? We'll stop by the Garrisons and let them know."

"I'd like that fine."

"Good." She reached out to ruffle his dark-blond hair, saw his suffering glance, and withdrew. "Sorry. I forgot."

Kit rolled his eyes and grinned. "It's all right. You can

do it this—" He broke off as the door to the classroom opened. Lydia had gone very still, her attention completely centered on the person in the doorway. Kit felt her shock. More than that, he sensed her fear. He looked over his shoulder to see who was standing there.

"Good afternoon, Lydia," Brigham said. Leaning casually against the doorjamb, an insouciant smile on his lips, Brigham Moore felt the full impact of Lydia's reaction and enjoyed it. "Father Colgan said I would find you here. He's always been helpful. Part of his nature, I suppose."

"Miss Chadwick?" Kit asked, his brows creasing. "Do you want—"

Lydia placed a hand on the boy's thin shoulder. "It's all right, Kit. Go on and wait in the hallway for me. I won't be but a few minutes, then we'll leave together." She gave him a nudge. "Go on."

Kit's look was skeptical, but he complied, his eyes darting between Lydia and her visitor right up until the moment he was closed out of the classroom.

Palms sweating, Lydia folded her arms across her midriff in a self-protecting gesture. Brigham looked much as she remembered him: square-jawed, even-featured, with a rakish cock to his head. His sandy hair and tawny brows were a shade lighter, the result, she thought, of spending a lot of time on a ship's deck without benefit of a hat. His face had the same open, pleasing expression he wore so well, and his green eyes were brightened by his easy smile. Now that she knew he was alive, Lydia had the luxury of wishing him dead. "You're a thorough bastard," she said calmly. "I'm glad for this opportunity to tell you so."

Brigham laughed, genuinely enjoying himself. He pushed away from the door and took a seat on one of the children's desktops. His long legs were stretched in front of him, his ankles crossed, and he picked up a pencil and tapped it lightly against his thigh. "I wondered what your

372

first words would be," he said. "Nothing so trite as 'My God, you're alive!' Still, that's what I sensed when you saw me. You thought you were seeing things for a moment."

Lydia did not respond to his baiting. "How did you find me?"

"First let me say that your mother and Samuel send their love. They're worried about you, Lydia. Your father hired me to bring you back to San Francisco. Set me up with passage money and a sizable down payment as a guarantee for your eventual return."

"That's a lie. He would never do that. He knows how I feel about you."

"Oh? How would he know that? You're probably referring to the bedroom-window incident. But you treated Nathan and me alike on that occasion, remember? And you're married to Nathan now, aren't you? I don't think Samuel knows what to think."

"Nathan said he explained everything to Papa in a letter."

Brigham shrugged. "The only one I know about is the one written in your hand saying that you eloped with Nathan. There was never any other. I stayed with Samuel and Madeline while I was recovering. Did Nathan tell you that? Yes, I see that he did. I would have known about a letter to Samuel if there had been one."

"It doesn't matter," Lydia said. Somehow Brig was responsible for her father not getting his letter. Lydia believed that just as surely as she believed Nathan had written one. "I've been here more than seven weeks. Not only has Papa received something from me by now, but I won't have much longer to wait for his reply."

Brig nodded. It was not unexpected that Samuel would eventually learn the truth from Lydia. He was philosophical about it. "It had to happen sooner or later," he said easily. "I really have never had any intention of taking

373

you back to Frisco. You needn't worry yourself on that account."

"What do you want, Brigham?" Every nerve in her body was stretched taut.

"Right now?" He came to his feet lazily and smiled. "I just wanted to let you know I'm here, Lydia. As for what I want later?" He dropped the pencil he'd been holding back on the desk. "That will have to be decided between Nathan and me. I'm afraid you don't have any say in the matter."

By the time a response came to Lydia she was alone.

Two days passed before she saw Brigham again. He was waiting for her when the school day was ended, standing on the steps of Saint Benedict's, squinting in the bright afternoon sunlight, and looking for all the world as if he hadn't a single worry. Because she didn't want to make a scene, and because the route back to Petty's Hotel was crowded with pedestrians, Lydia allowed Brig to accompany her. Kit, though he had been dismissed by Brigham, followed in Lydia's wake at a discreet distance.

"What is it you want now, Brigham? I haven't any liking for this cat-and-mouse game of yours." She pulled back her elbow sharply when he made to escort her across George Street.

Brigham pretended to take offense, giving Lydia a wounded look. "My, aren't you the haughty one. I think I detect your mother's fine influence. Tell me, have you heard from her yet? Or Samuel?"

"That's not your concern," she said. "Or it shouldn't be."

Her reply didn't bother him. He knew she hadn't yet learned of her mother's death and probably wouldn't for a while longer. He could hold back the news indefinitely if he could get Henry Tucker to give him her mail. He'd have to give some thought to what reason Henry would

374

most easily accept. "I understand you're staying at Petty's Hotel."

"If I thought you didn't already know that, you wouldn't be accompanying me now."

"There's definitely a shrewish side to your nature I don't recall on our previous encounters. It's not becoming, Lydia. Is that why Nathan sent you away from Ballaburn?"

Lydia was careful not to show her surprise. So Brigham Moore didn't know everything. He only thought he did. She ignored his question and asked one of her own. "Does Irish know you're back?"

"It's only a matter of time before he learns about it. Nathan, too. I had no intention of staying on in Sydney until I happened to learn that you were here. I hadn't expected you and Nathan would part so quickly. Perhaps you'd consider going back to Ballaburn with me. I'm leaving soon."

"I'm happy here," she said tersely.

Brig looked over his shoulder and saw Kit was still dogging their steps. "I heard your little shadow back there call you Miss Chadwick the other day, yet Father Colgan told me he performed the marriage ceremony himself."

Lydia sighed. Father Colgan probably never gave a second thought to sharing that information with Brig. No doubt he regarded Brig with as much affection as he did Nathan. "Nathan and I are most assuredly married, Brig. Ballaburn is his now."

"Not quite yet," he corrected her. "Until Irish dies it's strictly only Nathan's inheritance."

Steps faltering, Lydia glanced sideways at Brig. "No one told me that."

"Understandable, don't you think? Irish had two wills drawn up in the event of his death. Which one will be executed depends on the outcome of the wager."

"Which Nathan won."

He shrugged carelessly. "Only time will tell." Brig stopped on the corner opposite the hotel and faced Lydia. His smile was perfectly genial. "A lot can happen in a year."

"What do you mean by that?" Lydia reached for his elbow as he started to walk away from her. Brig brushed her off much as she had done to him earlier and kept on walking.

Lydia stayed with Kit and the Garrisons for the next four days, hoping to give Brigham enough time to leave Sydney. She made a habit of never going out unescorted and varied the route she took to and from the church. Believing she had eluded him, Lydia was stunned to return to Petty's and find Brigham waiting for her in her room.

Concluding that his presence had been made possible by Henry Tucker, who thought he was doing a favor for his friend, Lydia didn't bother asking Brigham how he got in her room. Lydia had no intention of entering her room while Brig was lounging in the only chair, one leg hooked over the arm, the back of his head cradled in his palms. He was studying her; she simply stared at him.

"You're going to have to leave," she said, clutching her books a little more tightly.

"Have to?"

"Or I'm going to scream, Brig. I'm going to scream so loud they'll hear me all the way at Ballaburn. Now get out."

Brig sat up straighter and raised two fingers. "Two minutes, Lydia. That's all I want."

She hesitated but said wearily, "Two minutes." She didn't move from the threshold and kept the door open behind her.

"You're acting as if I mean to do you some harm, Lydia. I can't say I'm flattered by that. I'm the one who should be concerned. After all, the last time we were together in Frisco, you shot me."

Lydia didn't think his statement deserved a reply and she didn't give him one.

"I might not have recovered at all if it hadn't been for Nathan. He made certain there was someone to take care of me. That's the kind of friends we are, Lydia. Until you, no one's ever come between us."

"It's not me, Brig. It's Ballaburn."

"You *are* Ballaburn."

"No," she said. "I'm not. And I won't let you or Nathan treat me as if I were a tract of land."

"Is that why you're not with Nathan now? Doesn't he know how to treat you like a woman?" Brigham stood. "I would do better by you, I can promise you that. You can't really be happy here, Lydia. If you'd divorce Nathan you could become my wife."

"*That's* the kind of friend you are," she said softly. "Get out of here, Brigham. I'm going to scream."

Brigham scooped up his hat from the end table and laid his coat over his arm. "If you won't consider divorce, then you don't leave me many choices." His green eyes were pensive, his smile a trifle sad. "G'day, Lydia."

She stood clear of Brigham as he walked past her, afraid that somehow the merest touch from him could contaminate her. She stared after him until he had disappeared down the steps at the end of the hall, then she went into her room and locked herself in. Still clutching her books, Lydia dropped to the floor and leaned heavily against the door.

Divorce. It wouldn't have to be divorce, she thought. An annulment would accomplish the same end. It would be as if the marriage had never been, as if she and Nathan had never shared anything important or intimate. Brigham would take it as a sign that she meant to marry him and he would have no reason to try to take Balla-

377

burn by any other means.

Dissolving the marriage, leaving Nathan free of both herself and Ballaburn, could be the only method of saving his life.

Father Colgan interrupted Lydia's class on Tuesday afternoon with word that she had a visitor in his office. She did her best not to show her frustration and left the priest in charge of a very competitive spelling bee. Brigham was sitting behind Father Colgan's desk in his high, leather-backed chair. He was turned away from the door, staring out the window into the children's barren play area.

Lydia shut the door behind her hard and was satisfied to see the chair jerk in response to Brig's surprise. "I don't like you interrupting my lessons," she said. "If you must see me, then leave a note with Henry at the desk. I'll meet you somewhere publicly, but not here. Now, if you'll excuse me, I'd like to get back to my pupils."

The chair swiveled around. Nathan's silver-gray eyes were expressionless in their regard, his features impassive. "Very well, Lydia."

"Nathan!"

There was no denying her shock was real. Nathan felt himself relaxing a little. He had given some thought to the kind of welcome he might expect from Lydia, but none of his imaginings were close to the coldly terse and dismissive greeting he received. Now it seemed that it was not meant for him at all. "Who were you expecting?"

Lydia's mouth opened and closed as every thought fled from her head. Nathan! Her heart was pounding so hard that she was sure he would hear it and know that she was not indifferent to his presence. "I thought . . . that is . . . I was expecting . . ." She sank slowly into the

378

chair on the other side of the desk and laid her hands lightly in her lap. "Father Colgan didn't say it was you. I didn't think you'd reply so soon to my letter and certainly not in person. It was good of you to come, Nathan."

"I haven't come in response to any letter, Lydia. If you wrote something recently I haven't received it. Perhaps it arrived at Ballaburn after I left today."

No letter. Her shoulders sagged a little. He had no idea what she wanted from him. Everything she had explained so carefully in her letter would now have to be explained in person. She wasn't certain she was capable of that sort of confrontation with Nathan. What if he saw through her?

"Then why have you come?" she asked. She blinked, her eyes widening anxiously as something occurred to her. "Is it Irish? Has something happened to Irish?"

Nathan shook his head. "No, Irish is much as you last saw him." Lydia would have to make of that what she would. He would not break his promise to Irish, but if Lydia was observant at all she would know her father was not doing well. "He sends his best."

"I miss him."

"You could do something about it," Nathan said, seizing the opening she had given him. It was difficult to sit where he was, pretending a certain emotional distance was between them, when what he had really wanted to do since she came in the room was kiss her. He'd release the tight coil of her hair and his fingers would sift through its length and thickness. His hands would cradle her head gently, hold her still, and his mouth would touch her, lightly at first, then when he'd just given her a taste of him his kiss would deepen, harden, and his tongue would . . .

"Nathan?" Lydia frowned, tilting her head to catch his attention. "I asked you if that's why you came—to convince me to return to Ballaburn?"

Nathan came back to reality. "I think you're putting the cart before the horse, Lydia. Tell me, can you leave the children for the day? I don't think this is the best place for what I've come to discuss. Why don't we go to Petty's? I've taken a room there for a few days."

Lydia blanched. "You took a room at Petty's? Oh, Nathan, how could you do that? What will people think—you in one room, me in another? Henry's certain to have told someone by now."

Dark eyebrows raised, Nathan's look was disbelieving. "If you care what people think, then your place is at Ballaburn, not here in the city. Can you leave for the day or not?"

"I'll meet you at Petty's when I'm finished," she said quietly. "My room number is—"

"Come to mine," he said. "It's the suite we had. I'm sure you remember it."

Too well. "I don't think that's a good idea."

"Don't you trust me?" he asked bluntly.

"Well . . . yes, I trust you."

You're foolish, he wanted to say. What he said was, "Then you must not trust yourself." He stood, skirted the desk, and touched Lydia's shoulder lightly on his way out. "I'll see you in a few hours."

Lydia got through the rest of the day on sheer nerves. Sister Isabel was helpful with the younger children while Lydia worked individually with some of the older ones. It was difficult for her to keep her attention focused when her thoughts kept straying to Nathan waiting for her at the hotel. He was right about not trusting herself with him. It was easy to think she could be cool and reserved when he was at the station and she was in the city, quite another thing when she was in the same room with him.

It wasn't fair that Nathan could turn her inside out when he looked at her in that certain way. She had always felt the pull of those predator silvery-gray eyes, and there was only a brief period of time when she hadn't run from the fiercely felt attraction. Lydia had known it again in the priest's office, and the urge to leave had nearly overwhelmed her. She couldn't run, though, not if she wanted to convince Nathan that what she felt for him was nothing so much as indifference.

"Come in," Nathan called. He was standing on the veranda when he heard Lydia's knock. She had come straight from the school. She was carrying a satchel of books, her reticule, and an armload of papers. She dropped everything on the bed, laid her coat and hat on top, and went to the fireplace to warm her hands. Nathan came in from the veranda and sat behind her in an overstuffed brocade chair. His gaze wandered over her trim back and the curve of her hips. Her plain gray gown was severely cut, modest, and proper. He wondered if she was wearing the lacy drawers and batiste chemise he had purchased for her under it. Glancing at her hemline, Nathan tried to get a glimpse of her pantalets. He was fairly caught out when she turned around but he didn't apologize or even pretend abashment. What he did was smile.

Lydia's heart started thumping again. "You haven't told me why you're here," she said calmly, taking the chair opposite him.

"You probably already know, Lydia. I've had time to think about your reaction when you came into Father Colgan's office today. You never told me who you were expecting, but it's become clear to me. You thought I was going to be Brig."

She nodded. "You've seen him then? He's already at Ballaburn?"

"No to both your questions. He hadn't arrived when I left. Did you think he would go there?"

"He said he would."

Nathan swore under his breath. He looked away from

381

Lydia and into the fireplace. "I'd hoped to get here before you had to talk to him at all. Word reached Ballaburn a few days back that he was in Sydney. I was in the bush until last night or I would have come sooner." He got up, poured himself a drink, and sat down again, this time on the arm of the chair. "How did he find you?"

"I'm not certain," Lydia said. "I don't think it was very hard. I wasn't really hiding from him. I know you said there was a chance he'd recover, but I suppose at the back of my mind, I really believed I killed him. When I saw him again . . ."

Nathan finished for her. "You wished you had."

"Yes." Her eyes closed briefly. "I'm not proud of it, but that's what I wished."

To keep from reaching for Lydia, Nathan's hand tightened around the glass he held. Keeping his voice carefully neutral, he asked, "How many times have you seen Brig?"

"Three times. Twice at school, once here at the hotel. He got Henry to let him in my room."

"He what?!"

"It's all right, Nathan. I've spoken to Henry since then. It won't happen again."

"You're right it won't. You're coming back to Ballaburn where I know you'll be safe."

Lydia blinked at his harsh tone. "I'll stay just where I am, thank you very much."

"This really isn't open for discussion." Nathan knocked back his drink and set his glass down. "I didn't come here with that intention, but knowing what I do now there's no better alternative. Irish told me that you think Brig's a killer. If you believe that's true, Lydia, then you need to be where I can protect you."

"If I believe it's true?" she asked. "*If?* You must know the truth, Nathan. I think you've suspected for a long, long time, but your misplaced sense of loyalty to Brig has kept you silent. If you didn't know him for what he was

382

you wouldn't want me back at Ballaburn, you wouldn't have followed him to San Francisco, you wouldn't have left me and Fa'amusami on the beach so you could question her father about another similar murder."

Nathan went to the French doors and stood with his back to them, his features blurring in the shadows. "I want you back at Ballaburn because I know Brig will continue to harass you anywhere else. I followed Brig to San Francisco because that was the only way I had a chance of getting the station for myself. And you don't know what I talked to Fa'amusami's father about because I never told you."

"Tell me now."

He shrugged. "Very well. I asked Fiame about a certain aphrodisiac I'd heard existed on the island. Do you know what an aphrodisiac is?"

"Yes, but I don't believe you." It was hard not to put her cool hands to her burning cheeks. "You left just as Fa'amusami was talking about that young girl's suicide."

"Coincidence."

Lydia went to the bed, routed through her satchel, and withdrew a blank sheet of paper. She gave it to Nathan. "Fold that," she said.

"What?"

"Fold it. Go on. I want to prove something to myself, then I'll prove it to you."

Nathan shook his head, bewildered, but did as she asked. He folded it once, patting the crease with his fingertips. "Again?" he asked. She nodded. He folded it several more times, each time patting the crease the same way, then gave the square back to Lydia. "Now what did that show?"

"The night I shot Brigham I went to your hotel room because I thought I was meeting you. Earlier that day I had been to Madame Simone's salon. I bought some dresses, was measured for a few others, and went home with a couple of parcels. One of those parcels contained a note, from you, I thought. It was neatly folded, tightly creased, so much so that when I opened it I had to be careful not to tear the paper." She opened the paper Nathan had folded for her with no such difficulty.

"I had never seen your handwriting so I had nothing to compare it to. There was something else in the parcel which led me to believe I was dealing with you—a square of fabric from my yellow ballgown. Remember it? It's the one I wore to my charity ball and later to the brothel in Portsmouth Square. I ruined it trying to deliver Charlotte's baby."

"I remember. I gave you something of Ginny's to wear."

She nodded. "Which you later returned to her."

"She was already dead then."

"I'm sure she was," Lydia said flatly. "Did you see my yellow bloodstained gown anywhere in her room?"

"It's been a long time, Lydia. I don't recall—"

"Let me help you. I left it hanging over the back of the room's only chair. Do you remember seeing it now? No? Allow me to help you again. The reason you didn't see it is because it wasn't there then. Ginny didn't do anything with it because I would never have gotten a piece of it delivered to me weeks later. No, Ginny didn't do anything with my gown—her killer did. My yellow ballgown was one of a kind, Nathan. The killer picked it up because it meant something to him; it placed me in Ginny's room some time that night. He held on to it because he didn't know how it might help him just then, but it was a kind of security against a day when things might not go his way.

"That day came when I sent him jumping out of my bedroom window. His best friend warned me that I'd made an enemy, but I didn't understand." She drew in a breath and released it slowly. "So . . . so when I received the parcel and the note and the fabric I thought it was from you. I went to your hotel room with a check to buy you off and a gun to kill you if nothing else worked.

384

Brigham met me at the door and I made it so easy for him to lie. I was already convinced you were the one I needed to be afraid of. Brig didn't have to do or say much to make his presence there seem logical. By the time I realized he had no intention of letting me go, it was too late.

"But there was something Brig did while we were talking that stayed with me, something that kept pointing to him as the author of the note had I been able to realize it then." Lydia began folding the paper in her hands. Each crease was made by running her fingernails sharply over the fold. The sound of her nails on the paper raised gooseflesh on her arms, but she kept on folding. "I gave him the check that was made out to you, and this is what he did with it. I can't stand that sound, Nathan. It makes me want to shiver and grit my teeth. But you see what it does to the paper, how pressed and neat the folds are? That was the condition of the note I received. You didn't send it to me. Brig did. Brig had the gown, not you. Brig's the killer, not you."

Flames licked at the logs in the fireplace. The stack shifted and crackled. Otherwise the room was oppressively silent. Nathan stared at the folded piece of paper in Lydia's hand, finally took it from her, and walked over to the fireplace and pitched it in. Fingers of fire traced its edges before it exploded into heat and light.

"How long have you known?" he asked. He stood with his legs apart, gently rocking on the balls of his feet, hands in his pockets, shoulders hunched.

"Not as long as you might think," she said. "The realization didn't happen until after I left Ballaburn, although once my memory returned I was troubled by the incident at the Silver Lady. I could never piece everything together."

"You never bothered asking."

"To what purpose? You told me once that you hadn't murdered Ginny Flynt. You said the same about the murder that got you transported. You avoided my ques-

385

tions about your conversation with Fa'amusami's father. If you had denied sending the note and fabric to me, I don't know whether I would have believed you."

Nathan flinched at her honesty. "Is it part of the reason you were so anxious to leave Ballaburn?"

"No. Did it ever occur to you I didn't ask because I was afraid to know the whole truth?"

"You seem to have gone after it anyway."

She shook her head. "Not intentionally I didn't. It took a room full of children all folding paper at the same time, making each crease with painstaking precision, setting my teeth on edge until I begged them to stop, to finally open my eyes. I clearly remembered the note, the way Brig toyed with the check later, and the way you folded a newspaper. I'd seen you do it several times, pressing the folds with your fingertips or using the side of your hand to flatten a crease. You never used your nails. I would remember." Her light laughter sounded tinny and nervous to her own ears. "It would have led me to murder."

Nathan didn't respond to her black humor. He continued to stare at the fire. He could feel Lydia approaching nearer, but he didn't turn. "In spite of what you think, I've never known with one hundred percent certainty. I've never had anything closely resembling proof. Coincidence does not equal proof, Lydia, and that's all I had. I never knew how Brig got you to leave your home and show up at the Silver Lady until you mentioned rather offhandedly at Ballaburn that there was a note. Since I didn't write it, I knew it was Brig. It was clear you still suspected me and I was too proud to tell you differently. This is the first I've ever heard about your ballgown. It's the only piece of evidence I know that puts Brig in Ginny's room. It doesn't make him guilty, Lydia. It only puts him there."

"But—"

"I know what you think. I think it, too. But I was the

386

one transported for murder at fourteen. I'm the one with the record. A person doesn't have to dig very deep to discover that the young woman's murder in London bears a striking resemblance to Ginny Flynt's murder. No matter what I suspected in San Francisco, I wouldn't have turned on Brigham. Suspicion would have fallen very quickly on me. There's little that I feel for Brig because of a misplaced sense of loyalty, as you called it. Most of what I do or don't do is guided by a sense of self-preservation."

"When you're not trying to protect others," she said.

He laughed dryly, without humor. "I'm hardly successful at it. You know of three murders: London, San Francisco, and Samoa. In Frisco Ginny's suicide was accepted. Sometimes that happens. I know of two suicides here, one in Sydney about four years ago, and one in Melbourne in November two years back, just around Cup day, that were probably Brig's work. I wasn't successful in stopping them. In fact, I wonder if I didn't somehow contribute to them. I'm always around when they happen, just close enough to be considered a suspect if I went to anyone with my information, but never close enough to stop it from happening. I never know when it's going to happen or who the victim might be. The woman in London was the mistress of a powerful lord. Ginny and the woman in Sydney were both prostitutes. The woman in Melbourne was the widow of a convict Brig knew. Fiame assures me the Samoan girl was an innocent. She may have died simply for saying no to Brig."

"Does Brig know that you suspect him?"

"I don't know. I've never said anything to him. It would be a challenge in his eyes."

Lydia sighed, her shoulders slumping. "God, what a horrible mess."

Nathan turned sharply and demanded, "Have *you* told Brig any of your suspicions?"

Startled, Lydia took a step backward. She shook her

head vigorously. "No. I've never said anything to him. He thinks I believe you had something to do with Ginny's murder."

The tight coil of tension in Nathan's abdomen unwound fractionally. "Good. Don't ever let him know differently. That's your best protection." He paused. "That, and coming to Ballaburn with me."

Lydia didn't say anything for a moment, marshaling her thoughts and her defenses. "Actually, Nathan, that's related to what I was writing you about. I wish you had received my letter before coming here. You may have decided the trip was unnecessary."

"Oh?" She hadn't said anything and already Nathan didn't like where the conversation was heading.

"I know I've said that I don't want a divorce . . ."

"And now you do?" His eyes had narrowed.

"No . . . oh, no. I've been thinking that an annulment would be a better solution."

"The word 'solution' implies there's a problem. I'd like to hear what the problem is."

"I want to go home," Lydia said. "I miss my family. I haven't heard anything from Mother or Papa. I can't be certain they've even gotten my first letter." None of what she said was a lie, yet Lydia did not feel the same urgency imparted in her tone.

"You promised you would stay here for a year. Is this how you keep your word?"

"I'm sorry, Nathan. I didn't make that promise lightly. I really thought I could keep it."

"Why do you want an annulment? You could leave without it."

She frowned. "But then we'd still be married," she said. "You wouldn't be able to marry again."

"I don't plan on marrying again." He was watching her carefully, noting the way her eyes never held his for very long, the way they shifted to a point beyond his shoulder. "Do you?"

"I've never thought about it," she prevaricated.

"You mean it's not James Early or Henry Bell you're running to?"

"I've never lied about James. He's a friend. I suppose he always will be. I never think seriously about marrying him."

"Henry?"

"Henry Bell was a victim of my mother's considerable charms. I *never* think of marrying him. Seriously or otherwise."

"Then an annulment hardly seems necessary. We'll remain married until you're certain you want another husband. You can write me in that event."

"You're going to let me leave?" she asked incredulously. She had expected an argument similar to the one over the annulment.

"I can't really keep you here, can I? I can only make it difficult for you to go, and my ability to do that is limited when I'm in Ballaburn and you're here. If you won't come back to the station with me, then you can go to San Francisco."

"But you'll lose Ballaburn."

"I'd lose it if we were granted an annulment, too. But this way I won't lose you."

"Nathan, I don't think—"

He held up one hand. "Let me finish. I know you'll be completely out of my reach, Lydia, but I'll also know you're still mine. As long as we're married Brig can't have you."

And therefore he can't have Ballaburn, Lydia finished silently. She and Nathan had arrived at a similar conclusion though their approach to the problem was wildly different. She did not want Brig to have the station, either, but it was Nathan's safety she wanted to guarantee, not her own. The surest way for Brig to end their marriage was to make her a widow. An annulment was absolutely essential. "I'm not leaving Sydney without the dissolution of our marriage, Nathan."

"Then you're coming with me to Ballaburn. I can make that happen."

Lydia's chin lifted a notch. "What are you going to do? Bind and gag me? Toss me in a trunk? Because that's what it will take to make me leave."

Nathan almost smiled at her dramatics. "I was thinking along the lines of cuffing you on that arrogant chin of yours and pitching you over the back of my horse. And if you think anyone will stop me, you still haven't learned much about the way things are done here. You're my wife, Lydia."

"I'm not your property!"

"You're exactly my property!"

Lydia's hands clenched at her sides. She could imagine herself slapping Nathan solidly on the cheek. The vision in her mind's eye appalled and frightened her. Instead of striking out she sank heavily into the chair behind her, bowed her head, and stared at her shaking hands. "I'm afraid," she said softly. "Nathan, I'm so afraid."

He dropped to his knees in front of her and took her hands in his. "Do you think I don't know? Lydia? Look at me, Lydia." She raised her eyes slightly. "When you thought I was Brig this afternoon you were all sharp-tongued and bluster, trying so hard to make him see that you weren't intimidated. Perhaps it would have worked with Brigham, but it doesn't have the same impact on me. I know he's frightened you and you've already shown plenty of foolish courage by being with him at all. You *know* what we can't prove. Brig's a killer. It's right that you should be scared of him."

"I'm not," Lydia denied. "I'm not afraid of what he might do to me." Her hands were trembling now. Nathan's attempts at calming her were inadequate. "I'm afraid . . . I'm afraid of what . . ."

"Lydia," he said softly. "What else is there to be frightened of?"

390

She took a calming breath, let it out slowly. Her smile was faint, meant to reassure. "Nothing," she said. "You're right, of course, there's nothing else to fear."

Nathan looked at her oddly, trying to gauge her truthfulness. He wasn't satisfied that he had it yet, but he had no clear idea of what she was afraid of. He released her hands, took a padded stool from beside her chair, and sat on it. "I'll make arrangements for you to leave Sydney. You can be on your way to San Francisco in a few days."

Lydia knew she couldn't do that. If Nathan had not realized how his own life would be threatened, she did. She couldn't leave him unprotected. Someone had to watch his back and Lydia nominated herself. "I already said I wouldn't leave unless our marriage was annulled. Since I doubt Father Colgan will help me do it without your agreement, that means I'm staying here."

"In Sydney?"

She touched her chin, raising her eyebrows a tad. "I don't relish the thought of your fist against my arrogant chin. I'll go to Ballaburn."

"It will be all right," he said. "You'll see. Brig won't try anything at the house. He'd lose even his right to the strip of land he won if he made a move against you there. There will always be people around."

"Why doesn't Irish do something about Brig? Put an end to the wager without waiting out the year?"

"I thought you knew," Nathan said, puzzled. "Irish doesn't believe what you told him about Brig."

Lydia's head jerked up. She was stunned. "He doesn't believe me? But he sat in the dining room in this very hotel and listened to every word I said. He never—"

"He listened, Lydia. He also reserved judgment. When he came back to Ballaburn he told me the whole of it. It was clear that he thought you were mistaken in your conclusions."

"Did you tell him what you thought?"

"He never asked. I didn't volunteer any information

because it wouldn't have been welcome. Irish doesn't want to believe that he misjudged Brig so totally and I'm afraid that nothing I say is going to change his mind. It's more than Irish thinking he's a good judge of character. At Ballaburn he thinks he's omnipotent."

"I've noticed," she said dryly. "It's one of the reasons we're generally at loggerheads. He thinks he's right about most everything and I *know* I am." She sighed, her dark blue eyes clouding over. "It's just as well, I suppose, that he doesn't believe me. He doesn't need this to worry about. The best thing about going back to Ballaburn will be having more time with Irish. I never understood how much pain he's been in until he visited. The trip must have been horrible for him. I realized then that I couldn't expect him to come often, perhaps never again."

"Don't let him think that you're returning because of him," Nathan warned her. "His pride couldn't stand it."

"What will we tell him? If it's not his health, if it's not concern about Brig, then what story will appease him?"

Nathan cleared his throat slightly and tried to respond casually. "I've been giving that a little thought. We might be able to convince him that we've really fallen in love. I think he'd accept it."

Lydia had difficulty catching her breath for a moment. She said carefully, "He'd probably congratulate himself."

"It seems likely."

"All right," she said quietly. "I think I can pretend. You?"

He nodded. "It shouldn't be too difficult."

She fell silent, then, "There's still the problem of our bedroom. I don't know if—"

"I can sleep on the floor," he said quickly. "No one will ever know but you. It won't be much different than sleeping in the bush."

Lydia was uncertain. She studied Nathan's impassive face. "Well . . . if you really wouldn't mind."

"I didn't say I wouldn't mind," he said. "I only said I could do it."

"Oh."

"It's settled then?"

"It's settled." Quite without conscious thought Lydia held out her hand to seal the agreement. Nathan accepted it with equal ease. The bargain struck, they both looked away guiltily as the touch of their hands lingered beyond the moment.

Chapter Fourteen

Somehow it worked. Against the realistic expectations of both participants in the truce, Nathan and Lydia were holding their own. Without ever discussing how they would practice their loving deception on the rest of Ballaburn, they arrived at a plan that helped them avoid difficult explanations and tempting situations.

In spite of the fact that Brigham had never arrived at Ballaburn, Nathan made it a point to work within sight of the house. He did not trust Brig not to announce himself suddenly and turn the entire station on its head. He wanted to be close to Lydia when that happened. Lydia had no objections to Nathan stationing himself near the house. She found herself wandering to the windows, searching him out to reassure herself half a dozen times during the day. It was a satisfactory arrangement now, while the sheep were still at pasture, but as spring approached they would have to be mustered for shearing and Nathan would start to travel farther afield. Lydia already knew she would be going out with Nathan on those occasions. If he thought she was afraid to stay at the house without him, he might agree to take her along.

Lydia tried not to dwell on Brigham or the reasons he had chosen not to come to Ballaburn. Her task was made easier by the demands Irish placed on her attention. He rarely asked for anything from her outright, but Lydia realized she was gradually assuming more and more responsibility for the things he wanted done. They worked daily on cataloguing the books in the library. He showed her how the accounts for the station were kept, how the revenue from the gold mines supported Ballaburn in lean years. She learned where the important papers were, had access to all of the station's earnings and receipts, and was finally given the task of doing the payroll. Warming to Irish's confidence in her abilities, Lydia was the only one surprised that she showed such aptitude. Over her bent head, as she worked on the accounts, Irish and Nathan exchanged glances that were at once pleased and amused.

"He's grooming you to take control of Ballaburn," Nathan told her one evening after Irish had gone to bed. He put down the book he was reading and crossed the study to where Lydia was working at the desk. Pushing one of the ledgers aside, Nathan rested his hip on the edge and casually leaned over her work.

Lydia's brow creased as she concentrated on the lines of figures in front of her. Nathan's shadow had fallen across the pages. "You're blocking my light," she said, waving him aside absently. "How can I know what I'm doing if I can't—" The book was closed over her hand. "Nathan."

"Nathan," he mocked, using her tone precisely.

Lydia laughed and slipped her hand out from between the pages. She glanced at the cherrywood grandfather clock standing in one corner of the room. "My, it's late. I hadn't realized."

"I know."

It had been her practice each of the eight evenings since returning to Ballaburn to make her way to bed first. She would set out Nathan's blankets and pillow, make certain there was fresh water in the basin for him, and turn back all the lamps but the one on his highboy dresser. He always gave her adequate time to prepare for bed herself before he came into the room. Lydia could have easily fallen asleep in that time, though she never did. Instead, she buried herself deep in the cool sheets and thick woolen blankets and pretended restfulness where none existed.

Lydia believed Nathan was probably aware she wasn't sleeping, but he never mentioned it. Just as she never mentioned that although he said his sleeping accommodations were fine, she knew he tossed and turned on the hard floor. There were things better left unsaid, and privately they believed it was what made being together bearable. Or almost bearable. Neither of them thought for a moment that not talking about the tension between them made it nonexistent, but talking about it would have led to doing something, and that was the very thing they wanted to avoid.

"If you're tired, I'll go up now," she said. She started to push away from the desk, but Nathan's foot caught the seat of her chair and stayed her.

"If I'm tired, I can go up first. The sky won't fall if we vary our routine a little." His smile was faint. "As it happens, I'm not tired. I was going to go in the kitchen and make myself a cuppa. Would you like some?"

"Please. And if you can find any of Molly's honey biscuits in there . . ."

"I'll bring a feast," he promised solemnly.

Nathan was as good as his word. Returning from the kitchen fifteen minutes later, he laid out a smorgasbord of treats in front of the fireplace and bid Lydia join him. She put her work away again and sat beside him on the edge of the woolen rug. Her dark-blue skirt was spread around her as Lydia drew her legs to one side. She smoothed the folds and began to pick and choose among the cold meats, bread, and sweets that Nathan had brought.

"What did you mean by Irish grooming me to take control of Ballaburn?" she asked. "You weren't serious, were you?"

"Very serious." He poured himself a cup of tea. "Do

you really doubt that's what's going on?"

"I've never thought about it. Ballaburn will be yours someday."

"And yours through me. Irish doesn't realize you intend to leave at the end of a year. He wants you to have a part in the success of the station. What he's teaching you to do now could well give you complete control."

"That's absurd, Nathan."

"Not so absurd when you realize that I don't know the first thing about the accounting procedures. Irish has always kept that part of running the station to himself. I know everything about Ballaburn as far as its livestock and lands go. I can muster and shear and shoot and track, but what you've been doing most of this week I can't do at all." Turning his attention toward the fire, Nathan sipped his tea. "Someday I'll have to hire someone who knows the things you know and hope like bloody hell they don't cheat me."

"I could teach you." *Or I could stay,* she thought.

Or you could stay, he thought. "I'd like that," he said. "It wouldn't have to be everything. Just enough so no one makes a fool of me."

"I don't think that's possible," she said.

Her quick defense of him made Nathan smile. He watched her eyes stray to his dimples and the heat he saw in their depths was warmer than the fire. He looked away quickly, his smile fading. "I think Brig's doing just that," he said. "I don't kid myself that he's not somewhere around here."

"You mean here at Ballaburn? How can that be? No one's said anything."

Nathan shook his head, angry at himself for bringing up the subject. Confronted with the sultry heat in Lydia's eyes, knowing she didn't mean for him to see it, he had said the first thing that came to his mind. "I don't know that anyone else suspects. Some of the stockmen are reporting damage that could be animals . . . or could be bushrangers. A mob of sheep were maneuvered onto a ridge just west of here and chased over the edge into the gully. Wild dogs would explain it. So would Brig. I thought I might go out to Lion's Ridge tomorrow and see if Brig's staked out his property. He's entitled to the land from the ridge to Willaroo Valley. He may have decided to camp there."

"Don't go," Lydia said quickly. Her appetite fled at the thought of Nathan going out to find Brigham. "That is . . . umm . . . couldn't you send someone else? Jack would go for you."

"Of course Jack would go, but I . . . What is it, Lydia? Do you think Brig's waiting for me to leave so he can come here?"

It had never occurred to her. "It's possible, isn't it?"

Certainly it was possible, he thought. Anything was possible with Brig. The thing that worried Nathan was that he didn't understand what Brigham was doing. If he was guilty of the attacks on Ballaburn, what was the purpose? If he wasn't responsible, then where was he? Why hadn't he returned home?

"I won't go," he said. "If it will make you feel better, I'll send Jack and Pooley out to look over the property."

"Thank you. It does make me feel better."

"You know, Lydia, I really don't think Brig's going to do anything here at the house. He's not going to want to reveal his true colors to Irish."

"Perhaps he already has," Lydia said. "Irish rarely mentions Brigham. If he finds his absence from Ballaburn odd, he has yet to say so. Sometimes I wonder . . . I don't know . . . it's hard to make sense of it all."

"*You* don't make sense. What is it that you wonder?"

"Well, I've asked myself if we haven't overestimated Irish's esteem and affection for Brigham. Perhaps he really does believe that Brig's capable of everything I told him."

"Then why hasn't he discarded the second will and ended the wager? Or are you saying Irish really wants Brig to have Ballaburn?"

"No!"

"Then what?"

Lydia studied her hands in her lap. Unconsciously she massaged the place where her wedding ring had been. Irish told her she hadn't earned it back yet. "If he ended the wager there would be no reason for me to be here. You would be entitled to Ballaburn outright and I would be perfectly free to choose where I wanted to live. I know Irish hated it when I went to Sydney. I think he may have used events to his advantage. I'm here now, aren't I?"

"He has no reason to think you're ever going to leave me," Nathan said. "You've played your part of the loving wife to perfection these past eight days."

"Perhaps neither of us is the actor we think we are," she said quietly. "Irish may be seeing right through our charade."

Nathan was silent, thoughtful. He added some tea to his cup and warmed his palms around it. "It's something to think about, isn't it," he said at last.

"Yes." Lydia began to organize things on the tray Nathan had brought in.

"Leave it," he said. "I'll take it all back to the kitchen. You go on up to bed."

Lydia's busy, fluttering hands stilled. She avoided looking at Nathan in the event he was looking at her. "All right." Getting to her feet, Lydia smoothed her gown across her abdomen. "Will you be very long?" she asked.

"Long enough."

Not certain she wanted to know what that meant, Lydia carried herself off to bed.

"Bail up, mates!"

The Cobb & Co. coach was already slowing down when the order to halt was given. Three men on horseback blocked the narrow road and a quick look over his shoulder assured the driver a fourth man was coming at the coach from behind. The driver dropped his reins and held up his hands as the order was repeated. The man riding shotgun put down his weapon without firing.

The bushrangers were a scrubby lot, heavily bearded, and four of them riding together gave rise to speculation among the Cobb & Co. passengers. The most famous highwaymen in Australia were the Kelly gang and four made up their number. They did whatever struck their fancy: looting, ravaging, drinking to excess, and dancing till dawn with an entire town they held captive. They were also murderers. As much as they were admired by the general population for their daring and defiance, no one particularly wanted to be on the wrong end of their pistols.

The Cobb & Co. riders were almost obsequious in their efforts to give the bushrangers what they wanted. The strongbox containing mail and money was handed over quickly. The passengers filed out of the coach and stood quietly in line while they were stripped of their valuables. In a few minutes they were herded back inside, a shot was fired, and the coach was on its way again, each rider formulating the tale that would be related again and again about the encounter with the infamous Kelly gang.

After the coach was out of sight Brig shot open the lock on the strongbox. "You blokes can have whatever you like when I'm done," he said, rummaging through the contents.

"It was as easy as you said it would be, mate," one of them said. "We were as game as Ned Kelly."

Behind Brig's heavy beard and mustache he sneered. "Don't let it go to your head. They thought we *were* the Kelly gang. Why do you think I asked only three of you to help? And you there, Zach, with your black beard and brows, look as like a Kelly as Ned himself." There was dead silence from his helpers as they considered the import of Brig's observation. "Right," Brig said, rising. He held up an envelope. "I've got what I want. The rest is yours. I think you know not to brag about this incident. Kelly may hear of it and wonder why he's not a richer

401

man for his exploits. G'day, gentlemen." Mounting his horse, Brig cut a path into the bush and disappeared over the crest of a hill.

While the horses were being exchanged, the passengers talked excitedly in the large kitchen at Ballaburn, recounting their face-to-face experience with the Kelly gang. Lydia helped Tess and Molly serve refreshments and listened as avidly as they to the tales being shared. Irish wheeled in his chair from the hallway and Nathan came in the back door, the coach driver at his side. As the driver moved farther into the room, Lydia went to stand beside her husband.

"He's told you what happened?" she asked in hushed tones.

Nathan nodded. He put his arm around Lydia's waist and drew her closer to his side. Above her head his expression was troubled. After a few minutes of listening to the passengers, Nathan bent his head and whispered against Lydia's ear, "Come outside with me a moment."

Lydia followed Nathan out of the house. The day was cloudy and breezy and she batted at her gown to keep it from billowing all around her. Nathan offered her his jacket, which she didn't accept. "A moment, you said," she reminded him. "What is so important that we need talk about it out here?"

"This isn't Kelly country, Lydia. Ned's gang raids towns farther south of here. If those passengers want to think they've been held up by Ned Kelly, then let them, but I don't believe it."

"What are you saying?"

"I'm saying that as long as I've known Brig he's always had a fancy to play the highwayman. 'We'll have two pops and a galloper,' he used to tell me." At Lydia's blank look he explained, "Two pistols and a horse."

Lydia pushed back a strand of hair that blew across her face. "Brig? One of the highwaymen was Brig? Nathan, you can't know that."

She was right, of course. He couldn't know it with complete certainty and now he regretted sharing his supposition with Lydia. She would never comprehend Brigham the way he did, never appreciate that it wasn't intuition that guided him now, but a deep understanding of how Brigham worked when his back was to the wall and desperation made him reckless. Nathan felt his own choices dwindling. He was going to have to face Brig and settle what was between them. It was the only way he could protect Lydia.

"You're right," he said, his expression shuttered. He jerked his head toward the kitchen. "Go on back inside. You can tell me all their stories later. I have work to do." He strode off without giving her a chance to question his easy capitulation.

Lydia wandered back in the kitchen and stood at the periphery of the excited chatter. The coach driver moved aside to let her in the circle. She shook her head, smiling. "I'm fine where I am."

"I'm sorry about your letter, Mrs. Hunter," he said quietly. "Perhaps we'll find it later. Not likely that Kelly and his bunch wanted more than the money in the strongbox."

"Letter?" asked Lydia. "There was something for me on the coach?"

The driver nodded. "I mentioned it to Mr. Hunter. Just happened to see there was something for you when they put the mail on at Sydney. Like I said, we'll probably find it later. Ned was after the money, not much doubt about that. He won't take what he has no use for."

"I'm certain you're right," she said, then hesitated. "I don't suppose you noticed where my letter came from? Did it originate in Sydney?"

"Oh, no, ma'am. That's why I was upset that we lost it. I supposed this was something important for you. The stamp is what caught my eye in the first place. The letter came all the way from San Francisco."

*   *   *

The passengers were all gone by dinner and the wave of excitement had vanished with them. Irish and Lydia were eating alone in the dining room, neither of them having the inclination to wait for Nathan, especially when Molly put the hot food in front of them and ordered them to eat.

Lydia heaped Irish's plate with Molly's special dish of rabbit with cherry sauce, potatoes, and green beans and onions. "I've noticed you've had a better appetite lately," she said when he stared at the plate she laid in front of him. "It won't hurt to indulge a little."

"Trying to fatten me up?"

"Fill you out," she countered. Her eyes darted over his face, noting the sallowness of his complexion, the hint of gauntness in his broad features. The robust man she had known a few short months ago was fading in front of her eyes. Conspiring with Molly to stimulate Irish's appetite was hardly helping. His spirits were good, but pain was a thin white line around his mouth and permanently engraved at the corners of his eyes.

He puffed his cheeks, got the laughing response he wanted from Lydia, and began to eat. "Nathan's going to be sorry he missed this meal," he said after a while.

"I'll have Molly put aside something for him. He can eat later this evening."

"I don't think he'll be back tonight. I heard Jack tell Tess that he's gone up to Lion's Ridge."

"What?" Lydia's head snapped up and her fork hovered in midair. She forced herself to relax. "You must be mistaken. He told me last night that he was going to send Jack and Pooley up there. Jack must have meant *he* was going, not Nathan. Nathan's still out repairing fences with Billy and Ed. I saw him leave with them earlier this afternoon."

"But he didn't return with them. Billy and Ed are eating dinner with the other hands right now. Where are you going? Lydia? Come back—"

"I'll just be a moment," she said without turning around. "I want to find Tess."

Lydia never returned to the dining room. When she found out from Tess that Irish hadn't mistaken what he'd overheard, she went in search of Jack. After extracting his promise to escort her to Lion's Ridge, Lydia went to her own room and began packing. Irish caught up with her again as she was hurrying down the main staircase. She had already changed into a split riding skirt and boots and was carrying a bedroll and saddlebag stuffed with a change of clothes, personal items, and a Remington revolver. She had thrown a jacket around her shoulders and her hair was pulled back and tied at her nape with a black velvet ribbon. The hat on her head was a shade too large for her head and the wide brim rested on the upper curve of her ears.

"Where do you think you're going?" he demanded, blocking her way with his chair. She tried to sidestep him, but Irish wheeled around quickly and blocked her again. "I think I have a right to know where you're going."

"To Lion's Ridge. I'm going to find Nathan."

"Bloody hell!"

"Yes, bloody hell!" she shot back. "Jack's agreed to show me the way. I'm not so foolish as to set off alone at night."

"I'll order him to stay here."

"Then I *will* go off on my own, Irish. I want to be with Nathan."

Irish's thick fingers gripped the arms of his chair as he took measure of Lydia's threat. Finally he wheeled out of her way. "All right," he said. "Go. Take Jack *and* Pooley with you."

Lydia released the breath she had been holding and came down the last step to the landing. "Thank you, Irish." She bent then, and did something she had never done before: she kissed him. Her lips brushed his cheek. "Thank you," she whispered. "I'll explain everything when I get back."

The hallway was empty by the time Irish found his

voice. "By God, you *do* love him." Rolling his chair into the study, Irish found his strongbox and opened it. He removed two wills, glanced at them both, then tore up one, hoping to God he had not left it for too late.

The ride to Lion's Ridge was as arduous as Jack had warned Lydia. Her escorts rode on either side of her when it was possible, but there were many times when the trails narrowed and single file was the only way to pass. The horses were sure-footed yet they grew restless and shied on some of the rocky sandstone ledges they were forced to negotiate. Jack led the way, carrying a lantern. The light was bright enough for him to see his breath misting in the cool evening air. He did not need another reminder of how cold it was going to get. Behind him he heard Lydia's teeth chattering.

Where there was forest it was thick with the evergreen gum trees. Starshine and moonlight were often obliterated by the spreading crowns of the eucalypts. The forest floor was littered with stiffened strings of bark the trees had shed the previous spring and summer. Beneath the horses' hooves, the ground crackled and sometimes the brush would snap loudly as a kangaroo was startled by their approach and leaped to safety.

They rode for several hours and Lydia stoically bore the silent censure of both her companions, not caring in the least whether or not they approved. Neither did she tell them anything that might have led them to a different conclusion about her journey. The business of Ballaburn that pitted Brig and Nathan against each other was a private matter, not meant for speculation by the stockmen. She didn't want to think about them choosing sides behind the man they wanted to head Ballaburn in Irish's place.

Jack reined in his horse and pointed a small flickering light in the distance. "That's probably Nath, Mrs. Hunter."

"Probably?"

He shrugged his shoulders. "Who can tell? It's Lion's Ridge, that much I know. You can't tell now, but in daylight it's golden sandstone with a slope carved out like a lion's mane. Your husband's up there or it's bushrangers. We'll go quiet as we can from here. No need to make ourselves known until we're certain." Raising the lantern, he blew it out, and night surrounded them like a shroud.

It took them another hour to reach the campsite, for the light on the ridge had been visible for miles. When they arrived there was no one around. All that remained of the beacon fire was a few embers and ash.

"We'll camp here," Pooley said. "The site's been cleared of scrub and we have the makings for a fire. There's no sense going on tonight. We'll have to wait until morning to track him."

The ridge was dotted with boulders and Pooley disappeared behind a grouping of them to gather some kindling. When he reappeared a few moments later, he wasn't alone.

Nathan was holding a gun. "I think an explanation is in order," he said flatly. He was not looking at Pooley or Jack. His silver-gray predator eyes had centered on Lydia.

She steadied herself not to flinch and answered as if nothing out of the ordinary was happening. "Of course I'll explain, but I'd rather it be for your ears alone."

Nathan looked from Jack to Pooley. "Go on," he said. "You can camp at the foot of the gully; that way you'll be too far away to stop me from beating her." Both men laughed but Nathan wasn't entirely sure he wasn't serious. Lydia's nervous laughter told him that she didn't know what to think, either. "Lydia and I will meet you in the morning and we'll all go back to Ballaburn together. Jack. Pooley. Thanks. I'm assuming she would have come with or without you. Better with you."

"Right you are, Nath," Jack said. He tipped his hat to Nathan and took the reins of his mount and began leading him away. He stopped suddenly and turned around. "How long ago did you hear us approaching?"

"Thirty minutes. As soon as you started climbing. The ridge is too full of loose stone to make a quiet ascent. That's why I chose to camp here."

Jack shook his head, his smile admiring. "Nothin' gets past you."

"There's a fact," Pooley added, grinning. He dropped the kindling in his hands on the cooling fire and followed his friend down the rocky incline.

Their noisy descent gave Nathan opportunity to talk without fear of being overheard. He holstered his gun. "Tell me now what you're doing here, Lydia, because I'm really of a mind to turn you over my knee."

Lydia bent close to the fire and began arranging the kindling so it would ignite. "You left me alone at Ballaburn," she said simply. "I didn't think you should have done that. I thought I was at Ballaburn so you could protect me, and suddenly you were here and I was there and I didn't like being left alone."

"I left you there because you *were* safer there! You're always safer at the house than you are in the bush! How dare you risk your life and the lives of two of the men by coming out here!"

She waited for silence to settle. "And what about your life?" she asked calmly. "It was only this afternoon that you told me Brig might have done the coach robbery. Then you disappear. Do you think I don't know what this is about, Nathan? If you want to confront Brigham, then wait for him to come to you. Let him come to the house where there's protection for everyone, not up here where . . . where . . ." She waved her arm to indicate her surroundings as words to describe their situation failed her.

"Where I have better position than I'd ever have at the house," he said tightly. "Look around you, Lydia, and try to understand what it is you're seeing. This ridge has its own natural protection. You couldn't get close without

408

me hearing you and neither can Brig. These boulders behind us offer cover. There is no higher ground in these parts. You probably saw my fire twelve miles off. So would Brig. It was built expressly for that purpose when I couldn't find any sign of him in the area. I *want* him to approach me here, Lydia. It's time Brig and I talked about Ballaburn, don't you think?"

"Talk?" she asked incredulously. "That's why you've come out here?"

"It's what I plan to do first." He didn't have to say anything else. Letting the sentence hang there, Nathan made Lydia understand what he would do if forced.

"Brig may not be out here at all," she said.

"You're right. He may not be. And with you out here now, I hope he's not. I hope he had nothing to do with the coach robbery or the random attacks on Ballaburn. That's what I hope, Lydia, but not what I believe." He kicked at a loose stone and sent it sailing over the ridge. "Tomorrow morning we're going back to the house and you'll stay there."

"But if you leave—"

"You'll *stay* there." He waited for her response and thought he saw a slight nod of her head. "All right. Let's get some sleep. Get your bedroll and whatever else you had sense enough to bring. I'll get my things." He disappeared behind the boulders for a few minutes, came back with his bedroll, and laid it out.

Lydia took the straps off her bedroll and laid it out a few feet from Nathan's. He glanced at it and shook his head. "You're going to be cold tonight," he said. "You'd better move closer. Take advantage of my body heat."

"You were going to be out here alone," she pointed out. "I'll manage."

"Don't be ridiculous. My coat is heavier than yours, my bedroll's thicker, and I've slept in the bush before. Even so, I don't relish the thought of it tonight. If you won't share warmth for your sake, then do it for mine."

"Oh, very well." She dragged her blankets beside his. "There. Satisfied?"

He answered her sarcasm in kind. "How gracious you are." Nathan set some stones around the small fire to keep it from spreading and saw to their horses before he went over to their blankets. He looked down at Lydia, all bundled up in her bedding, and shook his head again.

"What is it now?" she asked wearily.

"The idea is to share the blankets and share our heat under them." He hunkered down, yanked hard on one corner of Lydia's blankets, and rolled her out of it.

"Nathan! What do you think you're—"

"Don't press me, Lydia," he said tersely, a rough edge to his tone. "I'm still not happy that you're here, but since you are, you'll do things my way. Is that clear?"

"Perfectly."

"Good. Now get off the ground before you catch your death. I'll fix our bed the way I want it." He snapped open two blankets, laid them out smoothly, and told Lydia to lie down. Stripping off his jacket, he gave it to her. "Cover yourself with this."

"I have a coat, Nathan. What will you—"

"Do it," he fairly growled. "That's better." Getting their saddles, Nathan put them down to rest their heads on. He lay down beside her, fitting his body to the stiff contours of hers, spoon-fashion, and pulled two heavier blankets over them. He tucked them around Lydia and himself as best he could. "I can still feel you shivering," he said.

Lydia felt him move closer, something she didn't think was possible. The trembling he felt was not entirely due to the cold. His arm was heavy across her waist and his breath was warm against her hair. She tried to stay as still as possible until she couldn't stand it anymore. "Nathan?"

His sigh was long on suffering. His voice was short on patience. "What is it?"

"There's a stone digging into my hip."

410

"Move it."

Lydia shifted, and her buttocks pressed directly against Nathan's groin. Even through her skirt and his jeans she felt his arousal.

"I meant, move the stone," he said, gritting his teeth. "Not move your backside."

"Oh." She shifted again, heard him groan, then swear softly. "Sorry. I'll get it in just a moment. Almost. There." She pulled it out, a little disappointed to feel how small it was in the palm of her hand. She would have sworn she was lying on Gibraltar. Lydia pitched it away and it rattled the scrub brush.

"What was that?" Nathan reached for his gun.

"I tossed the stone."

He relaxed slowly. "God, I may have to beat you before the night's over."

"Please don't be angry."

"Angry? Angry hardly describes what I'm feeling right now."

"I'm sorry," she whispered. "I didn't know it was going to be like this. So . . . so *frustrating*."

"You didn't know? Lydia, how can you say that? I've been sleeping on the floor of our bedroom for the better part of two weeks because we know what happens when we're this close."

Lydia turned over and faced him. "Show me what happens."

Nathan sucked in his breath. "Don't tease me."

"I'm not. Please, Nathan, if you don't kiss me, I'll . . ."

"What?"

"I'll kiss you." She closed the distance between their lips. Her mouth was warm and hard and hungry. Lydia's hands touched his lean cheeks, keeping him still while her lips tasted his. Her tongue flicked at his upper lip, traced the line of it. She moved over him, kissing his jaw, his cheeks, his brow. Her breath was moist and sweet. She kissed his neck, nipping his flesh with her teeth. The

411

soft, excited groan she heard was encouragement enough. Her fingers fumbled with the buttons of his shirt, spread the material, and delved beneath it. Lowering her head, she placed tiny, tempting kisses on his chest. His heart was racing and his breathing was harsh and uneven, catching as he anticipated the touch of her mouth and the caress of her fingers.

"Lydia?" Nathan stilled the restless and eager exploration of her hands. "Are you certain? Do you know what—"

"Yes," she said, kissing him on the mouth. "Yes. Yes. Yes." She punctuated each affirmation with another kiss. "Let me, Nathan. Please let me love you."

Nathan turned her on her back. His lips hovered above hers. "You're going to freeze," he whispered.

She smiled. "Cover me."

His mouth slanted across hers, hard and searching. He kissed her over and over—her neck, her cheeks, the sensitive spot just below her ear. His tongue ravaged her mouth, wanting, then wanting more. She helped him loosen the buttons on her blouse and together they tugged the material free of her skirt. He kissed her breasts through her chemise, laving her nipples with the rough edge of his tongue. They were raised hard against the material, and when he worried them with his lips and teeth she arched in his embrace.

She pulled at his belt and began to unfasten the buttons on his fly. She pushed at his jeans, working them over his hips while he struggled to come to terms with her split riding skirt. "What the hell do you have on?" he demanded tautly. "And how do I get it off?"

"Not that way," she said, pushing at his hands when he tried to raise the hem of the skirt. "It's like a pair of pants. You can't just toss it up."

"Don't ever wear it again."

"I won't."

He found the buttons in the waistband, undid them, and with Lydia's help, got her out of the skirt and under-

412

garments. He lay between her open thighs and felt her adjust to his weight and position by hooking her heels around him. Her hand came between their bodies and she reached for him, arching as she found his hard arousal and guided him inside her. His thrust was hard and sure, driving her back. She lifted, pushing against him, and he came hard at her again. His breath was warm on her face. He whispered things against her ear she only partly understood, but everything he said, everything he did, excited her to a point past bearing.

Her mouth was open under his. Their lips played, tongues sought entry, and their kisses were like the joining of their bodies, powerful and erotic and filled with desire.

It was a fire that engulfed them, shooting flames that seared and licked at their sweat-slick bodies. The heat was intense and burned rapidly and they surrendered to the hot and aching pleasure of it. Nathan's entire body tensed. His head was thrown back, his neck arched, and he felt Lydia tightly around him, urging him toward release with just the slightest of movements against him. In his last moment of control he thrust again, breathing her name as his body pressured hers with shuddering passion.

Lydia's fingers dug into his shoulders and she held on, tasting the cold night air at the back of her throat as she sucked in her breath. Her body curved to his. She stretched and cried out and brought his mouth down on hers as every tight spring in her body uncoiled.

Their breathing seemed loud in the stillness of the night. He was warm and heavy on her, but Lydia didn't mind except for— "Nathan? There's a stone under my hip."

His laughter was soft, washing over her. "Move it."

Lydia's hand left his shoulder and reached under the blankets to find the stone.

Nathan shook his head. The tip of his nose brushed hers. "Move your backside," he said. "Not the stone."

413

Heat rushed to Lydia's face, but she moved her pelvis against him. "Like that?"

"Exactly like that," he groaned. He kissed Lydia and shifted his weight off her before he came completely out of his skin. "God, but you're sweet."

Lydia got rid of the stone, found her pantalets, and settled her backside against the blankets. Her skirt lay somewhere out of her reach and she didn't care. Nathan's jean-clad leg was thrown over hers and he tucked the blankets warmly around her. They shared his sheepskin-lined jacket like two caterpillars in the same cocoon. She could make out his features, the straight slope of his nose, the lightly colored eyes that studied her face, the shape of his mouth. His expression was grave now, intent, so completely at odds with Lydia's giddy smile that she wondered if she had mistaken his feelings again. Her smile gradually faded.

"Don't do that," he said quietly.

"Do what?"

"Stop smiling. I love to look at you when you're smiling. I don't think you can know how good it feels to be touched by it." His forefinger traced the line of her mouth. The corners lifted and she kissed his fingertip.

"You don't have regrets then?" she asked.

Nathan did not answer immediately. He searched her face for some sign that she was prepared to hear what he wanted to say. The glow from the fire washed her features in a yellow-orange light and tinted strands of her sable hair auburn. He cupped the side of her face gently. "One regret," he said.

Lydia's eyes closed briefly under the terrible pressure she suddenly felt. Her stomach twisted and there was an agonized groan that came to her lips which she could not hold back. Giving sound to her pain embarrassed her. She tried to turn away quickly and draw her knees fetally to her chest. Nathan's hand on her shoulder stopped her and kept her on her back.

"Look at me, Lydia."

She might have refused if it had been a rough command, but the manner in which Nathan said those words it might well have been a plea. She found herself staring into his eyes.

"I regret that in all the times I've made love to you, you've never known you were loved."

Lydia's lips parted fractionally and a tiny sound that was not pain, but surprise, rushed out.

"I've loved you for a very long time, Lydia." And because he was absolutely terrorized by the thought of her rejection, Nathan added carelessly, "For what it's worth."

It was Lydia who caught him this time as he made to move away from her. "It's worth everything to me," she said.

"Do you mean it?" he asked softly.

"Oh, Nathan, of course I do." Lydia lightly touched his cheek with the back of her hand. "You can't know how desperately I've wanted to hear you say those words."

"Perhaps I can," he said.

At first she didn't understand what he was saying. There was a hint of expectancy in his voice, but the cause of it eluded her. Her eyes widened as realization was brought home to her. "But you know," she said. "You must know the way I feel, the way I've felt all along."

"Must I?" he asked. "You ran away from me on the occasion of our very first meeting."

"I was frightened . . . and fascinated. Of course I ran."

"When I saw you later that evening you made certain I knew you didn't want anything to do with me."

"I was embarrassed and worried you'd tell my parents where I had been."

"You hated that I won the wager in your father's poker game."

"I thought you did it just to torment me."

"You wanted Brig then."

415

"I was stupid."

Nathan was caught off guard by her admission. He smiled slowly and his chuckle sent a delicious frisson of warmth through Lydia. "Yes," he said. "You *were* stupid."

Not at all offended, Lydia nodded happily.

"You also found out enough about the wager between Brig and me to set the both of us up."

"I was stupid only to a certain point."

"We deserved everything you did to us," he said, clearly remembering the jump from her bedroom window.

"Even the fertilizer in the flower bed?" she asked.

"Especially the fertilizer."

"It could have been deeper," she said.

Nathan kissed her smug smile and finally began to believe that she really did love him. There was no bitterness in her tone as she recalled the trick that had been played her, no resentment or ill will. In spite of how he had wronged her, she had come to love him. "I would have never wished for you losing your memory," he told her, "but there was a part of me that was grateful when it happened. I was being given a second chance with you, or perhaps it was my first real one, only I didn't know quite what to do with it. You accepted me so easily then, so trustingly, that I was afraid for you. I couldn't bear to see you hurt and yet I was the one who was doing it to you."

"You loved me then." It wasn't a question, but a statement of fact.

"I . . . yes, I suppose I did."

She smiled because he sounded surprised. "I loved you then, too."

Nathan shook his head. "You only thought you did."

"What I felt for you then was quite real, Nathan. Don't belittle my feelings because I couldn't remember the past. While we were on the *Avonlei* I was in love with you. I never understood how much in love until we arrived at Ballaburn and I discovered I couldn't hate you

416

as I wanted to. I left because I had so little control where you were concerned. I was afraid of surrendering my very soul if I stayed."

"Instead you took mine when you left."

Her eyes darted over his face. He meant it, she thought wonderingly. He really meant it. "I didn't know," she said softly.

"That's because you married a coward. I was afraid to tell you." He sighed and his smile was rueful. "God, Lydia, I think I've been afraid of you from the very beginning. I've never wanted anything the way I've wanted you."

Lydia chided gently, "Ballaburn."

"I've *never* wanted anything as much as I've wanted you," he repeated. "Ballaburn be damned."

She placed a finger over his lips. "No, don't say that. I've come to love Ballaburn, too. I know it was wanting the land that brought you to me."

Nathan hesitated. "It was partly that," he said after a moment. "It was partly something else. You suspected it a while back, I think."

"Brigham."

He nodded. "I didn't want to let Brigham out of my sight. If Irish's child had been a boy, Brig would have killed him. He wouldn't have settled for a third of Ballaburn. When I arrived in Frisco and discovered Irish had a daughter, I was only a little less worried. I know how Brig appeals to women and I didn't think Irish's daughter would be immune."

"I wasn't," she said honestly, and felt Nathan's wince. "But that's when I was stupid."

He brushed her mouth with his. "You know I don't really think you were that."

"I know. But I was painfully eager to accept Brig's attentions. He appeared to be wealthy, immune to my mother's attraction, and interested in my work with the orphanage. He was pleasant, attentive, kind, and—"

"All the things I wasn't."

"*Some* of the things you weren't," she corrected. "Don't forget, the circumstances of our first meeting were quite different."

Nathan laughed shortly. "*Our* first meeting wouldn't have happened without Brig. That altercation in the alleyway was his doing. Those thugs were his hirelings. He set the whole thing up to have the opportunity to rescue you. You don't know how often I wished I had never overheard his plans. Instead of being grateful for my interference you were resentful."

"I told you I was embarrassed," she said. "Not resentful. Why did you intervene at all?"

"Because I thought Brig had gone too far. You could have been hurt."

Lydia snuggled closer. "I was grateful," she whispered. "For that and other things."

"Other things?"

"For your help with Charlotte and her baby. No, don't say that you weren't helpful. You were. I know that it didn't end as we might have wished, but you gave Charlotte a chance that she didn't have with me or Dr. Franklin."

"I saw you at the cemetery. You bought a headstone for her and Ginny Flynt, didn't you?"

"You were there?" She remembered standing in the cemetery, George Campbell close at hand while she said a prayer by the graves. There had been someone on horseback higher up the hill and later a carriage had disturbed the silence. "You were following me?"

"Not exactly. I was following Brig. Sometimes it was the same as following you."

"I suppose it was," she said. One of Lydia's hands slipped inside his shirt. His flesh was warm, his heartbeat steady. "I know what you did for Kit, setting him up at Saint Benedict's and all. I realize you didn't do it for me, but I'm grateful just the same. Grateful, I think, that I've fallen in love with such a good man."

"I don't know what you're talking about."

418

She smiled. "That's all right. You can pretend you don't know. I even find your modesty becoming."

"I still don't know what you're talking about."

Lydia kissed him. "It's enough that I know."

He held her close, his embrace the secure circle of his arms. "Suppose you tell me something," he said. "What made you decide to come out here tonight?"

"I told you that already. I didn't want to be left at the house alone."

"I thought perhaps you'd tell me the truth this time."

"That is . . ." She stopped. Didn't she owe him something more than another lie? There had to be trust between them. ". . . not the truth," she said, sighing. "I came out here to protect you."

"I see," he said softly. "Where did you get the idea that I needed protection?"

"It's more puzzling to me why you think you don't. We both know how much Brig wants Ballaburn. To his credit he tried manipulation first. He wanted me to divorce you and marry him."

"Is that why you asked me for an annulment?"

"I wanted to hold out some hope to Brig, but I never would have married him. I'd have left the country and you would have been safe. Not being married to either one of you, Irish would have had to rethink what he wanted to do with Ballaburn. I suspect he'd have settled on a fifty-fifty split and you and Brig would come to some kind of agreement on how the place should be managed."

"I see," he said slowly. "So you've given this matter a great deal of thought."

"I had, but you wouldn't grant me the annulment. That changed everything. Nathan, if Brig makes me a widow, then I'm free to marry him. He'll try to get Ballaburn that way. I left Sydney with you so I could protect you, not the other way around."

"I was afraid it might be something like that," he said. "You're Mad Irish's daughter, you know that, don't you?"

419

"Let's say I'm beginning to understand what people mean when they say that to me."

Nathan chuckled. "It's not entirely a compliment."

"I'm learning that, too."

"So how were you going to protect me out here?" he asked.

Lydia did not mistake his tone for anything but patronizing. "I have one of Irish's guns in my saddlebag," she said. "No derringer this time. It's a Remington and I know just enough about using it to make Brig think twice about hurting you."

Nathan released her immediately. He sat up, looking around for her saddlebag. He found it and the gun inside. Swearing softly and succinctly he put them both down out of her reach.

"Nathan! Put that gun over here!" She started to sit up. The cold and the force of his arm drove her back down again.

"God, Lydia, that you could be so naive! You're not to do anything to Brigham, do you hear me? I'll handle him. I've known all along that he might use you to get to me, and if he succeeds, Lydia, he'll still use you. He'll make you his wife, take Ballaburn, and at the end of a year you'll have a very tragic suicide, your wrists slashed, the blood drained out of you. He might rape you first, your hands tied tightly to the headrails of your bed, and it won't matter if you struggle because I suspect that Brig would like that."

Lydia's hands were covering her ears. "Stop it, Nathan! You're not—"

He took her hands away and held her as closely and tightly as he could. "I love you, Liddy," he whispered against her ear, then her mouth. "I love you. I don't want anything to happen to you, do you understand?" He felt her nod and drew her head against his shoulder. His hand nestled in her hair. "I can't protect you if I'm dead and that's what I'll be if you get between Brig and me. That you're willing to risk so much means everything to me,

420

but I don't need proof that you love me. God only knows why you do, but I know you're telling me the truth."

"Yes," she said. There were tears pressing against her tightly closed eyes. "Hold me, Nathan. Please, just hold me."

Nathan did. In the stillness of the night, with Lydia's gentle breathing reminding him of the passage of time, he came to know the profound nature of love.

Chapter Fifteen

Nathan turned away from the small group of stockmen engaged in energetic conversation around him. He didn't wonder any more how he could always sense Lydia's approach, he simply accepted it as one of the unique pleasures of loving her so deeply. He strode over to where she had reined in her horse and helped her dismount, relieving her of the wicker basket she carried on her arm. A blue-and-white checked cloth covered the contents of the basket and the deliciously warm fragrance of Molly's spiced chicken and apple cobbler had Nathan's mouth watering.

"Well, I like that," Lydia said as she watched her husband investigate the contents of the basket. "Not so much as a peck on the cheek or it's-a-pleasure-to-see-you."

Nathan glanced up from the basket, grinning wickedly. His free arm snaked around Lydia's waist and he jerked her toward him, playfully rough. Bending his head, he caught her mouth with his and kissed her hard and long, breaking off only when his mind registered the light smattering of applause from the circle of men off to his right.

Lydia's theatrical curtsy in their direction prompted him to take a bow. There were several good-natured taunts that followed Nathan and Lydia as they linked arms and disappeared over the hillock for their picnic.

"Thought I told you never to wear that skirt again," Nathan said, settling against the trunk of a red gum tree. He felt about her split riding skirt the same way he imagined a randy knight felt about chastity belts: it didn't belong on his wife when he was around.

Lydia twisted the cloth basket cover and snapped him in the chest with it. "Perhaps my aim should be lower," she said, eyeing the taut fly of his jeans. "I thought you were going to ravish me back there."

Nathan routed through the basket, found a chicken leg, and bit into it hungrily. "You can't decide what you want," he said around a mouthful of food. "First I get taken to task for not welcoming you properly, then I get the same when I do. I'd be grateful if you'd make up your mind."

Lydia leaned toward him, taking aim with the twisted tea towel, but at the last moment she unraveled it and carefully tucked one corner in Nathan's shirt, smoothing the rest of it across his chest like a dinner napkin. She smiled innocently at him as she completed the small wifely task. "Don't get too used to it," she said, giving him an arch look. "I came out because Irish is napping and Molly and Tess said there's no room for me in the kitchen. The coach just left a little while ago. This came for you." She handed him a small square packet. It was surprisingly heavy for its size, as if it might hold a few coins.

Nathan glanced at it, smiled, and slipped it under his coat to put it in the breast pocket of his shirt.

"Aren't you going to open it?"

"Not now."

"It's from Kit," she said.

"Why should you think that?"

"I recognize his handwriting. I taught him, remember?"

Nathan continued to smile, refusing to say one way or the other.

"Oh, very well," she said, sighing. "Have your secrets."

"Thank you. And was there anything for you?" he asked.

She shook her head and her eyes were grave now. "Nothing. It's been a week since the robbery. I don't suppose my letter will ever be found."

"Probably not." Especially if Brig had it. There had been no robberies of Cobb & Co. coaches since the one a week ago and that only reinforced Nathan's belief that Brigham had been responsible. Nathan had no idea if Lydia's letter had been the motive for the robbery or if Brigham had been after money and chanced upon the letter. The strongbox had been found two days after the holdup in a thicket a few hundred yards from the road. The contents of the box were scattered, some of the mail had been opened in a hurried search for money, but it appeared that a large portion of it was recovered. Lydia's letter was not among the items. "You've written to your father again, haven't you? Told him what happened?"

"A few days ago, when I realized the Cobb people most likely would never have anything for me. But it will take so long, Nathan." She hugged her knees against her chest and stared off at the house in the distance. "Things that are happening to me now, things I want to share with my parents, won't be known to them for weeks and it will be weeks again before I know a reply. I wonder about them: what they're doing, what they think of the decision I've made to stay here. I wonder if they think I've betrayed them."

"Is that what you think?" he asked.

"No . . . well, sometimes I thought it when I was living in Sydney without you. I felt I belonged in San Francisco if I couldn't really be happy anywhere else. I worry that Papa will think my love for him has lessened in some way because of what I've come to feel for Irish."

"I think Samuel will understand."

"I hope so." She blinked back a sudden rush of tears

425

and glanced at Nathan, a sad half-smile on her lips. "Mother won't."

Nathan pitched the chicken bone over his shoulder, wiped his hands on his napkin, and caught Lydia by the arm and pulled her closer. When she was nestled comfortably against him he said, "Your mother's not old enough to understand. She may never be. She's still the reckless, spoiled girl she was of seventeen when she met Irish. Marriage and childbirth never changed her. She was jealous of Samuel taking Pei Ling to his bed, yet she never recognized that she bore some of the responsibility for their affair. She kept you in her shadow so it was a rare occasion when you shined, and when you did, she managed to make you believe you hadn't."

"Nathan." Lydia said his name quietly, wanting him to stop. "She's my mother. I don't always like her, but I do love her. I'm more familiar with her faults than you. I'm the one who could never be bright or pretty or accomplished enough to suit her. She tried to make me in her image and failed miserably."

"Thank God," Nathan said feelingly. "If you were any brighter, any more beautiful, or a fraction more accomplished, you would have married that James Early fellow years ago."

Lydia laughed. "Especially if I were brighter."

"Especially that."

She picked up the basket and put it on his lap. "You better eat something else, I'm not—" Lydia turned her head as something she saw out of the corner of her eye got her attention. Gray curling smoke was rising above one of the hills in the distance. "What's that?" she asked, pointing.

Nathan was on his feet immediately, pulling Lydia to hers. "Go back down to the house and tell anyone who's left at the stable that we've got a bushfire near Coolabri. They'll know what to bring." He caught her elbow as she started to go. "And don't come back yourself, Liddy. I mean it. Stay at the house with Irish. He'll want to come

426

rattling out here in that buggy of his and it won't be safe."

Lydia only looked behind her once as she raced her horse back to the stable. Nathan and the stockmen had already mounted and were charging in the direction of the smoke.

From high ground Brig watched the fire march forward. Occasionally the orange-and-red flames would break rank and leap ahead to lick at the stringy bark of a gum tree or a high tuft of grass. The sheep had corraled themselves in the valley's dead end and were bleating helplessly, struggling for position and protection as the fire approached.

Nathan was among the first group of men to arrive. Brigham saw immediately that they had nothing with them to fight the fire. That suited him perfectly; it meant he had perhaps as much as an hour before more help would arrive, if it ever did. The fire would spread and accidents could happen. It was what he had been waiting for since he seeded Coolabri with kindling.

The split among the men occurred more quickly than Brig anticipated. Most of them went to the far end of the valley in an attempt to drive the sheep out to safety. One man dismounted, tore the saddle blanket free of his horse and began beating out the small fires that broke free of the main block of flames. Brig was only interested in Nathan's movements, and as he studied his old friend, he made a succession of wagers with himself about the next direction Nathan would take. He watched Nathan check the wind and search the smoldering burnt-out area on horseback, but it wasn't until Nathan rode clearly into Brig's sights and out of the sight of the other men that Brig could do anything.

Brig dug himself more comfortably into the grass, steadied himself carefully, and raised his gun. He was an excellent shot, but he didn't overestimate his abilities,

427

wanting no accidents to remind him of the last time he tried something so risky. No matter how he felt betrayed by Nathan, he didn't want to maim him. Not for Nathan, the life of a cripple. The shot had to be clean and . . .

Nathan moved slowly along the outer edge of the flames. The heat must be enormous, Brig thought, following Nathan with the nose of his gun. He waited. The wind shifted.

He fired.

Lydia helped gather supplies from the stable and the house and load them on a wagon. Axes, shovels, blankets, and picks were thrown onto the bed. Molly and Tess packed food and drink for the men and drove the wagon themselves to deliver it all. Irish wheeled into the kitchen just as Lydia was waving them off.

"What the bloody hell's going on?" he demanded. "People running up and down the stairs. Everyone shouting."

"Bushfire," said Lydia. She drew his attention to the kitchen window and pointed northwest. A gray haze was lying flat on the horizon. "There. Nathan called it Coolabri. Everyone's gone but us. I think this is what's known as holding down the fort."

Irish swore colorfully. "Whoever heard of a nursemaid and an invalid holding down anything? That's what we are. Whose idea was this? Yours? Nathan's?"

"Nathan's. But I agree with him. Anyway, you're just feeling sorry for yourself and I'm not paying it the least attention."

"That my own daughter should treat me so," he muttered. Irish stopped rolling his eyes when Lydia flashed him one of her beautiful smiles. "How long ago did it start?"

"I don't know. It's only been thirty minutes, though, since we first saw the smoke."

"Wrong time of the year for bushfires," Irish said,

staring at the smoky haze. "Coolabri, you say? It's hard to tell from here."

"That's what Nathan said. We were on the hill over there."

"Well, he'd know from that angle." He wheeled to the back door and pushed his way out onto the porch. Lydia followed. "Wind's picking up. That's not a good sign." In the distance a flock of magpies took to the air. They soared and swooped and finally chose to settle in the boughs of some snow gums closer to the main house.

"What will the men do?"

"They'll try to clear a path to stop the fire in places where they can't beat it out. There's a stream near Coolabri that might help cut it off, but they can't get water to the fire. There's no pump, and running a brigade would be like trying to plug a volcano with sand, one grain at a time. The best they can hope for is containing it."

"Why are you frowning? Don't you think they can do it?"

Irish hadn't been aware that he was frowning at all. He made an effort to control it, rubbing the bridge of his nose as if he were only being thoughtful and not worried. Motioning Lydia to help him back in the house again, he chose his words carefully. "They'll contain it. It might take them a few days, less if we get some rain, longer if the wind keeps rising. Depends if the fire moves out of the valley."

"A few days," she said softly. Lydia was only now beginning to understand the nature of what Nathan and the others were fighting, the urgency that prompted Molly and Tess to send food with the other supplies. "No one explained it to me. I thought . . . I don't know what I thought. I've never seen a bushfire."

Irish didn't tell her about the wall of incandescent flame that ripped through dry sheep country in the summer. Ballaburn only had patches of land like that and Coolabri wasn't one of them. Lion's Ridge and Willaroo

429

Valley were more likely to be overtaken by fire, but this was still the wrong time of year. The paddocks were green and the scrub in the bush wasn't tinder dry. The stringy bark from the gum trees made good kindling, but it probably wouldn't have ignited spontaneously. There had been no storm in recent days, no lightning that might account for the fire. "Well, you're not going to see a bushfire now. Nathan left you here as much for your sake as he did mine. How about giving me a push to the study?"

Feeling a little sorry for herself now, Lydia did as she was asked. She had known there was some danger, of course, but Nathan hadn't tried to convey the full extent of the hazard. Now Irish was doing his best not to convey it, either. "What happens if they can't contain it? Will it come this way?"

"It's possible, but not likely. Wind's wrong for that. It'll burn itself out eventually. The question is, how much good pasture and forest will it take in the mean time? Coolabri is good grazing. Nathan and the men will try to move out the sheep that didn't trample each other in the first panic." Irish wheeled himself over to his desk and opened the bottom left-hand drawer. Pretending to leaf through a stack of papers in the drawer, he checked his Remington to make certain it was loaded. It was. He closed the drawer only part way.

"I feel as if I should be doing something," Lydia said. She went to the windows of the study and drew back the curtains, craning her neck to see. A thin film of smoke shadowed the underside of the lowest lying clouds. It was impossible to see anything else. "Perhaps I'll make some tea. Would you like some?" The kitchen had a better view.

"A drop of whiskey in it wouldn't be amiss."

"All right."

As soon as she was gone Irish went into the entrance hall and threw the bolt on the front door. He secured windows on the ground floor in his bedroom, the parlor,

430

the dining room, and when he returned to the study he checked those as well. Waiting for Lydia to come back with the tea, he wondered what else he could do. He'd have to send her upstairs on some pretext or other in order to lock the back of the house. Holding down the fort was more apt than Lydia could have known when she said it. How long before Nathan realized it was no ordinary bushfire he was fighting, but one deliberately set? How long before he understood the danger wasn't only at Coolabri but probably at the very heart of Balla-burn?

Irish wondered if telling Lydia his suspicions would make her safer or only cause her to panic. "Lydia!" he called. "Forget about the bloody tea and come here. I'll pour us two stiff shots. For what I—" He broke off, driven to silence by Lydia's presence in the doorway. She was carrying a china tea service on a wooden tray and her grip on the handles was white-knuckled. She was pale, her eyes large and vaguely bruised by the nature of her thoughts. She stared at Irish, unblinking. Behind her and a little off to the side, stood Brigham.

"I let her finish making your tea," he said pleasantly, giving Lydia a nudge to enter the room. "It was the least I could do."

Lydia set the tray down. When she attempted to go to Irish's side behind the desk, Brig stopped her, pulling her back by the waistband of her skirt. Her movement had been enough to permit Irish to see Brig's gun. "He set the fire," she said tonelessly.

"I thought as much." Irish's hand lay carelessly on the open drawer at his side. The Remington was within his reach.

Brig laughed as though he were genuinely pleased. "How clever you both are. It wouldn't be any good at all if you were slow to catch on. Nathan's been a bit of a dis-appointment today. I've already shown Lydia his coat and the bullet hole. She knows the truth. By now the bushfire's taken care of him and the coat's being

431

destroyed in your wood stove." He smiled faintly. "Everything consumed by fire."

Irish's upper body snapped to attention. His head jerked up. The sickly pallor that had shaded his complexion was replaced by the first flushes of deep, unforgiving anger.

Brig didn't respond to the accusation in Irish's eyes. "Get me the strongbox, Irish. I want to see the wills you drew up. Go on. Get them."

"Get them yourself. You know where the box is."

Lydia felt the nose of Brig's gun stop pressing on the small of her back. He turned it aside long enough to fire a shot in Irish's direction. The bullet missed Irish entirely because it was intended to and shattered one of the window panes behind him instead. Lydia's knees buckled. She was held upright by Brig until she recovered her balance and her strength. She hated him touching her, hated the fact that he was aware of her fear.

"Show me the wills," Brig said calmly.

Reluctantly Irish's hand left the drawer. With Brig using Lydia for cover it was impossible to use the revolver. He wheeled to the bookcase and opened one of the bottom cupboards, withdrawing the strongbox. A key he kept wedged between the arm and seat of his wheelchair opened it. "There's only one will left," he said, raising it to show Brig. "I destroyed the other a little while back."

Lydia's lips parted around a small gasp. She forgot Brig's presence for the moment. "You did?"

Irish nodded. "The night you went out to Lion's Ridge after Nathan."

"But you never said. I thought—"

"I wanted to be sure."

Brig jabbed at Lydia, infuriated that he was no longer at the center of their thoughts. "I'll have a look myself, if you don't mind. Put the box down." When Irish had moved out of the way, Brig pushed Lydia over to the table and sifted through the contents. Skimming the will that remained, he understood his worst fears had been realized. Everything would be Nathan's.

"I'm not entirely surprised," he said. "Father Colgan told me how taken you were with Lydia. It stood to reason that you'd be set on giving the land to Nathan, if you haven't been set on it all along. I had hopes their marriage might come to nothing, but apparently there is to be no divorce. The question that had been plaguing me was how to get Ballaburn?"

Irish slowly wheeled back to his desk, trying not to look purposeful about it. "There's no will, I told you. You've seen for yourself that there isn't."

"You'll have to write another then, won't you?" Brigham followed Irish's progress around the desk. When Irish was situated directly behind it, Brig said, "Put your hands flat on the top. That's it. Lydia, sit down." When he had compliance he went to the desk, found Irish's revolver, and tucked it in his trousers. "Did you think I would forget? Your actions are almost laughably predictable, Irish. I thought you might be waiting for me, and you were. With you and Lydia alone here it was the opportunity I had been waiting for, the one I created." Without turning his back on Irish, he went back to Lydia and seated himself casually on the arm of her chair. His gun rested comfortably on his thigh. "You need to start writing, Irish. The exact terms as before, then no one need know you got rid of the original. Do it, and I'll let you live out your days here naturally. More, I might add, than you were willing to offer me."

"I'll be damned if I'll—"

Lydia's glazed, grief-stricken eyes met Irish's. "Write whatever he wants, Irish," she said dully.

Brig smiled. "Your daughter has good sense. Listen to her."

Irish stared at his daughter and felt her pain more deeply than he felt his own. There was no accusation in her eyes, no reminder that they had come to this pass because of his wager, yet Irish could not have felt more

433

responsible for Nathan's murder if he had pulled the trigger himself. Several long, silent minutes passed. Irish's shoulders slumped at the moment of his decision. He found paper, a pen, and began writing. When he was done he pushed the document across the desk toward Brigham.

"There should only have ever been one of these," Brig said as he examined it. "The day you drew up two, you made the price of owning Ballaburn Nathan's life. I'd hoped to win the wager and make killing him unnecessary, but it wasn't to be. Don't think I'm not mourning his death."

A cry was wrenched from Lydia as she came to her feet. "You bastard! Don't you dare speak of mourning him! You had no feelings for Nathan when he was alive and surely none for him now that he's dead! You've always used Nathan to serve your own ends! You think Ballaburn is yours? Well, you're welcome to it, Brig, but you can't make me marry you."

"Can't I?" he asked. He raised his gun and leveled it at Irish's head. "Don't think I won't do it. There's people enough at Ballaburn who'd believe Irish would blow out his own brains. That's the kind of pain he's been in since the bushrangers put him in that chair."

Suddenly Lydia knew the truth. It was so clear to her in that moment she wondered why she hadn't known, or at least suspected, long ago. "It was never bushrangers," she said. "It was you. You're the one who put Irish in that chair."

Irish saw the truth of it in Brigham's face and in the reflex jerk of his head that he could not control. "You bloody whoreson!" Irish's hands gripped the arms of his chair and he raised himself up, pain twisting his features. "I'll kill you myself!" Forgetting his infirmity, one of Irish's arms shot out to wrest the gun from Brig. Immediately he fell backward against the chair. It began to roll away from him and before he could steady it or himself, Irish collapsed helplessly on the floor.

While Brig made no move toward Irish, Lydia ran for him, skirting the desk and dropping to her knees beside him. There were tears in his eyes, more humiliation than pain, and Lydia realized that Brig had broken the proud spirit that was Irish.

"Get away from him," Brig told Lydia. "Leave him. He needs to remember how helpless he's really been all these years. Even before he was a cripple in body he needed others to do his work for him. He couldn't have found you without me, Lydia. I was the one he meant to send in the beginning and I should have gone alone." He gestured to Lydia to move aside again, waving his gun at her this time. When she didn't move quickly enough to suit him, Brig leaned forward, grabbed her forearm, and forcibly dragged her toward him. She tripped, the toe of her shoe catching Irish in the thigh as she was pulled across his body. Wincing at the thought of causing him more pain, Lydia struggled with Brigham as she tried to attend to her father again.

Brig hauled her against him, securing her with one arm held tightly beneath her breasts and making it difficult for her to draw a breath. His gun was once more leveled at Irish. "See?" he asked, kicking Irish hard in the thigh. "It doesn't hurt him at all there." He kicked him again, this time in the side just above his waist. "He can feel that. Can't you, Irish?"

Lydia jammed her elbow into Brigham's middle and heard him suck in his breath. "And you can feel that!" She struck him again before he could recover.

"Bitch!" He pushed Lydia away from him so that she fell against the desk. He removed the gun that was wedged between his trousers and his abdomen before it jabbed at him a third time or fired accidentally. He tossed it away, saw it land harmlessly on the deep leather armchair, and hauled Lydia back in his arms. "Let's discuss our wedding plans upstairs, shall we?"

Cursing, Irish pushed himself to a sitting position. "Don't you touch her, Brig!"

One corner of Brig's mouth lifted in a parody of a pitying smile. "Or what, Irish?" He waited for a reply and when none came, he laughed softly and prodded Lydia out of the room at gunpoint.

He was still smiling when he forced Lydia into his old room at Ballaburn. He didn't bother to shut the door, believing the threat from his gun was enough to keep Lydia precisely where he wanted her. "There's no reason you shouldn't be comfortable," he said, pointing toward the bed.

"Go to hell."

"I wouldn't be so quick to condemn me," he said. "You haven't heard half of what I want to say to you."

"I don't want to hear anything you have to say."

"Don't you?" He reached in his vest pocket and pulled out an envelope. "I was going to read this to you, but then . . ." He shrugged, starting to put the letter back.

Even at the distance she stood from Brig, Lydia recognized her father's handwriting on the envelope. The letter was addressed to her. "That's mine," she said, holding out her hand. "Give it to me."

Brig shook his head. "I don't think so," he said. "But if you'll do as I want, I'll tell you what it says."

Lydia hesitated, looking from Brig to the letter and back to Brig again. She cared far less about the letter than she did about the gun, but nothing was served if Brig should realize it. Moving with obvious reluctance and fear that was not entirely feigned, Lydia went to the fourposter and sat down on the very edge of the bed. "You took the letter from the coach," she said.

His tawny eyebrows lifted. "You knew?"

"Nathan suspected. I wasn't as certain."

"You should have trusted him. He knows me better than anyone. It was difficult to hit on something that would draw him away from Ballaburn without making him suspicious at the outset. The fire worked well."

A blessed numbness settled over Lydia. It touched her heart first, which thudded with a dull, steady beat, then her eyes, where there were no tears to blink back. The ache in her throat disappeared as the heavy lethargy spread to her arms and legs and finally her head, weighing her down so that it seemed impossible to move or even want to. It was hard to remember that she wanted the gun. "You've always used Nathan to get what you want. Even when you were boys."

"He told you how we came to be here, did he?" He laughed shortly, shaking his head at the memory. "Poor Nath. He wasn't so wise then. He never would have agreed to set out on this adventure if I hadn't forced it."

"So you killed that woman in London."

"One whore more or less doesn't matter. No one mourned the passing of my mother when she took her own life—including me. She left me to make my own way when I was eight. I found her, you know. Her wrists still had ropes on them. I was much older before I realized her last lover had tied her to the bed before he used her. She didn't bother to take them off before she slashed her wrists."

Thinking of the twisted manner in which Brig later honored his mother's memory, Lydia shivered. "You allowed Nathan to take the blame for what you did."

"More than that, actually," he said without remorse. "I made certain he was arrested. Put the evidence in his shoe that placed him at the whore's home the night of her death. The truth is, I never meant the whore to die. She came upon me as I was looking over her property. She thought I was a beggar and invited me inside. I didn't want or need her pity."

"So you killed her."

For a brief moment a look of helplessness passed across Brig's face. "It just happened."

"Oh, God," Lydia moaned softly.

Brig blinked suddenly and the small action seemed to jerk him into the present. "It wasn't like that with the others," he said. "I got better at it. No one's ever known the other suicides were murders."

"Nathan knew."

"But he couldn't say anything, could he? Not with hi[s] past." He held up the letter. "It's important you hear thi[s] from me, Lydia. Samuel writes about it, of course, but [I] wanted you to hear it from me. Your mother kille[d] herself."

The numbness Lydia felt everywhere finally extende[d] itself to her brain. She fainted.

Irish was sweating hard by the time he pulled himsel[f] back into his chair. His skin was cold and the gray pallo[r] of his face had deepened. Wheeling himself around th[e] desk, he searched for the gun Brig had tossed and found i[t] on the chair. His hands trembled as he picked it up an[d] checked to be certain it was still loaded. Wiping his bro[w] with his forearm, Irish pushed himself to the staircase, feeling each breath he took as a heavy burning in hi[s] chest. At the bottom of the stairs he paused and looke[d] up. The steps rose above him as the face of a mountain might to an able-bodied man. Tucking the gun in hi[s] trousers at the small of his back, Irish reached for th[e] newel post and raised himself out of the chair. Using th[e] banister rails and the steps themselves, he bega[n] the ascent with his hands and arms, dragging his useles[s] legs behind him.

Lydia was only unconscious a few minutes, but it wa[s] long enough for Brigham to secure her wrists to the post[s] at the head of the bed. Her initial struggle merely tightened the scarves that had been used to bind her. Her eyes settled on the gun lying on the bedside table, completely out of her reach now.

Brig leaned forward in his chair, his forearms resting near his knees. "I know it's a shock," he said quietly. "That's why I wanted to be with you when you heard."

Lydia tried to sit up. Her bonds prevented her. "You[

438

killed her."

"Samuel wrote it was suicide. Perhaps she missed me. I think you suspected Madeline and I were lovers. Apparently she killed herself shortly after my departure. I was sorry to learn of it."

Tears gathered in Lydia's eyes now and Brigham's face blurred. Her hands curled into fists.

"You're probably wishing you had killed me at the Silver Lady," Brig said. "That's understandable. It's difficult to know what's to be done about you, though. I'm not usually indecisive. For instance, it was not hard at all to know what to do about George Campbell." Lydia's short gasp told him that she understood. "Your father didn't completely trust me, I think. He sent George with me to bring you back to Frisco." His palms turned upward in a gesture of mock helplessness. "There was an accident during the voyage."

He stood and went to the bed, sitting down near Lydia's waist. For the longest time he didn't touch her, but simply studied her features. "You have such an odd little face," he said. "So plain sometimes, almost beautiful others. But your eyes . . . your eyes are always magnificent. When you look at me as you're doing now, I don't think I mind at all that you hate me." He lifted one hand and grazed her cheek with the back of it. "Madeline had skin like this. Soft and pure. She was a whore, though. You knew that about her, didn't you?"

Staring back at him, refusing to look away, Lydia said nothing.

"I'd kill you now if I thought I could get away with it," he said. "But everyone for hundreds of miles knows about Mad Irish, his wager, and his bloody will. I can't have anything if I'm not married to you."

Lydia's mouth was too dry to spit. She told him to go to hell instead.

"Irish's life hangs in the balance," he said. "Think about that. He's the last person whose life you can save. You couldn't help George or your mother or Nathan, but you can help Irish. I have nothing to lose, you see. If you don't marry me, I can't have Ballaburn. It doesn't matter to me then whether Irish dies now of a new wound or later of an old one. I think, though, that it matters to you."

Irish pulled himself to the open doorway and drew his gun. He was breathing hard and his heart hammered in his chest. "It doesn't matter to me," he said. "Untie my daughter."

Lydia strained to see Irish. He was lying on the floor, his gun raised with remarkable steadiness. "Brig's gun is on the table," she called. "Don't let him—"

Irish fired as Brig tipped the table and rolled to the floor. The bullet missed and the gun skidded a few feet. Using the table for cover, Brig reached the revolver. A bullet splintered the wood directly above his head and imbedded harmlessly in the wall behind him. Lydia's fingers worked frantically on the knotted scarves. She felt one give a fraction just as Brig returned Irish's fire. The bullet caught Irish in the shoulder and he fell on his back. His entire body shuddered once, then he was still. Brig stood up cautiously, his gun held in front of him, and approached Irish slowly.

The scarf that secured Lydia's left wrist slipped another knot. She forced her forefinger through the opening, widened it, and when she found she could grasp the loose tail, pulled hard. She saw Irish blink suddenly, and knew that Brigham had seen it, too, when he pulled back the hammer on his gun. With her free hand she flung a pillow at Brigham's head, screaming to distract him. His hand jerked up, the bullet went wild, and Irish had the moment and range he needed. Grunting with the sheer pain of his effort, Irish raised his revolver and fanned the hammer in quick succession, sending three bullets powerfully into Brigham's chest.

Brig staggered backward and collapsed, dead before his body sprawled at the foot of the bed.

Lydia pulled her feet up sharply as the bed jarred with

Brigham's weight. Only the hem of her gown was caught under him. Bile rising in her throat, Lydia yanked it loose, then worked quickly to free herself from the bedpost as Irish called her name.

Her eyes wet with tears, Lydia sank to her knees in the hallway beside Irish. She ripped part of her gown to make a bandage for his wounded shoulder.

"It's a hell of a thing," Irish said weakly, trying to raise a smile. "He could have shot me in the leg and I wouldn't have this pain now."

"Hush. Don't talk. I have to get help for you." Her tears slipped past her cheeks and fell on Irish's ashen face. Blood was pumping steadily from his wound and she couldn't stem the flow.

"There's no help for me." His dark-cobalt eyes were sad but resigned. "I'm sorry for most of it, Daughter, but not for wanting to know you. I can't be sorry for wanting to know my child."

Lydia slipped an arm under Irish's shoulders and raised him so that his head was in her lap. Her fingers stroked his iron-gray hair. "I'm proud to be your daughter, Irish . . ." She paused. "Father."

"Thank you for that," he whispered. Another of Lydia's tears touched his face. He smiled because he knew he was forgiven. "I love you."

Lydia said the same words and she believed in her heart that he heard them. When her vision cleared the pain was gone from her father's eyes. She wept softly for her own.

It was much later that there was noise in the yard, the sound of doors opening and closing, and the rapid tattoo of feet on the staircase. The arms that came around her were strong and steady and familiar. They smelled pungently of smoke. She didn't ask how or why they were suddenly there, reaching for her, holding her. She accepted them, turned in their loving circle, and leaned against the solid wall of Nathan's chest.

Epilogue

December 1869

The sun had set on Christmas Day but heat still hovered over Ballaburn. Samuel Chadwick patted his forehead with a handkerchief and marveled that his daughter and son-in-law hardly seemed affected by the temperature. Even Pei Ling looked comfortable. Kit was a little subdued, but Samuel didn't know if it was the weather or the dinner in his belly that had finally quieted the boy.

A cross breeze swept the parlor. The delicate, waxlike red-and-yellow blooms on the potted Christmas Bells swayed gently. The fringe of hair on Lydia's forehead was ruffled. Nathan raised his hand and with just the tip of his finger brushed back a strand that had fallen across her cheek. Samuel watched his daughter turn to Nathan and smile and he was struck once again by the depth of love Lydia and her husband shared.

"So," he said, addressing the room at large. "Is anyone going to show me this medallion I've heard so much about? If it saved your life, Nathan, I'm surprised Lydia hasn't built a shrine around it."

"Oh, Papa," Lydia chided. "Don't be blasphemous. Kit, it's in the jewelry box on my dresser. Would you get

443

it for me? I can't believe I haven't shown it to Papa and Pei Ling yet."

Glad for the opportunity to do something, Kit hopped to his feet and disappeared into the hallway.

"That's a good boy you have there," Samuel said when Kit was out of earshot. "Very earnest."

"And bright," said Lydia. "Father Colgan says that Kit has nearly caught his classmates. Nathan and I discussed letting him stay on here. I could tutor him while Nathan taught him about the station, but we agreed he also needs to be with other children. He stays with a good family in Sydney and visits us now and again. Father Colgan has visions of Kit going into the priesthood, but I think he'll settle here at Ballaburn someday." Lydia leaned into Nathan's shoulder and laid her hand across his. "God knows, he's welcome."

"Because of the medallion?" Pei Ling asked.

Nathan shook his head. "The medallion was a miracle. None of us, least of all Kit, take any credit for what happened, or *didn't* happen because of it."

"Nathan was sponsoring Kit at the school," Lydia said. "Though he'd never admit it outright until after the shooting at Collabri."

"I didn't have much choice," Nathan explained. "Lydia gave me a package from Kit just minutes before the bushfire was sighted. I pretended she was wrong about who sent it and put it in my shirt pocket. I remember thinking it was a little heavy, but I never gave another thought to what might have been in it." Nathan saw Pei Ling's dark eyes lift toward the doorway and realized Kit was standing on the threshold. "Bring it on in, Kit, and show it to Samuel."

Kit ducked his head, embarrassed, but the smile he couldn't quite hide was proud. He crossed the room to Samuel's chair and held out the medallion. It was the size and thickness of a sovereign. The edge of the medal was ridged and the face was engraved with a portrait of Christ; the obverse had Kit's initials. The portrait and

he initials were difficult to make out because the center
f the medallion was mishapen now, dented by the bullet
. had stopped.

"Father says it's the medal of Saint Jude," Kit said as
,amuel passed the medallion to Pei Ling. He watched her
urn it over in her hand, touching it with delicacy and
we. "He's the patron saint of hopeless causes. Father
Colgan gave it to me when I won the class spelling bee."

Samuel smiled. "A hopeless cause, eh? And what was
our winning word?"

Kit straightened smartly and became the model
tudent attention. He said clearly, "Lugubrious. L-U-G-
J-B-R-I-O-U-S. Lugubrious."

"That's very good," Sam said. "But what the hell does
t mean?"

"Papa! Your language."

"Excuse me," Samuel said. "But what the *bloody* hell
loes it mean?" Everyone laughed, including Lydia.
"Well?" Sam asked.

"It means very sad or mournful," Kit said, and added
.or good measure, "We shall all be lugubrious when you
nd Pei Ling return to California in the New Year."

"Good God." Samuel looked suitably impressed.

Pei Ling handed the medallion back to Kit. "It is very
'ine honor, young sir. Also very fine that you send to
Nathan."

Kit's hand closed over the medal and he bent his head
again, embarrassed by the attention. He shrugged and
stared at his feet. A lock of dark-blond hair fell over his
.orehead.

Nathan took pity on him. "Why don't you go out to
the stable, Kit? Pooley said he was looking for someone
to help him with the horses. He probably could use you."

"Oh, yes, sir." He tossed the medallion to Nathan.
"Thank you, sir."

The adults managed not to smile at Kit's eagerness
until he was out of the room. Nathan turned the
medallion over in his hand and fit his forefinger against

445

the indentation. "I was on horseback at the edge of t[he]
fire. I still don't know what made me turn. It might ha[ve]
been the heat, my mount, perhaps something I heard—
none of those things. But I did turn, and the impact [of]
Brig's shot knocked me down. I know I was unconscio[us]
for a while and that probably helped save me as well. B[rig]
came out of his hiding place long enough to take my co[at]
as proof for Lydia that I was dead. When I came arou[nd]
the fire was licking at my boots and the heat was seari[ng]
my lungs." He could laugh at the memory now, and di[d.]
"I thought I was in hell. It wasn't until I found Ki[t's]
packet in my shirt pocket that I realized I was alive. T[he]
bullet was still imbedded in the medallion."

"He came back for me then." Lydia looked at t[he]
raised flesh on her forearms. "I can't seem to help b[ut]
shiver when I think about it."

"Quite a feat in this weather," Samuel said flatl[y,]
dabbing at his brow again.

Pei Ling rose to her feet. "Samuel cannot apprecia[te]
miracle when he so hot," she said. "I prepare cool ba[th]
for him now." Making a slight bow to Nathan an[d]
Samuel, she left the room.

"When are you going to marry her, Papa?" Lyd[ia]
asked baldly.

The heated flush in Samuel's cheeks deepened. "I'[m]
not." He held up his hand to stay Lydia's objection. "It[']s
not what you think, Lydia. We both know I was sa[d]
dened by your mother's death, horrified at the manner [of]
her murder at Brigham's hands, but it would be a lie t[o]
say that I'm mourning her. I would take Pei Ling as m[y]
wife tomorrow if she would have me. The truth is, sh[e]
won't. She says it's quite acceptable for me to have [a]
Chinese mistress, but not a Chinese wife. She will sta[y]
with me as my mistress, honor me with her love an[d]
fidelity, but she won't marry me. I can't make her chang[e]
her mind." His light blue eyes flashed a warning to Lydi[a.]
"And it's not your place to try to influence her. Pei Lin[g]
and I will manage."

"I would never interfere," Lydia said solemnly.

446

Nathan bent his head and kissed her on the temple. "Liar," he whispered, when his mouth was close to her ear.

Lydia's smile was serene and inscrutable. "Nathan and have another present for you, Papa," she said. "I'm going to have a baby."

Later that evening when they were in bed, Lydia turned on her side to face Nathan. Her knees were drawn up and they bumped his. "I think Papa was pleased, don't you?"

He reached for her hand under the covers and threaded his fingers through hers. His thumb brushed back and forth across the fleshy pad of her palm. He said dryly, "I'd say pleased was an understatement. But then, I'm only judging Sam by how loud he shouted when you told him."

Lydia laughed softly. "One *would* think it's never been done before."

"It hasn't . . . not by us." His eyes were suddenly grave. "You really don't mind that our child will be Currency?"

"*I'm* Currency, Nathan." She squeezed his hand. "Irish's daughter, remember? He never had a pardon. If there's such a thing as convict stain, then it's mine to pass on, not yours. You're not a prisoner any longer. You never were."

Nathan shook his head. "It's a state of mind," he said. "You'll never be Currency, and a thousand pardons from the governor can't change what was done to me in Van Dieman's Land."

Nathan heard no bitterness in his voice and his smile was gentle. "Our child will be loved," she said. "Let's think about that and forget Sterling and Currency."

Easing his hand out of Lydia's, Nathan placed his palm across the faint swelling of her abdomen. "Do you ever feel the babe?"

"No, not yet. Molly says it will be a few more weeks

447

before the quickening." At his look of disappointmen[t] Lydia smiled indulgently. "I'll be sure to let you know a[s] soon as it happens. But if I have to come out to the pa[d] dock, the men will rib you mercilessly."

"I don't care."

Her eyes darted over his face. "You really don't, d[o] you?"

He bent his head, touched his forehead to hers, an[d] whispered huskily, "I really don't."

Lydia snuggled closer, folding her arms around h[er] back. His hand moved from her belly to her breast an[d] cupped the underside. "I love you, Nathan Hunter."

Sometimes the words were still difficult for him to sa[y], not because he didn't feel them, but because he felt the[m] so deeply. It was one of those times.

"I know," Lydia said, her mouth a mere moment fro[m] his. "Just show me."

He did so gladly, loving her slowly at first, gently savoring the closeness, the touching, building a fir[e] against her skin with his fingertips, raising desire with hi[s] mouth. Whispering, kissing, a timely caress, were th[e] small exchanges that gave pleasure in the beginning an[d] brought peace in the end.

Afterward Lydia slept in his arms and Nathan watche[d] her, listened to her breathing, was eased by the com[-] forting warmth of her body and the fragrance of her hai[r]. It was Lydia who made him a free man, not because sh[e] had tirelessly petitioned the governor for his pardon, bu[t] because her love was unconditional. In the eyes of th[e] law Nathan Hunter was no longer a prisoner, but in hi[s] heart he was bound to Lydia for life.

It was a just sentence, and in Lydia's hands, a lovin[g] one.